CW00621729

Published 2007 Grace Publishing / Enspiren Press Gorrie, Ontario, Canada
www.enspirenpress.com

Printed in the USA

Copyright © 2007 Anita Davison

Catalogue #

ISBN 978-0-9739502-7-4

DUKING DAYS
Rebellion

By Anita Davison

Dedication and Acknowledgments

To my family, Clive, Michael and Alexandra;
who have been so tolerant during the writing of this novel.
In memory of my Mum, Eileen Hahner, who always told me I could do it.
With special thanks to Lisa and Ginger, my wonderful critiquers who
believed in me.

To my editor and friend, Anne Whitfield, who fought my corner and
saw me through.

And for everyone in the Historical Fiction Critique Group, who gave
their attention, skills and advice willingly and enthusiastically.
You made it fun.

For Liz

Who was the first
one to buy this book,
I hope you enjoyed it
Much love
Anita Davison
x x x
31/7/07

Preface

In 1675, a private Whig society met at rooms in the King's Head Inn, Chancery Lane. Calling themselves, the Green Ribbon Club, on special days their votaries wore ribbons in their hats, of 'Leveller Green'.#

Their patron, James Scott, 1st Duke of Monmouth, the eldest illegitimate son of King Charles II, was a regular visitor. He wore 'the green', and they honored him by tilting their hats and brims over one eye in the 'Monmouth Cock', toasting him openly as 'Prince of Wales'.

In those days, their members swaggered across the cobblestones of Whitehall, talking of the days when 'Jemmy' traveled through the West of England, 'dancing the green' and 'carrying of the Plate'*

Toasts were drunk to, "Bless his Majesty and confound the Duke of York', with little fear of the pillory or Newgate prison. Monmouth's popularity was high, particularly in the West Country, with its mines and rich woolen trade owned by non-conformists who had been severely punished for their dissent.

The eleventh of June 1685 was known as the first of the Duking Days: - so called because that was the day Monmouth sailed into Lyme Bay accompanied by eighty-one hopeful men.

His aim was to wrest the British crown from his uncle, James II, the newly crowned king, and within days, six thousand West Countrymen had rallied to his cause. Monmouth was declared 'king' in Taunton market place in front of an enthusiastic crowd, but his army was poorly armed, badly disciplined, and many of the promised gentry did not arrive to support him.

James II retaliated by sending his troops to the West under Lord Feversham, with John Churchill as second in command. On the night of July 5th, Monmouth launched a surprise attack on the royal army on marshland outside Bridgwater in Somerset.

The Battle of Sedgemoor was the last ever fought on English soil. A battle that included the men of the Woulfe family.

> # Salute to Thomas Rainborough, a popular Leveller leader and sailor, murdered in 1648
> * 1675 the Duke of Monmouth, an excellent rider and sportsman, had carried off the international plate at the St Germain horse race.

Author's Note

As part of my research for this book, I visited the Blake Museum in Bridgwater, which contains memorabilia of the Duke of Monmouth and the Battle of Sedgemoor. A guide sat in a corner of the room, dressed in the uniform of Monmouth's army and when I identified, correctly, a uniform of one of 'Kirk's Lambs' on display, the guide stared at me levelly and said, "We don't talk 'bout him round 'ere."

They have long memories in Somerset.

CHAPTER ONE
Exeter, June 1685

Helena clung to the hanging strap of the Woulfe family carriage as it clattered down the hill and turned onto Northgate Street, two haughty footmen clinging to the rear. This would be the first time they had gone to church without their father, Sir Jonathan and their brother Aaron. Her heart twisted and she sent up a silent prayer that, wherever they were, they, and Uncle Edmund were safe.

She looked up and met Bayle's gaze, too anxious to return his smile. Nathan Bayle, body servant to Sir Jonathan, had been part of Helena's life forever. 'Ask Bayle.' was the watchword at Loxsbeare Manor. House servants and estate staff alike called him Master Bayle, whether in earshot or not. To the family he was Bayle. Only her father ever called him Nathan.

A broad shouldered man, he kept his wavy brown hair slicked back from a high, flat forehead over expressive brown eyes. Despite his imposing size, he was a non-threatening figure with a calm expression. Occupying the majority of the seat opposite, he dwarfed her younger brother Henry, who would have surely fidgeted more had there been room for him to do so.

The smells of hot leather and horses, sun-baked grass and starched linen assailing her senses within the confined space made Helena queasy as iron-clad wheels bumped over the cobbles in Arches Lane.

Beside her, Lady Elizabeth sat staunchly upright, her delicate features turned to the window. Helena couldn't see her face, but sensed her unease as she watched her fiddle with a lace lappet falling from her headdress; tugging at it with nervous fingers.

Exeter sported few private carriages, so as they rolled to a halt outside St Mary Arches Church, the knot of curious onlookers gathered to watch the Woulfes handed down at the lytch gate was not a cause for concern.

Helena bowed in greeting to several acquaintances at the church door; others looked away as they took their usual pew in the cool and lofty interior. She stared straight ahead, ignoring the curious eyes boring into her back and the low mutterings echoing from adjacent pews.

Let them whisper and gossip; she was proud the men in her family had stood up for their principles and were willing to die for them.

Master Triske, a thin, humorless man, completed his self-indulgent sermon. Under the eye of the magistrate in the front pew, and with some reluctance, Helena thought, the minister announced the Duke of Monmouth's declaration, made a few days before from Taunton market place.

After several nervous starts, he informed them Monmouth claimed to be the rightful king and that James the Second had murdered his father, King Charles.

Helena went rigid with shock as murmurs of dismay rippled round the congregation. Beside her, Henry murmured, "Father said Monmouth did not seek the throne."

"Hush!" Helena nudged him, her gaze on their mother, who stared stonily ahead, a spot of color developing on each cheek.

With an undertone of warning, the minister recited King James' pronouncement that his nephew and all his 'adherents, abettors and advisers' were traitors and rebels.

Helena felt warmth creep into her face. Traitor? How dare this insipid cleric call Sir Jonathan Woulfe such a thing? Rebel indeed! Didn't he realize he was trying to protect the very church where Triske condemned his loyalty? "If the king had his way, you, Master Triske, would be chanting in Latin," she murmured under her breath.

Her self-righteous anger sustained her through the rest of the service, when Lady Elizabeth gathered her and Henry in her wake to glide regally down the aisle, watched by their erstwhile friends and acquaintances.

Helena stayed close to her mother's skirts like a child, eager to be away from what she felt were disparaging murmurs and hard looks. A friend of Henry's started forward, most likely to offer his greetings, but a male hand clamped down on the boy's shoulder and after a murmured exchange, he was guided away. Helena narrowed her eyes, angry for Henry, who had harmed no one. Was this what they were to expect from a community who had always held the Woulfes in high regard?

She turned away, telling herself they would feel differently about their son associating with her brother once the Duke of Monmouth was in Whitehall.

"No one trusts Catholic James," her Uncle Edmund once told her. She hoped it was true.

Lady Elizabeth exchanged polite greetings with the minister at the church door, but did not pause to chatter with friends as was her usual custom. Instead, she walked rapidly down the path toward their coach, past a glowering Lord Miles Blanden and his wife.

The Blandens owned an ancient manor at the top of St David's Hill; richer than the Woulfes, but according to her father, the respect of the city's citizens so far eluded them. Helena practically shared a nursery with their son, Martyn, and when she reached seventeen, they were betrothed. Helena liked him well enough, but she had been disappointed; expecting to feel something quite different for the man destined to be her husband.

Helena's father granted her a generous portion, commensurate with the Woulfe name, and dazzled by his generosity, she had moved through a haze of over indulgence, exhilarated to be the center of so much attention.

Despite the heat of the churchyard, Helena shivered at the memory of that morning last December, when Martyn fell ill during a visit to Loxsbeare. His manservant half-carried him, in obvious pain, to his horse and bore him away before Helena could bid a proper farewell. Her enquiries as to his well-being were deflected with vague responses, and two days later, a messenger rode over from Blanden Manor to tell them Martyn was dead.

Helena feigned her tears; her overwhelming emotion at the time being relief. Even Lord Blandon had appeared more frustrated than grief stricken, making Helena wonder if he had instigated their betrothal so he could bathe in the reflected glory of the Woulfes' reputation.

She offered them a perfunctory curtsey, but kept her face expressionless; conscious of their eyes boring into her back as Bayle helped her up the step into the carriage.

"What do you suppose he wants?" Henry nodded to the black-garbed city magistrate, who strode grim-faced down the path in their direction. The man raised a hand to attract their attention, but the carriage already lurched towards the North Gate, leaving him standing in the middle of the road, frowning.

"His duty can wait a little longer," Bayle muttered.

Helena gave him a thin smile, unable to bring herself to ask what that duty might be.

The carriage rumbled beneath the stone gatehouse to climb the steep Longbrook. Images crowded Helena's head of the days before her father left, when he would shut himself in the great hall for hours with a succession of anonymous men. Visitors their Father forbade her and Henry to see, much less ask about.

She had once tried to listen at the door, but heard only a low murmur of male voices, the chink of glass on glass and an occasional brief laugh through the thick wood. The distinctive sound of a chair scraping back had alerted her to fear of discovery, and Helena swung round in preparation for flight, right into the arms of Tobias Lumm, her father's steward.

His strong hands closed on her upper arms and his eyes danced with amusement. "I beg your pardon, Mistress."

Helena froze, her thoughts racing to formulate a good reason for being crouched outside the door, but she couldn't think fast enough. A flush warmed her face as she realized he had not released her. Indignant, she squirmed out of his grasp, slapping at her skirt in an attempt to restore her dignity.

Tobias dropped his hands with no show of self-consciousness, as if what he was holding had no more effect on him than a sack of flour. He smiled, and then reached for the handle, saying, "May I assist you, Mistress?"

"No." Helena bobbed on her heels. "Er . . . no, Lumm. I have changed my mind. I shall speak to my Father in the morning."

He gave an exaggerated bow in her direction before the door of the great hall clicked shut behind him. Helena stomped up the stairs, forgetting to lift her skirt and almost falling when she trod on the hem. Hoisting it away from her foot with a vicious tug, she fled upstairs to the window seat on the half landing.

She and Henry kept long vigils there together, waiting, wondering, as the atmosphere in the house changed from light-hearted happiness to nervous tension.

Helena looked to where Henry sat huddled in the corner of the carriage; his sandy brown hair concealed under a dark peruke that made his skin seem paler than normal, his boyish grin nowhere in sight. He looked troubled and subdued today, as they all were.

Helena jutted out her lower lip and blew air upwards to create a breeze, lifting the 'favorites' at her temple. She would be glad to get out of this stifling coach, but suspected the rest of their Sunday would be no more restful.

* * *

Taking advantage of the warm weather, Helena and Lady Elizabeth occupied a bench beneath a stone arch cut in the garden wall. Bayle, Tobias and Henry sprawled untidily on the grass, the roar of the River Exe discernible below the Weare Cliffs behind the enclosing garden wall.

Helena stared up at the rear of the house, its soft gold ham stone facade almost glowing in the sunlight. She loved Loxsbeare and never tired of looking at it, sitting square on its grass embankment perched on the top of the cliff above the river. The clinging white blooms of trailing eglantine roses drooped in the afternoon sun, softening the walls. A window opened and a hand appeared, waving a white cloth, and then pulled it closed again with a bang, the leaded panes winking in the sunlight.

Set on one side of the house, the rose garden gave a view of the gravel road curving from St David's Hill, through a set of impressive wrought iron gates into a cobbled courtyard. Tall, mullioned windows marched across the southern front reaching two stories high, with ornamental battlements built above.

Helena's great-grandfather, Julius Woulfe, built the house for his fifteen-year-old bride when the first King Charles occupied the throne. To make her transition to married life easier, and perhaps the prospect of her twenty four year old groom less terrifying, he named their new home after the village near Tiverton where she was born.

His son, Thomas, Helena's grandfather, possessed an artistic nature and had the interior white plasterwork painted with swathes of leaves and flowers trailing up the staircase and across the tops of doorways.

Helena waved her fan back and forth across her face, the feathers catching on her damp skin, making her feel sticky and uncomfortable. She pulled her skirt away from her prickly legs, shifting on the bench; her gaze sliding toward Tobias, unnerved by the easy way he slouched on the grass. He would never have relaxed so completely in her father's company, with his shirt unfastened at the neck and his thick brown hair loose on his shoulders.

Tobias had been estate steward for the past year, although where he came from, or admitted to, Helena had not demeaned herself to ask. A few years older than her elder brother, he was proud for a servant, with a knowing manner as if he were a possessor of secrets. He was strong-featured, many said handsome, with deep-set brown eyes, and a wide, ready smile. She would have denied it if challenged, but Helena found him interesting.

His station in life certainly did not hinder his fondness for flamboyant clothes, which he purchased second-hand and wore like an impoverished cavalier. She heard him once giving half-threatening instructions to the laundresses for the care of his garments.

Her father ignored her mistrust, which infuriated her when she saw them together around the house and grounds, their heads close together, more like equals than master and servant. Even Bayle regarded him as hard working and efficient, giving her no choice but to accept the man, but she did so at a distance.

As if he sensed her thoughts, Tobias glanced across at her and gave a slow wink. Helena lifted her chin and stared off, annoyed he had caught her looking at him. He's impertinent too!

"Lord Feversham has been put in charge of King James' forces sent to the West." Bayle confirmed Helena's suspicion that his frequent visits to Exeter had little to do with obtaining supplies.

Squinting against the sun, Tobias handed Bayle a glass of lemon water from a tray. "Churchill will feel slighted by that," he tutted. "To be overlooked in favor of a Huguenot. The man has a long memory."

Helena looked up at his reference to Huguenots. There were quite a number of them living in Exeter; refugees from the unyielding French king. She had heard about how King Louis dragged families apart, forcing children of Protestants to accept the Roman faith. St Olave's Church in Fore Street had been renamed the French Church, where the émigrés gathered to seek alms.

"You don't think King James would let such a thing happen here. Force us to be Catholics, I mean?" Henry looked up at Tobias, shielding his eyes with one hand.

"Let it happen?" Tobias thumped his knee with a fist. "I fear he might make it happen."

Helena watched the steward and the manservant, marveling at the change in them since her father left. Bayle deferred to Tobias naturally and they shared duties with no rancor, despite Bayle having been at Loxsbeare since his boyhood. Despite her misgivings about Tobias, Helena found their presence reassuring, and they both took special care of her mother, for which she was silently grateful.

Henry sat cross-legged in breeches and shirt, his wig discarded and the latest newssheet on his knees. "Monmouth has gained possession of Axminster!" he read aloud. "They were barely ahead of Lord Albermarle's militia and when they encountered Monmouth's men outside the town, some of the Somerset militia ran away." He looked up with a bright smile. "That must have pleased the Rebels."

"Don't call them Rebels, Henry. It makes a chill run through me." Helena snapped her fan shut and gave a shudder.

Henry ignored her. "It says, when they reached Taunton, the townsfolk lined the streets in welcome. A party of schoolgirls presented Monmouth with a pennant bearing the initials 'JR' topped by a crown." He turned bright eyes on his mother. "You see, Mother? They want Monmouth for their king."

"It's not all good news, Master Henry." Bayle batted away a persistent fly with a hand the size of a small shovel. "There was that skirmish at Ashill." Helena's gaze flew to his face. "Was it serious?"

"Four of Monmouth's men were killed and some wounded, I believe." Tobias offered Bayle a lace kerchief, which he dismissed with a snort.

"Did they kill any troopers?" Henry pulled a wide leaf from a nearby shrub, chewing at the woody stem.

Tobias pocketed the kerchief with a flourish and leaned back on one elbow. "Churchill lost three men, including one of his best officers, a Lieutenant Monoux."

Henry raised a fist, giving a loud whoop, and Helena's heart beat a little faster, wondering if her family was among the casualties.

"Jonathan promised there would be no bloodshed." Lady Elizabeth nibbled at her bottom lip. "Monmouth and Churchill used to be friends." She stared off as if remembering. "Perhaps the king does not trust Churchill, so he put the Frenchman in command." She gave a small sigh and discarded the embroidery she had been holding, but not working on.

Helena looked away, embarrassed for her mother, whose thoughts lately seemed discordant and rambling, but not knowing what to do about it.

A warm breeze brought the sound of the river into the garden, ruffling Helena's hair. Insects buzzed in nearby flowers and the snap-snap-snap of a startled pigeon disturbed the quiet. She cast her mind back to the day her father had left with Edmund and Aaron. The messenger who came to tell them Monmouth had landed at Lyme with eighty men, was not a dark, brooding stranger galloping a sweating horse into the courtyard under cover of night, but a nondescript laborer who kicked his ancient mount into a lumbering trot through the manor gates.

Helena shivered in the heat, recalling an image of her father, brother and uncle riding away with a group of the Loxsbeare servants; watching them grow small on the road. She hadn't understood then why she was afraid, just as her fears confused her now. Loxsbeare was where she felt safe, the only home she had ever known. Her father had been adamant that the Duke of Monmouth was what the people wanted, but since then, he had declared his uncle a murderer and himself king. Surely, that changed things?

A bank of cloud appeared on a stiffening wind and a long shadow slid over the garden, sending a tremor of foreboding down her back.

CHAPTER TWO

Helena laid down her quill and poured sand onto the page, then set the book upright to let it run off in a thin stream. She leaned back with a smile; triumphant at having remembered in such detail, the day she accompanied her father to Taunton the previous winter.

Dressed in her new riding habit, they had set off under a high winter sky, so clear and blue it might have been summer, with two liveried outriders as escorts. The ground was deeply rutted and initially, Helena struggled to keep her seat, wishing she had not ridden cross-saddle quite so often with her brothers.

Her father had looked severe but handsome in a dun colored long coat, pinched at the waist over a matching long vest, his hair gathered at his nape and fastened with a black ribbon. In a household of two healthy sons and a beloved wife, Helena accepted early in life that she took last place in his affections, but that day she felt he was wholly hers.

As she rode beside him, she hadn't known then it was to a secret Rebel meeting in John Trenchard's clubroom at The Red Lion Inn. Helena was charmed at the gentleman's effusive welcome at the inn door, but then his demeanor had altered, become secretive. Without meaning to, Helena heard them talk of muskets and troop ships, but they quickly changed the subject when they noticed her presence.

On the morning they left, Helena had taken her leave of Master Trenchard expressing the not altogether truthful wish they might meet again soon. "Most assuredly we shall mistress," he had said, bowing over her outstretched hand. "For we have fellows in scarlet to take off, do we not Jonathan?"

The bustle of the inn yard had stilled with an expectant hush and her Father's face turned black with anger. He brought Buchan round to stand beside the offender, "Hush man, you know not who might be listening!"

A voice made her jump. "You have been writing for hours, Helena. What can have kept you occupied for so long?"

"Oh, Mother," she looked up, "I did not see you there. I have been compiling a journal, see?" She held up the book. "In a year or two, the events of these days will recede into the past and I might forget how we all felt."

Without warning, Lady Elizabeth's eyes glinted and her voice turned cold. "I do not need a journal to tell me how I feel!" She walked over to the cold fireplace and stared into the grate, one slim hand pressed against the white marble. It trembled as she held in there. "I shall never forget the horror of this summer."

"I didn't imply we would forget, Mother. I thought. . ." Helena broke off, all her good feelings about her writing banished by the harshness of her mother's voice.

"This is not a game, Helena." Lady Elizabeth gave a brittle laugh. "Nor is it a country excursion for you to read aloud at the fireside on winter evenings. This is war."

Helena felt close to tears, her mother had never spoken to her so cruelly before. "I am sorry, Mother. I did not mean..." She sat twisting the leather fastener of the journal between shaking fingers. "I know this is difficult for you with Father gone."

"Difficult!" Her stance as she stepped toward Helena was almost menacing. "You have no conception of how . . . difficult this is for me."

Tears glinted in her blue eyes, sending guilt coursing through Helena to have been the cause.

"He took my son." The words were drawn out, one hand pressed to her bodice. "Aaron was mine, and Jonathan took him without a word. He turned him into a soldier, telling him what a great adventure they would have with their duke." She spat the words out in contempt. "But he didn't ask me if I was willing to lose my precious boy."

Mesmerized by her ferocity, Helena sat frozen as her mother sagged against the window; glaring sunshine highlighting her papery skin and the blue shadows beneath her eyes. Helena rose and drew her away, as if by removing her from the light, she could restore her vitality.

"I am so sorry, Mother. You are right, I did not understand. I miss Aaron too." At her mother's hard glare, Helena rushed on, "But not in the way you do, of course. We must pray for his safe return." Repelled by the feel of the fragile bones beneath her fingers, Helena forced herself not to drop her hands.

"Pray?" Lady Elizabeth spat. "You pray if you will, I will make my pact with the devil if needs be." She tore herself from Helena's grasp and fled the room.

The salon lost all its peace and summer beauty with her going, leaving Helena isolated in the echo of her mother's venom, horrified, yet proud of her passion. Feelings she had kept well hidden when her father and Aaron had been at home.

Helena wandered over to the window to stare out at the deserted road. 'I wish she would feel that way about me,' she whispered against the glass. She squinted at the dirt road, imagining them there, returning to Loxsbeare where they belonged. And what if they don't come home? She reached for the journal and slipped it into the pocket of her gown, resolving not to let her mother see her writing in it again.

* * *

Scattered news reports filtered through to the manor as the long days passed; some were contradicted days, or even hours later; but Helena dutifully recorded every skirmish and where it took place, the number of casualties and the names of the regiments on both sides in her journal.

When King James sent thousands of men to stop a second rising in Scotland and a third in the north, she copied the details meticulously from the London Gazette.

Bayle returned from Exeter one afternoon and laid two sheets of parchment on the table at dinner. "They are copies of both proclamations. Monmouth's denouncing his uncle, and King James' countering his nephew's claim of kingship."

"Where did you get these?" Henry's eyes were round in admiration as he fingered the heavy parchment. Lady Elizabeth took them from him, her lips quivering as she read.

Bayle shrugged in reply to Henry and turned to their mother. "His majesty was bound to take a stand, Mistress." Lady Elizabeth lifted her gaze briefly from the page to stare up at him. "It changes nothing, Monmouth's cause might still prevail."

"Might?" She waved the parchment at him. "Monmouth accuses his uncle of killing his father and usurping his crown while the rightful heir was out of the country." She jabbed at the other sheet with a fingernail. "And here, King James says his nephew is a traitor and a Rebel and must be 'seized and apprehended', together with all his, 'adherents, abettors and advisers'." She threw the pages onto the table. "They are writing their own death warrants."

Helena had never seen her so upset, and while their dinners went cold on the table, she tried to offer a comforting arm; but was cruelly shaken off.

Henry leaned forward to run a finger under a line of print. "Monmouth says King Charles was poisoned."

"Monmouth says," Lady Elizabeth mimicked. "James the second is our crowned king, and Catholic or not, anyone who says otherwise is putting themselves on the side of traitors."

Henry's brow furrowed in concentration. "Is father a 'divers traitor' or a 'traitorous complice'?"

Alarmed, Helena snatched the documents out of his hands. "It's not funny, Henry."

"I am married to a traitor and we are all doomed," her mother cried, covering her face with her hands.

"Mother," Helena entreated. "If that were true, then so was Grandfather when he joined the Parliamentarians."

Lady Elizabeth looked bewildered. "Sir Thomas Woulfe was no traitor!"

"Perhaps not in the days of the commonwealth, Mistress." Tobias picked up the documents Helena had discarded on the table. "But he fought against the first King Charles with Lord Fairfax, in which case. . ."

"That was entirely different," Lady Elizabeth interrupted him, lowering herself into a high backed chair, her knuckles standing out white on the wooden arms.

Tobias dropped the papers and strode to the door, calling to a servant to fetch her maid. "My lady is in need of her," he ordered.

Ruth appeared like a silent apparition to usher her mistress toward the door, raking them all with rodent eyes before it clicked shut behind them.

Helena slumped in her seat, her food forgotten. Her mother's outbursts were becoming more frequent and their ferocity frightened her, but her words made sense. To the world outside Loxsbeare, Sir Jonathan Woulfe was a traitor. Traitors were executed weren't they? They lost all their possessions and their families were disgraced.

Her throat felt dry and tears threatened, but unwilling to let Henry see, she palmed them away. Henry was meant for the army, but how could that be possible if the king seized their father's possessions? Where could they go? Would their mother sink into apathy and wither away? What would life offer her, for surely no respectable man would wish to marry a traitor's daughter?

Unbidden questions crowded into her mind, each one conjuring worse images than the last. Distraught, Helena rose to her feet to follow her mother from the room, mumbling an excuse in response to the puzzled enquiries thrown at her.

CHAPTER THREE

Bayle strode across cobbles slick with rain from a brief, but welcome summer storm. Taking advantage of the stables being half-empty, he ordered the remaining horses moved from out of the stalls for cleaning. When he spotted Henry approaching, he gave a weary sigh. The boy had been trying to question him since the Gazette arrived, but thus far Bayle had avoided him.

"Who is this Percy Kirke?" Henry asked, stomping over clumps of wet hay scattered across the yard.

"Why do you ask, Master?" Bayle spoke slowly, playing for time.

"The Gazette says he commands the Queen's Foot Regiment. He is on his way to Dorset with John Churchill and the Oxford Blues."

"We shall talk about soldiers later, Master, I have duties to attend to." Bayle retreated into the tack room, glancing back over his shoulder to see Henry glaring after him.

He saw Helena watching, and when Henry left, she handed a leading rein to a groom before picking her way across the yard toward him. Knowing she would not be so easily deflected as her brother, he sat astride a milking stool and waited. The door creaked behind him, but he didn't turn round.

"Who is this man Kirke?" she asked, coming to stand at his shoulder.

He stood up, preparing to bow, but she made an impatient gesture and he sat down again. Her skirt was grubby, her hair scraped back under a white housewife cap. She looked incredibly young standing there, her eyes wide and gray as a pigeon's wing.

He picked up a small tool and applied it to a piece of frayed leather. "The Queen Dowager brought Tangier as part of her dowry when she married King Charles. Kirke maintained the garrison there in command of the regiment."

Helena bunched up her skirts and perched on a hay bale, her gaze fixed on his face.

"He has a bad reputation, Mistress Helena." He twisted the softened leather round his fingers. "His men are brutal and they take pride in their savagery."

"How do you know?" she whispered.

"I grew up with a man who served with him. He has been dead these two years." He gave a shrug, as if this made a difference. "Kirke is a drunken brute, in charge of a drunken regiment, who would kill a man merely to test the edge of a new weapon." At her horrified gasp, he tried to soften his words. "But who knows the truth of it. When a man is full of cider he will say anything to make others listen."

"And these men are being sent to the West?" Helena's voice was thin.

Bayle nodded. There was no point in lying to her. "They saw off the heathen Moors in Tangier." He exhaled slowly, muttering, "May God protect those poor boys."

He searched his mind for a way to give some hope, but before he could speak, Helena leaped to her feet and ran outside, the bottom of her skirt heavy with rainwater from the stable floor.

Dismayed that he had spoken his fears aloud, he remembered too late that Helena had lived a sheltered life and was, in many ways, younger than her years. She may look and act like a lady, but inside she was still a girl. He called after her to wait, but heard only the slam of the heavy front door.

* * *

Dispirited, Helena wrenched off her filthy clothes and dressed in a lighter gown, she went to sit on the window seat on the half landing, where a warm breeze lifted the curls at her temple. The weather had turned from rain to cloudless heat in the space of an hour, and the only sound was the call of a bird or the odd stable noise drifting through the open window.

Henry's rapid footsteps clattered down the hall, breaking the peaceful silence. "I'm bored," he muttered, throwing himself down on the seat beside her.

Helena's gaze was fixed on the road outside, visualizing Kirke's men marching toward the house. In her head, she could hear the rhythm of the horse's hooves and the clink of bridles. She forced the image away to concentrate on what Henry was saying.

"Have you noticed how bad tempered mother is lately?" Henry shifted closer, positioning himself so she had to look at him.

"She misses Father, and all this talk of fighting makes it worse." He gave a resigned nod, but he still looked miserable.

"She shouted at me a while ago." Henry stared at his hands as if the admission pained him. "Bayle wouldn't tell me, so I asked Tobias about Percy Kirke. She heard me and ordered me to my room."

"Is that where you are supposed to be?"

Henry looked sheepish but evaded the question. "She stays in the winter parlor all the time, with Ruth."

"You miss her don't you?" She kept her voice low.

He shrugged. "How can I miss her when she is still here?"

Helena leaned back against the cushions, not bothering to reply. She knew he craved their mother's attention. She did too.

Their Mother was an increasing source of worry. She had abandoned her elaborate gowns to spend most of the day déshabille in a loose mantoe over a plain linen shift. Helena's presence appeared to irritate her and Henry, with his boyish appetite for news of the fighting, tried her patience.

Her mood teetered between anger and hysterics; when she would storm out of a room after a barrage of anger, or sink herself in apathy. Sometimes she was even openly unkind. Helena began making excuses not to be in her company; her recent demonstration of love for Aaron having awakened feelings of jealousy. She knew Aaron was her father's pride, but it appeared he was her mother's too. Where did that leave her? And Henry? She couldn't hate Aaron for it, she loved him unreservedly, but why wasn't there enough love to spare some for her?

"She will be better when Father gets back." Henry brightened.

"When father gets back," Helena repeated.

Their mother had never been what some people called, 'delicate', but Helena had chatted with Betty Humbold, the housekeeper, often enough, to know that Lady Elizabeth had suffered her own share of tragedy. It was from Betty she had learned that within a year of her mother's marriage, her firstborn, a tiny, mewling kitten of a son, had lived two weeks.

Helena could only imagine the heartache it must have caused her mother, a devastated young girl pained by the loss of a child, coupled with the guilt of knowing she had not done her duty to the Woulfe family.

Aaron had arrived next, so different from that first sickly child. He had entered the world screaming for attention and had done so throughout his life. A year later, another son was born who lived for a year. "Your arrival was very different," Betty told her. "You were a lusty, noisy baby who brought joy to both your parents, together with the hope of more healthy children."

A second girl and another son followed, both conferred to the family vault in St Mary Arches within a year. Then Henry arrived, but there had been no sign of a child since. Lady Elizabeth had buried her disappointment and expended her energies on her surviving family.

Helena's gaze drifted to the wall, where a framed parchment hung. The faded ink dimmed the writing, but the royal seal was very much in evidence. She knew the words by heart, having learned her first letters from it with her mother.

> Charles, by the grace of God King of England, to all to whom these letters come, greetings.
>
> Know that we have granted on behalf of ourselves and our heirs that our beloved and faithful Thomas of Exeter and Eleanor his wife that they may fortify and crenellate their house named Loxsbeare Manor in the county of Devon with a wall of stone fortifications, and that they and their heirs may hold it, thus fortified and crenellated, forever, without let or hinderance of us or our heirs or any of our officials. In witness whereof we have caused these our letters to be made patent.
>
> Witnessed by myself at Whitehall Palace, on the twenty-third day of May in the fifth year of our reign.
> *Signed and sealed by Charles II*

By the time she reached the end, the sun had gone behind a cloud and the temperature had dropped. She shivered and reached up to close the window.

"What is going to happen?" Henry murmured, chewing at a cuticle.

"I don't know, Henry."

"Then tell me about great grandfather Julius, building Loxsbeare for his child bride."

Helena groaned, she had told the story so often, he knew every word. She was about to refuse, but at the pleading look on his face, she threw her head back and laughed, shattering the tension.

* * *

From blistering heat that dried up ponds and baked the grass, the weather changed to relentless rain, battering the standing corn in the fields to the ground. Musky damp crept into every crevice of the manor, leaving traces of green slime on north facing walls and dragging Helena's spirits even lower.

During the brief lull in one of many summer storms, a visitor arrived.

The figure of Master Samuel Ffoyle, riding through the gates of Loxsbeare, was an image Helena would always carry. Never hurried, always composed and yet relaxed. "A good man in a crisis", her father always said of him.

Tall and serious, he habitually dressed in unadorned earth colors, a legacy of his Puritan parents. Her father intimated this was less a religious display, than an aversion to wasting time visiting tailors. Yet Samuel was brought up in a household where Christmas was a fast day and singing and dancing considered sinful.

Helena had learned through childhood that the changing times of Charles Stuart's reign had fostered the close relationship between Samuel Ffoyle, sheep-farmer-turned-merchant, and Sir Jonathan Woulfe, landed gentry and courtier. She ran lightly through the open front door and greeted him with a curtsey. "Good morning to you, Master Ffoyle."

"How are you this fine day, Mistress Woulfe?" He walked beside her into the great hall, but refused her offer to sit in her company while he awaited the lady of the house.

Before the thought had properly formed in her head, she found herself asking, "Why are you not in Somerset, supporting the Duke of Monmouth, Master Ffoyle?"

Brown eyes flicked to her face in startled surprise. He gave a long, unhurried sigh and placed his hat on a table; opened his mouth, and then closed it again. When he finally spoke, Helena was convinced he had intended to say something else.

"I have been occupied ensuring my sons remain at home." He folded his hands across his waist. "They would have been off to Somerset by now, had I not reminded them of their familial duty."

Helena pictured the faces of Patrick, who was Aaron's age, and Seth, a year older than Henry. "You forbade them to go?" Aaron had been so proud to be accompanying their father. It would have crushed him had his wish been refused.

"I did indeed." Samuel was apparently unmoved by her shocked expression. "They have a duty towards their mother and their siblings. When they have their own households to manage, they may be free to abandon them as they choose."

"But they would be upholding the Protestant religion!" Even as the words left her, Helena knew how pompous she sounded. But her resentment overrode her good sense at the thought that the Ffoyles were safe at Ideswell, while her family faced danger far from home.

Lady Elizabeth swept into the room on a rustle of heavy silk to take charge of their guest. Helena was summarily dismissed and went to sit on a chair by the window; imagining it was much to Master Ffoyle's relief.

The clattering of hooves drew Helena to her feet. Through the window she saw Bayle ride into the courtyard. It had rained in the last half hour and she watched him hand dripping reins to the groom before bounding up the steps to the front door.

Helena frowned at the sight of the unfamiliar lad who took Bayle's horse, wondering why he was not Parry. With a pang, she remembered that the cheerful lad with the permanent grin had gone to join the Rebels.

Bayle had discarded his saturated cloak by the time he joined them, but brought the smell of wet wool and mud into the room with him.

"Good day, Bayle." Samuel looked up expectantly. "And what news have you brought?"

Bayle nodded to Helena before taking his seat. "The king has commanded William of Orange return the Scots Brigade from Holland, to add to the forces against Monmouth."

"Prince William did not acquiesce, surely?" Lady Elizabeth frowned. "Monmouth was brought up with the Princess Mary, they are very close."

Bayle sighed. "He cannot refuse, Mistress, those troops are the king's men after all."

Her delicate hands fluttered to her throat. "Do you think Monmouth knows?"

"If we know, Mistress, then we must assume he does too," Bayle sounded resigned.

Helena stared out of the window, where slate clouds were gathering their skirts to bustle away and deluge another part of the Devon hills.

"Do we know what happened to Argyll in Scotland?" Samuel asked.

Bayle glanced at Lady Elizabeth before answering. "Hardly any dared to turn out for Campbell, the enormous militia presence made sure of that. He was arrested almost straight away."

"Bad news indeed for Monmouth," Samuel murmured. "What of the rising in Cheshire?"

Bayle closed his eyes briefly. Helena saw the gesture and began chewing the base of her thumb; convinced her growing anxiety was well founded.

"Their numbers are diminishing," he replied. "Their supplies are nearly gone, and they have resorted to pilfering and free quartering on the locals."

"I doubt that made them very popular." Samuel crossed his ankles and leaned forward with a frown. "Is it King James' Pardon which is reducing their numbers?"

Bayle placed his glass on a table and leaned forward, knees splayed; a casual stance Helena did not see him use often. He nodded. "The king sent hundreds of copies to the villages to be shown to the Rebels, promising no retribution would be taken if they returned home. Many have taken advantage of it."

Samuel sighed and her mother looked stricken.

Master Ffoyle declined Lady Elizabeth's invitation to dine and, when he left, Helena walked with him to the courtyard. When the groom brought his horse, he did not mount straight away; his attention apparently caught by an approaching figure who stopped to engage him in conversation.

Helena retreated to the entrance hall to watch them through the window. She would have given half her dowry to know what they were talking about. If she still had a dowry.

*　*　*

"You didn't show her the other newssheet then? Samuel Ffoyle slapped his hat against his thigh, signaling the boy who held his horse to wait.

"I couldn't, Master Ffoyle, what good would it have served?" Tobias lifted both hands in a gesture of helplessness.

"What does it say?" Samuel nodded to the folded pages peeking from the steward's jacket.

Tobias looked down but didn't remove it from his coat. "Monmouth's half brother, Grafton, was attacked by a force of rebels manning a barricade outside Philip's Norton, two days ago."

"Grafton fighting his half-brother," Samuel mused. "Eager to prove disloyalty does not run in the family, I suppose. Go on."

Tobias's gaze raked the courtyard. "It was not a success for Grafton, but many rebels were killed, too. They say the blood ran like a river down the lane where the hedges penned them in."

Samuel winced. The lad holding his horse shuffled and the animal whickered, prompting him to reach back to stroke the soft muzzle. "There are no names of the dead yet?"

"Not that I have seen. Monmouth cut his losses and retreated. He is on the march again."

"He'll never get to Bristol now, let alone London." Samuel stepped up onto the mounting block and eased himself into the wide saddle. Released, the boy loped away.

"He's making for Frome, I think." Tobias squinted up at the mounted man, shielding his eyes from the sun with one hand.

Samuel paused before replying. "The gossip at Mol's yesterday put the Earl of Pembroke and the Wiltshires in Frome. Monmouth will gain nothing by it."

Tobias looked uncomfortable.

Samuel took pity on him. "Don't fret, man. You are right not to upset your mistress further." He turned the horse toward the gate. "But I would keep that newssheet away from Mistress Helena, she will be asking awkward questions soon enough."

Tobias pulled a wry face. "She distrusts me, that one."

"She doesn't know you, Tobias."

"Doesn't know who I am you mean?" His voice held some bitterness.

Samuel grimaced. "It would be better not to talk of it."

26

"Before maybe, but now?"

"It's a bad time, Tobias." Samuel turned away, indicating he was not prepared to discuss the subject further.

"It's always a bad time," Tobias muttered, loud enough for Samuel to hear.

Once out of sight of the Loxsbeare gates, Samuel slowed his horse. His visit to Lady Elizabeth had not quelled any of his fears. Monmouth was on the run, and God knew what might happen to Sir Jonathan.

He had kept to himself the fact his own family were under scrutiny since the Duke's landing. Although a professed Anglican, Samuel's father was a Puritan, a militant one at that, who saw his duty as being an irritant to whoever opposed his beliefs. Samuel's upbringing had been difficult, and having risen to the position of Master of the Guild of Clothworkers, there were those jealous enough of Samuel to point the finger of suspicion.

In London, two hundred Whigs had been arrested; two of them prominent cloth workers and members of his guild. Samuel wrote letters of protest on their behalf, but imagined nothing would come of it.

So far, he was able to reassure the city magistrates of his loyalty, but if the situation worsened for Monmouth, would Samuel be torn from his home and thrown into the Exeter gaol? A shiver ran through him as a sharp gust of wind lifted his hat. He pulled his cloak tighter, peering upward at a darkening sky that threatened more rain. The animal snorted and picked up his hooves. Samuel patted the steaming neck; his horse didn't like the rain.

Tobias Lumm's image came into his head and Samuel gave a sigh which was carried off on the fresh wind. A year before, he had encountered Tobias, looking bored and with an eye for mischief, lounging on the cobbles outside the Ship Inn in Martins Lane. It occurred to him then that the lad's indolence could lead to his ruin if he didn't find something to inspire him.

On impulse, Samuel had stepped into the inn and over a jug of fine ale, he struck up a conversation with the landlord; a man he knew tolerably well. "Tell me, Jim," he lifted his jug to indicate the slouching figure flirting with a serving girl. "Why is your Tobias hanging about with nothing to do but annoy the wenches?"

Jim's bovine gaze slid sideways and then rolled in resignation. "Aye, he's a puzzle that'n." He poured a jug of ale and served another customer, then balanced an elbow on the back of the chair opposite Samuel. "Too proud fer this place." He indicated his surroundings. "Restless he is, and him all 'o three and twenty. Dunno what's to become 'o him."

Samuel remained silent, staring into his ale. Then Emily Lumm had sauntered into the room. "Master Ffoyle," she had drawled, bobbing a curtsey, which for all its simplicity held an invitation. She impaled him with her brown-eyed stare far longer than was seemly. There was that look again. Even as a child she had that look. As if she knew something and was promising not to tell. The years had given her a more voluptuous body, but she still possessed the clear skin and stride of a girl. And that look.

Samuel had felt a certain responsibility toward her lad, and when he approached Sir Jonathan with his suggestion, it had proved a simple matter to secure a position for Tobias at Loxsbeare.

Sir Jonathan found Tobias to be entertaining and intelligent, with ideas of his own for making the estate run more smoothly. Even Bayle accepted him as an asset without resentment, and Henry certainly liked him.

Aaron didn't seem to take much notice. His position as crown prince of Loxsbeare had always been secure, so he had no reason to be on the lookout for usurpers. Helena, well she was different. Samuel had seen her cast suspicious eyes in Tobias' direction. And Tobias, headstrong young man that he was, openly stared back, teasing her occasionally and even winking at her, without a thought for how the other servants might view it.

But Sir Jonathan was gone, and who knew if he would return. What did Tobias' future hold? Samuel sighed again. He could not wrestle with that particular problem today.

Fat drops of rain drummed onto Samuel's cloak. His horse nickered, shaking his long head to shake off the water trickling into its eyes. Samuel gave himself up to a jolting canter, not stopping until he turned into the farm gate and his own stable.

CHAPTER FOUR

The narrow staircase of St Mary's church tower forced the group of soldiers into single file. Heavy boots scuffed the well-worn steps. An occasional clang of a sword against stone, followed by a muffled curse, indicated Sir Jonathan was not the only one finding the climb a chore in the early July heat.

A tall, handsome man was the first to emerge onto the roof. The summer wind lifted his black wig from his shoulders, threatening to tear his wide brimmed hat from his head and launch it into Cornhill below.

Jonathan watched his irritated expression; on any other day this would have amused him, but James, Duke of Monmouth was a troubled man and in no mood for levity.

Lord Grey handed the Duke a spyglass as Captain Hucker and Major Wade joined them at the parapet; all five men gazing out over Bridgwater to the flat expanse of marshland beyond. The silver snake of the river Parret curled through the centre of town, the streets tailing off into the distance where the king's troopers were encamped.

Monmouth surveyed the horizon. Those he commanded to defeat the Scots Covenanters at Bothwell Bridge in '79 were now his enemy and waited there on the marsh.

"I know those men." Monmouth lowered the spyglass. "They will fight."

"How many troops does Feversham have?" Grey turned to a nervous looking man who hung back by the tower door. Introducing himself as Godfrey, he had sought an interview with them that morning, claiming he possessed useful intelligence.

"'Bout four thousand, sir," Godfrey muttered. "'Two thousand on the moor, with another thousand each in Middlezoy and Otherey. But they don't know the ditches like I does." Godfrey sidled up to the Duke. "I could show you the way across and surprise 'em."

"The three divisions lay far apart." Jonathan nodded. "Our spies tell us their discipline is not good."

"Besides," Hucker gasped, still winded from the climb. "They drink themselves into a stupor each night on local cider."

"It might work." Nathaniel Wade arched an eyebrow at Jonathan, who stayed silent, his arms folded across his chest. There was no need for either man to voice an opinion; Monmouth was enough of a soldier himself to know the odds were stacked against them.

Jonathan was thoughtful. Feversham and John Churchill led trained men with battle experience. Percy Kirke was there with his infamous 'Lambs', men who wouldn't be cowed by a bunch of farmers wielding scythes.

Only days before, Jonathan convinced himself the Duke was ready to retreat; but the arrogant Lord Grey still spoiled for a fight and advocated a full on attack. Jonathan blew air through his lips in a silent whistle; he supposed it would be better than dodging Ogelthorpe and his troopers through the countryside until they ended up back at Lyme where they started.

"If you make for 'ere, sir." Godfrey pulled a hand drawn map from his coat and dragged a grubby finger across it. "Go along the old Bristol road towards Bawdrip, and then turn south along Bradney Lane and Marsh Lane. I could get you the other side of the Bussex Rhine and right into their camp before they know what's happenin'."

"The cavalry could lead, your Majesty." Grey's lips curled into a leering half smile. Jonathan turned away, irritated with his use of the title. He had been against Monmouth declaring himself king, but Grey's influence was strong. He mentally shrugged; it was too late anyway, the whole countryside knew what they were about.

Jonathan rubbed both hands across his face, dry washing it. I'm simply tired. His lodgings were mean and the landlord sour-tempered, although more civil since he had been assured his guest intended paying his bill.

Most of their men were camping out in people's houses, eating their food and ransacking their stores for horse feed. No wonder the town had been less than happy to receive them this time.

Those June days seemed so long ago, when they even turned away would-be soldiers for lack of weapons. The march into Taunton had been the high point, with the entire town turned out to welcome them; the celebration, which followed at Captain Hucker's house, had lasted until dawn. It was almost like those heady days of the Green Ribbon Club, when they would drink the night away at the Kings Head; speculating on the world they would live in under Monmouth's leadership.

It occurred more and more to Jonathan lately, that those days were an illusion; King Charles, aware of his son's involvement in a traitorous society, had protected him, and in doing so his friends. And should King James not meet his nephew's demands, would England be willing to rid themselves of their monarch a second time?

Monmouth too seemed more introspective with age; his devotion to his mistress the Lady Henrietta, vying with his loyalty to his wife, Duchess Anna. Was the Duke's resolve still strong? Edmund seemed to think so, but then Edmund had been straining against his domestic tethers in search of adventure for years. Now, they were cornered, unable to get to Bristol, let alone London; with that Frenchman out on the moor biding his time.

"We shall do it." Monmouth snapped the spyglass shut. His handsome face broke into a wide grin and they turned to clatter down the tower stairs again in better spirits. When they emerged onto the street, a group of Rebels lounging nearby straightened with respect at the sight of the Duke.

Monmouth turned to his officers. "We march in silence, with every man charged with dispatching the man next to him with a knife, should he utter a sound to betray us." He looked into each of their faces in turn, gave a curt nod and then turned to stride off down St Mary Street with Lord Grey beside him.

As he set off for the inn and his flea-ridden bed in the hope of a few hours sleep, muttering to himself, "How many of the men even have knives?"

* * *

Buchan, Jonathan's bay Iberian, grew restless, his master even more so as he and Wade led their infantry onto the mist-shrouded moor. They had been marching for almost an hour, the smell of peat marsh in their nostrils.

The pressure of keeping the men silent was proving a burden. It was difficult to see where the causeway ended and the marsh began, but at least they had passed the Black Ditch without mishap.

He imagined they should be near the Langmoor Rhine by this time, although he had not noticed the rock Godfrey said marked it. The moon was full, but the fog lay so thick, his troop began to break ranks and wander about in the gloom. With the command for silence, he dared not issue orders to call them back.

They found the crossing more by accident than design, and in moments they had crossed the pludgeon and were on the moor. The only sounds were of heavy breathing and feet squelching into the mud with every step. Jonathan peered into the gloom where he could just make out the cavalry ahead. They appeared to be bunching up and colliding, with horses neighing and men cursing. *Where is that infernal Godfrey? He told us he knew the way.*

A shout came from his right. Then a shot broke the heavy silence.

Jonathan gave a groan of dismay, reining Buchan to a halt, hoping for a second the discharged weapon meant nothing. He heard drums in the distance—the sentry calling the Royal troopers to arms. A ripple of fear ran through him, knowing their enemy would be upon them within minutes. They were still almost a mile from Feversham's camp.

A command to charge went up ahead, followed by thundering hooves heading off at speed. Jonathan cursed; Grey had taken his cavalry forward too soon. Aaron was among them. "May God go with you, my son," he murmured under his breath.

Wade pulled up beside him, his horse turning and twisting in agitation. "The royal troopers have been alerted," he gasped.

"That's obvious, man!"

"We are too far behind and must get the men across that ditch to back up Grey's cavalry." Wade jerked his horse round to relay the message to the other officers.

With all thought of secrecy gone, the infantry marched at double speed. "Hurry it up men. Or Lord Grey will have taken them all out before you get a chance," Jonathan yelled, smiling as loud cheers drifted back over the mist.

In the distance, the king's dragoons formed a shadowy black line, preparing to launch against them. *God's blood they move quickly.* Jonathan positioned himself behind his men, but the rhine ahead ran deep, with no obvious way to cross. They would have to fire from this side, or risk a savaging by the troopers.

The click and slide of muskets being loaded filled the air as a horseman he did not recognize appeared out of the mist with a shout. "Francis Compton is wounded. He's holding off until the royal infantry are lined up on the other side of the Bussex!"

Jonathan knew Compton by reputation; he was one of Churchill's cavalry officers. He raised a fist to indicate he understood, but as he watched the horses ahead, something unexpected happened. Instead of breaching the ditch, Grey's cavalry split into two columns, one swung to the right towards the distant glow of hundreds of tiny lights coming from the direction of the town.

Jonathan rode up and down the line, shouting orders and rounding up disoriented stragglers, his eyes growing accustomed to the dim light. As his vision cleared, he realized what the lights ahead were and called for a runner. "Get over to my Lord Grey and tell him those lights aren't the town. They are the matchlocks being made ready to fire."

The runner sped away. Pray God he reaches them, if they fire first, they will take our cavalry unawares.

A volley of gunfire screamed across the field making his fears real; a plume of smoke drifting across the horse's heads as they wheeled in fright, plunging backwards into the upcoming infantry.

Offering a silent prayer that Aaron had been able to keep Strider on course, Jonathan kicked his own mount nearer the ditch where his men wandered about in all directions, disoriented. "Go forward. Turn about and line up by the ditch. Keep to the ditch men."

The men obeyed; organizing themselves into a ragged line along the edge of the Bussex Rhine. Most of Grey's cavalry had fled the field. A blow, but there was nothing Jonathan could do. He hoped the handlers of the ammunition carts left at Peasey Farm would stand fast, as the horsemen were heading that way.

By this time, troopers streamed across the ditch to tackle Rebels at first hand, although Wade ordered the infantry to hold fire. From the corner of his eye, Jonathan saw a familiar figure and halted, his blade held high. It was Monmouth, his half pike in his hand, waving his men onto the edge of the ditch, ordering them to fire.

Jonathan's orders were to storm the trench and tackle the royal troops, but with the noise and chaos in the dim light, the men hesitated and instead, fired across it. He swore in frustration, but there was nothing for it but to keep them loading and firing. It was their only chance.

He heard the continuous boom of cannon in the distance. Thank God for their Dutch gunners. From the shrieks and chaos, the Rebels seemed to be wreaking havoc among the Dumbarton's Infantry; the indignant yelling of their officer to return fire confirmed it.

The Rebel muskets fired, but seemed to be making no impression. "Fire lower," Jonathan yelled, riding up the line and back again, hollering until they obeyed and the rounds hit their mark. A mixture of swords and farm tools cut into heads and limbs, accompanied by yells of shock and pain. Jonathan did his own share of maiming and killing, trying to keep the enemy from cutting down his men.

He lost sight of Monmouth, but heard Feversham's officers ordering the bringing up of the Cavalry; the Life Guards, Horse Guards and Dragoons, forming up rapidly into an imposing barrier behind the ditch. But that was all they did.

What are they waiting for?

Then it came to him. Feversham was holding off until daybreak; then he would order a full charge in better light. His head ached from the roar of the royal cannon; his throat burned from shouting above the clamor, ordering more ammunition from men who were too dazed to hear him, or too terrified to obey, for none came.

Jonathan's chest swelled at the sight of his ill-equipped troops, running full pelt at the royal horse, keeping up a constant fire on the foot battalions.

He tried not to hear the repeated wet whoosh of steel slicing into flesh, or the primal cries of men in agony; doomed to be trampled by his enemy's horse, or his friend's.

Fingers of dawn light crawled across the horizon, harbingers of a summer day so many would not see. How can the night be gone so soon?

The dawn came fast, and with it a lull in the attack. The swampy field was waterlogged with blood and mud from hundreds of boots and horses. An undulating line of royal troops were visible through patchy mist on the other side of the rhine, fixing their plug bayonets, biding their time.

Well, come if you are coming, you bastards.

As if in response to his silent scream, a wave of horses and men flooded across the ditch, the jingle of bit and bridle and the clang of sword on scythe resounded in Jonathan's head as the troopers fell on his men. The remaining Rebels broke and fled under the devastating onslaught; only to be slashed and shot without mercy as they ran.

Buchan wheezed and panted in fear and exhaustion, but Jonathan had more to ask of him. He had to find the Duke and plan a new strategy, their options were few but the decision was not his to make. Pounding over fallen men of both sides, he closed his ears to the shrieks of the wounded as they cried for help, the big horse's flanks shaking with exertion.

Lord Grey and Monmouth stood by a massive tree at the edge of the field; their armor piled at their feet. He recognized Buyse and Anton nearby, their faces haggard in the weak light. Jonathan halted beside them. "What now my Lord? Our men are being slaughtered."

Monmouth turned away as if unable to look at him, but Lord Grey stepped forward. "We have no choice; we must get away as best we can."

"You are leaving us?" Jonathan's anger made him reckless. "Look at them!" He waved an arm at the devastation on the field. "They are being massacred. You cannot abandon them to their fate."

Grey winced and made to step nearer, but Buchan gave a half rear. Holding up a hand to fend the massive horse off, he raised his voice. "If the Duke is no longer here, the troopers may show some mercy."

The group mounted and Monmouth turned his horse about, bringing it to stand beside Buchan. "You have been one of my best and most loyal, Jonathan." He held a hand toward him. "Come with us."

Jonathan stared toward the Polden Hills, temptation pulling at him. Then he met the duke's gaze and Monmouth flinched. He dropped his hand and turning to signal the others, kicked his horse into a gallop.

Jonathan followed them with his eyes, wondering if they could hear the sound of their faithful Rebels behind him, dying in the mud.

He knew with certainty, he would never hear anything else.

* * *

After daybreak on Monday morning, Bayle ushered the landlord of The Ship and a companion into the kitchens of Loxsbeare. Tobias greeted him with the distance he usually reserved for his father, ignoring the travel stained man with him. "How are ye lad?" Jim Lumm asked, snatching off his hat and dipping his head at Bayle.

Bayle saw Tobias roll his eyes at the ceiling, embarrassed at his father's sycophancy. "What can we do for you, Jim?" Bayle offered the man a seat, which he only accepted after Tobias gave a nod of approval. The second man slid onto the bench beside him, his gaze on the breakfast Tobias had been about to enjoy. He was well-built, with the tanned, leathery skin of someone who worked outdoors. His clothes were of good quality, and his wide brimmed hat looked new.

With an accepting sigh, Tobias slid the plate towards the newcomers. The stranger began to eat, but Jim shifted on the bench.

"Please, help yourself," Tobias urged.

Jim waved the food away. "This here is Walter."

The man beside him nodded, his mouth already full.

"He's a merchant from Plymouth way. His young brother joined the Rebels."

Bayle looked up at Tobias who gave an almost imperceptible shake of his head.

Jim sneered. "Ye don't hav'ta pretend our Tobe, I know you wants to 'ear this." He nudged his companion. "Tell 'em Walter."

Walter swallowed, taking another swig of ale. "Well, I took a copy of King James' offer of pardon to Bridgwater to persuade that bone-headed brother of mine to come home."

"Nah then, Walter." Jim's thick eyebrows did a dance on his forehead.

"I presume your brother did not heed you." Bayle fought a smile at this comic pair.

Walter wiped his mouth on his shirtsleeve. "Ungrateful brat. Threw the paper in the mud he did, and let all his cronies laugh at me."

"How did you find him?" Tobias leaned against the doorpost, watching cold meat, bread and cheese disappear down the man's throat.

"T'wasn't easy I can tell you." Walter spoke round a mouth full of bread. "All those Rebels were camped out on castle field and I must have spoken to at least half on 'em." He held a small knife, awkwardly trying to cut a wedge of cheese, then gave up and crammed it into his mouth whole.

Bayle glanced at Tobias, standing with his arms crossed on his chest, a look of hostility directed at his father. He knew they did not get on, but had no idea why and supposed it was because Tobias wanted to put some distance between his family and his new station in life. A mistake the young often make.

"What was Bridgwater like?" Bayle kept his voice casual. Dull as this man was, he did not want to alert him to the family's interest. Then he saw Jim's face, and realized the innkeeper knew more than he would have liked.

"Crowded," Walter mumbled through his food. "Rebels were in church half the morning, so I 'ads to wait. I left it almost too late to secure a room for the night. The streets were full to bursting with weeping women, come to say goodbye to their husbands, brothers an' sweet'earts."

"The townsfolk knew there was going to be an attack?" Tobias sounded surprised.

"Aye, everyone for miles around knew, 'cept Feversham's lot. They was getting drunk and abusing the locals. Hey, is there any more 'o that ale?" His expression was hopeful.

Bayle refilled the jug. "Did you see anything of the battle?"

Walter did not so much as shake his head as swing it from side to side. "Nah, I heard the guns in the night, so I got up around dawn. That's when I saw a whole crowd of Rebels come running over the bridge from the marsh. Covered in blood some on 'em were." He chewed noisily for a moment. Tobias gave a cough and Bayle held up a hand, urging patience.

"One fell in front of me and died, right there on the cobbles." Walter slapped the table in a 'can-you-believe-it' gesture, making Jim jump. "Then hundreds of troopers came right on after them, yelling and cursing as if they was on a hunt." He frowned. "Which I s'pose you could say they were."

"What about your brother?" Bayle's question was perfunctory.

"Never saw 'im. I was scared for my own skin by this time, with all those soldiers about. So I got my horse and got out o' there." He gestured with the knife.

"You were fortunate to ride so far without attracting attention." Bayle crossed his arms and leaned against the wall.

The man shrugged. "Soldiers had plenty of real Rebels to go after, without botherin' wi me."

"Did you hear what happened to Monmouth?" Jim sounded almost sympathetic. Bayle wasn't surprised; many wanted to see the duke triumph, but few seemed willing to take the risk involved and Jim had an inn, five children and a flighty wife to look after.

Walter held up a hand. "Now there's the thing, talk is he left the field. Upped and rode away with his officers."

Bayle stared off, his thoughts on his master. Did he ride with him? Or had he already been lost?

Walter went on, "But then, rumors say he was hit in the chest by a cannon ball, which is why the Rebels fled. As I s'pose they would do with their leader dead." His big head swayed again.

With nothing more to impart, Jim elicited a promise from Tobias to visit his mother soon and tugging his forelock at Bayle, the two men left. Tobias poured himself some ale, cutting more cheese and bread to replace his breakfast. "Do you want me to go and tell the family?" He hooked a thumb in the direction of the yard.

Bayle rose wearily to his feet. "I'll do it."

CHAPTER FIVE

Henry and Helena made slow progress across the courtyard from the stables. With several of the stable lads gone to the rebellion, everyone had to help with the outside chores. The extra work made no one more willing, and after an hour spent feeding horses and sweeping stables, Helena took out her temper on her hapless brother, who trailed behind offering complaint.

Glancing up, she saw Bayle and hastily smoothed down her stained skirt in embarrassment; aware of her dirty apron and without a single ribbon anywhere. Uncomfortable warmth crept up her neck as she realized Bayle must have heard her shouting at Henry.

Then she saw his face and the yard seemed to tilt around her. Henry, awkwardly carrying a bucket, walked straight into her, spilling soiled water on his breeches and shoes. "Hoy! Helena, look what you are doing, I nearly tripped. . ." his words of dismay cut off when he followed her gaze.

"What has happened?" She lifted a hand to her throat, her voice strangled by dread.

"There was a battle," Bayle began. "A terrible battle and hundreds are dead."

"Who is dead?" Henry asked, alert.

"The Rebels, the king's troops have slaughtered hundreds of them."

"Where?" Helena gasped. "When?"

"Outside Bridgwater, near Westonzoyland, sometime during last night."

Helena wanted to scream that he was wrong, but the words wouldn't come. Don't let them be dead! "What else have you heard?" Her knees felt weak and she had to concentrate on remaining upright. Could the roaring in her head mean she was about to faint?

"Troopers rode into Bridgwater early this morning looking for Rebels, capturing whoever they found." Bayle shrugged. "That is all I know, we may hear more later."

The leather bucket fell from Henry's hands, hitting the cobbles with a thud and sending muddy water over the sides. Heedless of his soaked breeches, he clutched at Bayle's arm. "What of the Duke?"

Helena glared at him for mentioning that man's name when his first thoughts should be of their family. But what was the use?

Some of the house servants and a groom drifted out into the courtyard, watching curiously from a distance. Bayle's glance drifted to them and he gripped Henry's shoulders, murmuring at him to keep control.

Helena's eyes filled with gathering tears. "Father?" she whispered, knowing the question was unanswerable.

"Is Monmouth dead?" Henry was distraught.

Bayle closed his eyes briefly. "He fled the battlefield, so they say." At Henry's cry of dismay he rushed on. "But the stories are wild, no one knows where he is."

Helena felt her brother's misery, but couldn't find words to comfort him. Instead she faced a new terror. "Will the king's troops come here?"

Her panic transferred itself to Henry, who looked as if he might cry. "Will they arrest us?"

Bayle wrapped a protective arm around him. "I think not," he whispered.

"Everyone must know Father joined the Rebels." Helena didn't care who heard her, appearances were the last thing on her mind. She threw a fierce look in the direction of the huddled servants, who stared back with no more expression than a flock of sheep.

Sir Jonathan Woulfe's name would have the word, 'traitor' appended to it wherever it was spoken. But it didn't matter, not to her. She wanted him home again, to feel his laughter rolling in his chest as he held her against him, the scratch of his rough coat on her cheek and the smell of his skin in her senses. Father.

"Which is why you must leave here," Bayle said, his voice measured.

"But that makes no sense." Henry rubbed has face with a dirty hand. "If we are not to be arrested, why must we leave?"

"Because, Master. Condemned traitors forfeit their property to the Crown."

"They will take Loxsbeare?" Henry's face was white with shock and he groped for his sister's arm.

Bayle's face twisted in anguish. "Henry, they will take everything Sir Jonathan owns."

Grief vied with rage as Helena watched her brother's distress. What value did their father's high principals for the Anglican Church have now, when they were to be driven from their home? Where would they go, and how? She felt panic building up inside her and her breathing quickened. Bayle stepped forward to close the circle, an arm around each of them, his hard glare holding the inquisitive servants at bay.

With no idea where the thought came from, Helena blurted, "I must go and find them."

Henry's child-like misery was replaced by incredulous horror, and in a harsh voice he demanded. "Go where, Helena?"

"To this Zoyland place, or wherever the battle was."

Fielding further questions, she lifted her skirts and pounded towards the house, calling for Chloe as she ran.

They caught up with her on the upper landing. "A battlefield is no place for a gentlewoman," Bayle argued.

Helena waved him away. What was a battlefield like? Whatever she might find, she couldn't spend another day waiting anxiously in the house, with her mother growing more self-absorbed by the hour.

If she could find them, and bring Aaron back, perhaps it might rekindle some of the spirit which had deserted her these last weeks. With Aaron restored to her, she might forgive her father too, for taking him away in the first place. And, Helena reasoned, perhaps then, she might be able to lover her too.

Henry's voice broke into her reverie with more fear than anger. "You cannot leave, Helena. It is too dangerous."

They followed her into her chamber, where she turned on them, ordering them out. Henry's pleading turned to shouting. "You have no idea where they are!"

"I will find them," she shouted back.

Bayle's reasonable voice cut through their bickering, but she flung away from them both, opening the chest at the bottom of her bed. As she hurled items of clothing onto the coverlet, Chloe appeared, her confused gaze moving from one animated face to another. She started when Helena ordered, "Fetch me one of father's traveling bags, this instant!"

Chloe threw Bayle a beseeching look as she left the room, but he paid her no attention. Helena's oldest shifts and two plain, worn gowns joined the pile heaped on the bed. She glanced down at the muddy skirt she wore; bits of straw still clinging to it. At least she looked the part.

Bayle harangued her steadily, the ensuing commotion exacerbated by the arrival of the housekeeper. Betty Humbold blamed Chloe for the fuss and demanded an explanation. Several housemaids had followed Betty upstairs, curious to see what the excitement was about. Into the chaotic melee stepped the elegant figure of Lady Elizabeth, a hopeful and enquiring expression on her face.

Helena's heart lurched and she pulled garments into a rough pile, murmuring under her breath, "Not me, please don't let it be me who tells her."

Bayle stepped forward to detach her from the crowd, drawing her out of Helena's line of vision. When they returned, Lady Elizabeth was pale, her blue eyes clouded with pain. Helena's shoulders slumped, angry with herself for even thinking of leaving her. "Mother I-"

Her mother held up a shaking hand to silence her. "Go. It may be possible for you to travel where others cannot, and we need to know . . ."

"But Mother!" Henry was aghast.

Her face crumpled and Lady Elizabeth put an arm round her son, shushing him. Bayle's next words lifted Helena's heart. "I will go with her, Mistress. We can take the heavy cart and two of the moor ponies. We can go under the guise of a traveling wool merchant and his..." Helena thought he was about to say daughter, but he changed it to 'niece'.

He stepped onto the landing and called for Tobias to pack for him. When he strode back into the room, Bayle's gaze flicked to Helena's bag and the journal poking out of it.

"You cannot take this." He held up the little brown book, its fastening trailing like an appeal. "We are traveling merchants who know nothing of the rebellion." He thrust it at her. "This would give us away in an instant."

Embarrassed, Helena handed the journal to Henry. At her pleading look he nodded, folding the little book in his hands.

Bayle hoisted the bag onto his shoulder and shoved through the huddle of curious servants at the door. "We will put our story together on the way," he said, leading the procession down the stairs and out into the courtyard.

Their leave taking was very different from that of the joyful Woulfe menfolk almost a month before. Lady Elizabeth held her daughter in her arms, which might have proved Helena's undoing had Bayle not pushed her almost roughly towards the cart.

Helena could not help but notice there were no fine horses and best garments for Bayle and his young 'niece', simply two of the hardiest moor ponies the Woulfes' owned, fastened into the traces of the provisions cart.

Helena eyed them uncertainly. "Must we take these?" She asked, dismayed. "They are not even proper horses, we could move faster on the bay and the chestnut."

"No doubt," Bayle offered with a cynical smile. "But would you set them to pull this?" He indicated the heavy cart. "Or shall we take the carriage? The one with the Woulfe crest on the door?" His sarcasm cut into her and she felt a burning flush creep up her neck.

His expression softened. "They are superior horseflesh. What would you do if a trooper asked where you got them? Or he attempted to take them from you because they are finer than his own?"

Helena groaned at her own stupidity, aware of the listening servants. Watching his face, it occurred to her that being left with two women, a boy and a houseful of the weaker and less able servants, must have been hard on Bayle these last weeks.

She suspected he did not approve of the rising, but had her father commanded him, he would not have hesitated to accompany him to Somerset. No wonder he welcomed the opportunity to do something positive for his master. For the first time she saw him as a person in his own right. with feelings she could not fathom. Helena's world shifted and the stark fact came to her, that not everyone's ambitions were the same as the Woulfes.

Helena watched Tobias packing horse feed into the cart. When she caught his eye he gave a slow, courteous half-bow. She was saved from responding with a curt retort by Henry, who lunged at her and wrapped his arms around her waist.

"I know you will say it is not possible, but I would do anything to go with you," he pleaded.

His words broke her heart, but she had to refuse him, even before she saw her mother shake her head and press a fist to her mouth. "I cannot, Henry. Boys like you are known to have joined the Rebels. If the troopers decided to take you, I would have no means to prevent it."

"What if they should take you, Helena?" he whispered, too low for their mother to hear. "Do you think they wouldn't hang a woman?" Helena stiffened, the thought hadn't occurred to her. But she couldn't weaken.

She pulled herself out of his embrace and Henry stepped back. He reminded her so much of Aaron then, she ducked her head away and climbed into the cart. She had to find them and bring them home.

With a last, longing look at her mother, who stood with her arm round Henry in front of the only home she had ever known, the cart lurched out onto the road. Would anything be the same when she returned?

* * *

Henry looked up as Samuel trotted into the courtyard; halted his mount in a flurry of choking dust and dismounted, discarding the reins. Comfortable with well-known surroundings, the animal waited for someone to lead it away. Benjamin, the new head groom loped forward to take the bridle. The man had come into his position since the departure of the original incumbent for Monmouth's army, but Henry didn't like him.

Henry changed direction to fall into step beside Samuel, he two of them striding toward the house. Lady Elizabeth waited beside the casement window in the entrance hall; bathed in a shaft of light like a nervous ghost. On catching sight of their visitor, her lovely face closed as if in anticipation of more bad news.

Samuel bowed over her hand. "Lady Elizabeth." He wasted no time on preliminaries. "With Monmouth's army routed, the king will show no mercy to known Rebels, you must leave here."

She snatched her hand away, but Samuel persisted. "We are not as far from trouble as you might believe. Somerset is swarming with troopers, and Devon will be too in a day or so."

"My husband could return at any time. I cannot leave." She lifted her chin defiantly but defeat was in her face.

"Madam, if you don't go of your own volition, you may find yourself taking flight with only the clothes you stand up in."

Henry placed a hand on her shoulder. "We must listen to Master Ffoyle, Mother, he would never give us bad advice."

She stared about wildly. "Where would we go? Who would risk their own life to help us?"

"Master Ffoyle will help us, Mother," Henry saw Samuel's face relax and said, "My father asked you to do this?"

Samuel nodded. "There is no time to explain, but I promise we shall talk later. You must pack up everything you need. Hide your valuables, or send them away with someone you trust."

"You are the only one we can trust, Master Ffoyle." Henry knew he sounded bitter, but he couldn't help it. He should have been proud to take over as man of the house, but he felt discarded, inadequate.

His father, uncle and brother had gone off to fight for a cause they believed in. Even Helena had followed her own impulses; and where was he? Caretaking an empty house occupied by a distraught woman, who, up until that afternoon, had scorned his care.

Samuel patted his shoulder and beckoned a footman to take his hat and cloak. "Three carts are on their way to take your goods to my home. The servants must bring horses, plate, anything you don't wish the king's men to steal or destroy."

Samuel turned serious eyes on Henry. "You and Helena must dress yourselves in simple clothes, no silk or taffetas, you must pass for local farming people and-"

"Helena is not here," Henry interrupted. A sob escaped Lady Elizabeth and he felt warmth creep into his face. "She left for Somerset this morning."

"Somerset, alone? Why?"

"Nathan Bayle is with her. They have gone to find father and the others."

Samuel blew air between his lips in a silent whistle. "Well, Bayle at least knows the plan, so when they return." He paused, the word 'if' hanging in the air between them. "They will know where to come."

Lady Elizabeth recoiled as a shadow passed the window, followed by the sound of cartwheels rumbling into the yard.

"Ah. My men are here." Samuel strode across the floor, turning back at the door. "When the carts are loaded, cover and conceal them in the stables. Don't leave them out in the yard, they can be seen from the road."

Henry called after him, "Master Ffoyle, what about Helena?"

Samuel halted with one hand on the door. "Pray for her."

Lady Elizabeth's face twisted with anguish and she hurried away, leaving Henry alone in the hall.

He felt perilously close to tears as everything seemed to be spiraling out of control. He had promised to take care of his mother and yet they were about to abandon their home. Watching Helena ride away with Bayle still gnawed at him. If anyone was going to search the countryside for his father and brother, then it should have been him, not a girl. Was I too afraid to insist? Dread knotted his stomach at the thought of how he would explain it all to his father when he returned.

A maid came running into the hall, slowing her steps when she saw him, a frown on her face. Henry straightened his shoulders and brushed past her, taking the stairs two at a time. He could at least help them save everything they could from the house.

He descended the stairs again some time later, balancing two paintings of long dead Woulfes in his arms. He paused to watch two servants emerge from the steward's room, struggling to carry a heavy oak chest between them.

Samuel followed behind, his arms full of ledgers topped by two gold candlesticks. The estate accounts, Henry knew, were almost as valuable as the contents of the chest. His stomach knotted again. They were really leaving Loxsbeare.

* * *

The heavy cart rumbled down the Honiton road. "Don't look so terrified Mistress." Bayle admonished her good-naturedly.

Helena forced herself to relax, lifting her face to the sun.

Bayle glanced at her and looked up. "Let us hope the sun dries up the roads. Some have been impassable by flash flooding these last weeks."

The gentle jolting of the cart was not too uncomfortable, a half filled woolsack was placed between Helena and the wooden seat. "I know our purpose is grave," she gave a long sigh. "But it is almost a relief to be out in the countryside after being cooped up at Loxsbeare for so long.

Her gaze followed the flight of a bird over her shoulder and she heard scuffling in the hedgerows above the steady clop of the ponies' hooves. A deer crossed in front of the cart, its soft eyes regarding her steadily before disappearing into the woods beyond the hedge.

"Why so many sacks?" Helena indicated the flatbed of the cart.

"To sleep on, Mistress." At her shocked expression he added, "There are plenty of inns, but who knows when we might have to keep off the main roads."

Her mouth formed a silent 'O', as another thought occurred to her. "Do we have any coin for innkeepers?"

"Yes, Mistress." He smiled, arching an eyebrow. "And for horse feed, if we can find any."

"But there is horse feed in the cart." She indicated a second sack.

"That is to sell, not for these brutes to eat."

Helena fell silent, aware of Bayle's indulgent smile on her profile. Had she really anticipated, for one moment, making this journey alone?

Beyond the low hedges, Helena saw workers in the fields, their backs bent as they sliced rhythmically with their scythes, heaping cut wheat into piles and tying them together, heads uppermost to dry out.

"It's early for the harvest," she murmured.

"The bad weather has flattened the corn." His nod encompassed the fields of gold off to their left. "It is swollen and difficult to gather, they are saving what they can."

It must have been hard, dirty work and the men who silently watched their progress looked tired and haggard. Apart from an almost ruined harvest, Helena wondered if they too scoured the horizon for royal patrols.

Several images came together in her head as she asked, "Does the Green Ribbon Club still exist, Bayle?"

He frowned. "Not as it once did, Mistress. Many of its most prominent members are dead. But there are plenty in these parts who uphold their beliefs." He did not mention her father's name, leaving the implication hanging between them.

"Is John Trenchard one of them?"

"I believe so. He ran a Rebel club out of the Red Lion Inn in Taunton."

Several of Helena's questions were answered at once. "Ran?"

"He has fled the country since the arrest warrant went out for him. Why do you ask, Mistress?"

"No reason, just something I heard once about buying muskets."

He frowned, but she chose not to elaborate about the time she spent in Taunton with her father. Idly she wondered what had become of the weapons Master Trenchard had bougt. He wouldn't be using them now, against the king or anyone. Then another thought had her gabbling again. "Suppose the soldiers come to Loxsbeare when we are gone?"

"As well they might, Mistress." He did not look at her, occupied at that moment with guiding the ponies around a hay cart blocking the road.

"But Mother . . ." she stammered, horrified at herself for not considering this eventuality before. She had quit her home without a thought in search of her father, but the parent she should have been caring for was alone. How would Lady Elizabeth manage without her, and more importantly, without Bayle?

They will be gone by tonight, your mother and Henry."

"Gone, gone where?" She turned to stare at him.

"To the Ffoyles," he replied, "that is what was arranged."

Helena experienced a moment of clarity as several disjointed conversations replayed in her head. "Father arranged this before he left? He knew this would happen?"

Bayle shot her a look. "Your father was committed to the cause, never doubt that." He flicked the reins to make the ponies gather pace. "But taking arms against a king brings certain risks."

Helena felt anger bloom and grow inside her head. If there was any possibility her father thought the rising might fail, how could he have ridden off and left them like he did?

She twisted in her seat to face him. "Samuel Ffoyle is not a Monmouth man. He told me himself he forbade his sons to go. For which he must now be grateful." She tried, but failed to keep the bitterness from her voice.

"Perhaps not," Bayle arched an eyebrow at her. "But he is Jonathan Woulfe's man."

Several questions sprang into her head, but Bayle seemed to know what was going through her mind.

"You will have to accept, Mistress that Loxsbeare Manor is no longer your home."

"It will be taken from us? Soon?"

Bayle gave a slow, thoughtful nod, his gaze fixed on the road ahead.

How could it be happening? Her great grandfather had built the manor. In her head she strolled through the massive oak door into the lofty entrance while sunlight played on the polished floor. The upper room overlooking the garden had been hers since she was small. She didn't sleep well anywhere else. A silent protest rose up inside her. The manor belonged to the Woulfes. It should always belong to them.

Then her rational self told her otherwise. Circumstances had changed and they were no longer in control.

The thought of strangers at Loxsbeare gave her a physical pain. She gripped the rough wood of the cart so hard, she felt splinters cut into her hand.

The thick branches above them swayed and collided in the wind, throwing off the remains of the last storm to sprinkle the cart with droplets of cool water.

Helena took a deep breath. "Then you had better stop calling me Mistress."

CHAPTER SIX

Elizabeth Woulfe fought the creeping lethargy threatening to overwhelm her. How could their comfortable life at Loxsbeare have ended like this? Always outwardly loyal to the Whig cause, privately she had been suspicious of Jonathan's friends.

The fanatic Lord Shaftesbury seemed to bewitch him, and she never understood why Jonathan tolerated the odious Lord Grey. A man who had kidnapped his wife's sister and lived quite openly with her. Then there were the others, Wade and Prideaux and those ambitious Speke boys; all of them with their ludicrous plans to oust the Duke of York.

It had gone on for years and had seemed harmless enough when all it amounted to was boisterous talk. Even when Monmouth himself visited Loxsbeare, she had never quite believed they were in earnest.

Then King Charles died, and the gravity of what Jonathan planned left her horrified, but silent. She had never voiced her misgivings aloud, knowing her husband's beliefs would not be swayed by what he called, 'a woman's weakness'. What sustained her was her ability to pretend their clandestine meetings were not traitorous at all.

She stared around the deserted entrance hall, bitterness making her angry that Jonathan's folly had brought them to this; while he could be lying dead or dying on a field in Somerset. And the very worst of it; was that he had taken Aaron. Her Aaron. Taken him without an apologetic word. Not caring that he was ripping out her heart.

She drifted from room to room listlessly, sighing at the sight of the dismantled house as she packed household items in bags and wrapped them in oiled cloth; Betty Humbold waddling in her wake.

By mid afternoon, seventy years and three generations of accumulated trappings of the Woulfe family were piled onto the hall floor, it's volume surprising her. It was impractical to remove everything; the massive wooden beds and heavier furniture had been constructed inside the house and would take a team of carpenters to dismantle.

When the housekeeper appeared with a pile of linen, Elizabeth lifted her arms in a gesture of bewilderment. "I don't know what to leave behind, Betty. I could not bear to think of one pewter plate ending up in the home of some undeserving magistrate, or sold by some soldier for ale money."

Betty surveyed the jumble of belongings, chewing her bottom lip. A tall woman with wide hips and heavy bones, she had arrived at the manor as a ten-year-old kitchen maid, when Sir Jonathan's mother, Eleanor, was a young bride. The unchallenged mistress of the servants' hall, she had buried three head grooms during her tenure, one of whom she had married.

Betty's voluminous skirts swung as she lifted a hip over a pile of books, patting her mistress's shoulder. "If you give those men outside the things you and the children will need for a while, I know a place we can stow the rest." Her plain face softened into an enigmatic smile.

Blinking away tears, Elizabeth could only nod gratefully. Betty's flat brown eyes twinkled with amusement. "We shall come through this terrible time you and I, and live to tell stories round the fire when we are old."

Elizabeth smiled at that; when would Betty consider herself old?

* * *

On reaching Somerset, Helena could not help but notice every village buzzed with talk of Monmouth's defeat. At Wellington, villagers huddled at public pumps and outside the inn to repeat what they had heard, while others appeared to be watching for strangers who might threaten their existence or bring more news. Once Bayle convinced them that he and Helena occupied the second category, they clustered around to ask them what they knew and claim sightings of Rebels in the surrounding fields.

At Staplegrove, Bayle stopped to buy small beer and allow the horses some rest. Helena climbed down to stretch her legs and Bayle removed the wheat stalks which had wound their way around the cartwheels. He struck up a conversation with some wary locals at the entrance of a tumbledown farm.

They learned Lord Churchill's patrols were systematically searching farms and cornfields, assuming fugitives would try to make their way back to their homes. "Troopers have been through here already today." An elderly man with cracked, sun-baked skin told them.

"Where is the patrol now?" Bayle asked.

"They took off through those fields over there after a couple o' poor wretches on the other side of that wall." He pointed a dirty finger down Fore Street, back where they had come. "But I don't think they woz Rebels, they had 'orses with 'em."

Thanking him, Bayle urged the cart onwards through villages with names like Cheddon Fitzpane, West Monkton, Adsborough and Thurloxton; a route Bayle seemed familiar with, although there were few signposts. Helena scanned the fields and roadways with narrowed eyes, half expecting to see ragged and blood-splattered figures crawling through the undergrowth, or peering out from behind trees as they passed. She saw no one.

The landscape remained quiet and still, the empty fields baked and glowing in the early evening light. As hunger intruded, she picked at the package of bread and sliced meat prepared for them, handing morsels to Bayle. Nibbling the still-soft dough, Helena pictured her mother and Henry at home in the dining hall eating their supper. Then she remembered, they would be leaving Loxsbeare soon.

Daylight faded into pink and yellow evening, the road stretching ahead onto a wide, flat plain with empty fields on either side; a few low trees scattered in the distance.

With the sun lowering behind the horizon, the temperature dropped swiftly. Helena's back was stiff from being bumped against the unyielding wooden seat, her jaw so sore, she could swear her teeth were loose from being cracked together. "Are all Somerset roads so narrow and bumpy?" she complained.

Bayle gave a wry smile. "I'm afraid so."

She was about to ask if they intended to spend the entire night traveling, when a cluster of houses materialized out of the gloom. A squat church with a thin spire rose on their left behind a row of houses. A misty, range of hills was visible in the distance, but the village, if that's what it was, contained little else.

With only the sound of the rumbling cart to break the silence, they entered the main street. Helena peered at a hanging sign above their heads, sporting what resembled a white bird in flight, the bottom half obscured by dirt and grime.

Small, square windows were dotted along the façade, the upper storey overhanging the ground floor. Soft yellow light streamed out of the lower windows onto the road and the sound of chattering voices within, mingled with the clatter of pots and plates.

"Where are we?" Helena whispered, her hunger awoken by enticing cooking smells drifting in the air.

"Weston is about five miles on the other side of that marshland." Bayle nodded toward flatlands outlined by clumps of trees. "We shall stay here tonight, there will be soldiers all over the roads into Bridgwater tomorrow."

"Would they bother with us, do you think?"

"Whatever they intend, we are at their mercy. Remember not to show any interest in the Rebels. Churchill's men will be well organized after the initial chaos of today and every soldier in the county will be searching for fugitives."

"Do you wish I had not forced you to come?" she asked, hauling her pain-filled body onto the road.

"We are here now," his response was curt. "By tomorrow or the next day, pray God, we may be home again, but I fear the countryside has seen nothing of the king's vengeance yet."

* * *

Samuel's men loaded the last cart, the previous one having left half an hour before. During a lull in the activity, Henry sat on a hay bale in the stable out of the sun, whittling a piece of wood. Two grooms idled outside, pitching horseshoes at a stake in the ground, an occasional clang the only sound above intermittent birdsong.

Henry had enjoyed the responsibility of supervising the Ffoyle servants to load the carts. He didn't even mind when Samuel stepped in to call a halt because he was allowing the men to stack the goods too high.

"Not only would it slow us down," Samuel said, issuing new instructions, "but they are too obviously the possessions of a wealthy man in flight and bound to attract attention."

By mid afternoon, three loaded carts and four horses from the Loxsbeare stables had left for Ideswell, although to Henry's dismay, it seemed to make little impression on the contents of the manor.

Samuel joined him in the stable, leaning against an empty stall with his arms folded across his chest. Henry thought he might be dozing, until Samuel opened one eye and gave him a reassuring grin. Henry liked Master Ffoyle, who had always treated him as someone whose opinions were worth listening to. As a child, while his older brother practiced his swordsmanship on the Weare Cliffs behind the house, Henry had begged to accompany Master Ffoyle and his father into Exeter.

When he became bored with merchants' talk in the Customs House, or the pipe smoke in the Bishops Blaize inn irritated his chest, Samuel came to his rescue. He would take him to Tuckers Hall to gossip to the wool men, or to walk among the flapping sails of the drying racks in the Crulditch outside the city walls. Recalling those times with a pang of sadness, he wondered if he would ever spend days like that again.

The door creaked and Henry looked up, startled, but it was only Benjamin. Samuel rolled his eyes and Henry gave a nervous laugh as the groom sidled through the door and paused, his hands in his pockets, morosely silent.

Benjamin had elected to remain behind at Loxsbeare, from cowardice or loyalty, Henry could not decide. While everyone else worked, the groom had been neither help nor a hindrance. He was little more than an irritant, so Samuel had sent him to keep watch for approaching soldiers.

Samuel scowled at him. "Well?" he demanded, apparently puzzled by the servant's lethargy.

"Dragoons," Benjamin muttered under his breath.

"Where?" Samuel and Henry leapt to their feet.

"Came up Shepcote Hill s'morning," he mumbled, glaring at his questioner.

"Where are they at this moment, man? Not this morning?" Samuel cuffed him in frustration.

"Prob'ly near North Gate b'now," Benjamin sneered, ducking away from the blow.

"God's Blood," Samuel shouted. He ran outside, Henry at his heels.

"You!" He pointed at Benjamin, then seemed to change his mind, "No, you man." Another groom froze at the sound of his voice. "Move this cart into the rear stable out of sight." The man leapt forward to obey.

Henry cast a terrified look at the upper windows. "Will they search the house?"

"We shall have to bluff it out and hope that isn't why they have come." Samuel leaned his weight into the shoulder of a stocky pony in an effort to force the animal to move.

Tobias came running from the rear calling instructions to the servants, but panic made Henry hesitate, stranded in the middle of the courtyard as figures and animals rushed past him. He contemplated running back into the stable and hiding in the hay byre, but only for a second. Perhaps he should make for the house to help his mother, but indecision left him not knowing which way to turn.

"Churchill's men won't have got this far west so soon." Tobias struggled with a skittish gelding. "Like as not, they'll be militia patrols, surly, tough men but none too bright." Henry didn't understand the distinction, but in an effort to make himself useful, he ran to fasten the stable doors.

They were just in time. The sound of hooves and the jingle of bridles signaled the approach of horsemen on the road beyond the gates.

* * *

"Welcome to The Dove." The barrel-chested landlord greeted them at the entrance, leading the way into a low-ceilinged hall with a scrubbed board floor, its bulging walls covered with mottled yellow lime-wash. A narrow, uneven staircase stood at one end, fingering its way to the upper story like a series of elbows at odd angles.

Bayle negotiated their accommodation while Helena stood fidgeting under the suspicious stare of the landlord's wife, a brown faced woman with mousy hair peeking out from under a grubby white cap.

"Do they have rooms for us?" she asked Bayle when he rejoined her.

"For you certainly." He guided her to a table in the corner of the room, amongst a motley collection of tradesmen and merchants. "But the one I was offered is at the front. I cannot see the horses from there." He kept his voice so low, she had to bend forward to hear him. "I shall sleep in the stable to make sure no one deprives us of them during the night."

Helena was about to offer a protest, but the guttering, smoky candles made her cough.

"The hay there will probably be fresher than the mattress you'll be sleeping on." Bayle laughed aloud at her horrified expression.

They had arrived too late to avail themselves of the evening meal; instead they were offered a supper of soup, coarse bread and strong ale, followed by sliced ham and potatoes fried in bacon fat. The food was hot and appetizing, the bread still warm and the soup reminiscent of a meaty stew.

As Helena expected, the conversation around them centered on the defeat of the Rebels and the progress of John Churchill's troops. She learned Lord Feversham was on his way to Wells with three battalions of Guards and the Wiltshire Militia.

Some claimed to have seen Rebels running away through cornfields, others to have witnessed hangings at the roadsides. A florid man with stained teeth, told them that six Rebels had been hanged the previous night at Glastonbury from an inn sign. He tried to draw Bayle out as to his allegiance, but received monosyllabic answers, while others in the room shifted nervously. Sidling away, he tried again with another group of diners, but ceased his probing when they responded with mild threats.

The meal over, a maid in a food-stained apron escorted Helena to her room, through narrow corridors and up several short flights of stairs. Set under the eaves, the room was small and sparsely furnished, with a crooked door hanging lop-sided against the latch.

The bed bore thin, rough sheets and a coarse blanket; set lower to the floor than Helena was used to, bringing images of rats to mind, which she pushed away. It at least looked clean.

Helena peeled the bodice of her gown away from her itching skin, letting the skirt fall to the floor. She was more weary than she could ever remember; and yet proud of how far she and Bayle had come since the morning. In only her shift, she crossed to the low window, its grimy glass giving a view of the darkening countryside, the road they arrived on running beneath.

She leaned her hands on the cracked sill, bending a little to peer out. She squinted at the shadowy outline of Bridgwater in the distance. The smell of grass and wildflowers drifted on the air, combined with the sharp tang of the stable. She remembered Bayle was there and hoped he would not be too uncomfortable sleeping on the hay; her smile fading as a thought came to her. Where was her father sleeping tonight? Beneath a hedgerow somewhere, or in the Taunton gaol house? The other alternative, that he lay dead on the battlefield made her shiver, though the night was warm. And where were Aaron, and Edmund? Were they together, or alone, running from the troopers?

The sound of riders invaded her thoughts, but at first she was too preoccupied to be alarmed. Then voices on the road grew louder, followed by a shout and the slam of a door.

Then she saw them, a jumble of moving brown shapes huddled together, merging and separating again to become riders; coming from the direction of Bridgwater. Her stomach turned over as ten mounted men moved nearer in a steady, rhythmic canter, their bridles rattling. Their faces were white blurs in the dim light, but they sat their mounts with an arrogant air, leaning over their saddles to stare into windows as doors were slammed shut ahead of them.

Helena stepped back and fastened the window, retreating to press her back against wall. The sounds of shouting and running feet on wooden boards reached her. What should she do? Run and fetch Bayle or stay where she was?

The seconds stretched and she frowned as the sound changed pitch. The hoof beats were receding. They had ridden past the inn without stopping. She exhaled slowly, feeling almost dizzy with relief.

No longer caring that she had no means of washing the dust from her hair and that Chloe was not there to help her, she climbed into the creaky bed. Despite her exhaustion, she lay awake for what seemed like hours, listening for more hooves in the distance. The tiny patch of sky beyond the window darkened to black as she teetered on the edge of consciousness. Her father's face swam into her head and seemed so real, she mumbled into her lumpy pillow, "I am coming, Father."

* * *

The patrol cantering through Loxsbeare's massive gates consisted of twelve soldiers riding in double file. Their bridles rang and their hooves clattered to a halt on the cobbles. Betty Humbold was crossing the yard with a kitchen maid and muffled an oath as they halted in front of her. Hoisting her skirts, she ran up the steps, dragging the maid with her to slam the door shut behind them.

The officer's glare raked the courtyard, fixing on Samuel who strolled forward, a puzzled frown on his face as if their appearance was a mystery.

Henry had left it too long to do anything but watch as they crowded into the yard, larger and more menacing than he had imagined. He felt, rather than saw Tobias at his shoulder and was reassured; although his legs shook.

The officer dismounted, his boots ringing on the cobbles as he approached Samuel with calm authority. The Master of Cloth Workers drew himself up to his full height to return the man's arrogant stare.

A black-coated figure, who had been slower getting down from his horse appeared at the officer's shoulder. Henry knew this man. It was the Magistrate, the same one who had tried to waylay them outside the church that day. Samuel apparently knew him too. "What can I do for you, Master Penecost?"

The magistrate looked sheepish, avoiding Samuel's gaze. "I apologize for our unannounced presence, Master Ffoyle, but these officers have business with Sir Jonathan Woulfe."

He indicated the man beside him, whose face sported a livid scar running from beneath his right eye to the corner of his mouth. At the magistrate's ingratiating tone, Henry saw a grimace of distaste pass across his face. He shoved past the magistrate to withdraw a folded parchment from inside his coat. In a rough voice he snarled. "I have orders here for the arrest of Sir Jonathan Woulfe, on the charge of treason against His Majesty King James the second and the seizure of his goods and property."

Henry groaned and felt his knees about to give way. How had they arrived so quickly? Had they captured Father?

Tobias gripped his shoulder, and Henry realized he had spoken aloud.

Two soldiers dismounted from the column and climbed the front steps to pound on the door, demanding entry.

Samuel took the document from the officer, taking his time to read it through. The soldiers had gained the house and the sound of booted feet on floorboards drifted across the yard, accompanied by a man's shout and a shrill female protest.

Samuel held his hands out in surrender, the paper held aloft as if its contents confused him. "Sir Jonathan is in London, sir, on court business I believe."

The officer narrowed his eyes and said something Henry couldn't hear above the sound of a crash from inside the house. At a shouted order, the rest of the troop dismounted and fanned out through the grounds.

In a harsh whisper Tobias ordered, "Go and find somewhere to hide., Henry. There may be trouble."

Henry was about to argue, but the steward's fierce expression changed his mind. He scampered behind the stable toward the kitchen garden. It appeared empty, but he had no intention of hiding, not with his mother still in the house. He had to protect her. Listening for the crunch of footsteps, he made his way around the fruit bushes in the kitchen garden. He reached a side door and dragged it open as a rough hand grabbed his collar.

"And where might you be goin'?" a burly soldier snarled close to his ear. A massive fist struck Henry in the back, the momentum barreling him into the wall. He bounced off the stonework and slid to the ground, the breath knocked from his lungs.

"Hopin' to hide the valu'bles wuz we, lad?" The man grinned, revealing brown stained teeth.

Dazed, Henry staggered to his feet, but the soldier cuffed him again, sending him sprawling. This time, he stayed put, his cheek pressed into the gravel. With an obscene oath and a throaty laugh, the soldier moved away.

Henry wobbled to his feet, heart thumping; giving silent thanks to Samuel for insisting he wear groom's clothes that morning. He staggered into the rear corridor, where two soldiers had apparently found the meat locker and were tussling over a joint of cooked ham. Sara, the kitchen maid, stood with her hands on her hips, glaring at them as if they were naughty children.

One of them turned and saw Henry, who froze. The soldier had greasy hair hanging in rats tails, the lower half of his face covered with stubble. He raked Henry with speculative eyes, which dulled when he saw nothing to interest him. With a contemptuous snarl, he gestured him away.

Henry turned and fled before the man changed his mind, this time toward the main hall, but there was no sign of his mother. Another soldier came down the stairs, his arms were full of linens and what appeared to be a hanging from one of the bedrooms.

Betty Humbold followed behind; but she was stout and at least thirty years older and made slow progress. She showed no more fear than Sara had, and Henry heard her muttering enraged curses.

The soldier grinned evilly over his shoulder as he gained the front door, while Betty held on to the newel to hurl a final insult. Henry waited until the soldier had gone, then crept along the corridor, peering into each room as he passed. They were all empty, the floors strewn with items dragged from drawers and chests. Where was mother?

He wandered back into the entrance hall in time to hear the stable door flung back hard on its hinges. He ran toward the front door, almost colliding with Tobias, who dragged him backwards by his collar. "What are you doing here, Master?"

"The horses!" Henry waved in the direction of the yard.

"It's too late. There is nothing you can do to prevent them." Tobias tightened his grip on Henry's coat.

They watched from the covered porch as soldiers lead the last of the Loxsbeare stable away; trotting three chestnut geldings toward the gates on leading reins. The sight of the fourth made Henry's heart contract.

Verity was hauled out into the sunlight. She flattened her ears and rolled her eyes in fear at the unfamiliar hands. "Don't pull her, she has a soft mouth," Henry moaned. Tobias made sympathetic murmurings at his side, but his hold on Henry's collar stayed firm.

"One of those geldings was to be mine," Henry growled, the closest he had come to rage since the soldiers had invaded his house.

His gaze shifted to two uniformed men in the courtyard, glowering at each other over a turkey rug on the ground. One drew his sword, but a third soldier intervened to separate them by ordering them away.

Tobias leaned down to whisper in Henry's ear. "A pile of fine bed linens, a silver candlestick and a whole ham, are real treasures to them. In all their lives they would never own such luxuries." He reached into a pocket and brought out a kerchief, holding it out. Henry stared at it, uncomprehending. "You're bleeding." Tobias cocked his chin at Henry's head.

Henry dabbed at his temple, pulling the cloth away with a frown; his eyebrows rose at the large red stain left there.

The officer with the scar was nowhere in sight. His second in command and the magistrate remained in the courtyard, idly watching the rest of the troops carry the more portable goods out of the house. Then a curt order came from somewhere and the troopers re-mounted their horses, most with heavier packs than when they arrived.

Samuel came through the front door, flinging his head back toward the courtyard. "They have my ponies." He looked accusingly at Tobias, who shrugged. "They must have found the cart."

Samuels' eyes narrowed as he caught sight of Henry. "You are not badly hurt at least," he murmured.

Henry looked up at a sound from above. The officer with the scar stood at the top of the stairs; his arms full of plate and what looked like a bed hanging. Lady Elizabeth followed close behind him as he started to descend, her face a mask of anger demanding he stop.

They reached the half landing together, her eyes ablaze with indignation. Heedless of any threat, she placed herself in front of the officer as if to challenge him, but he sneered and shouldered her away.

Henry gasped as she lurched against a post, swayed, but remained on her feet. The officer turned and halted, as if noticing her for the first time. His chin jutted forward, like a fox spotting its prey. He dropped the bed hanging and with his free hand, groped for her throat.

She gave a gasp as her sapphire pendant came away, reaching out a hand to reclaim it, one foot hovering over the step. Her position was already precarious, and with her equilibrium gone, she lurched forward and toppled down the flight of stairs with a startled cry.

As she fell, her head struck the wall and her body slammed headlong onto the floor at the bottom of the stairs.

"Mother!" Henry screamed, throwing himself forward across the hall to slide the last few feet on his knees.

The officer froze on the half landing, surveying the scene below him with uncertain eyes. Samuel lurched forward, muttering a threat and made to climb the stairs toward him. "No, Master Ffoyle." Tobias wrapped both arms around him and held on, grunting with the effort.

Henry lifted his mother's head onto his knees with shaking hands, stroking her hair. "Mother? Mother can you hear me?" She lay eerily still, her pale curls fanned out around her head, her face serene as if in sleep.

A trickle of viscous, almost black blood slid from her ear down her jaw. Alarmed, Henry stared at it, his stomach churning. "She's hurt, Master Ffoyle," he sobbed. "Someone, fetch a surgeon!" He stroked the pale curls away from her face. He must call a servant to fetch a cloth and some water, Mother wouldn't like to get blood on her hair.

Tobias reached past him to press his fingers gently against his mother's throat. He would help her. Tobias would know what to do. Samuel bent forward, his hands held flat above his knees. Tobias glanced up at the older man and gave a slow shake of his head.

The soldier halted on the stairs, watching them.

Samuel heaved a long sigh and clenched both fists. He drew himself up to his full height, his mouth working.

Samuel tugged at Henry's arm. "Come away, Master Henry."

"What do you mean?" Henry swung his head between the two men. "You have to help me get her to her chamber. Someone has to fetch the chirgeon."

When no one made a move toward him, the soldier's expression turned to an insolent grin. He descended the stairs slowly, the sapphire necklace hanging loosely from his fingers. His back to the wall, he skirted them and the body on the floor, then loped out of the door without a backward glance.

The hall fell ominously silent. Henry stared up at Tobias, holding his gaze for long seconds before he understood. "No!" he whispered.

Tobias reached out a hand, but when Henry looked away, he withdrew it again with a useless shrug.

Hesitant footsteps approached and Betty Humbold appeared from the direction of the kitchens. Her curious expression changed to abject horror when her gaze fell on the prone figure of Lady Elizabeth. She dropped to her knees with a groan to fling her arms around Henry, but he shrugged her off.

Betty sat back on her haunches, her hands pressed to her mouth and fat tears pouring down her face.

Tobias encircled Henry with both arms and hauled him upright. "Let go of me, Tobias. I want to stay with her."

"You shall, Henry," Samuel murmured. "But we cannot leave her here, like this."

Henry slumped down on the bottom step, his hands held limp between his knees to stare at the bundle on the floor as Tobias and Samuel bound his mother in the discarded hanging. How had it happened so quickly? Bile rose into his throat and his stomach heaved. Mother. Helena.

CHAPTER SEVEN

Helena bolted upright in the narrow bed, startled at the sight of the landlady's pinched face leaning over her with a mocking expression. "Your ladyship's bath awaits," she crowed, dumping a bucket of hot water unceremoniously on the floor, before sweeping out of the room.

Helena decided the woman's insult was almost bearable to be able to rinse red dust from her hair, and scrub her gritty skin. Accustomed to having Chloe standing by to deal with unreachable fastenings, the effort required to dress herself came as a revelation.

Pulling the draw cords on her shift was easy enough, but attaching the bodice to her skirt proved frustratingly difficult. She gave her discarded gown a shake, bundled it into her pack and went to find Bayle.

He sat in the dining hall, a large breakfast spread before him. "The woman who brought the water was positively insulting," Helena complained, helping herself to eggs and pork. "She barged into the room without knocking and... What are you grinning at?" She frowned, a chunk of buttered bread halfway to her mouth. Bayle gave her a lop-sided smile and turned back to his plate.

Their host made a show of hospitality, sauntering over to their table to enquire if they had spent a comfortable night. Repelled by the falsely ingratiating set of his bloated features and his enormous black-nailed hands, Helena suppressed a shudder and pretended to stare through the leaded window inches from her face.

"Aye," the man said. "We've 'ad troopers in and out of this place since yesterday morning." The landlord wiped his nose on his sleeve. "Pretty angry they are too with all the Rebels loose hereabouts."

Maybe Helena imagined it, but he spoke the word 'Rebel' with a disdainful inflection. Bayle forked food steadily into his mouth, saying nothing.

"Caught plenty of they poor devils too. Hanged some 'on em on the trees outside St Mary's Church at Weston yesterday. It will be a while before those bodies will be cut down, I can tell you." Then he asked the question Helena expected since she and Bayle arrived. "And where, sir, does your journey take you when you leave us this fine morning?"

Bayle lowered his tankard. "We are bound for Bristol, but have no wish to cross paths with angry soldiers. Can you offer us some advice?"

The landlord looked puzzled for a moment, and then mumbled something about soldiers on all roads leading east and there was no avoiding them. With a surly good day, he moved on.

Her appetite gone, Helena acquiesced willingly when Bayle suggested they be on their way.

"Do you think the landlord suspected why we are here?" Helena tucked her bag beneath the seat and scrambled into her seat.

"It cost me more than the price of our breakfast to ensure he did not." He cocked his head backwards at the receding inn. "He's making a tidy profit keeping his guest's business private."

"What do you mean?"

"Our host is charged with reporting the names of all strangers and suspicious persons staying at The Dove. He would only fail in his duty if he is sufficiently recompensed beforehand."

Helena's felt her jaw slackening in shock.

Bayle gave a dismissive shrug. "He might be a rogue, but his lax morals served us well. There are those who suffer and die in times like these, and others who will use it to line their pockets." He gave a sigh. "T'is the way of the world."

Before Helena could voice her outrage at injustice in all its forms, he told her to keep a look out for troopers. "There will be patrols on all the roads soon."

In Middlezoy, his warning proved accurate; they were not even in the village before Helena spotted them. Troopers hammered on doors and pounded through houses, thrusting aside anyone brave enough to disobey.

For no greater sin than not responding fast enough to a shouted command, they forced men and boys alike to endure cuffs and insults; administering hefty whacks across shoulders with the flats of swords.

A soldier insulted a local girl with rough handling, tearing her clothes. A man, Helena presumed to be the girl's father, rushed forward to defend her and received a slash of the soldier's whip across his face. The man fell to the ground, bleeding, while his persecutor delivered a vicious kick.

"Don't react to it, Mistress," Bayle whispered, flicking the reins to urge the ponies on past them.

Helena gritted her teeth, her sense of justice demanding an explanation. "What is happening, Bayle? And stop calling me mistress."

Bayle threw her an apologetic smile. "They hate us, they hate us all. In their eyes, the West Country has committed the ultimate act of treason, and we must pay. Few armies are merciful in victory. It is often too hard won."

"But these people aren't Rebels, they're villagers. They offer no threat."

"It hardly matters, they are savage because they can be. There is no fairness to it."

Helena never measured her courage before, and cowardice burned in her. She had left Loxsbeare full of arrogance, determined to find her family at any cost. But that cost was only now becoming real. She was laying herself open to possible arrest, even a beating. Or worse. No one had authority over these vicious soldiers, and Bayle would be helpless if they turned their attentions on her. Her enlightenment came too late as she realized that turning back, was as dangerous as pressing on.

The day remained hot as they ventured into the flat, open countryside.

"Where are we?" Helena scanned the low horizon.

Bayle pointed toward a clump of trees ahead, beyond that, Helena could make out rooftops on a rise. "Up the road there is Westonzoyland, where my aunt and uncle live."

Helena studied his profile in surprise. It had never occurred to her before Bayle had a family. "What are they like?"

"That's a strange question."

"Yes, I suppose it is." She grinned. "Would they know anything, do you think?"

"I know no more than you do." He sounded weary. "But it's somewhere to begin and the best lie to tell is one wrapped in truth."

Helena didn't understand what he meant, but remained silent as they entered the well-kept village with its pleasant green. A row of substantial stone houses clustered round a church with a square spire. "St Mary's," Bayle murmured, nodding toward it.

She was about to ask where these relatives of his lived, when without warning, he hauled the hood of Helena's cloak over her head, pulling her into his side and holding her there.

The ponies snorted and struggled between the traces as they caught a whiff of something unpleasant, while Bayle cracked the reins against a round rump shouting, "Get on there, go." Helena felt their panic at his ferocious growl, and the cart sprang forward.

After a short but jolting sprint, he released her. Helena emerged spluttering. "Why did you do that?" she demanded. "And what is that dreadful smell?" She twisted round to look behind her.

"Don't look," Bayle snapped, but she barely heard him.

Her first impression was of four men seated above her in a tree, but there was something unnatural about their posture. When she recognized what she was looking at, her jaw slackened in horror. Four corpses swung from the towering oak, metal chains looped about their necks and torsos, hands tied behind their backs. Their faces were frozen in grotesque parodies of human expression, which showed their deaths had been neither quick nor easy. She choked back a scream, clamping her eyes tight shut to block it out, but the image remained seared behind her eyelids.

"Is it? Are they. . ."

"Calm yourself, Helena. It isn't them."

Hot tears of relief trickled down her cheeks, which turned to pity for the poor wretches who had died so horribly. She kept her gaze fixed on the churchyard, its beauty marred by groups of unkempt soldiers languishing against gravestones, while others trampled the grass.

"Don't stare at them," Bayle warned. "It will alert them we are strangers."

He halted the cart at the edge of the green and helped Helena down. Her legs still ached from the journey of the previous day as he guided her down a pathway to an oak door, which showed evidence of violent treatment - scars and splinters gouged in the wood at eye level.

In response to Bayle's knock, the door swung inwards, revealing a diminutive woman in a brown dress, covered by a white apron with a housewife cap on her head. Her eyes widened and wordlessly, she ushered them inside, casting a fearful look over their shoulders before closing the door.

"Nathan," she whispered, her hand to her throat. Helena watched as the years drained from her face, giving a glimpse of the lovely woman she had once been. "I had not thought to see you here, and at such a time."

She was delicate featured and pale skinned, with a trace of worry lines around deep brown eyes, identical to Bayle's. It was her smile that told Helena they were related, for it lit her face in the same way a smile lit his, with warmth and intelligence. A face you could trust.

She showed them to an upholstered settle by the fireplace where Bayle explained. "Mistress Fellowes is my father's youngest sister."

"I thank you for your hospitality, Mistress." Helena inclined her head.

"So this is Mistress Woulfe?" Sharp eyes took in Helena's face, drifting towards her dusty gown before she fixed her gaze lovingly on her nephew. "You shouldn't have come. These are dark days, Nathan."

Her warning delivered, she excused herself to issue orders to an unseen servant while Helena took in her surroundings.

The old stone built house had low ceilings and lime washed walls with flat, mullioned windows under a thatched roof. The ground floor consisted of two large adjoining rooms, with a narrow corridor leading into what she supposed was the rear offices. An aroma of wood smoke and wildflowers overlaid by the tang of vinegar and heady beeswax, combined with a cloying, sickly smell she did not recognize. Mistress Fellowes returned with a female servant, deferential but obviously anxious, who set down a tray of cool ale and small cakes before shuffling away.

Their hostess turned to Helena. "I gather Sir Jonathan joined the Duke's men?" Helena could only nod, the sound of her father's name on the lips of this kindly stranger made her want to cry.

"Edmund Woulfe and Sir Jonathan's son, Aaron, are also amongst them." Bayle took a jug of ale and handed another to Helena.

Mistress Fellowes' eyes darkened in dismay. "And you want to know what happened here." It was not a question. She folded her hands together and spoke in a measured voice stripped of emotion. "When Monmouth returned to Bridgwater last week, the mayor begged him not to lay siege to the town, but hemmed in as he was by Feversham, he had little choice."

Helena sipped her ale, surprised at its freshness, her gaze fixed on the lady's face. "Lord Feversham arrived and billeted the royal troopers in every house they could." Her mouth twisted in recollection.

"How were you spared?" Bayle glanced around as if looking for signs of hostile occupation.

"We were not. But the two soldiers quartered here are dead." She gave a dismissive wave to signify that was another story. "Dragoons occupied the rectory and Weston Court, the manor close to here." She nodded toward the front window. "So arrogant and sure of themselves. They spent every evening drinking, and we have barely slept for days-." She broke off, as if embarrassed to mention this inconvenience in the midst of such tragedy.

"Were you ever in danger, Jane?" Bayle was obviously concerned.

Helena smiled at Bayle's use of his aunt's given name. Jane, it suited her, simple and plain, but she seemed kind and quick-witted as well.

"Colonel Wyndham insisted the whole village pledge loyalty to King James. But that was nothing." She offered an apologetic smile. "Our guests," she stumbled over the word, "showed us no disrespect, and we aren't grand enough for the officers." She gave a bitter laugh.

"What about the battle?" Bayle asked, consuming three tiny cakes in quick succession. Helena frowned and he grinned. "My aunt is a good cook."

Jane went on. "No one in Weston knew about the attack, not until we heard the gunfire in the middle of the night. All we could do was sit here and listen. It stopped soon after dawn and we watched them bring in the dead and herd the prisoners into the church."

Her voice rose in anguish. "I feel I betrayed those poor men. We offered to tend the wounded, Gil and I, out of Christian charity, but the officers said the Rebels did not deserve help and their suffering was God's judgment on them for their treachery against the king."

"Where is Gil?" Bayle gazed about the room. Helena assumed he referred to the lady's husband.

"At Langmoor Drove." Her voice dropped to a whisper. "He's helping cover over the pit where they laid the dead."

"Kings men or Rebels?" Helena's voice was strangely calm.

"Rebels, my dear. About a hundred and seventy of them. Five kings' men were given Christian burials yesterday at the church, but the Rebels. . ." She held up her hands in silent apology. "Colonel Kirke complained to his superiors about the state of the graves." She smoothed nervous hands down her skirt. "He demanded a digging gang build a mound over them."

"Kirke did not strike me as a humanitarian." Bayle's voice was bitter.

"He is not." Her eyes clouded. "But the mass grave is a pitiful sight. They did not dig it deep enough and. . . well, the stench will encourage animals to forage."

Helena made a choked sound and Jane pressed her hand. "I am sorry, my dear."

"What is happening now?" Bayle plucked another cake from the plate, chewing thoughtfully.

"Most of the soldiers have returned to Axbridge to collect their cannon and then to London to report to the king." She turned sad eyes on her nephew. "Lord Feversham took his men to Wells yesterday, and Churchill and his troops rampaged through Bridgwater scaring the townsfolk. They found some poor wretches, but not so many as they hoped." She blew her nose on her kerchief. "The Tangier regiment is staying to guard the prisoners and take them for trial at Taunton." Her eyes flashed. "They are less than men, Nathan. Yesterday, without benefit of a trial, they hanged six Rebels. Monmouth's Dutch gunner, and a deserter from the Hampshire Militia. We have no idea who the others were."

"We saw some of them," Helena mumbled. "I can still smell that sweet, fetid stench." She halted at the look Jane exchanged with Bayle.

"The smell is still here, Helena," Bayle explained. "Those men in the church, their wounds are festering in the heat. They are what you can smell."

Helena went rigid with horror, her breathing quickening.

Jane threw her a sympathetic look. "They are being taken to their home towns, either tonight, or in the morning. The parson says they will have to fumigate the building when they are gone. The churchwarden is already complaining about the expense to the parish." She gave a loud sniff.

Bayle rose to his feet and adjusted his hat. "I will see if I can find Gil. He might be able to help us."

"Yes, I am sure Gil will know more. But be careful," Jane warned.

Helena opened her mouth to protest, frustrated that everything was being taken out of her hands, but the wooden door clacked shut behind him, leaving the two women together in uncomfortable silence.

CHAPTER EIGHT

The soldier who kept watch at the rear door of St Mary's church greeted Gil with grudging respect. Bayle focused on the musket the fellow held loosely at his shoulder, but the man made no threatening moves.

"This is my nephew," Gil offered, gesturing to Bayle, who nodded, leaving the soldier to assume he was a local. "How's the arm?"

The soldier glanced down at his forearm, a grubby bandage visible beneath a ragged tear in his sleeve. "The pain is almost gone, thanks to you, Master Fellowes." He gave a lop-sided grin, displaying a gap between his front teeth.

"May we take some water in to the wounded?" Gil indicated the bucket and cup he had brought with him from the alehouse.

The soldier looked way, his gaze flicking to the building behind him. "My Captain has given orders no one must go in."

"Perhaps you won't see us." Bayle kept his face bland, inwardly thankful his uncle knew this soldier well enough to enlist his help. They had to get into the church and search the prisoners for the Woulfe men and this was the only hope they had.

The soldier hesitated, then muttered, "I need the privy, I will be gone a while."

The nauseating stench of unwashed bodies, blood and decay assailed his senses like fog as Bayle stepped across the threshold into the airless church. With the pews shoved aside to make room for the prisoners, dusty flagstones served as beds for the wounded. Sunlight streamed through the arched windows, sending beams of white light onto piles of rags lying on the floor – rags, which moved.

Prone figures with dull, uncaring eyes that sharpened with urgency as Gil leaned down to offer water. The fittest slurped greedily, while the more badly injured needed assistance propping up their heads.

Bayle went from one pitiful form to another, searching for familiar features or recognizable signs, picking his way over broken limbs with open wounds he tried not to see.

"There are so many," Gil whispered, his eyes bright with compassion. Bayle pressed a kerchief over his nose and mouth, easing his way along the wall.

He rounded a stone pillar, nearly colliding with a huddle of men who lay between the altar and the back wall. "How will I find anyone in this?" he murmured aloud, bending to peer into dirty faces and unfocussed eyes. A sudden jolt went through him when he found himself staring into a young face, one side caked with blood from a long head wound. He lay on his back staring at the ceiling with glazed, unseeing eyes.

Gil joined him. "Is he one of them?"

"It's Parry."

Gil frowned, uncomprehending.

"One of our stable lads," Bayle whispered, his gaze fixed on the boy.

Gil dipped a cup into the bucket and brought it to the boy's dry lips, but he had no strength to swallow. The water dribbled down the side of his face. "He's barely conscious," he whispered. "He'll not last another night."

Bayle gave a resigned nod, having come to the same conclusion. Then his gaze locked on something a few feet away. He stepped closer. A man lay on his side, one arm flung over his head clad in a brown plush coat. The sleeve held a row of silver buttons Bayle had polished with his own hand. He crouched down, rolling the man onto his back.

A roaring began inside his head. His breath caught in his throat as he stared down at a face he knew. A face that was void of animation and life.

Gil came to his side. "Who is he?"

"Was," Bayle emphasized. "He was, Edmund Woulfe."

Gil bent down to move the stained cravat to one side. "Slashed across the neck," he murmured. "Must have bled to death on the field, for there is little blood here but on his clothes."

Bayle turned to an uninjured man who sat watching them. He handed him a cup of water. The Rebel reached for it with trembling hands and drained it. "Almost dead when they brought 'im in," he whispered through parched lips. "Never woke up."

With one graceful movement, Gil lifted Edmund's body into his arms as if it weighed no more than a child's and approached an arched door. Leaving the bucket for the fitter men to distribute, Bayle followed, fastening the door behind him. He found himself in a short corridor leading to another arched door, which Bayle assumed led into the vestry.

He slipped through this door and was brought up short against Gil, who stood perfectly still inside the door; his gaze fixed on someone seated at a table. The remains of a scratch meal lay in front of the man; a half-eaten heel of cheese, some coarse bread and a jug of ale.

The three regarded each other in expectant silence as the third man rose slowly to his feet. He wore a long cassock and Bayle noticed his hands were white and soft. A cleric. The stranger's gaze flicked to the body Gil carried. "You will be arrested, Master Fellowes."

Gil offered no argument. "We must hide this man, Master Pelham," was his response. At Bayle's questioning look he muttered, "churchwarden."

Pelham cast a swift glance toward the window, and then seemed to make up his mind. "This way." He took them through an even lower arch where a flight of stone stairs dropped away into blackness. "The crypt," he explained. "No one will think to look there."

With a grateful nod, Bayle helped Gil manhandle their grim cargo down the steps. Curious, the churchwarden looked into the face of Edmund Woulfe and gave a shocked gasp. "He's dead!"

Bayle glared at him. "He is my master's brother. I will not leave him here to be consigned to a pit. I am taking him home."

The nervous cleric stepped back, cast a terrified look at the door, then back at the two men. "T-transporting a body through the roadblocks won't be easy," he stammered.

For several seconds, Bayle impaled him with an unyielding stare. The churchwarden looked away. His shoulders slumped and with a silent nod, he left them to their task.

* * *

Helena jumped at the sound of the latch as Bayle re-entered the house. A broader man, whom she took to be Gil Fellowes, followed him. Shorter than Bayle, he was strong and stocky like many West Country men, with a kind, open face. Jane sent the maid to fetch them a cooling drink, those first minutes spent on introductions and polite enquiries like ordinary visitors making a call on a summer day.

Bayle lowered himself onto a chair beside Helena, his hands hanging between his knees. He seemed to have difficulty speaking.

"Is it so awful out there?" Helena attempted to break the tension.

Bayle blew air between his lips. "We took some water into the church for the prisoners."

"How did you manage that?" Jane asked in amazement. "I could not get near them yesterday."

"You remember that soldier of Churchill's whose arm I stitched, Jane?" Gil gave a short laugh. "He let us in, albeit reluctantly."

Helena's eyes narrowed and she fidgeted in her chair, uncomfortable to think her hosts helped king's men. Then guilt rose to the surface when Bayle gave her a look. The same look he used when she had been caught doing something she shouldn't as a child.

"He seems less eager to torture the sick and dying like some. He has been charged with listing the names of all those brought in, so he may be able to help us." Bayle said.

Helena nodded and looked away, mortified her feelings showed so clearly on her face. Had Mistress Fellowes seen it too? Her mother was always telling her she must learn more...what was the word? Composure.

"He's a local man," Gil explained, his gruff voice rumbling from somewhere deep in his chest. "There are near five hundred men in St Mary's, Jane. It looks and smells like Hell itself."

Jane looked away, a hand to her mouth as if words were inadequate.

"What can this soldier do for us?" Helena asked, her resentment receding. "Can he help find my family?"

Gil exchanged a look with Bayle, whose face took on the same expression as the previous morning, when he came to tell her about the battle. Could it have been only yesterday? His next words chilled her. "Helena, we found your Uncle Edmund."

In another life, Helena would have leapt up to throw her arms around him to congratulate him on his cleverness, then issue an excited demand he take her to her uncle at once. But instinct told her this was not good news.

"Where is he?" Helena had to force the words past the lump in her throat.

Bayle swallowed. "They brought him in yesterday morning." He reached for her hand, but she snatched it away. "He must have lain in a cornfield for a day and a night. I don't think he woke up in that time."

"He's dead?" She trembled, willing him not to say the words, but already knowing the truth.

He lifted his hands in mute appeal, and beside him Gil gave a sigh. Jane dabbed at her eyes with a crumpled kerchief.

Helena fought dizziness, making it an effort for her to speak. "Where is he?"

"We took him down to the crypt. The churchwarden helped us." She frowned. "Why did you do that?"

Bayle gripped her hand. "They would consign him to the pit, Helena. And we want to take him home, don't we?"

"Home, yes of course," she murmured, her head spinning. "But you said we cannot go home." She rocked back and forth, a pain in her chest expanding and threatening to burst out of her.

"We shall take him to Ideswell, to Samuel Ffoyle's, where your mother and brother are."

Helena nodded silently as the dreadful words kept repeating inside her head. Edmund is dead. He has not gone to the city for a day and will be returning with white fullers earth on his clothes. There would be no more teasing, no secret winks behind her mother's back; no one to sneak food to her room when she was banished without supper for disrespect. He would never open his arms to enfold her in his strong hug, while she laughed in protest that he was crushing her, ever again. He was gone.

Helena leapt to her feet and paced the floor, her throat scratchy. Hot tears trickled down her cheeks, which she palmed away with tremulous hands.

Bayle rose and grasped her by an elbow, stilling her frantic pacing to guide her back to her seat. "I have seen the lists of prisoners. Neither Sir Jonathan nor Aaron is on them, so they haven't been captured." The word 'yet' hung between them. "However, there is no way of knowing if they have been killed in battle or escaped. Perhaps we will find someone who can tell us something."

Helena stiffened. "No."

Jane and Gil stared at her.

"You have been very kind to us," she addressed them both. "But we have no right to endanger you further." The horrors of the past two days made her realize what a perilous situation they were in.

Gil inclined his head with a sad grin. "This is a dangerous place whether you are here or not." Jane nodded silently beside him.

"You have to live here when we are gone," Helena persisted, "where so many are being arrested on the flimsiest of excuses."

Jane was about to respond, when a shout and the sound of scuffling feet came from outside. They all moved to the window to watch as lines of uniformed men gathered on the green in front of the church. Muffled orders were relayed, followed by the thudding of boots on dirt and the clinking of bits as the officer's horses trotted onto the green.

"The Tangiers are marching the prisoners out," Gil announced.

Helena gripped the sill, staring at the men in their distinctive knee length scarlet coats with turned back cuffs faced with sea-green. Their coats unfastened due to the hot day; their broad brimmed black hats with green bands over sweaty faces. Each man wore a leather baldrick and sword, carrying knapsacks, ready for a march.

"Kirke's men," Gil growled by her side.

The church door opened, and several soldiers broke rank, surging forward to haul out a group of slow moving prisoners, each one shackled and tied to his neighbor. Some shuffled unsteadily, others required support from those beside them, dragging wounded limbs, bound and encrusted with dried blood.

They emerged like moles, squinting and ducking their heads, with chains hanging from their waists and wrists. Soldiers shoved them aggressively to move faster, with one or two losing their footing, stumbling into the men ahead.

Helena could not see their faces, but their defeat emanated from them and she bit her lip so hard, she tasted blood. Some of the wounded had difficulty keeping up with those beside them, surrounded by haughty, uniformed men who pushed and harried the slow moving column. A crowd of silent villagers gathered at the edge of the green, but the soldiers paid them scant attention.

The column set off down the road they had arrived on that morning, with two carts at the rear carrying the more severely wounded.

Helena turned away, visualizing her uncle amongst them, although knowing he wasn't brought her no comfort. He was dead, and she had never felt more wretched in her life.

"Poor beggars," Gil murmured at her shoulder, echoing her thoughts.

* * *

Bayle went out again before nightfall. Helena did not ask where he was going. She spent a restless night in the room under the eaves, her dreams filled with scenes of her childhood and her uncle Edmund, who had always been more like an elder brother than an uncle; spoiling her with trinkets and making excuses for the boys when they got into scrapes.

A younger son, albeit by less than an hour, he left Exeter for London when he was seventeen to work for Master Samuel Pepys in the Navy Office administration. With a promising career ahead of him, Edmund purchased a house in Greenwich and married sixteen-year-old Catherine Jenkins, a merchant's daughter from Kensington. Within two years they had two sons, and life held promise.

However, as philosophers and the dispossessed will testify, when men make plans, God laughs. The plague which came to London that year, was the worst it had been since the middle ages. Edmund escaped the infection, but his pretty wife and their infant boys died within days. Her father had told her many times of his frantic ride to London to find Edmund standing silent guard over three wrapped corpses, waiting for the dead cart to take them to the lime pits.

Her uncle's occasional need for solitude was accepted as part of her early life. Helena would often discover him standing morosely on the Weare Cliffs, a faraway look in his eyes as if he were imagining a happier time.

The images of him were so vivid, Helena woke with a smile on her lips until the truth crashed in, making her groan aloud in her grief. She turned puffy eyes into the pillow, her chest constricted with dread that she would have to tell her mother, and when they came home, if they came home, Aaron and her father too.

When she rose at dawn, Jane and Gil waited for her in the rear kitchen, their drawn faces showing their night had been no more restful than her own. Refusing their offer of food, she sipped some milk without interest.

Nathan is waiting for you in the back lane with the cart." Gil hooked a thumb at the rear door. "The soldier helped us load it earlier."

Helena nodded, unwilling to ask about the load he referred to, postponing the moment when she would have to see for herself.

"You must go quickly, child." He handed over her bag with a wry smile. Helena thanked them both, at which Jane shed a tear and Gil bowed self-consciously. Unable to bear their compassionate kindness a moment longer, Helena hurried out of the rear door into the lane.

Bayle stood talking to a soldier with a short plug bayonet hanging from his leather baldric, heavily stained with a blackish crust. A white bandage peeked through a badly torn sleeve. She slowed her approach, and sensing her, the ponies nickered. At the sound, the soldier glanced up. His eyes widened for a second before looking away; with a sharp nod at Bayle, he disappeared in the direction of the church.

"Can we trust him?" Helena whispered, taking the soldier's place. "He looked terrified when he saw me."

"He has as much to lose as we do, Helena." Bayle glanced round at the lane. "And he would rather not have seen you either." He walked round the cart, checking the traces and bits. "The churchwarden has written a letter," he patted his coat. "It says we are transporting a Weston man, who died of smallpox two days ago."

Too heart-sore to respond, Helena nodded, inwardly congratulating him on his foresight. As she climbed onto the wooden bench beside him, she glanced into the flatbed and her eyes instantly clouded with tears.

A length of black cloth hung down over the upright sides of the flatbed and secured at the corners. A white ribbon was arranged on top in the shape of a cross, with miniature roses and sprigs of wildflowers draped around the sides, their subtle scent drifting into the morning air.

This simple and touching display of respect left Helena speechless. Bayle busied himself with their bags, as if to allow her a moment of private grief.

In a choked voice she whispered, "Wrapping a lie in a truth."

He heaved himself onto the platform and inclined his head, flicking the reins so the cart lurched forward. Helena turned to wave at the two figures standing in the shadows at the rear of their house, wondering if she would ever see them again.

The cart rolled through the silent village, the corpses hanging from the trees following them with dead eyes. A row of gibbets had appeared on the Bridgwater Road overnight, from which swayed the bodies of summarily hanged Rebels dragged from their hiding places, their captors eager for blood. Repelled yet fascinated, Helena looked into sightless eyes in distorted faces, frozen in their last attempts to draw breath.

Bayle talked soothingly to the horses, who threw up their heads at the swaying limbs and the stench of blood. Helena bit her lip, aware it would shortly to turn to a decay the villagers would be forced to endure.

When they reached Taunton, they avoided the main street, although Bayle's caution proved only partially successful. About a mile on the other side of the town, they encountered a roadblock, manned by pike carrying guards who ordered the cart to halt.

Bayle took his place in a short line of travelers, some with pack ponies, others on loaded carts, like their own. Even a coach and six horses - with an indistinguishable crest on the doors – waited in line. This vehicle wasn't detained long, making Helena wish she might have been with the gentleman inside who abused the officer roundly and saw him off with a flick of his cane.

A disgruntled soldier stomped toward the cart, ordering Bayle and Helena onto the road, his rodent eyes alert for signs of disrespect. She tried not to tremble, aware of an imperious, mounted officer observing the proceedings from a safe distance. When they obeyed, he stepped closer and thrust his face close to Bayle's to demand their names.

"Nicholas Bone," Bayle indicated Helena, "and this is my niece, Ann."

He stared at them with suspicion. "Where bound?"

"Exeter, sir."

"For what purpose?" He slapped his hand against his thigh, demonstrating impatience with Bayle's clipped responses.

Bayle's gaze went to the cart and back again. Taking her cue, Helena gave a moan and began sniffing into a kerchief. "We are taking my brother home for burial." Bayle handed him the churchwarden's letter.

The soldier snatched it, continuing to peer at them both with doubtful eyes. "A lot of Rebels come from Tawnt'n."

Bayle bowed. "I'm a King James's man, there are no Rebels in my family."

For long seconds the man's eyes raked Helena insolently, then he spat at the ground, making her grimace in distaste. He opened the parchment and began to read, his lips moving as he labored over the words.

His eyes widened. Thrusting the paper at Bayle, he backed away, turning to the mounted officer with whom he conducted a short, fierce conversation.

The man on the horse nodded. With a final, defiant sneer, the soldier signaled them to leave. Bayle folded the letter unhurriedly and returned it to his pocket before retrieving the reins.

One of the younger soldiers, not party to the whispered conversation, started forward as they climbed back onto the cart, his eye on the traveling bag on the seat next to Helena.

Before he could reach for it, the officer hauled him back by his collar, answering the man's furious look of enquiry with a shout, "Nay, leave them, you don't want smallpox."

Helena did not breathe normally again until they had traveled half a mile down the road, her nerves causing her to gabble as she recounted the event to Bayle as if he hadn't been a party to it.

CHAPTER NINE

They reached the other side of Sampford Peverell without having to show the churchwarden's letter again; passing through roads strangely silent, scanning the horizon in each direction for more patrols. Despite Helena's vigilance, when three figures stepped out of a copse of trees to block the road in front of them, she gave a startled shriek and clutched at Bayle's arm. "Keep going."

He shook his head. "The ponies won't run down a man."

She huddled into his side, as if his bulk might shield her. One of the men grabbed the reins, although it was unnecessary, the ponies had come to a halt at the human barrier.

"Where are you going?" the stranger asked, his other hand stroking the pony's ears.

Helena sat up straighter at the sound of his voice. She had expected a rough demand delivered in the local dialect, but his voice was calm; unexpectedly cultured for a man with streaks of grime obscuring his features. She stopped cowering and looked at him properly. His skin was unblemished and his teeth were good. He wore his sandy hair long and it hung in greasy clumps under a dirty hat—a gentleman's hat. He met her gaze with intelligent eyes, and although she still clung to Bayle's arm, her initial panic receded.

"What do they want?" she whispered. "They don't look like soldiers."

Beside her, Bayle seemed relaxed, almost unconcerned. She glanced up at him in enquiry but he looked quite calm as he addressed the stranger. "More importantly, where do you want to go?"

The man smiled as if accepting a challenge, but Helena saw he was nervous, his dirty fingers fiddled with his soiled cravat, torn and hanging loosely down his front, barely concealing a stained shirt.

The second man moved closer, halting a few steps from Helena's side of the cart. She stiffened, but his interest did not include her. He stood with his arms folded across his chest, his gaze raking the horizon, head tilted as if listening for a far off sound. His face, beneath a wide brimmed hat, sported a crust of dried blood above one eye.

The third was no more than a boy. He shifted from foot to foot, fidgeting at every sound, shoulders hunched as if ready to run. All three of them wore somber coats and breeches with buckles on the straps and shoes, not workmen's boots.

Helena knew then, if not who, then what they were. Not soldiers, they were Rebels. "They don't have any weapons," she whispered, feeling more confident.

Bayle gave a slow nod to indicate he had seen that too.

The first man released the bridle, leaving the ponies champing at their bits. He leveled a stare at Bayle which asked a question and gave a warning at the same time. "We need to get to Tiverton." His gaze shifted toward the direction they faced. "But there is a patrol ahead. The fields here are too open. There is no cover and we would never get through like this." He indicated his clothes.

Bayle handed Helena the reins and climbed down into the road.

"What are you doing?" she asked, alarmed.

He nodded to the copse on their right. "Move the cart into the trees, Helena."

Puzzled, she did as she was told, securing the reins on a low hanging branch. The horses stood placidly, snatching the grass with their teeth and flicking their tails to dislodge flies.

Bayle beckoned the men to follow as they moved into a clearing, positioning himself between the men and the cart, apparently taking stock of the three bedraggled figures. His self-possession seemed to give them confidence and they slumped down on the grass as if waiting to be told what to do. Helena hung back, watching uneasily.

"My name is...." the first man began.

Bayle held up a hand. "We don't need to know your names." His voice softened at the fear that sprang into the younger one's face. "It is best we know nothing about each other."

He nodded. "Given names then. I am Joel. This here is Simon and the lad there is Harry." He pointed to each in turn.

Bayle took a leather water bottle from the cart, shaking it onto linen cloths, which he handed to each of them. "Clean each other up as best you can, especially the blood." He waved at the streak of dried brown on Simon's head. "Are any of you injured?"

"Harry's arm is gashed." Joel pushed the boy forward.

"What about your head?" Helena's curiosity overcame her fear as she pointed at Simon.

He fingered his hairline absently, then waved her away. "It's nothing."

Harry winced as Bayle peeled his coat away from his shoulder, but he offered no complaint. Helena crept nearer, forcing herself to look at the exposed flesh of his arm, and at the sight of the wound, she breathed a sigh of relief. It was less serious than she had first imagined. Ripping a linen cloth in half, she dabbed at the cut, which oozed a little once the encrusted blood was removed, then bound it tightly to keep the jagged edges of flesh together.

"Have you been running all the time?" Helena asked, gathering up the bloodied cloths and leather water bottle.

"Since the battle, yes." Simon looked more animated, as if the encounter gave him hope they might survive their ordeal.

"We got separated from our regiment," Joel explained. He was quieter than the other two, almost surly, with suspicious eyes peering out of a swarthy face.

"Soldiers are everywhere." Simon cocked his chin at the fields around them. "We were forced to spend most of the time hiding." His tone screamed impatience at his own failure.

Bayle hung their coats from tree branches and while he beat the dried mud from them, Helena rooted through her bag for a comb, pushing aside the tortoiseshell one she used herself and handing them a cracked, bone one. They could have lice. The man Joel accepted it gratefully, tugging at the tangles and rubbing the encrusted dirt from his scalp.

"You wouldn't pass in many drawing rooms, but you don't look too bad," Helena said, when they had finished.

"When did you last eat?" Bayle asked.

Simon sniggered, and Joel snorted. Their response spoke volumes.

Bayle produced the food Jane had given them from beneath the seat, setting it down on the grass. They fell on it ravenously and as Helena watched, the crusty brown bread, cheese, cold sliced pork, apples and raisin cakes disappeared within minutes.

They sprawled in the clearing, backs against trees with a soft wind lifting the branches overhead. Helena leaned against a wheel, watching the breeze rippling the cornfields on the far side of the hedge. She nibbled at an apple with no appetite, thinking the scene looked more like a country picnic than an escape attempt.

"May we ask who you are?" Simon asked around a mouthful of food. "And why you are traveling at this inauspicious time?" He gave a sardonic grin.

Bayle appeared to consider for a moment, leveling his gaze at Helena. She gave a tiny shrug.

"My name is Nicholas Bone, and this is my niece, Ann." He waved a hand at Helena.

Joel stared at Bayle with sharp eyes. "You called her Helena a while ago."

Instead of a response, Bayle draped his wrists over his knees and stared off. Helena studied Simon through lowered lashes. He looked like a man not used to taking orders. "We are on our way to Exeter," she said, hoping to distract him from the discussion about names.

"You aren't Rebels." Simon relaxed against a tree. "But I'm thinking you know more about them than you pretend." His speech was measured and educated. Had Helena encountered him in other circumstances, she would have taken him for a gentleman.

Helena rose and wandered to where Bayle stood. "I don't think they would harm us," she whispered. "They need our help."

"How did I guess the lady was the master here?" Simon exchanged 'I told you so' looks with his companions.

Bayle ignored the taunt and reached back into the cart for Helena's bag. He set it down in front of Harry and pulled a gown and bodice from it. "Put these on," he instructed the astonished boy, who looked to Simon for support.

Simon gave an admiring nod. "Do as he says, it might work."

Harry looked quite credible as a girl, with his beardless face and thick fair hair falling to his shoulders in waves. The skirt kept wrapping itself round his legs, tripping him. Each time it happened, his cheeks burned bright red.

"Shorten your stride," Helena suggested, grinning.

While Helena taught Harry to walk like a girl, Bayle spoke to the men in low voices. She watched them from a distance, wondering what Bayle had in mind. With a sudden protest, Joel took a few steps back. He gaped back at the cart and gave a barked protest. "You have a body in there?"

Simon let out a throaty laugh. "What did you think these were for?" He flicked a hand at the flowers attached to the sides.

"We carry a document stating the man died from smallpox." Bayle tapped his coat. "It should get us through the patrols without a search." His gaze challenged Joel. "If you keep your nerve and don't move."

"You want me to get in there, with a pox'ed corpse?" Joel fidgeted as if something unpleasant crawled on his skin.

Simon slapped his companion's shoulder hard. "Take a chance, Joel, or risk the hangman!" He gave them a glimpse of his ready smile as he heaved himself over the side into the flatbed, wrinkling his nose as he wriggled against the wooden sides and away from the rolled sacks supporting the body. "Cover us over well, Master Bone."

Joel followed, obviously reluctant, muttering to himself as Bayle pulled the cloth tight over them before climbing back onto the driving platform. Helena covered Harry's fair hair with a grubby cap, tying the strings under his chin to leave hanging locks on either side obscuring his face. With the hood of the cloak ruffled round his neck, he looked very girlish.

With Harry perched between them, the cart bumped and swayed back onto the road. Bayle cast him a sideway grin. "You don't make a bad maid."

Harry flushed and hunched his shoulders.

Helena spotted the patrol as they topped a small rise, her heart hammered for a moment, then settled down again when she saw there were only two of them. "Not much of a patrol," she sniffed, intending to reassure Harry, who looked terrified, but her own hands felt clammy.

"Don't be deceived, one musket can kill as well as six," Bayle spoke out of the corner of his mouth, giving a low warning to the men behind.

The soldiers looked hot and tired, their coats flung open and hats tilted back. Their horses were tethered to a tree at the side of the road, tails lazily flicking away flies, heads down as if they had been there for a while.

One of them held up a hand and with a sharp swiping motion, signaled them into a verge. Bayle obeyed.

Helena shivered. These two were professional soldiers. Their long-coats were faded across the shoulders, now reddish-brown from marching long distances in all weathers. Patched in places, the turned back cuffs were no longer crisp. The younger one had a front tooth missing, while the other sported a cropped ear and two hacked-off fingers.

"Where are ye bound?" the officer demanded in a rough voice, indicating for Bayle to climb down.

Helena sat quite still as Bayle complied, proffering the churchwarden's letter. The soldier gave the parchment a contemptuous look and ignored it, which told Helena he could not read. This did not bode well.

The second soldier stared at her, a leering grin on his face, his musket held across his body at waist level. She could not take her eyes from it, although when the man ducked his head to attract Harry's attention, the boy glared at the ground as if frozen. The soldier sniffed and moved away, but Harry fidgeted, stilling only when Helena placed a comforting hand on his arm. The cart creaked and a bird called in a nearby tree, the tension growing as they waited. Helena glanced over her shoulder to watch the officer circle the contraption, flicking a contemptuous hand at the arranged flowers.

Without warning, he flipped up the edge of the makeshift pall, coming face to face with Simon, whose head lay inches from his hand. Helena gave a moan and for long seconds, the Rebel and the officer stared at each other as if immobile with shock.

The Rebel moved first. He lunged out of the cart, grabbing the officer round the neck with both hands. They tumbled onto the road as one, with Simon's full weight on top of the soldier. Neither man had a chance to call out.

In the split second it took for his companion to register what was happening, Bayle closed the space between them. The second soldier lifted his musket, but at the same second, Bayle pulled his arm back and punched him squarely in the face. He hit the ground with a dull thump, and stayed there.

Helena's shocked cry was smothered as the ponies crabbed sideways, threatening to trample Simon and the man beneath him. She hauled on the reins to keep them still and Harry scrambled down, almost colliding with a moving wheel. The soldier beneath Simon pulled a knife from somewhere, but as Simon's fist connected with the man's face, Harry sprang forward to wrestle it from his hand.

Joel hauled himself out of the cart and grabbed the musket the other soldier had dropped. Harry leapt out of the way and Joel stepped over the unconscious man, checked to see the weapon was loaded and shouted. "Roll, Simon!"

Simon reacted immediately, flinging himself to one side as Joel fired into the exposed soldier's chest.

The sound of the shot echoed across the fields, sending up a flock of crows in a nearby tree, dying away quickly into the afternoon quiet. A crimson bloom spread over the front of the officer's shirt and with a final grunt he relaxed into the earth, dead eyes staring at the sky. The ponies whinnied once, stamped, and then fell silent.

The other soldier stirred, groaning. In two strides, Joel raised the musket and brought the wooden butt down on the man's temple with a sickening crack.

Helena thrust her fist into her mouth to muffle a scream, transfixed by the unnatural dent in the man's skull. She looked down at her skirt, where spots of blood stood out for a few seconds before soaking into the fabric.

The horses whinnied in fear, pulling against the reins so that all Helena's strength turned to keep them standing. When she could bring herself to look, Bayle and Simon were dragging the shot soldier toward a deep ditch running along the side of the road.

"Harry," Simon shouted. "Go and collect ferns and branches, as many as you can."

Wide-eyed, Harry stumbled away, hampered by his skirt.

The three men had turned their attention to the body of the officer. "There should have been six of them," Simon grunted with the effort. Bayle looked up, his gaze sweeping the horizon. Helena looked too, but nothing stirred; the only sound was that of insects in the long grass. They rolled the limp bodies into the ditch, flattening the long grass on the incline.

Joel collected the other musket and threw both guns in after them. Harry returned, his arms full of branches and wide leaves they all set to spreading over the bodies and the disturbed vegetation, hiding them as best they could.

"How long before they find them, do you think?" Simon asked no one in particular.

"The others, if there are others, could be back at any time." Joel jerked his head toward the road ahead. "They are always in packs, like dogs." He brought a contemptuous foot down on the brittle twigs, their sharp crack making Helena jump.

Harry tore off the skirt and bonnet and hurled them into the cart. "What about their horses?" He nodded toward the docile animals grazing a few feet away.

"Get rid of anything which marks them out as soldiers' mounts," Bayle told him. "You and Joel will have to ride them. We cannot leave them here."

Joel examined the docile horses. "Two knapsacks and a blanket with a military crest." He held them up for inspection. "Their saddles are ordinary."

The men gathered up their meager belongings from the grass. For want of something to do, Helena climbed down and scraped a mound of soil in her hands from the side of the ditch, sprinkling it over the patch of bright blood in the road. Somehow she felt better having done it.

Clambering back onto her seat, she fixed her gaze on Bayle's face, willing him to get them away from there. Joel held both horses reins in one hand, their heads straining forward. As he passed the cart, his eyes narrowed and he hooked a thumb backwards. "He's beginning to smell."

Bayle scowled at him, but Helena pretended she hadn't heard, tucking her skirt around her legs, avoiding the damp blood. The horror of the past few minutes had rendered Joel's comment as little more than a distant idea.

With the men mounted, Bayle flicked the reins and turned toward her, his voice filled with sympathy. "Let's get Master Edmund home and give him a proper burial." She was trembling too much to answer, biting her bottom lip to stop it quivering

They maintained a fast pace for the next mile or so, while Helena kept a careful eye on the horizon, alert for the sound of pounding hooves. She held fast to the seat as they bumped over the uneven road, the vibrations running through her as Bayle urged the horses to go faster.

At the Appledore turnoff, Bayle hauled the cart into the verge. "Get everything tidied away," he ordered. "If there's another patrol, this would arouse suspicion."

Helena looked back and understood. The cart no longer resembled a funeral wagon. The cross and the flowers had been ripped away in the brief conflict, leaving the black cloth draped untidily over the body; her skirt and cap jumbled in a heap in one corner.

Her legs shook as she climbed down onto the road and made for the rear of the cart, the image of the dead soldier's battered skull imprinted in her head. She gathered up her discarded clothing and paused, transfixed by the sight of the body in its linen wrappings. It had shifted slightly and lay to one side; its head, torso and legs clearly defined, like a large doll with no face.

Her practical self told her it was Edmund, but she could not reconcile the slight, lifeless shape with the moving, breathing man she loved. Her throat closed and tears spilled down her face, leaving her breathless and shaking. It was really him.

With a muttered curse, Bayle stepped forward and flipped the cover back into place, painstakingly securing the sides.

Harry appeared at her shoulder. "Was he a close relative?"

"He is...was my uncle." She faltered on the words that consigned Edmund to the past.

"He didn't have the smallpox, did he?"

"No." She knuckled tears away with both hands.

"I got this at Weston." Harry indicated his bandaged arm. "We scattered after the first charge and found ourselves on the wrong side of the ditch." He shrugged apologetically. "We could see our men, but couldn't reach them, and by the time we found our way round, well. . ." He sighed as if embarrassed. "Then Joel got knocked out, and Simon and I carried him off the field."

Helena stayed silent, her gaze fixed on the body. Harry was no longer a shy boy, she had seen the look on his face when he grabbed the fallen soldier's knife. She was convinced he would have used it, had Joel not shot the man.

"What was his name?" Harry asked.

"Edmund Woulfe." She examined their faces for a reaction. There was none. Disappointed, she jammed the clothing back into her bag.

"We part company here, masters," Bayle called, startling her. Her nerves were so on edge. "I am worried about the rest of that patrol arriving."

Joel gathered what meager belongings they had and led the horses closer.

As Simon bowed over Helena's hand in farewell, unexpected warmth crept up her neck. He was a gentleman.

They re-mounted the trooper's horses, and with Harry perched behind Joel, set off toward Tiverton.

They were still in sight when Helena turned to clutch the manservant's arm. "Bayle." Her tremor turned into heavy shaking as she fought hysteria. "We killed two men."

"We didn't kill anyone." He snatched the rein and flicked it hard against the nearest pony's flank. "Those men would have been hanged, and us with them." He glared at her steadily. "Forget them, and tell no one what happened today, ever."

CHAPTER TEN

Helena awoke, nestled between clean sheets in a bedroom she didn't recognize. Bleary from sleep, she pushed aside the coverlet and stumbled across bare floorboards to the window. Undulating green fields lay under a heat haze. A scattering of sheep grazed on a hillside and silhouettes of field workers stood framed against the sky in the field beyond.

Bewildered, she wondered what happened to the red city walls of Exeter. With a groan, she turned away from the window, realizing they had come home, but not to her home; not to Loxsbeare.

Tears stung her eyes. Would she ever live there again? When she had left for Somerset, it was with determination to find her family, battered and weary perhaps, but whole and alive. But she had returned with a corpse and no news of either her father or brother. It was an ignominious defeat.

A new maturity had thrust away her innocent and happy childhood, replacing it with a harsh realism she felt ill equipped to handle. She longed for her mother's smile, and Henry's laughter; but would anything be the same after what she had seen?

It was very late when they arrived, and apart from Samuel and Meghan, the household was sleeping. Bayle had looked so tired, steadying himself against the cart and pressing one hand to the small of his back. Despite her own exhaustion, Helena berated herself for drawing him into her misguided folly, hoping he would forgive her impetuosity someday, if he had not done so already.

She had offered neither resistance nor co-operation as her heavy, dirt-caked gown was peeled away. Clad in her grubby linen shift, a garment she swore to burn as soon as she was able, she collapsed onto the bed and almost instantly, sleep claimed her.

Helena turned from the window, surveying the room in which she had spent the night. It was large and comfortable; with low ceilings, sparkling white walls and black oak beams. The heavy oak furniture, polished to a rich glow, conjured up images of previous generations of Ffoyles.

It surprised her how many of her belongings there were in the room. Her bone and tortoiseshell combs lay on a side table, her dressing mirror propped above. An achingly familiar wooden chest sat beneath the window; her prayer book lay on a table by the poster bed, beside a carved wooden box containing her unimpressive collection of jewels.

A small cabinet from her closet stood nearby, and with a sudden urgent thought, Helena rummaged through it, expelling a sigh when her hands closed on the brown leather book. Her journal was safe. Henry must have put it here, knowing where she always kept it.

Gazing round the room, she bit her lip, frowning. Mother must have left Loxsbeare in a hurry, even with all these things were. Is this where they intended to stay? And if so, for how long?

At the sound of footsteps in the corridor, Helena searched frantically for something to put on. Mother and Henry might be downstairs waiting for her and she was wasting time staring out of the window. Before she located her clothes, the door swung inwards with a sharp click, revealing Samuel and Meghan's eldest daughter. Susannah carried a pitcher from which wisps of steam arose; over her arm was draped one of Helena's own gowns. With her hands full, closing the door was a tricky process culminating in a swift backwards kick.

"Good morning Helena," she greeted her shyly.

Susannah was nineteen, with similar looks to her father. She was tall, with red-brown hair and the same nut-brown eyes and open expression. Apparently, she shared her father's tact, and apart from asking how Helena felt, made no mention of how she had passed the previous two days. Helena discarded the gritty shift, which chafed her skin, washing luxuriously in the hot water.

Fond of Susannah, Helena could not describe them as friends. When they met at holiday gatherings or the Lammas Fair, they gravitated together and enjoyed each other's company.

"I shall never take cleanliness for granted again." Helena laughed as she dried her skin. "Is my mother awake yet?" Her voice muffled amongst the folds of the gown Susannah pulled over her head. "I was so tired last night I could barely stand."

Susannah's hands stilled on the fastenings, but she did not reply.

Helena frowned. "Susannah?"

"Master Henry is here." Susannah collected pitchers and the discarded linens. "Your maid too."

"Chloe?" Helena gasped in surprise. "Why did she not come and help me dress?"

Susannah turned for the door, her back stiff. "I will send Father to you." Before Helena could question her further, she hurried out.

Puzzled, Helena sat on the bed, listening with growing unease to a murmur of voices in the corridor outside. The words were indistinct, but the timbre indicated there was something wrong. She jerked to her feet as the reassuring figure of Samuel appeared, but her greeting froze on her lips when she saw his distraught face.

"How are you this morning, my dear?" Samuel couldn't meet her gaze.

"I am well, Master Ffoyle. I must thank you for allowing us to seek refuge in your home, Mother and I are. . ." she trailed off when he flinched.

"There is something, I have to tell you." He opened his mouth and then shut it again, his gaze drifting past her. Helena grew uneasy, and the quaver in his voice heralded some new terror. A flutter of dread opened like wings in her stomach and threatened to fly into her throat to choke her. "What is it?" Her fear overcame her good manners.

He closed his eyes and took a deep breath. "Your mother is dead."

For a moment there was no sound in the room. Blindly she reached for the bedpost, clutching it to keep from crumpling to the floor. Her grip was so hard, the carvings cut into her hand, but the pain helped her concentrate.

Helena flew at him, clutching at his coat. "What are you saying?" Anger gave her strength and she hauled on the heavy serge, shaking him. "How can she be dead?" It couldn't be true, Mother was alive when she left. That was only three days ago! Her mind refused to absorb it. What kind of cruel trick was this?

Samuel's brow furrowed, his large hands closed over hers and held her still. "I cannot tell you how distressed I am." His eyes pleaded for understanding.

Everything about his demeanor gave truth to what she refused to accept. She flung away from him as if his touch burned her, thumping a clenched fist against the bedrail. "What happened? I insist you tell me!" Helena screamed, staring at her white knuckles on the bedpost.

Still shaking, Helena listened to his account of what happened the day the soldiers came to Loxsbeare, the catch in his voice slowing him down. When he had finished, she released her breath in a long, shuddering sigh. "She fell?"

He held his hands out in supplication, but she glared at him in disbelief. "And you stood there and did nothing?"

He gave her a pitiful look. "Helena, there was nothing we could have done."

A red mist appeared behind her eyes. "Father did this to us," she shouted. "He left us all alone at the militia's mercy, and for what?" Her breathing grew rapid as her emotions raged inside her. She paced the room, ignoring the pounding in her temples. "Uncle Ned too; with his obsessive hatred of Catholics. And Aaron, he followed Monmouth's men simply to impress father; leaving Henry, Mother and me to suffer for their folly. Her words tumbled out and she collapsed against the bed. "And now she has been taken from me too."

Samuel attempted to help her upright, but she recoiled from his touch. "I care nothing for who rules the country," she yelled into his face. "Kings, bishops or cloth workers, it does not matter. I want my home and my life back as it was."

Her loud ranting brought Meghan and Susannah to the doorway, their faces a mixture of pity and amazement. Samuel retreated from the room, his shoulders slumped.

Uncaring of the shocked faces around her, Helena curled herself into the covers on the unmade bed. Drawing her knees into her chest, she gripped the linen tightly beneath her chin. "It was because I didn't bring Aaron back," she whispered into the pillow. "Mother's dead, because I couldn't do the one thing she wanted. And now I never can."

Her eyes burned, her face becoming sticky from tears and mucus as she wailed; first in anger, then at the injustice of a loss she had to hear about from others. "She could have waited for me," she cried, knowing her words made no sense.

When the storm abated, comforting hands massaged her shoulders. She blinked in confusion as someone else smoothed her hair away from her face. Through swollen eyes she peered at two children's faces, staring at her from the doorway.

Meghan Ffoyle's soothing voice broke into her lethargy from a distance, then another pair of strong hands helped lift her upright. She felt disoriented as her hot face was dabbed with a damp linen cloth. She could smell lilac and soap, a far off scent of freshly baked bread, but her taste buds were as dull as her mind. Then a female voice issued a scold. Was it Meghan? And the faces disappeared from the door.

From violent sobbing, Helena reverted to numb silence, as if she had expended all her grief in one outburst and there was no feeling left in her. Eventually she grew calmer, aware of her surroundings again. Pulling away from Susannah's touch, she avoided Meghan's pitying gaze. "Where is Henry? I want to see Henry."

He must have been waiting outside in the hall, for as the women withdrew, Henry dashed past them to halt awkwardly in front of her. He looked so young standing there, his eyes filling with tears and his lower lip trembling. He held his hands away from his sides, dropping them again in a gesture of helplessness. "Helena?"

At the sound of his voice, she opened her arms and he threw himself into her embrace. "She did not even have the passing bell," he gasped between muffled gulps.

When he grew quiet, she held him away from her, her gaze shifting to the bandage. "You are injured?"

"It doesn't hurt much any more." He stood, passive, as she adjusted it.

"I shouldn't have left her." Helena sniffed.

He grasped her shoulders so tightly, she winced; his gaze locked with hers, no longer distraught, but determined. "I couldn't save mother, any more than you could have saved Uncle Ned."

"Oh Hal, I didn't mean...it's just..." Weariness and misery overcame her. What could she have done when the soldiers came to Loxsbeare? Henry was no more responsible than Samuel, or Tobias. The troopers killed her mother, even though Samuel insisted it was an accident. "You are right Henry, I'm being unjust. My presence would have made no difference."

Shame made her face burn at the thought of her outburst at Samuel and wrapping her arms round Henry, she murmured into his hair. "I must go and apologize to Master Ffoyle."

"He will understand." Henry accepted the kerchief she handed him and blew his nose nosily. "I thought he was going to kill the man who. . ." he broke off, with a shudder.

She held him tighter, wondering how she could have not realized before. The troopers could have hurt Henry too, or worse, had Samuel not been there. And she had blamed him.

They found Samuel slumped in a chair in the parlor, staring morosely into an empty grate. Meghan looked up when they entered, cast a concerned look at her husband and then rose regally to her feet to welcome them.

In her stiff white apron and spotless cap, Helena found her serene presence reassuring and found she felt calmer than she had since waking that morning. "It is very kind of you to give us..." What was Meghan giving them? Refuge? Escape? The very idea she needed either of those things made her start trembling again.

"You are welcome to all we have, Mistress." Meghan placed a broad hand on her shoulder. "And I am so sorry about your mother, and your uncle."

She cupped Helena's cheek briefly before resuming her seat. Meghan was born in the damp hills of Wales, tall and sturdy with broad cheekbones and near black eyes that betrayed her foreign origins.

When the solitary bachelor Samuel Ffoyle, visited Caernarvon in search of welsh sheep for his farm more than twenty years before, he had surprised everyone by bringing more than thirty healthy ewes back to Devon with him.

The woman's handsomeness struck her and Helena stifled a shudder, realizing Meghan wasn't much older than her own mother, who would never become old now. "Where is my mother?" she asked. Beside her Henry gave a small groan.

Samuel lifted his head and turned haunted eyes toward her. "Nathan Bayle has taken her to St Mary Arches. The minister has agreed to bury her tonight."

Helena's mouth fell open in shock. "Tonight? But it happened three days ago, why haven't...?"

Samuel held up a hand. "Forgive me, Helena. We could do nothing. The Minister was too afraid to conduct services for her. He was cowed by the troopers and virtually shut the church against all the Woulfes."

This new horror was too much for Helena. "You couldn't even bury her?" She groped for Henry's hand.

"Calm yourself, my dear." It was more like an instruction. "Master Triske has capitulated. Tobias Lumm convinced him."

"Tobias?" This was the last thing Helena expected to hear. "He interceded for us?"

Samuel gave a considered nod. "Yes, well intercede is a good term for it. However I believe some. . .persuasion was required."

A sharp pricking of tears threatened to rob her of her hard won self-control. "And Edmund?" she whispered hoarsely.

"The Minister will inter them both. But we must be circumspect." The defeated look had gone and Samuel sounded more like the capable man she knew. "No one must know your uncle died at Sedgemoor."

"What can it matter now?"

"Because your father, and your brother may still be alive. We must preserve the illusion they were not involved."

"Even with our home seized?" She knew she sounded hard, but she couldn't stop herself.

"Denial is sometimes the best course, no matter what rumor and speculation might say."

Helena sighed. What he said made sense.

She wouldn't let go of Henry's hand and kept stroking his hair. As if embarrassed at these repeated shows of affection, he took the first opportunity to slip out of the room. When she looked up to see he had gone, Helena retreated to the chamber where she had spent the previous night.

She drifted from the newly made bed to the window and back again, edgy yet lethargic too. Her restless fingers found her journal, and for a moment she stood holding it, running the strip of the fastening through her fingers. After a brief search, she found quills and when she asked Meghan for ink, the lady acquiesced without comment.

Helena spent the rest of that afternoon writing. She hesitated over the words Simon and Joel, but defiantly recorded that encounter too, telling herself no one would see it.

Her handwriting reflected her shaking hand when she came to the part about her mother's death. How much worse it must have been for Henry, who had witnessed it. Poor Henry, though the impulse to go and find him receded as her pen traveled across the page, the compulsion to finish keeping her in her seat.

Hunger eventually drove her to the parlor as servants scraped chairs and benches up to the solid oak table in readiness for the main meal of the day. The low buzz of activity in the kitchens grew to a noisy crescendo as the family appeared from different parts of the house and yard to eat. Too warm for a fire, the fragrance of summer flowers and dried herbs filled the handsome room.

As everyone took their places, Meghan inquired after each of her children in turn, admonishing them for chores left undone and transgressions recounted by the others, squabbling and teasing the younger ones. Unaccustomed to such boisterous companionship, Helena watched from the sidelines, as did a sad but bemused Henry.

Patrick, the eldest son, was the first to formally welcome Helena. Two years older than Susannah, he was proud of his position as firstborn and the image of his father. Seth, at sixteen, sandy haired and hazel eyed, had a ready grin and gentle, friendly manner. Aware of his good looks, he greeted Helena like a great lady, bowing over her hand and making a leg as well as any gallant, despite his clothes being plain and in drab colors.

Deborah at thirteen was the pert and pretty darling of the household. Like an exuberant puppy, she was full of high spirits and endless questions. Rebekah, the middle girl, at fifteen, was more demure, with light brown hair and green-flecked brown eyes, she offered few opinions, but when something was required, she was the one who ran silently and obediently to do her elder's bidding.

The youngest was Robson, known as Robin, ten years old with ruddy cheeks and big brown eyes. Shy one minute, noisy and energetic the next.

Conversations, stilted at first, rapidly turned to curious questions concerning Helena's journey into Somerset. She responded with a mixture of evasion and half-truths, the faces of Joel, Simon and Harry never far away from her thoughts.

Henry, billeted with the two younger boys, appeared delighted to have a contemporary in the charming and friendly Seth, while Robin gazed at him as if he was a hero.

Seth complained in Helena's hearing, that he had carried Bayle's bags up three flights of stairs into an attic room, so she knew he could not be far away. She had not seen him all day and longed to talk with him, yet dreaded the moment when they must acknowledge the loss of her mother.

During grace, Samuel made a reference to 'those lost to us', but left no pause in which to grow maudlin, for which Helena was grateful. Meghan ordered the roasted piglet brought in, whose tantalizing aroma had filled the house all afternoon.

Three kitchen maids bore steaming platters of onions and potatoes into the room, followed by leeks with fennel, cabbages and boiled carrots. Samuel served wine to his guests, ale and small beer to the younger members of the family.

The food disappeared quickly, although Helena ate sparingly, despite her initial enthusiasm and Henry pushed his plate away, disinterested. Megan watched them both, alert, Helena knew for signs of melancholy, which could sour their humors and poison their systems.

Helena recalled her mother's similar fears. Lady Elizabeth had lived every day with death's shadow hanging over those she loved. She had guarded them all from the harmful influences of bad air, evil miasmas and melancholy. "Who do I have who will protect me from those influences now?" Helena mused aloud, fighting fresh tears.

* * *

The daylight faded and a dust haze hung over the fields as the Ffoyle carriage rolled through the West gate and up Fore Street. Turning left at the summit to roll into Mary Arches Lane, halting outside the church. The windows of the square tower hovered above them like blackened eyes as Helena and Henry climbed down from the carriage and approached the door.

Somehow, news had spread and the road outside was lined with curious onlookers, some of whom Helena recognized. Her gaze flicked over their faces, but the Blandens were not amongst them. As it was to be a private ceremony, the crowd remained outside on the road.

Before they reached the church door, a clutter of hooves thundered into the street and all eyes turned to stare at the soldiers halting their mounts in the road.

Helena fought to calm her rapid breathing, but they did not dismount, watching them with surly expressions.

Henry scanned their faces. "I don't know any of them. They weren't the ones who came to the house when..."

Helena glared at them. "Let them do as they please, they cannot hurt us any more."

Her words were sheer bravado, for she spent the entire ceremony darting furtive glances at the door, half expecting them to burst in and stop the proceedings.

The tiny congregation consisted of Samuel and Meghan with their four eldest children, plus Helena, Henry and Nathan Bayle, all huddled into the front pews of the near empty church. Helena coughed in the musty air, the sound echoing into the cavernous roof.

Her gaze were drawn and held by the two coffins laying side by side in front of the altar. How could her vivacious uncle and tall, beautiful mother be contained in such small wooden boxes? Henry followed her gaze and groped for her hand.

The passing bell rang for Lady Elizabeth, six slow rings to signify the death of a woman, followed by one ring for each year of her age. Edmund Woulfe went to his final rest in silence.

Master Triske intoned the Anglican service in low tones, although he never mentioned her uncle's name, simply 'our brother'. Helena thought how sad it was to be committed to your grave without your name.

Almost before she realized it, the service ended and the churchwardens helped Bayle, Samuel and the elder Ffoyle boys carry the coffins inside the vault behind the altar. When they emerged, the iron door clanged shut, the sound resonating in Helena's head as she stumbled from the gloomy building into the summer night, blinking back tears.

Master Triske caught up with her outside the church. "Don't neglect your devotions, my dear. It is times such as these, that your faith is tested. Even in your sorrow, you should not fail your savior."

Helena fixed him with a contemptuous stare. "Take your platitudes and expend them on someone who wants to hear them. God has taken more from me than you could ever imagine. I have not failed him, he has failed me." The minister stepped back, affronted.

Samuel stood a few feet away, the surprise on his face indicating he had overheard. The minister waved the Master of Clothworker's apologies away and fled back to the vestry, his cheeks scarlet and gown flapping.

Helena watched him go, the last vestiges of her anger dissipating into the summer night. The wind ruffled her hair and tiny pinpoints of light appeared in the deep blue canopy of sky above her. The crowd had dispersed and it was a clear night, and so still. An owl called from a tree in Bartholemew Street and a carriage horse whickered in impatience.

Helena breathed in the heady scent of wildflowers, the vengeful grief that had twisted inside her all day had dissipated into quiet sadness. Her mother and Uncle Ned were both safe; nothing could ever hurt them again. "When my time comes." Helena linked her arm through Susannah's. "I should like to be buried by moonlight."

"There is no moon," Henry muttered flatly from behind them.

CHAPTER ELEVEN

Troopers came to the village the following day to search houses, question villagers, bully women and strike out at young boys for imagined insolence. Helena watched fearfully from an upstairs window as a uniformed Colonel halted his men at the lynch gate. With two officers following, he rode down the dirt drive, dismounted and hammered on the heavy door, shoving his way past a terrified servant.

Helena crept down the stairs to join Meghan and the girls in the parlor, where they listened in fearful silence to unfamiliar upraised voices, followed by the softer tones of Samuel's responses.

The door latch clacked and Seth's face appeared round the doorjamb. Meghan gasped and Helena released a pent up breath. "Father bade me tell you the soldiers have gone," he said brightly. "And there is to be no search of the manor."

"I have accepted responsibility for any Rebels who may be hiding in the village," Samuel announced gravely during the afternoon meal. "About twenty fugitives have been rounded up, so the militia's appetite has been satisfied temporarily, but no quarter will be given to others being harbored."

"Are they still making searches?" Patrick asked between mouthfuls.

Samuel nodded. "Captain Morton suspects those who managed to get this far, will most likely have disappeared by now."

"The locals would never give them up, if that's what they are expecting." Patrick gave a snort.

"I do not believe so either." Samuel helped himself to bread. "The militia will stay in the area for a few more days before they are dispersed."

Meghan handed platters of seasoned chicken marinated in honey around the table and as the two youngest tussled over a plate of onions and cabbage, the door to the garden swung wide and Bayle stood framed in the doorway. Conversations ceased and knives stilled in mid air. "I am sorry to interrupt your meal, Master Ffoyle, Mistress." He nodded at Meghan. "But I thought you would want to know..."

His hesitation made Helena's stomach turn over.

"They have captured the Duke of Monmouth." A groan of dismay went round the table. "He was hiding in a ditch on Cranbourne Chase, he and Lord Grey."

Seth dropped his bowl with a clatter. "So it is over?"

Helena kept her head down and pushed food round her plate. Were her father and Aaron hiding in a ditch somewhere? Would they too be dragged out, cold, wet and hungry and cast into some dank prison? Her spoon clattered to her plate and she abandoned any pretence at eating.

She looked up at the two elder Ffoyle sons, remembering how these two had pleaded to join the Rebels. She wondered what where their thoughts were at that moment.

The meal ended abruptly and the family dispersed to different areas of the house. Helena offered to help in the kitchen, but Meghan waved her away. "I have strapping girls enough to help me here and a kitchen full of servants who need no excuses to avoid work." She bustled away, dismissing her.

Helena heard Meghan's warning follow her down the hallway. "Debs! Not three jugs at once, you will break them."

In her room, a sulky Chloe prepared Helena for bed. At the sight of the girl's pinched face in the mirror, Helena recalled what Susannah had said earlier; that the kitchen maids had teased Chloe for calling herself a lady's maid.

"Chloe is my lady's maid," Helena had responded, puzzled.

"This is a working farm, Helena," Susannah scoffed. "There are no ladies here."

Helena didn't really belong here ether, and for the first time, she felt sympathy for Chloe.

It was still light outside, and with Chloe snuffling in her sleep on her truckle bed in the corner, Helena watched the evening breeze ruffling the branches of the apple trees. For the first time in her life, she had no idea what would happen to her tomorrow. Or the next day. No one remained in her life but Henry. A shiver passed through her, although the night was warm.

The candle burned down and the light faded, the fields beyond the window disappeared into the twilight, leaving Helena's stark reflection in the uneven glass. Her lids grew heavy and before she climbed into her bed, she whispered against the cool glass, "God keep you Father. Goodnight Aaron."

* * *

A declaration was nailed to the door of Exeter Guildhall, declaring James Scott, 1st Duke of Monmouth, Duke of Buccleuch, Earl of Doncaster, Earl of Dalkeith, Baron Scott of Tindale, Lord Scott of Whitchester and Eskdale, was executed in front of Westminster Hall on the fifteenth of July 1685.

"The king granted him a final audience," Samuel read to his wife from the latest newssheet. "He did it to torment Monmouth, for it's a privilege usually extended to those about to be pardoned."

Meghan's hands moved skillfully over a petticoat she was mending. "How cruel," she murmured.

"It seems Monmouth pleaded for his life and even offered to convert to Catholicism."

"Oh. He shouldn't have done that, King James would despise him for such weakness." Meghan's keen intelligence warmed him; it was a quality his friends envied.

Helena and Henry arrived in the kitchen from the yard, with Seth and Debs close behind. Henry was in plain country breeches and Helena wore a deep green gown with a white housewife cap over her flowing hair.

Their faces, if not carefree and happy, at least looked healthy from good food and time spent in the sun. Henry's wound had healed well, a yellowish bruise above his eye the only evidence, which Meghan assured him would not leave a scar.

Seth straddled a stool and started to remove his boots. "Two troopers offered Henry and me five shillings for turning in fugitive Rebels."

Meghan said nothing as she counted the eggs from Helena's basket, pausing only to throw him a reproachful look. Samuel placed a firm hand on Henry's shoulder, imagining how hard it must have been to conceal his hatred in front of the soldiers.

"May I see the Gazette, sir?" Henry looked down at the newssheet in Samuel's hand.

"Samuel." Meghan's voice held a warning, her hands moving constantly transferring eggs into a bowl.

But Henry had already began reading. "There is an account of the execution." He raised the page higher. "Listen. Jack Ketch took several blows at the Duke's head before throwing down his axe, saying he couldn't do it."

Helena gasped and Debs dropped an egg onto the floor with a distressed cry. Meghan tutted at her through pursed lips and Rebekah ran forward to wipe up the mess.

"The crowd was so angry, they were about to turn on Ketch. He had to finish the job with a knife-" Henry's voice cracked and dropping the newssheet, he fled the room, ignoring his sister's plaintive cry for him to come back.

* * *

Henry's sour mood did not improve as the days shortened and cooled, the nights drawing in. Samuel surprised him one morning with a suggestion that he might ride into Exeter with him to visit the fulling mill.

"I am no longer a wool man, Master Ffoyle," Henry murmured, his eyes on the floor.

"Are you not?" Samuel asked enigmatically.

Aware his father's former acquaintances would be gossiping at his presence, Henry resisted. Someone had informed on Sir Jonathan's involvement in the rising and the coming assize would decide the fate of the remaining Woulfes.

But Samuel proved persuasive and when Henry ran out of excuses, he gave a resigned shrug, collected his cloak and followed him to the stables.

Their ride took them past fields empty of workers; showing only stubble where the wheat had been gathered. Fieldwork earned no more than a handful of shillings for long hours, so most workers' homes had looms installed in their upper rooms, where their winter days were spent weaving the cloth the city was famous for.

Henry guided his horse into the steep alleys of St Mary Steps and All Hallows on the Wall, where the ramshackle workmen's cottages were. A cart followed behind to carry the lengths of untreated cloth collected from the weavers for delivery to the fulling mill.

Henry received respectful bowing and bright greetings from the workers; a community he had known all his life. No one mentioned Sir Jonathan Woulfe.

At the fulling mill, the cloth was taken away for soaking, and as he had done the previous year and the year before that; Henry went to the row of hooks where the workmen's aprons hung, donning a canvas coverall to protect his clothes.

Local children arrived with the buckets of sheep's urine

used to soak the cloth and soften it. Henry doled out their earnings at a penny a bucket into small, reaching hands; chasing them away when they pretended to throw stones into the troughs to annoy the fullers.

While Samuel discussed business with the overseer, Henry chatted to the workers, relieved to be able to forget his ignominious position for a while. After the soaking, the serge was soaped and scrubbed to remove the urine, the lengths then pounded in water by huge wooden timbers with notched teeth.

It always amazed Henry that the cloth did not get torn into shreds by the malicious hammers, but somehow it was better for this treatment. The only means of communication between the workers was a combination of shouts and sign language over the relentless noise.

His mother often objected to these visits; insisting a gentleman's son should not be exposed to such things. Sir Jonathan had refused to listen, saying it was all part of Henry's education. Henry learned from a young age to check the rows of tenter hooks without trapping his fingers. His eyes misted as he fastened the hooks in place; after all his mother's tender care, it was she who had suffered harm.

Henry's strengthening arms were put to good use when it came to loading the heavy lengths of wet cloth to take to the Crulditch outside the city wall to be fastened to oak racks to dry.

It had been a long day, and near sunset, the carter called to him, "We be goin' back d'rectly Master Henry, do ye wants a ride?"

Henry looked up. "No Sam, I will walk back to Tucker's Hall and meet Master Ffoyle there."

The carter left and Henry stood alone on the incline, shading his eyes from the lowering sun. The rows of serge lengths were spread below him over the sloping fields like flat sails, the wooden supports creaking in the wind.

Henry could still hear his father explaining how, once the cloth was dry, the surface was scoured by hand with teasels to remove loose particles. Teasels he and Aaron used to collect from the hedgerows as children.

Henry dropped his hand and stared off toward the north gate, conjuring Loxsbeare in his mind's eye. He had no desire to go there; his memories were tainted forever by the sight of his mother, lying so horribly still at the bottom of the stairs. An image he saw every night in his dreams.

He turned and strolled back to Fore Street where Samuel waited for him, bidding a silent farewell to his childhood.

CHAPTER TWELVE

Samuel Ffoyle strolled towards the Broadgate, beneath the stone archway leading to Cathedral Yard and turned into the entrance to Tom Mol's. They served coffee and ale on the upper floor, although it was not a coffee house in the sense such establishments existed in London. He climbed the stairs where the proprietor waited to show him to a seat, and ordered.

In the Guildhall that morning, Samuel occupied one of the wooden stalls reserved for members, to endure the spectacle of Judge Jeffreys haranguing the men brought before him, his abrasive voice tearing into the wretched creatures huddled in the dock.

In Dorchester the previous week, they tried three hundred and forty men in batches, but only with thirty or so appearing that morning, Jeffreys took pleasure in berating each one for their treachery.

Jostling onlookers packed the spectators' benches. Relatives of the accused and the curious crammed into the paneled public area to watch. The heat and stink of unwashed bodies in the airless building made the atmosphere almost unbearable.

Samuel baulked at the idea of watching the condemned being led off to the gallows at the Heavitree, unlike the horde gathered outside, who considered it a culmination of an entertaining day. In need of some pleasant surroundings and refreshment, he strode to the rear, intending to let himself out into Gandy Street.

Before reaching the door, a warden stepped out of a room to accost him. "His Lordship wishes to speak with you, Master Ffoyle." The man's voice held a sneer, as if in possession of superior knowledge he had no intention of sharing. Suppressing rising panic, he followed the clerk into the presence of Judge George Jeffreys.

Samuel accepted the cup the serving maid placed before him, contemplating that interview as he sipped the brew. His thoughts were far away when a familiar voice drifted up the stairs and two men entered the room.

Samuel peered around the decorative screen beside him as Lord Blanden and his companion scraped back chairs noisily, taking seats at the table on the other side of the wooden screen. Samuel intended acknowledging the newcomers, but to make his presence known, he would have to stand up and move into their line of vision. He decided the effort required more energy than he was willing to expend and instead, turned his attention back to his coffee.

They ordered ale in aggressive voices before resuming their conversation. When Samuel heard the word, Loxsbeare, his back stiffened. Pulling his hat down to conceal his face, he leaned closer to the screen to listen.

"That greedy blackguard, Jeffreys has ordered an examination of the property." Blanden gulped his ale, banging the jug on the table.

"Do you think he has his eye on it for himself?" his companion suggested.

"I doubt it. He's a Somerset man, and has a small manor near Taunton. He sees this only as a profitable exercise."

"Your loyalty to the king should be rewarded." The other man's voice was ingratiating.

"I shall be, with the house and the land." Blanden thumped his chair with his fist. "Despite it costing me twice what I originally offered." He gave a harsh, unattractive laugh. "And I'll wager our esteemed judge keeps it himself when it's all settled."

"Even at that price, it's still a bargain." The second man sounded envious.

"Aye, I know, and soon Loxsbeare will be mine."

"Have you heard that the younger Woulfe boy has been seen in the cloth market?"

"In the company of Ffoyle?" The first man gave a derisive snort. "I heard, but I haven't seen for myself. I thought he left Exeter with his sister after their mother died."

"There have been rumors about that too."

"What sort of rumors?"

"That she was murdered by the militia for her jewels."

The hairs on Samuel's neck stood up and he had to force himself not to burst from behind the screen and confront them.

Blanden sniggered. "It makes no difference to me how it happened. But they would do well to be out of the district before I take possession of the manor."

The men drained the last of their ale and left.

Samuel sat frozen in his seat, his coffee cold in front of him as the implications of the conversation sunk in. No wonder the militia was at Loxsbeare so soon after news of the defeat came.

He allowed some time to put some distance between himself and Blanden before emerging onto the street. The road was deserted when Samuel retraced his steps to the Guildhall.

The crowds had dispersed and the judges long gone when he got there. He located the clerk he had spoken to earlier. The man answered his questions without curiosity, even flipped through a few documents Samuel asked to see.

On the High Street, he summoned a link-boy to call his carriage, while Samuel waited beneath the porticoed entrance, mulling over his discovery.

* * *

Helena glanced up from her journal as Samuel entered the room. She had waited for his return all morning, but dreaded hearing what he had to say. She watched him in silence as he took a clay pipe from a box on the mantle, rolling it between his fingers without lighting it.

"What an unhappy day, my dear." Samuel pressed Meghan's shoulder as he took his place by the empty hearth.

"What happened, Father?" Patrick asked, as spokesperson for his siblings.

"The sentences were harsh. But no less than expected," his father responded. "Sir Jonathan and Aaron Woulfe were on the list of those ordered to account for themselves. But they did not appear in court."

Helena breathed a sigh of relief, but Henry didn't sound reassured. "Which means they are still wanted fugitives?"

Samuel gave a slow nod. "Over thirty men were tried today, two will be whipped and seven transported. The others..." he looked away.

"So much misery meted out in one day." Meghan stabbed her needle into a piece of linen.

"Hundreds of Rebels died in an hour and one half on Sedgemoor," Henry blurted. "With hundreds more cut down by dragoons with pikes and plug bayonets as they ran or-"

"Henry," Helena snapped, nodding toward Deborah and Robin, who stared at him wide-eyed.

He fell silent, fidgeting with the buttons on his vest.

"What does transported mean, Father?" Rebekah asked, blushing.

Samuel patted her shoulder affectionately. "The condemned are the property of Queen Mary Beatrice. She collects a price for each man, paid by the master who buys them as indentured labor and who ships them to work on the plantations owned by Englishmen in Jamaica and Barbados."

"Like slaves." Henry pulled a little too hard on a button, which came off in his hand.

"How long do they have to stay there?" Susannah looked up as Bayle entered the room, sliding along the bench to make room for him.

Helena looked across the room and gave him an acknowledging nod. He had been to Loxsbeare that morning to see Tobias, but she resolved not to ask what was happening there. It would hurt too much.

"At least ten years," Samuel replied. "If they can buy their passage back to England after that time, they can return home."

"Although most of them don't survive the journey to the south seas." Bayle locked gazes with Susannah as he spoke.

"What of the Taunton schoolgirls, who presented the Duke with the banner?" Meghan asked.

Her husband shook his head. "They will be ransomed back to their parents."

Meghan sighed. "Not one of them was above ten years old."

Helena thought Samuel seemed nervous, his fingers fidgeted with the clay pipe. "What else happened in Exeter, Master Ffoyle?" she asked.

Samuel frowned. "Benjamin Hobbs was at the Guildhall. He sought a private audience with Judge Jeffreys when the trials were done." He paused to light a taper, holding it against the bowl of the pipe for long seconds. "I was asked to act as a witness."

Henry looked about to say something, but Meghan spoke first. "What did he want of you?" She discarded her sewing, picked up a kerchief from the table, folded it in her lap, and then refolded it.

Samuel blew smoke into the air before covering one of her hands with his. "Do not distress yourself, my dear. He merely wanted me to confirm Hobbs was who he claimed to be." Meghan exhaled slowly in obvious relief. "Hobbs accused Sir

Jonathan of being a Rebel and I, of course, expressed suitable shock." He shrugged at Helena, as if apologizing for the lie. "I inferred a mistake had been made, but I doubt Jeffreys believed me."

"Benjamin saw you at Loxsbeare that day the soldiers came." Henry sounded panic-stricken. "He knew you helped us!"

"What did Hobbs want?" Helena's voice was icy calm.

"He demanded a reward for informing on his master."

Helena slumped in her chair, disbelieving. Samuel held up a reassuring hand. "He got nothing. Jeffreys had him thrown out of the Guildhall."

"Serves him right. The traitor." Henry folded his arms, scowling.

Samuel tapped the pipe against his lower lip, smiling at Henry. "A man like Jeffreys would never take the word of Benjamin Hobbs over mine, Henry. I refused to give credence to any of his claims, much to Hobb's fury. Jeffreys declared he had done no more than the duty his sovereign required of him."

Helena silently congratulated the dreadful judge on his good sense, but the fact changed nothing. They could not go back to Loxsbeare. An image of Hobbs came into her head, but she barely remembered ever speaking to him. She wondered what prompted his disloyalty.

"He was not the only one." Samuel's statement halted a spate of speculative chatter. He had taken only a few puffs of the clay pipe, but turned it upside down and tapped it against the hearth, dislodging the smoldering contents. "In May, a letter was sent to the city wardens, setting out Sir Jonathan Woulfe's involvement in the rebellion. It told of private meetings held at Loxsbeare in the weeks before Monmouth's landing. The document named Grey, Younge, Speke and the others."

Helena whispered in horror, "They knew from the beginning?"

Samuel nodded.

"Who sent the letter?" Henry clenched both fists on his knees.

Samuel paused before answering. "Lord Miles Blanden."

Bayle blew out a long breath and Helena gasped.

"But he's father's friend." Henry thumped the arm of his chair with a fist. "It couldn't have been him!"

Samuel held up his hands. "The letter is in his hand and carries his signature, Henry. I saw it myself."

Henry turned to Bayle. "What did he hope to gain by betraying us?"

"Everything," Samuel replied. "Lord Blanden has petitioned the Court for possession of the house and lands of Loxsbeare."

Blood roared in Helena's ears. This is my fault. Guilt slammed into her like a blow. If she had welcomed her betrothal to Martyn more willingly, this might not have happened. Lord Blanden would have had access to Loxsbeare and the links with the family he craved. Common sense told her she could not be blamed for Martyn's death, but Blanden had been casting covetous eyes at Loxsbeare for years, and the rebellion was the opportunity he needed. She felt nauseous and looked to Henry for sympathy, but he was staring the empty fireplace, his mouth working silently in shock.

Distracted by the turmoil inside her head, Helena caught only part of what Bayle told Samuel.

"...magistrate came to Loxsbeare this morning. He was angry the manor has been stripped bare and told Tobias the house was to be made ready for a new owner and furnishings would have to be arranged."

Henry gave a triumphant snort. "Serves Blanden right, I hope the soldiers pulled it to pieces."

Helena frowned. Loxsbeare had been stripped. Where were her family's possessions? The cartloads standing wrapped in the Ffoyle stables were only part of what Loxsbeare held. Is that what Benjamin had been doing, emptying the house of valuables left behind? Did Tobias Lumm discover this and throw him out? Or . . . were they in league together? And if they hadn't taken them, then where was it all? The conversation had moved on, and she had missed her chance to ask questions, leaving her frustrated and annoyed.

Bayle withdrew without ceremony, which Helena attributed to his sense of responsibility for Benjamin Hobb's actions, although he could not have known of the man's treachery. She resolved to speak to him about it later. Helena lingered by the window as the rest of the family bade goodnight to their parents and drifted out of the room.

Samuel laid down the clay pipe. "No, Henry, please stay. What I have to say concerns you." Henry paused at the door and returned to stand beside Samuel's chair. "You both have a decision to make."

"What kind of decision?" Helena asked warily, turning to face him.

"If you wish to remain in Ideswell."

Helena exchanged a look with Henry. "Leave?"

"I imagine you might want to go somewhere Sir Jonathan Woulfe's disgrace is not so well known."

Panic rose in Helena at the prospect of leaving the Ffoyles. "Are we to be driven from Exeter because of our father's questionable loyalty?" Is this what her life had become, moving from one house to another as displaced guests?

"Helena, you were the most important thing in his life," Samuel said.

"Not more important than his religion and his Duke," Helena snapped back. "He abandoned us for them."

"His religion and his Duke were intrinsically linked with his home and his family. One day you will understand."

"I don't want to understand." Her voice rose in anguish at the sight of him sitting there, his hands folded together like a cleric. "I want him back! I want them both back. Our mother and uncle are dead, what are Henry and I to do?"

As if speaking her worst fears aloud made them real, her defiance crumbled and she started shaking. She knuckled hot tears away.

Samuel leaned forward, his gaze on her face. So far, Henry had said nothing. "Your father was concerned with what would happen to you if he had chosen the wrong side."

"He never believed the rising would fail," Henry insisted.

Samuel ignored this comment. "He knew he could trust me not to cheat his children, so he signed certain properties over to me, to be held for you."

Henry's practical nature surfaced. "What properties?"

Helena blew her nose, her tears forgotten.

"Apart from the sheep, which have been grazing on Ffoyle land since May. There are the houses in Magdalen Road, the warehouse at the Quay, your mother's jewels."

"You have mother's jewels?" Helena looked incredulous. "We thought, I thought he had sold them for Monmouth."

"No. They are yours. Yours and Henry's, and Aaron if. . ." He let the thought hang in the air.

"Not her sapphire necklace though." Henry's voice was hard. "That soldier will have sold it by now."

Samuel blew air between his lips as if bad memories surfaced. "You will have an income from the wool manufacturing and rents from the houses. There will even be sufficient money for a dowry for Helena."

"We won't be rich." Henry gave an accepting shrug.

"Not without the Loxsbeare lands, no."

Helena began to think logically again. What Samuel was offering was more than she could have imagined. She smoothed the folds of her skirt with trembling fingers. "Where can we go?"

Henry turned horrified eyes on her. "You want to leave Devon?"

She lifted her chin. "You heard Master Ffoyle, we have some means. Do you want to see Lord Blanden occupying Loxsbeare?"

Henry started, then as if a thought occurred to him he asked, "Could we go to London?"

Helena felt her stomach turn over. London? She had always loved Exeter, but the thought of its familiar streets felt hostile, as if she had no place there any more. Like an animal fleeing from the scene of its distress, she felt in need of somewhere to regain her strength. And if not London, then where?

Their father had friends in Frome and Winchester, even Taunton. Then she remembered, there had been an assize held in all those places. A Rebel's daughter would hardly be welcome.

Samuel held up a hand. "Do not decide tonight. Allow me to write a letter or two to some associates of mine. Between us, we may have something to offer."

As they took their leave, Samuel's discrete cough made Helena pause at the door. "I want you both to know," he began gently. "Sir Jonathan was a dear friend."

"You believe he is dead then?" Helena blinked hard, her heart twisting.

"I do not know." He frowned. "But to my mind, the numbers don't add up."

Henry stepped back into the room. "Numbers?"

"At Sedgemoor, Monmouth had four thousand men. Thirteen hundred Rebel bodies were collected after the battle." Helena gave an involuntary shudder. "Some eight hundred or so have since been captured and convicted. Say five hundred deserted, although reports claim that figure is high. That accounts for two thirds. Where are the others?"

Henry stared at him, his lips moving. "That would mean almost fourteen hundred men are unaccounted for."

Samuel nodded admiringly. "Which suggests more must have escaped Sedgemoor than originally believed. Don't give up hope on your father yet," his face softened, "or Aaron."

Outside in the corridor, Henry told Helena he was going to find Bayle and try Samuel's theory out on him. She watched him go, noticing he moved differently somehow. His shoulders had broadened and his stride seemed slower.

She wandered through the kitchens, stepping outside into an empty yard bathed in watery sunlight. Susannah was there, throwing handfuls of grain to six fat geese, which nudged her and scrabbled at her feet.

Pulling the cords of her cap free, Helena lifted her face to the sky and let the wind take her hair, blowing it around her head. She pretended to chase the indignant geese as they flapped and squawked in panic.

She perched beside Susannah on the garden wall, her gaze on the soft green hills around them. For the first time in weeks, Helena felt her future held hope. As to finding happiness, she would have to wait and see.

CHAPTER THIRTEEN

In his travels around the county, Samuel could not help but acknowledge that King James stayed true to his promise to, "Teach the Rebels a lesson". At every crossroads and market place and on the green of every large village that gave their sons to Monmouth, hung chained or roped corpses; sometimes just their heads and torsos, stuck on poles with orders not to remove them.

The stench of rotting flesh permeated the countryside through the hot summer days, poisoning the atmosphere with the king's revenge. The locals could not even attend church to pray for their fallen sons, without passing a gibbet by the lynch-gate, or a dead face hung above the church door.

A week after the assize, Samuel took an early morning ride into Exeter. Mol's was empty of customers at that time of day, and when his companion climbed the stairs to take the chair opposite, he felt it was unlikely they were observed.

Samuel's lip curled into a cynical smile as he sipped his coffee. "The whole city knows of Blanden's betrayal. He will find few friends here."

"He is taking occupation in a few days." Tobias said. At Samuel's questioning look, he smiled. "And before you ask, I left last night."

"Have all the servants gone?"

"Most of them. I am staying with my parents at The Ship."

"You surprise me. I thought inn-keeping was not to your taste."

Tobias' troubled eyes stared off. "Lately I have changed my thinking about what suits me and what doesn't, Master Ffoyle."

Samuel watched as first anger, and then resignation crossed Tobias' handsome features. Hi fingers tapped the tabletop restlessly. "I sought to improve your life, Tobias. Not make you dissatisfied." Samuel sighed. "For that I am sorry."

Tobias gave a weak smile. "I don't blame you for Sir Jonathan's political loyalties."

"He was proud of you."

"Not proud enough to ask me to go with him." His eyes flashed fire, his hurt plain on his face.

"Had he done so, would you have gone?" Samuel lifted his cup to his lips, watching him over the rim.

"I don't know." Tobias folded his arms and stared off toward the cathedral on the other side of the window. "But he entrusted me with his women." He gave a harsh laugh. "And I allowed one to run off to Somerset and the other..."

"I am more to blame than you." Samuel gave a dismissive wave, unwilling to discuss such a raw subject.

"Still, at least he managed to preserve some of his assets for his remaining children. I hear Helena and Henry will be going to London." Tobias' voice held no bitterness, and only a trace of disappointment.

Samuel smiled. "There are arrangements to make, but I feel it is a possibility. And tell me, Tobias, what would you like to do?"

"With my position as steward terminated?" He arched a well-shaped eyebrow. "What I want is not the issue, but I shall not remain at Loxsbeare, not with Blanden as master."

"Your father would applaud your loyalty."

"My father is most probably dead." Tobias' tone held regret. "My foster father, on the other hand, has asked me to take over the Inn." At Samuel's surprised look, he went on. "My brothers are too young yet to be of much use."

"Will you take up his offer?"

Tobias sat back in his chair; his gaze swept the room before settling on Samuel. "He brought me up. I feel I owe it to him, now he is no longer healthy enough."

"He is sick?" Samuel was surprised. Jim Lumm had seemed the same as ever when they last met. But some illnesses could creep up on a body and drain the lifeblood from them. He resolved to call on Master Lumm, and soon.

"Aye. And then there's mother." Tobias grinned, wry amusement animating his face.

Samuel pictured Emily Lumm's sensual walk and inviting smile. Always loyal to his flighty mother, yet Tobias had no illusions about her. She had made no secret of the fact that the kindly, if bovine Jim Lumm was not Tobias' father. This knowledge, Samuel knew, had instigated some of the young man's youthful rebelliousness.

Samuel reached into his coat and removed a folded parchment, which he placed on the table.

"What do you have there?" Tobias looked at it with no more than mild interested.

"Your inheritance."

Tobias blinked. Samuel held it out and he took it, examining it briefly. Tobias raised his head, startled. "This is the deed to the house by the east gate. Sir Jonathan's house."

"It is yours." Samuel summoned the serving man to bring more coffee. Tobias declined, his agitation made it clear he was impatient for the man to leave so he could ask questions.

Tobias leaned forward. "How can you give this to me? It should be Henry's, or Helena's." He sounded confused, but his expression was hopeful.

Samuel smiled. "I am not giving it to you. Sir Jonathan is." He raised the dish of coffee and took a slow, appreciative sip. "I meant it when I said he was proud of you. When he came to me before the rebellion to ask if I would look after his children, you were included."

"I was?" Tobias held the parchment reverently, turning it over in his hands.

Samuel nodded. "I won't pretend he ever loved your mother. It was a youthful liaison and she was a-"

Tobias held up a hand. "I know what she was, Master Ffoyle; in many ways she still is. I also realize Sir Jonathan could not acknowledge me publicly, but he gave me a good position at Loxsbeare."

"You don't feel he showed you a way of life you could never have?"

Tobias gave a sigh, studying the decorated ceiling for a moment before replying. "Who knows what I might have had? Had he lived, he might have furthered my career in other ways."

Samuel was as unwilling to admit his friend might be dead, any more than Helena; but this wasn't the appropriate time to argue the point. "He wanted you to have something of his, and he decided on this." Samuel indicated the parchment. "It belonged to his father, and his grandfather."

"Thank you, Master Ffoyle." Tobias's voice broke a little as he slid the document into his coat, resting his hand on it for a moment. When he spoke again there was no softness in his voice. "About Benjamin Hobbs."

Samuel tensed, wary. "What about him?"

"I caught him loading a bag with some items of plate left behind. When I ordered him out, he boasted about what he had done in betraying Sir Jonathan."

Samuel snorted. "Blanden pre-empted him there. Did he know about you?"

"He didn't taunt me with it, so I am certain not. We had an . . . altercation." Tobias steepled his fingers in front of his face, staring over the tips. "Suffice it to say he won't be returning to Exeter, not in my lifetime."

Samuel held up a hand. "I would rather not know the details, but thank you for the reassurance."

Tobias pulled himself to his feet, looking down on Samuel with a sad smile. "Thank you, Master Ffoyle."

Samuel smiled and nodded, knowing he meant more than the delivery of a piece of paper. "And please, wish Helena and Henry happiness in their new life. I hope someday to see them again." He turned abruptly and left, his boots echoing on the stairs.

Samuel watched him go, saddened that Helena and Henry might never acknowledge him. Tobias Lumm was a fine young man, a brother anyone would be proud of.

* * *

As the horror of the previous weeks began to recede, Helena spent her days in tasks she would have scorned at Loxsbeare. She prepared vegetables, sorted linen, made candles, or sewed shirts and underclothes with the girls in the front parlor. In contrast, the nights passed slowly as she ran disturbing scenarios through her head as to the possible fate of her father and brother, from whom still no word came.

In late September, Samuel received a response from London. Master Robert Devereux was offering himself as guardian to Helena and Henry, expressing a willingness to establish them in his own home.

He read some of the words aloud to himself.

'being mindful of their situation, I would willingly offer safe haven against any disadvantage which may be visited upon them as the offspring of a known Rebel'.

Darkness came earlier with the arrival of autumn and Samuel waited until the family gathered in the parlor after the evening meal before revealing the contents of the letter.

"But London is a terrible place, of sin and Catholics." Susannah said on hearing the plan. "A city of 'evil and debasement."

"Oh, you are such a goose Anna." Deborah laughed. "It is a wondrous place full of interesting and wealthy people. Why, you could do anything in London, live in a fine house, and go abroad in a carriage every day. See the king if one wished."

"I doubt anyone can go and see the king if it took their fancy, Debs." Rebekah hovered between one sister's censure and the other's excitement, molding her opinions to suit whoever spoke last.

"But it is so," Patrick contradicted her. "The king and his entourage parade through Whitehall Palace every day. Anyone who has a mind to has the right to enter the grounds to see him. All they require is the patience to stand around for hours in draughty corridors."

"What manner of man is Robert Devereux?" Helena edged forward, finding the excitement catching.

"A fine gentleman who will introduce you around the city." Samuel smiled.

Helena was dubious. Were they still respectable enough to be taken into society?

"Does he have a fine house?" Deborah's demanded.

Samuel smiled indulgently at his youngest daughter. "He does indeed. Lambtons is still, I believe, the best alehouse in Holborn."

"Alehouse?" Helena and Henry repeated together.

Meghan looked up from her sewing with a secretive smile. "Samuel, I do believe Helena and Henry are shocked you would consider sending them to live in such a place?"

Samuel pretended to be affronted. "Why ever should they be? Lambtons is a fine chophouse, patronized by the best of London society. It has an excellent reputation."

"But an alehouse, Father..." Susannah's voice trailed, uncertain.

"They serve their ale in real silver tankards, even in the tap room," Samuel teased.

Helena listened to the banter with mounting anxiety, lacking the confidence to challenge Samuel. They had nowhere else to go and no one to go to. If a London chophouse was willing to shelter them, she was in no position to questioning it.

Henry surprised her with his enthusiasm. "I never supposed to live in an alehouse. It will be an adventure."

"Will Helena be a serving girl?" Deborah asked, wide eyed.

"No, of course not, child." Samuel snapped his newssheet. "Lambtons is not that sort of establishment."

"An alehouse without serving girls?" Seth's mocking gaze slid towards Helena. She glared at his grinning face, half-furious, half-apprehensive.

"They have an army of serving girls." Samuel laughed. "And serving men, but there would be no requirement for Helena or Henry to perform duties of that kind." His eyes twinkled with amusement at the relieved look on Helena's face.

Henry looked disappointed. "I would have enjoyed being a serving man in a London chophouse."

Helena pulled a face at him, but he pretended not to notice.

Speculation and discussion continued until Samuel announced he could bear the inquisition no longer, and banished them all affectionately from his sight.

* * *

Helena and Susannah sorted linens for packing in the parlor, while Samuel and Nathan sat with heads bowed over ledgers and work sheets. Helena watched Bayle with possessive admiration, realizing again he was a younger man than she had ever perceived. She let her mind drift back to their days in Bridgwater, when he had been solicitous, entertaining and sympathetic by turn.

Helena was shocked to learn Bayle was not going to London with them. The idea of living without him panicked her at first, and in quiet moments, her doubts still lingered.

The only contact she would have with her old life was Chloe, who would be accompanying her. She gave herself a mental shake. Her life had changed, irrevocably, and it was time she accepted it.

She owed Bayle more gratitude than she could ever repay, and though she would miss him, her 'selfish bone' welcomed a new life, free of all past entanglements. Her mother's words came to her then with a pang. "You have a 'selfish bone', Helena." When questioned as to what it meant, Lady Elizabeth explained, "It's a tiny, misplaced bone, which hides from you most of the time. It surfaces when you make a decision based on self-interest." It became a family joke, and used to get her into trouble when she was younger.

Helena knew Bayle was tortured by the fact he had not been at Loxsbeare to prevent their mother's death, but he forbore to talk about it with anyone. Nor did she reveal her own feelings of culpability, or that her sleep was disturbed with thoughts of 'what if'. What if she had not dragged Bayle off to Somerset, what if Bayle had been there when the soldiers arrived instead of Samuel. But if she had learned anything in her short life, it was that choice had a price.

Lately, Bayle had discarded his working clothes, taking to formal attire consisting of a dun-colored long coat nipped at the waist, worn with soft cambric shirts, cravats and polished leather shoes. Quietly respectful to Samuel, he was solicitous of his new master's family and Helena felt sad, aware his concern would be for others in future and not for her.

Turning to her companion to share her thoughts, she saw Susannah too watched Bayle, with a soft, almost longing expression on her face. Bayle looked up from the papers spread before him and gave them a broad grin, his eyes lingering a fraction longer on Susannah's face, before dipping his head to his work again.

Helena smiled. Perhaps Bayle would not be so lonely without them after all.

CHAPTER FOURTEEN

Helena opened her eyes and sat up, startled to see an unfamiliar room. Then she remembered; they had stopped at Kingston the night before. The inn was pretty and ancient; its overhung upper windows leaning precariously toward the river.

The thin light told her it was early still and she wondered what had woken her, until the harsh shout of a street peddler came to her, calling his wares underneath her window. The lone voice joined swiftly by others, until there seemed to be a new call for every commodity and foodstuff she could imagine. Helena grimaced, the smell of herrings and oysters at that time of the morning made her queasy.

She stretched in the watery sunlight flooding onto the bed, easing her stiff muscles. Four days of confinement in a coach, large and comfortable though it was, had proved a testing time for her joints.

Helena's fingers closed over the sheets and with a smile, she remembered Meghan's words as they packed Lady Elizabeth's precious bed linen, recalling her night at The Dove.

"We cannot have you abed on inn linen, Helena." She smiled. No, Mistress Helena Woulfe does not sleep on inn linen.

Her farewell to the Ffoyles had been poignant, and as Chloe's deft fingers fastened her into her riding gown on the morning they left Ideswell, Helena's hand had drifted down to smooth the skirt. An image of her father came into her head on the last time she wore it; the memory making her throat hurt.

Helena had watched as Bayle bade goodbye to Henry as they stood close together beneath the overhanging porch. She was too far away to catch what they said, but their earnest expressions illustrated how difficult it was for both of them. Then Bayle offered a stiff bow, which Henry returned, and then he brushed past Helena on his way to the coach, his eyes bright with tears.

Bayle's gaze remained fixed on Henry's back when Helena approached him. His smile when he saw her was not reflected in his eyes. Never had she seen him look so dispirited as his gaze skimmed her from head to toe.

"You look every inch Lady Elizabeth's daughter today, Mistress."

Then Helena was the one who fought back tears. "I am Sir Jonathan's daughter too," she reminded him.

"You always shall be, never forget that."

"Thank you, Nathan. For everything you have done for me, for all of my life, as well during this summer."

He held his hands toward her, palms upwards, and then dropped them to his sides again. An impulse drove Helena forward and she enfolded him in the briefest of embraces; over almost before it began. She pulled away and without looking back, strode to where Samuel held the coach door open.

The carriage jerked forward and Henry held up the leather window flap, one arm raised in farewell. She had longed to make a reference to their mother, or Loxsbeare, but resisted for fear of opening the floodgates for them both.

The square, wooden Ffoyle carriage sported a new coat of brown paint; its faded leather curtains replaced with stiff, new hide. The iron clad wheels and axels were new and the Clothmakers' coat of arms were recreated in bright new colors on the doors.

Two heavy carts followed, each with a brace of armed servants aboard for protection, piled high with the possessions Lady Elizabeth had rescued from Loxsbeare Manor.

The journey was a revelation, with Samuel's authoritative manner working like sorcery on indolent maids to procure both the best rooms and frequent and copious hot water at the inns. All the previous night, Helena had lain awake in anticipation, listening to the watch call out every hour.

"We are nearly in London," she said aloud to the ceiling, hugging herself.

Chloe hobbled through the door, almost as if she had heard her. "'Tis a lovely day, Mistress. If a trifle cold. Are ye ready to get up yet?"

Once dressed, Helena hurried down the stairs; almost colliding with Samuel in the entrance hall. She stepped back in surprise at the sight of him attired in a bright blue long coat and black periwig; items Helena had no idea he possessed. In the dining room he haggled with the innkeeper in threatening terms, declaring their bill was extortionate and the food barely adequate.

Helena exchanged an incredulous look with Henry at this tirade, for the fare had been exceptionally good. Out on the street again, Samuel bellowed at insistent traders who sprang forward to pester Helena; cuffing grooms who did not respond quickly enough to his orders.

"Life in London is harsher for servant and master alike," he said, as they rumbled toward Hammersmith, "and far less forgiving."

As if to demonstrate, he shrieked at linkboys who clung on the coach, offering to guide them through the traffic for a penny. "If we are set on by footpads, I will strangle you first," he roared, declaring all street hawkers to be in league with ambushing villains.

He hollered at their driver to harangue other coachman and chairmen to force their way through any obstacles. "Use your whip, man. We shall never get anywhere in this throng, else!"

"Master Ffoyle, you are frightening Chloe." Helena's gentle scold was rendered ineffective when Samuel glared at the maid, who shrank back in her seat. Helena was convinced that for all his ferocity, Samuel enjoyed the faster pace and he seemed more alive in the city than at home.

"London has more new buildings than anywhere else in the country," Samuel told an impressed Henry as the carriage swayed along cobbled streets. "The great fire of '66 destroyed many of the old wooden houses and churches."

Helena tried to imagine the magnificent city in flames, but the image eluded her. "How did the fire start?"

Samuel gave a shrug. "Some say it was Catholics." Henry gave a disbelieving snort. "But I fear it was simply a dry summer and   a fire not extinguished properly in Pudding Lane. Whichever it was, it made thousands homeless and some left London, never to return. But only a handful of people lost their lives." He shuddered as if dispelling bad memories. "Christopher Wren drew up plans for rebuilding, based on an Italian piazza system with the streets radiating from a central point." His tone changed to one of regret. "But it fell by the wayside."

"Why, sir? It would have served far better than all these crooked alleyways and courts." Henry pointed out.

"When your house is a charred mass on the ground, you cannot wait for the ambitious schemes of kings to be completed. These people." He waved at the crowds beyond the carriage windows, "had families to put roofs over and businesses to run. They simply re-built them in the same places. However the new building regulations should ensure such a tragedy never happens again."

"I still think the Italian piazzas would have looked wonderful." Henry sounded disappointed. Then the scene beyond the coach windows caught his attention again. "It's so vast, and there are so many people!" He craned so far forward; Helena had to warn him he was in danger of losing his hat.

The streets became narrower, and the winter afternoon was fading into a colorless dusk by the time they entered a cobbled street; lined with half-timbered black and white houses, with uneven leaded windows.

"This area is called Holborn." Samuel pointed his cane through the window. "The great fire did not reach this far, so most of the buildings are original."

"Are all these shops?" Helena stared into dingy leaded windows as they passed.

"Mostly; the living quarters are on the floors above."

The carriage halted in front of a timbered building with wooden balconies along the length of the upper floor. A long row of windows covered the lower façade, the individual panes twinkling with golden light.

"It looks like several houses joined together," Henry observed when Samuel announced they had arrived.

"It's enormous," Helena whispered, staring up at the painted wooden sign stretched over the front, with 'Lambtons Inn' in green and gold lettering. Shadows moved behind the glowing windows, and the sound of laughter and shouted greetings reached them, together with the enticing smell of cooking.

Samuel handed Helena down from the coach and a portly man clacked toward them on high-heeled shoes. Helena could not take her eyes off him. Was that a patch on his cheek?

The man fluttered around them, tiny black eyes skimming over Chloe, to settle admiringly on Helena. "I am Lubbock," he gave a dainty bow. "Master Devereux's manservant and I welcome you to Lambtons on behalf of my master."

A brace of grooms appeared in a livery of buff jackets over black breeches to direct the carts and the Ffoyle carriage into the stable yard. Lubbock ushered them into the inn, skipping around them as if he were herding sheep. Helena stepped across the threshold into a double height entrance hall, its interior shimmering with rich fabric, paint and tapestry in varying shades of cream, white and gold. Mirrors arranged on the walls reflected light from myriad candles and a thick, pattered carpet spread like a colorful sea at their feet.

"This, is an alehouse?" Henry whispered, spinning on his heels as his gaze slid around, then up and back again.

Helena glanced with awe through a row of open doors on the right of the staircase as they passed. Two revealed the busy dining halls of the inn, the sounds of clinking glasses and loud conversation drifting toward them. One room, arranged as a salon, had ornamental brocade furniture and rich hangings: a long table laid out for dinner filled another.

At the bottom of an ornate staircase, three females and a man waited. Their hosts, Helena assumed. Samuel bowed to a man of middle height; alluding to a past Helena had no knowledge of, giving her time to study him.

A little taller than herself, Master Devereux possessed an oval, friendly face and blue eyes which twinkled as if constantly amused. When beckoned forward, Henry made his most gracious leg and Helena dropped a curtsey, her gaze fixed in fascination on his clothes.

Around his shoulders was a patterned brocade garment of palest blue, gathered on one hip over a shirt with flounces peeking out at the front. The robe reached to below his knees, decorated with birds and flowers beneath which his spindly legs poked through.

In place of a heavy periwig, a fur turban covered his shorn head, evident by the rough short hairs protruding from above pink ears. Low-heeled mules of black velvet encased his feet, embroidered to match his coat.

He indicated a lady beside him." This is my wife, Adella."

This person too, took Helena by surprise. Somehow, she had imagined a London version of Meghan Ffoyle, but the magnificent creature that enveloped her in perfumed, satin arms was almost girlish. She wore a silver-colored mantoe, which shimmered in the candlelight, pleated and fastened to reveal the top of an elaborate corset holding in her tiny waist and showing an ample décolleté.

The split skirt pulled back and up, was a new fashion to Helena, fastened on the woman's still slender hips and draped to reveal a blue underskirt. Her glossy mahogany hair was piled in large curls on top of her head; with looped ribbons and feathers in creamy pinks and grays, making her appear taller than her husband.

Close up, Helena realized she was older than she first appeared, her years hidden under a careful veneer of face paint, with a crescent moon taffeta patch next to her carmined lips.

"I am delighted you have come to live with us." Her voice was husky and she enunciated each word carefully, caressing Henry's shoulder with one hand. Helena tried to catch her brother's eye, but he appeared mesmerized by her.

"This is my elder daughter, Celia." The lady waved a hand toward a plump, pretty girl of Helena's own age, dressed in aquamarine. Her corseted bodice was worn open, held together at the waist, the gap in between filled with a stomacher covered with rows of ribbons, or 'echelles', each one wider than the last like the steps of a ladder. Her décolleté, cut straight in the current fashion, had decorative edging and a bertha of exquisitely worked cream lace.

"Welcome to Lambtons," Celia's voice was soft and high-pitched. "I hope London is all you wish it to be."

A younger girl stood beside Celia, this one dark and vivacious in deep yellow silk. She possessed all the daring, self-confident look of her mother as she greeted Henry warmly. When she turned to Helena, her penetrating gaze took her in with a sweep of long lashes, obviously not liking what she saw.

Helena bobbed a brief curtsey but the girl lifted her chin and stared, until Adella nudged her, hard. "Phebe, offer your respects to Mistress Woulfe." When the girl made no move, Adella forced a laugh. "Please forgive my Phebe, Helena dear, she can be rather shy on occasion."

At Helena's shoulder, Celia gave a derisive snort and flapped her fan.

"Mistress," Phebe murmured, her curtsey barely discernible, before she turned pleading eyes on her father. "Papa, it is so late for dinner, please may we eat?"

Ignoring this awkward exchange, Master Devereux beckoned them all into the private dining room where a long table awaited them, one silk-clad arm around Phebe's shoulders.

"Who looks after those people in the alehouse, if they are all here with us?" Henry asked.

Helena shrugged, her mind too occupied with Phebe's hostility.

Master Devereux turned at this observation to give a full-throated guffaw. "My dear boy, we have an army of staff who run the chophouse and public rooms. I rarely have to make an appearance, unless a member of the Court happens to grace us with their presence. Do come into dinner, my dears, and sample the best Lambtons Inn has to offer."

Helena dropped back, whispering to Samuel, "What is that extraordinary garment Master Devereux is wearing?" She had hesitated to ask, but was transfixed by it.

Samuel grinned at her. "It's called a banyan. It's made of silk brocade from India. You will find many gentlemen have adopted them as indoor attire." Helena found this hard to believe, and wondered if she would ever see another.

Dinner was a new experience. Helena had heard of the French style of eating, with all the dishes arranged on the table at once, but she had never dined that way before. At her hesitation, Samuel helped identify the meats and pastries, piling her plate high as he regaled the company with their crossing of Blackheath.

"We had to wait for other coaches to join us, so we could cross in convoy," Henry ventured between mouthfuls, his eyes round at the memory.

"The heath is a dangerous place," Robert acceded with a nod. "I always travel with an armed escort against footpads and highwaymen."

"Well, I think you were all very brave to venture into such inhospitable country," Adella fluttered her eyelashes. "One dare not even imagine the consequences had you been attacked."

Helena's nervousness quickly dispelled at their friendliness and she began to enjoy herself, marveling as more dishes were carried in and set on the table. "What is that?" Henry asked, pointing at an oval dish giving off a savory aroma.

Helena frowned. "I think it might be Beef a la Mode, but I cannot be sure."

"Indeed it is, my dear," Robert said, forking several thick slices onto Henry's plate, "The finest English buttock beef larded with bacon and stewed in claret, cinnamon cloves, mace and pepper."

"It is a favorite of my William's." Adella batted her eyelids, stroking Henry's cheek familiarly. Helena stared, but Henry didn't seem to mind.

"William is our brother," Celia twirled her spoon in the air, answering Helena's unspoken question. "He is not in London just now, but you will meet him one day."

In response to Henry's compliments over the beef, Robert launched into a recital of each dish as it appeared.

"Here we have venison pasties and sallets, carrots mulched in vinegar, a cow's tongue garnished with capers and 'spinnage', rabbit in butter and some plump radishes."

Helena noticed that despite encouraging them to eat, Adella pushed her food round her plate after the first few mouthfuls.

Celia spent the entire meal with her arm looped through Helena's, as if to announce they were to be inseparable. Phebe imitated her mother in both her appetite and flirtatiousness, fluttering between the men like a bright butterfly, gazing at them from under her lashes or a coyly held fan.

She issued any servant moving into her field of vision with pointed, but needless instructions, exercising her position as daughter of the house.

The talk was lively, if superficial, each testing the experience and opinions of the others. Adella probed for details of their family life at Loxsbeare. "I have never been so far west." Her inflection intimated it was a daring thing to do.

"Why should you wish to, Mama?" Phebe made a moue of disgust.

"Have you ever visited the theatre?" Celia asked Helena.

When Helena replied she had not, Adella insisted she would personally correct that omission in her education. "Until one has seen the magnificent Anne Bracegirdle, one simply hasn't lived, my dear."

Master Devereux quizzed Henry, probing for details of what kind of life he saw for himself in the city. Helena listened avidly, intrigued as to where the conversation might lead.

Their father had planned for Henry to enter the army, but these days Henry refused to discuss soldiering; so Helena was curious as to how he would answer Robert's question.

Adella's husky voice distracted her. "I am determined you shall see the New Exchange shops and stalls, my dear, and there is of course Covent Garden and the Hungerford Market to visit. I guarantee you will have seen nothing like them in the provinces; you are in for a treat."

When she turned back to her brother's conversation, Helena discovered they had moved on to horses and dogs. Disappointed, she listened to Samuel telling Celia he planned to stay in London for a week or so, to oversee his warehouse in Freemans Yard before returning home to Exeter.

Grateful he was not leaving too soon, Helena suppressed a yawn. The warmth of the room and the good food conspired to remind her of their exhausting day.

"I feel it is time you retired, my dears," Samuel said, winking at Helena. She gave him a grateful smile and rose slowly to her feet, her hand on his arm as he escorted her into the hall.

The dining room was still half full of chattering patrons issuing orders for food and drink; the noisy activity feeling alien to Helena, who simply longed for bed. Celia collected a candle from a bureau at the bottom of the stairs where a row of candlesticks stood beside a basket of candles and tapers.

With a hand curled protectively around the flame and a footman following, Celia led them up the wide staircase, their elders calling cheery good nights from the hall below; Phebe beside them still wide awake.

Although Helena observed the upper floor was sumptuous, with wide corridors and walls covered with richly patterned wallpaper, once away from the lower rooms, the mirrors and gilt paint diminished and the candles stabbed into dark corners.

The footman led Henry off down a hallway and Celia took Helena to the opposite side of the building. "Your room is across the corridor from mine," she whispered.

The chamber she showed Helena into contained a high tester bed with heavy pattered hangings, a turkey carpet and full height paneling. A leaded window overlooked the back of the house, although it was too dark by this time to see anything.

Wishing her new friend goodnight, Helena leaned against the closed door, relieved she no longer had to stretch her weary face into a polite smile. Helena propped her elbows on top of a spindly legged bureau while a yawning Chloe combed out her hair; leaning her chin into her hands to whisper excitedly at her reflection."I am in London."

CHAPTER FIFTEEN

"Mistress Devero' 'as sent your breakfast mistress," Chloe declared the next morning when Helena stirred awake. Limping to the bed, she balanced a large tray awkwardly on the coverlet.

Helena smiled sleepily, examining her breakfast of tiny pastries, a beautifully crafted silver pot containing hot chocolate and a plate of thinly sliced bread and butter.

"They sleeps late in this 'ouse." Chloe tutted disapprovingly.

Helena pulled a negligee round her shoulders without comment, plucked a pastry from the tray and slid out of the bed to cross to the window.

"They have a garden!" She braced her arms on the wooden sill to peer into the space below. Completely enclosed, neat flowerbeds were arranged in geometrical patterns with pathways bordered by dwarf shrubs; so different from the semi-wild expanse of lawn bordered by tall, ancient trees at Loxsbeare.

"Look at this, Mistress." Chloe opened a door to the left of the bed to reveal a closet containing Helena's clothes chest and bureau, the heavy craftsmanship incongruous in the neat space, but achingly familiar.

Winter sunshine flooded into the room as Helena sipped the sweet hot chocolate. For the first time since crossing the city boundaries, she could not hear ironclad wheels or rough voices, clattering buckets, braying animals or noisy peddlers. She decided this must be because her room stood at the back of the house, the garden acting as a buffer from the street.

A light knocking came at the door and before Chloe could respond, two maids carried steaming buckets of hot water into the room and a third dragged in a hipbath and set it in front of the fireplace. A fourth set to laying the fire, which bloomed into life and warmth with surprising speed; livliness invading the room and filling it with activity.

Linen cloths were draped over the side of the bath; the fragrance of lavender and chamomile drifting into the air as they poured in the water.

"Do all Londoners bathe in the mornings?" Helena asked no one in particular. The maid closest to her concealed a snigger as if the idea was monstrous. "Not every day, Mistress."

"Mistress Devereux's instructions," the maid kneeling on the hearth responded. Chloe stood sulkily to one side, watching them with resentful eyes.

The maids stepped back, two on either end of the hip bath, waiting. With a small shock, Helena realized they expected her to disrobe while they were still in the room. Unwilling to appear unworldly, she allowed her shift to fall to the floor, but they barely glanced at her. Her embarrassment disappeared as she slid into the hot water, relaxing her still sore back into the fragrant heat that worked instant miracles on her stiff muscles. She trailed her hands under the water, her skin glistening beneath the surface as she lay back and took in her surroundings.

The room was not as large as her chamber at Loxsbeare, but she could hardly count that as a fault. The high, wide bed had green and gold hangings draped on either side, with a thick piled rug displaying a whorled pattern of yellow, green and gold beneath. Paneled walls added warmth and richness, one side of the room taken up by the leaded window.

Helena waited until the water began to go cold before stepping out of the bath, reluctant to leave its soothing caress. Instantly a maid wrapped a warm towel around her, while another was attempting to assist Chloe arrange Helena's clothes for the day. Chloe nudged her sharply aside and tended to it alone.

Their jostling brought a wide smile to Helena's face and at that moment she knew this was how she wanted to live, how she ought to live; with the entire magical city of London spread out on the other side of her window. She belonged here, and nothing was going to dislodge her.

Removing the hipbath took a deal of effort and some muffled cursing from the maids, but once they had gone, Chloe helped Helena dress in a russet silk brocade gown. The plain cut skirt, split down the front to reveal a cream silk underskirt, accentuated her slender figure. Deep lace ruffles fell from the sleeves, the bodice lined at the neck with an almost transparent lace bertha. Satisfied she would not disgrace herself in front of her hosts, Helena twirled before a long glass.

"I remember when Sir Jonathan brought this cloth, from right here in London." Chloe fingered the heavy material lovingly.

"Do you?" Helena's voice was nonchalant, but at the same time she felt an uncomfortable warmth creep up her neck.

"He intended it for your mother." Chloe's voice grew wistful.

Helena stayed silent. Of course she remembered. The instant she had seen it lying on the carriage seat, she was fully aware the silk was not for her. Determined to have it, she had thrown herself into her father's arms gabbling her gratitude for his generous gift. The resigned smile on her mother's face in response to his dismayed shrug, confirmed she had won.

Having to listen patiently while he recounted the fate of the Huguenot silk makers from whom he had obtained it, proved a small price to pay.

French made silk was very expensive and heavily taxed, its importation restricted. But since the arrival of the Huguenot émigrés, there was an abundance of reasonably priced silk available in London.

Her mother had taken her to the seamstress the next day to have the gown made up, but as she looked down at herself, Helena felt shame spread through her. Lady Elizabeth would have looked beautiful in this color.

"My selfish bone again," Helena whispered, shaking her head when Chloe asked her to repeat it.

Chloe withdrew and Celia erupted into the room without knocking, enquiring as to how she had slept. Without waiting for a response, she peered into Helena's jewel case and trailed plump fingers through her closet.

Helena felt her gown seemed drab beside the floating, pastel silk Celia was wearing, but when she mentioned it, Celia was complimentary. "It suits your dramatic coloring perfectly," she said, from her supine position on the unmade bed. Then she leapt to her feet, grabbing Helena's hand. "I must show you the Inn."

Helena looked toward the door. "Where's Phebe?"

Celia rolled her eyes. "She's sulking. Ignore her. She always wants to be the pretty one, and your arrival was something of a surprise."

Helena acknowledged the compliment but was instantly worried. Phebe had been so sharp with her at dinner. Celia gave her no time to ponder the dilemma as she pulled her down the wide staircase, giggling and chattering as they went. Together they toured the three dining areas, each one more luxurious than the last, their arched and curtained doorways decorated with rich hangings in red and gold.

The larger one had sectioned off booths for diners with wood and glass partitions. Candles sat in pewter and glass holders on walls and on tables, and as Samuel had promised, rows of silver tankards were lined up in rows in the taproom.

"We serve the best wines here," Celia called over her shoulder as they sauntered through the elegant space around the serving girls who swept and scrubbed them to shining brilliance. "The duty is high, which makes it expensive, but our ale is also the best and we add fruit and herbs for flavor."

"Do you brew ale here?" Helena asked, knowing this was the custom in Exeter.

"Oh no." Celia's bright curls bounced on her shoulders. "We buy it from brewers somewhere in the Norfolk. Father says it is a messy, smelly process and not worth the space required."

The kitchens, located behind the rear staircase, were the largest and busiest Helena had ever seen. Rows of massive wooden dressers lined the walls, loaded with platters and trays, pitchers and trenchers with silverware, jugs and bowls, all ready for the diners who would fill the public rooms.

A long, low hallway led away from the main kitchen, with storerooms, a dairy, meat lockers and storage areas on both sides; culminating in a rear yard where the stables and coach house were located. The main cooking area was a steamy, airless space where shouted instructions were hurled across the room. Everyone seemed frantically occupied and the atmosphere strained, but it all fascinated Helena and the smell of onions, herbs and cooked meat was compelling.

Henry, apparently up for some time, was chatting to the serving men when they arrived. He complimented the girls, who bobbed curtseys to the handsome young gentleman, welcoming him to Lambtons with shy smiles and blushes.

To Helena's relief, Celia made it clear neither she nor her brother would have much contact with the alehouse customers, or the hot, airless kitchen. "Even Mama rarely steps in here. Carstairs manages the staff."

Carstairs turned out to be a jovial but strict, middle-aged housekeeper, whose role was to marshal the serving girls into their various duties. A skill she performed, Celia told her laughing, like a mother hen.

The woman eyed Helena with mild suspicion. "Our taproom girls are from good families," she said, as if defending them. "Not ignorant slatterns like those employed in The Sunn, or Even Thompsons."

These establishments meant nothing to Helena, who accepted Mistress Carstair's judgment in polite silence.

"Our servers are all men, naturally," Celia announced, with all the authority of a chatelaine. "Lubbock trains them to keep everyone's personal orders in their head." She bent her head toward Helena to whisper, "They are more discrete than the girls when it comes to the private dining rooms."

Helena listened intently, slightly confused, but confident it would all make sense in time. On the second floor, they discovered Phebe loitering by the stairs. Helena was convinced she had been waiting for them, but when Celia invited her to join them, she looked disinterested. "I have little else to do this morning, I may think about it." When neither girl attempted to persuade her, she trailed behind him at a distance.

The ceilings were lower on this floor, the windows smaller, with rooms containing a table and two chairs in an alcove. Others were furnished with elaborate canopied beds as well.

"These are our private dining rooms." Celia waved a hand. "Exclusively for the use of our married guests."

"How do you know which of the guests are married?" Helena asked ingenuously.

Phebe raised an eyebrow. "Only respectable people come to Lambtons."

Helena wanted to contradict her, but Phebe's mischievous smile told her there was no need. Helena felt a small thrill of excitement, wondering what her father would think. Then it struck her, this was her life. A life he was not part of. Until he returns, a small voice sounded hopefully in her head as they descended the stairs to the girls' rooms.

The noise of the street could be heard clearly from there, but neither girl seemed to mind it. "I could not bear the silence of the country." Celia gave a slight shudder. "I love the clamor of city streets."

The girls came and went between each other's domains, bringing their exquisite gowns and elaborate headdresses for Helena's approval. Phebe appeared to have overcome what her mother called her 'shyness', at least for long enough to obtain Helena's awed admiration.

She produced a box of 'mouches', holding up a sheet of Spanish paper with a flourish. "I use it to color my cheeks," she explained unnecessarily.

"It can barely be seen when you do use it, Phebe." Celia rolled her eyes. "You already possess such high color." She threw a pointed look in Helena's direction, indicating they had had this conversation before.

"Well, I think it becomes me." Phebe lifted her chin. "When I am older, no one will venture abroad before asking what Phebe Devereux is wearing today, for fear they will not be quite the thing."

Helena perched on Celia's bed, their high-spirited chatter flowing over her as she cast her mind back to the summer in Ideswell. The Ffoyle girls were kind hearted, loving creatures, but their lives were narrow and Helena had soon outgrown their homespun kindness. She wanted more, and to have the sophisticated, colorful city of London laid out before her was more than she could have hoped for. She could not wait to be a part of it.

While Phebe and Celia bickered good-naturedly, Helena moved to the window to look down on the street where coaches clattered on the cobbles; sedan chairs flipped roofs and doors open to disgorge their occupants onto the swarming street.

It was not yet noon and Lambtons already bustled with activity. Despite the cold, the inn doors were thrown open, and even from where she stood, Helena could hear the enthusiastic welcomes of Lubbock, combined with muffled greetings and chattering of the diners as they entered the halls.

Helena stared, fascinated at the swaying headdresses and billowing skirts of the ladies, the ornamented coats and impossibly full wigs of the men with their oversized muffs and silver topped canes, strutting through the doors.

Celia came to stand beside her, pointing to a black contraption pulled by four bay horses in the street. "Oh look, there is Lord Marlborough's carriage."

Helena strained forward to see, exhilarated at being close to the famous John Churchill. Yet shouldn't she have felt more resentment than curiosity? This was, after all, the man who had led the king's forces against her family at Sedgemoor.

Celia nodded. "He is very handsome, and his wife, Lady Sarah, has the loveliest golden hair. They have been married seven years and he is still madly in love with her."

"Hmm," Phebe muttered from her position at her sister's bureau. "She is proud that one, and thinks she is more important than the Princess Anne."

Helena pressed her nose against the glass, but the street was so crowded, he disappeared before she saw his face. Mildly disappointed, she turned to lean against the sill, taking in her opulent surroundings. "I had no idea an alehouse keeper could be so-" She stopped, aware she was about to be insulting.

"Father isn't exclusively an innkeeper, Helena. He is a goldsmith as well." Phebe beamed with pride.

"Master Ffoyle often uses his services." Celia turned her gaze on Helena. "And I believe Sir Jonathan Woulfe too when he came to the city to trade wool."

"Master Devereux knew my father?" Helena felt her heart lurch to hear his name on Celia's lips.

"Of course." Phebe turned from her study of her own reflection. "Though we saw him but twice." She looked to her sister who confirmed this with a nod. "Sir Jonathan stayed here at Lambtons when he came to town." Helena thought she saw triumph in Phebe's face at her sudden discomfort. She decided to ignore it, at least until she could think of a way of making Phebe less hostile. She would need all the friends she could find in this vast city.

A worry had nagged at Helena all the way there from Devon, that if their father lived, and she dared not believe otherwise, how would he find them if they left. But he knew Lambtons.

She could not wait to tell Henry.

CHAPTER SIXTEEN

Henry picked his way across the cobbles towards the high wooden fence, almost colliding with a man pushing a handcart down the hill. He darted backwards, only to be nearly run down by a laden pony coming from the other direction. When he finally reached the fence, he was relieved he had managed it without mishap as he followed it in search of the gap in the boarding he had been informed was there.

When he found it, he gave a small cry of triumph; peering through it to see an entire side of the massive building site laid out before him. He craned his neck at the white façade which rose like a cliff face, the winter sky visible high above through the glassless windows.

Distantly aware of the hubbub of people and vehicles moving about in the street behind him, he watched workmen and stone carvers clambering over a cobweb of wooden scaffolding. Men in workman's' breeches hefted planks and stones, carrying strips of wood, tools and leather buckets of water expertly over rubble without spilling any. Young boys lugged mortar to the base of the stone façade, hoisted up by massive baskets to stonemasons perched on platforms high above the ground.

Master Devereux had spotted Henry wandering about the entrance hall of Lambtons an hour before and had invited him to go with him in his carriage. Bored and a little lost, Henry had accepted, and as they bowled along Fleet Street, Robert pointed out where the old houses which had survived the great fire ended and the new ones built since began.

When the carriage halted on Ludgate Hill, Robert gathered up his muff and walking stick. "I imagine you might like to take a look at Wren's cathedral while we are here, Henry. It may be more entertaining for you than my booksellers." He pointed his black japan cane at a fence opposite. "Building work has started again, and Wren has employed an army of stonemasons. It's a busy site these days and worth a look."

"The new St Paul's Cathedral, sir?" Henry asked, fascinated.

Robert Devereux smiled. "It is indeed."

"Was there anything left of the old one?" Henry asked as they alighted the coach.

"The statue of John Donne survived intact, and there is still some stonework left from Inigo Jones' original choir." Robert had to shout to make himself heard above the yelling, banging and general noise taking place on the other side of a wooden hoarding. "But I fear Wren will be removing that in due course. The lead roof of the old building melted and ruined everything inside. They say there was molten lead running through the streets here."

"It must have been a terrible sight, the fire." Henry kept his face solemn, but he was eager for more details. "Did you see it, sir?"

Robert stared off as if remembering. "I was a young man then, Adella and I had an alehouse at the rear of Fleet Street." He glanced sideways at Henry with the ghost of a smile, "I was not quite so respectable in those days. It burned to the ground and I had to begin again." He gave a deep sigh as he arranged his muff over one arm and hefted his cane in the other hand.

"It must have been a terrible sight." Henry stared down the hill toward the river, visualizing the mess the ruined city left behind.

"It was indeed. Master Wren, as he was then, had to engage a team of thirty laborers to operate a battering ram to demolish the ruins of the old cathedral."

"A battering ram?" Henry glanced over at the site, almost hoping it might still be there.

"Of his own design. However it was slow work, and to speed things up, he enlisted the services of a gunner from the Tower to explode gunpowder under it." Robert gave a throaty chuckle. "That worked too, although it frightened the residents hereabouts."

"How long have they been building?" Henry peered through the fencing, but he could not see much.

"It began about a year after the fire, but work has been intermittent over the years, much to Wren's frustration."

"Why was it stopped?"

Robert balanced both hands on top of his cane, his head on one side as if considering. "Well, Compton, the Bishop of London, voted for the Exclusion Bill, so King Charles withdrew the funds."

Henry cocked his head, listening. "But there is work going on now. I can hear it."

Robert nodded. "King James called his first Parliament this spring and reinstated the coal tax revenues, which funds the building work. For the next fifteen years at any rate."

"And shall it stay like this, sir?" Henry nodded at the building rising above the fence. "With a flat roof?"

Robert looked up at the towering edifice. "Indeed, no. Sir Christopher's plans include a magnificent dome, painted with ecclesiastical murals visible to the congregation from the cathedral floor. It will be the highest building I shall see in my lifetime."

"Is this to stop thieves?" Henry indicated the fence.

"Partly." Robert nodded. "But many say Wren prefers to hide his masterpiece behind this." He tapped one of the panels with his cane. "He has been criticized for his design. Some say the dome is too Catholic."

"I wish I could see it properly." Henry glared at the fence, willing it gone.

Robert brought his cane to his nose with a knowing smile. "Well my boy. There is a gap in the boarding a little further on, from which you can see the workings. However, I advise you to stay in sight of my coachman, lest you become a target for footpads." Robert turned on his heel and strode across the cobbles of Paternoster Row, disappearing inside a shop.

"Stand aside, boy, for my master to pass."

Lost in the spectacle before him, Henry had not heard a carriage pull up. A surly footman glared at him from the backboard.

"I-I beg your pardon," Henry stammered, pressing against the fence as an elderly man alighted from a coach. The watchman hopped from his box and scurried forward with an obsequious salute to open a door in the fence for the visitor.

The newcomer, slightly stooped and not much taller than Henry, wore an embroidered longcoat and a voluminous white wig falling halfway down his back. Sharp eyes in a lined, but well shaped face scanned the site possessively.

Several men in leather aprons hurried forward to engage the newcomer in urgent conversation. He addressed each one in turn, standing amongst the piles of rubble, discarded pieces of scaffolding, sheets of sacking and bits of stone, with as much aplomb as if he presided in a drawing room.

A male servant stood a few feet away, one hand resting on the shoulder of a small boy; the child's eyes looked vacant, as though unsure of his surroundings.

Satisfied with the man's responses, the workmen bowed and backed away, dispersing into the crowded site. With a final glance and a nod at the industrious hive before him, the man turned and made his way back toward the carriage, his small procession following.

Awestruck, Henry froze as shrewd eyes raked him from his polished shoes to his face, the man's lips curling upwards into a benign smile. "Do tell me, young sir, what you think of my cathedral?" he asked in a soft, lilting voice.

Henry gasped with enthusiasm. "It is a wondrous structure, sir; I have never seen anything like it." Then he frowned. "Did-did you say, your cathedral, sir?"

His questioner's face looked pensive for a second. "I certainly feel it is mine, for it is my design and I have petitioned two Kings to provide me with funds to complete it." He inclined his head. "But, my dear young sir, you are not from London, I can tell by your speech."

"No...no, sir, I am from Exeter."

"Ah! An historic city indeed, and with a fine cathedral of its own." He laid a finger against the side of his bulbous nose and gave an amused chuckle." And a proper Norman structure at that."

Belatedly, Henry snatched off his hat and gave a bow. "My name is Henry Woulfe, sir."

"I am honored to make your acquaintance, Master Henry Woulfe." He returned the bow. "And I am Sir Christopher Wren."

The servant's face appeared round the side of the open carriage door, but Wren dismissed him with a backward wave. Henry had guessed who the stranger must be, but hearing his name spoken aloud brought a wide smile to his face.

"I should have been disappointed had you never heard of me." His new acquaintance inclined his head so far to one side; Henry wondered how the heavy wig remained in place. "I am, after all the Member of Parliament for Plympton, in your own county of Devon."

Henry, having no idea at all of this fact, stayed silent, storing the information to tell Master Devereux later. "Sir, my host and patron has told me much about this wonderful structure."

"And who might your host be, young sir?"

"Master Devereux, sir, of Lambtons Inn."

"Ah." Wren lifted his cane to his nose. "I know your patron; I have dined often in his excellent establishment. He crossed his elegant hands over the silver-topped cane and leaned backwards. "And you, Master Woulfe are you by any chance interested in architecture?"

Henry grinned. "Indeed, sir, I had no notion of it before I arrived in London. But since I saw this magnificent cathedral this morning, I should like to know more."

With a look of pleased satisfaction, Wren's gaze followed Henry's and they stood side by side looking at the half-finished building. Encouraged by his companion's easy manner, Henry ventured a question. "Do tell me about this white stone, sir. It is somehow familiar, although most used in my home county tends to be red or gray."

"Quite so, and I shall tell you why, Master Woulfe. Exeter Cathedral is built of the same stone, which is why you find it familiar. There is nothing like it. Smooth and soft enough to carve, but its consistency weathers well after exposure to the elements."

The servant's face appeared in the window of the coach at intervals as they talked with varying degrees of annoyance, but his master ignored him and pleased to have such a famous man's undivided attention, Henry's heart swelled.

"London air is not good for the stone either," Wren sounded, dismayed, "see how dull this façade has become." He indicated one of the pillars on the unfinished structure before them. "Coal fires belch out smog which impregnates the surface with soot; see the difference." He lifted a piece of sacking a few feet away to reveal several slabs of pristine whiteness, beckoning Henry to look. The stone almost sparkled as if it had tiny shards of glass embedded within. The half-finished building seemed almost dull in comparison.

Dropping the sacking back in place, Wren slapped his hands together to remove the dust. "So, Master Woulfe, would you have a fancy to see inside my cathedral?"

"Tha-that would indeed be an honor, sir," Henry stammered. He paused, his enthusiasm vying with his duty to Master Devereux. "However, my patron will have finished his business for the day and I have to return. Although there will be other occasions if you would allow, sir. And if I have to use my two feet to get here from Holborn, I shall certainly do so for the privilege."

His words appeared to please the old man and when the child leaned out of the carriage, flapping his hand in agitation, Wren inclined his head to Henry to make a brief introduction. "This is my Billy."

Henry bowed and murmured, "Your servant."

He assumed the boy was his son, but Wren offered no further explanation. Instead he climbed into the carriage, calling to Henry through the open flap. "I will send my man to Lambtons to call for you; shall we say, Friday at ten of the clock?" Before Henry could give a response, the driver cracked his whip and the carriage rolled away up Ludgate Hill.

On the short journey back to Holborn, Henry treated a bemused Robert Devereux to an animated account of his meeting with the acclaimed architect.

Henry chose not to mention the empty-eyed boy. Not because the child discomforted him, more from a desire to protect a weakness he saw in his new acquaintance's life. A weakness he did not yet understand, but instinct told him it was one he should not speculate upon with others.

* * *

Everyone agreed Helena could not take her place in London society, or rather Lambtons' society, without suitable clothes; the procurement of which Adella Devereux launched herself into with wild abandon.

Heedless of Helena's insistence that she was of sufficient means to finance her own wardrobe, Adella waved her aside saying the honor was hers as she sent messengers to summon every seamstress, milliner, hosiery peddler, wigmaker and cosmetic merchant Cheapside had to offer.

"Why, my own girls have more than enough for this season, so there is no pleasure to be found there. But you my dear are darker, a little taller." In a small aside so as not to let her daughters hear. "Far more striking, so I shall have a wonderful time dressing you."

The veritable army who arrived in response to her summons, trooped up the stairs and into Adella's lavishly decorated private salon next to the chamber she shared with her husband.

"That's Mistress Groves," Celia whispered, indicating a haughty woman accompanied by two frail-looking girls whose arms were laden with parcels.

"Who is she?"

Phebe fixed her with a stare. "She is the Duchess of Somerset's dressmaker."

Helena made a face, showing she was impressed, but had no idea to whom she referred. Despite Phebe's frequent barbed remarks and attempts at belittling Helena, she appeared to want to be included in their girlish chatter. Helena wondered how long their uneasy truce would last.

Mistress Groves barely addressed her young client, as if aware of who was paying the account, apparently oblivious to her luxurious surroundings.

"She is used to Somerset House," whispered Celia, when Helena mentioned her apparent disinterest.

Both sisters remained in attendance during the measuring session, chattering happily and pouring over the items laid on the bed for inspection. Helena was convinced they stayed purely to see which items might be discretely acquired for themselves.

Helena felt awkward standing in her shift in a room full of strangers, but was unwilling to make a fuss which might demonstrate her inexperience. Silently she submitted to having bolts of cloth draped over her shoulders and around her waist with lengths of lace, silk and ribbons. There was so much to choose from; Helena found she was unable to make a decision about anything.

There were so many pins in the satin Mistress Groves fastened around her, she dared not move, amazed at how complicated everything in London seemed to be, although even that was somehow exciting.

"I shall entreat Master Devereux to let you girls take the carriage to the New Exchange tomorrow," Adella announced. Helena was about to offer her most enthusiastic thanks, but Celia's acccpting expression and Phebe's near boredom prevented her. She forbore to tell them she had never traveled in a carriage without an adult present.

CHAPTER SEVENTEEN

Bundled up in outdoor cloaks with a heavy rug tucked around their knees, the carriage bowled through the open spaces of Holborn into noisier, busier thoroughfares toward the river. Helena hung out of the window in what Celia declared was an unladylike pose. "And you may lose your necklace or headdress ribbons to a scoundrel."

Helena giggled, fascinated at the attention a fine coach attracted; "I am sorry, Celia. But the city is still such a novelty to me."

When forced to halt, traders dodged in between the traffic trying to attract their attention; thin, brown hands thrust through the leather flaps, or clung dangerously onto running boards until a footmen dislodged them with a well-aimed whip.

Celia adopted her haughtiest pose and looked away in distaste, but Phebe smiled prettily, pretending to be interested in the trays of gaudy stuff placed under her nose.

They left the coach in a side street and entered the pillared main hall with its vast concourse covering two floors, lined with open shops under a vast canopied ceiling. Each one bore an impressive display of brightly colored trinkets, laces, hats, gloves and fans arranged on trays and boxes to attract the shopper.

The female stallholders raked Helena with expert eyes; taking her enthusiastic interest as encouragement to their wares in her direction.

"They marry well," Phebe whispered, indicating the well-groomed and painted girls behind the stalls. "They meet so many fine gentlemen here."

Helena tore herself away from one stall, only to be accosted by the occupant of the next; faced with so many gloves and fans, ribbons, muffs and petticoats, she found making a choice was beyond her.

Determined to purchase something, she settled on a pair of silk hose from Philip Hanbury's shop, and a small ornamental japan box. Celia and Phebe trailed behind with bored expressions, while Helena was entranced, admiring phrases constantly on her lips.

A housemaid trailed behind with a sullen expression, her presence completely ineffective as a chaperone, for Phebe greeted every young man she knew with fulsome compliments, ensuring the entire hall must know Mistress Devereux was in the building.

She paraded up and down the concourse between the shops, alert for anyone whom she felt able to call out to. A flamboyant conversation would follow, and then came the bow and separation so the process could begin all over again with another gallant.

As one gentleman left them, having failed to elicit more from Celia than a cold stare, Phebe hissed at her, "Why are you so sharp with them? They are being no more than amiable in paying their respects; they are not trying to rob you of your virtue!"

Helena stifled a shocked laugh but Phebe was in full flow. "...and even if they were, they are unlikely to announce the fact publicly, here in the 'Change. You are quite safe."

Phebe stood swinging her muff from one hand to the other, scanning the hall as she spoke. "Why every one of them has been to Lambtons at one time or another, and those who have not, are known by those who have. If I should emulate you and simper like a schoolgirl, I shall never be noticed."

"You are bold and indiscreet Phebe, what will poor Helena think of you." Celia sniffed. "She cannot be used to such outrageous attention seeking."

Phebe pulled a face, bowing to mutter a polite, "Sir," to a slightly built young man in brown velvet who approached them. With a sweep of her arm, Phebe introduced him. "You know my sister Celia of course, and Mistress Helena Woulfe, who has lately come to town from Exeter."

The young man gave a careful bow and Phebe inclined her head. "Helena, Master Jack Montague, cousin of Sir Charles Montague," she added.

Helena accepted his admiring look silently, her gaze fixed on his impossibly high periwig which almost overwhelmed his narrow face.

He spoke in a high, almost feminine voice with a pronounced lisp. "Shall you be attending my Lord's soiree this evening to celebrate his majesty's birthday?" he asked, gazing at Phebe with an enraptured expression. "I assure you it will be a well attended occasion."

"I am sure it will, Master Montague." Celia imitated her mother's haughtiest tone. "However we cannot attend, although I am sorry not to see Master Evelyn, whom I am told shall be there."

"Oh...oh yes, he certainly shall." He caught himself before Celia had to repeat the question. "A remarkable old man is he not? So full of Court stories I never tire of listening to him," he concluded, indicating the opposite was true.

After a polite interval and much bowing, he moved off down the concourse.

"Huh!" Phebe flicked her fan back and forth. "When shall I be invited to a Court Ball, and not simply the parties held afterwards?"

"Never, you are not aristocracy, Phebe," her sister snapped, taking her arm to draw her in the opposite direction.

"Do you have a preference for that young man, Phebe?" Helena asked, glancing back at her new acquaintance.

Celia gave a loud snort of laughter, earning her a hard glare from her sister. "Not at all," Phebe smirked. "But he is very satisfying to practice on, don't you think?"

Helena felt instant admiration for Phebe. She was obviously a young lady determined to make the best of her opportunities.

Their return to the coach was precipitated by Celia complaining her feet hurt; where Phebe banished the housemaid to the outside seat, leaving them to gossip inside on their way back to Holborn, their prettily wrapped parcels balanced on their knees.

Celia attempted yet again to warn her sister of the dangers of forward behavior in public, but Phebe waved away her criticism. "It is all very well for you to eschew flirting, Celia, but we don't all have a Master Maurice dancing attendance upon us."

Celia blushed furiously.

"Who is Master Maurice?" Helena tried to recall those people she had met since her arrival, but it was an impossible task. The constant social round at Lambtons, with its never-ending parade of characters, was bewildering as well as exciting.

"He was that pale creature at dinner the other night," Phebe giggled. "The one with the dog eyes, who quivered each time father spoke to him."

"He did no such thing." Celia bridled. "Ralf Maurice and Father have much to discuss in the way of business." She lifted her chin. "He is a goldsmith, like Father. Which is why he may give the impression he is listening to Papa so intently."

Phebe smirked and Celia grimaced at her.

"Have you been acquainted with him long?" Helena asked.

Celia looked startled. "Well, actually I know him hardly at all. We have met but three times."

"He is Father's choice, so naturally, my sister docilely agreed to the match." Phebe sounded almost accusing.

"It is my duty to be obedient to Father, Phebe, as it is also yours. The contract has been drawn up and there is only my portion to be settled."

"I offer my congratulations." Helena attempted a smile, although she felt a sudden sense of loss at the prospect of losing her new friend so soon. Phebe's cheeks held high spots of color. "You disapprove?" Helena asked her.

"It would be inappropriate for her to approve or disapprove," Celia retorted, "and if Father decreed Master Maurice would be her husband instead of mine, she would still have no grounds on which to object."

Helena fell silent, recalling that no one had asked her opinion on Martyn Blandon either.

Phebe glared at her sister. "Well, I shall not be sold like a commodity to the highest bidder. I shall marry whomever I choose."

Celia looked hurt. "Can you not be happy I am to be the wife of a man who may one day be as rich as Father?" Her round brown eyes widened in pleading. "I shall have a house and servants, a carriage every bit as grand as this one, and Master Maurice will take me out into society far more than I am permitted to at present."

The threatening sky opened and heavy rain began pounding the wooden roof of the carriage so they had to raise their voices to be heard. Phebe gave a contemptuous sniff, then appeared to soften. "If you are content, Celia, then I shall be happy for you. But I shall choose my own husband, then if the marriage is not happy, there is no one to blame but myself."

"Why would it not be happy?" Helena pulled the rug tighter around herself as water began to find its way through the leather flaps. She remembered the servant girl and the coachman getting drenched on the outside seat, but felt it inappropriate to mention it. "Your father would take every precaution the man he found for you would be good hearted and well bred."

Lifting her pert chin, Phebe held Helena's gaze. "Perhaps you should ask Millie Bryant that same question, and see how she answers."

"Phebe, you are not to talk about such things!" Celia hissed.

Her brown eyes shimmered. "Millie Sanders, or Mistress Bryant as she became, married such a young man, chosen by her father."

Celia tutted, but Helena was intent on what Phebe was saying. "They were married less than a twelvemonth, but he spent her entire portion and turned her out of the house, where he lives with his mistress. Poor Millie is the sweetest, kindest girl who ever lived, yet she had to beg to be allowed her back into her family, as if the disgrace were her own." Phebe's voice cracked as she went on, "Her family treat her like an upper servant, an investment which went wrong. She cannot find a better husband as she is still tied to that brute Bryant, who cares not a fig for her and is still received into society, where poor Millie is not." She slumped back in her seat, breathless.

"You must be very fond of her, to champion her in this way." Helena said.

"I am forbidden to see her." Phebe blinked rapidly.

Impulsively, Helena leaned forward to grasp the younger girl's hand. A start of surprise replaced the cold light in her eyes, but she didn't pull away.

"I am so sorry." Helena strained to make herself heard above the drumming rain. "But it is not to say such a fate would be yours. Your family would never tie you to a man who discards a good wife."

Phebe stiffened her voice strong when she replied. "They certainly will not, for I shall find my own."

"But perhaps he - "

"Leave her, Helena," Celia interrupted. "She will change her mind, when she is reminded of her duty."

With a final glare in her sister's direction, Phebe threw back the leather flap covering the window, heedless of the cold rain lashing her face. Helena heard her say firmly. "I shall never change my mind."

* * *

When Samuel left to return to Devon on a November morning, Helena blinked back tears and held onto his arm through the carriage window to delay the moment of parting, eliciting a promise that he would return before too long.

Despondent, she turned away as the coach lurched forward, then a smile spread across her face when she heard him berating the coachman, before they had even rounded the corner.

The noisy street teemed with peddlers, hawkers and beggars, together with the sound of carriages rumbling past. Fearing the inn would be worse, Helena collected her cloak and crept downstairs, avoiding the rest of the household.

She tiptoed through the kitchens, moving unnoticed through the frantic activity. Cooks shrieked at the serving men, pans clattered and meat sizzled as she slipped through the door into the walled garden.

Her breath forming wispy clouds in the cold air, she noted the walled space suffered from lack of attention. The plants not been properly trimmed back for the winter and the hedges were ragged and overgrown in places; but it was quiet, and offered solitude. Flowerbeds and small arbors nestled into the walls, with ornamental hedges bent to form a covered archway, which, Helena imagined, would give cool shelter on sunny days.

During Helena's first hectic weeks in London, a constant stream of guests paraded through Lambtons; some to pay their respects to the orphans of the ill fated rebellion, others she felt sure, out of open curiosity.

When she had expressed bewilderment at so much attention, Adella had tried to explain. "Your distracted grief gives you an enigmatic quality, my dear, which will secure you a husband before you know it. Men adore mysterious women."

Helena had not known how to respond, but despite her forthrightness, she liked and admired Adella Devereux; it was only willful Phebe's occasional bouts of jealous resentment which soured her contentment in her new surroundings. However, Helena noticed that Phebe was making an effort to be agreeable since their moment of mutual understanding in the carriage.

Helena found being surrounded by people at all times of the day stifling and sometimes, she sought the luxury of solitude. On her second tour of the pathways, she turned at the bang of the kitchen door to see Henry hurrying toward her. "Here you are!" He called brightly, then pulled his cloak tighter with a dramatic shiver. "God's blood, it's cold out here."

"Walk with me, it will warm you." Ignoring his curse, she looped her arm in his." Tell me, how do you like living in an alehouse?"

"I'm enjoying it, and besides," he placed a finger to his cheek a gesture characteristic of Master Devereux. "Lambtons is no ordinary alehouse."

Helena's laugh rang across the dormant winter garden. "You don't think Father would disapprove of us being here?"

He frowned. "What made you say that?"

She shrugged, suddenly overcome by sadness. "I would not care if he came back and dragged us away in a rage. But I doubt more and more it will happen."

"That he will drag us away?"

"That he will come back."

Henry stared off with a frown, making Helena sorry for being the cause of his melancholy. He had been so much happier lately, spending every moment he could with his new friend, Sir Christopher Wren. She asked the first question which came into her head. "Have you been at St Paul's again today?"

His face showed surprise. "How did you know?"

She raised both eyebrows in response.

Henry stamped his feet and blew on his hands. "I met Master Hawksmoor this morning."

"And who might he be?" Helena feigned enthusiasm.

"Sir Christopher engaged him as his pupil, when he was not two years older than I am now."

Helena waited, suspecting there might be more.

"He is taking me to see the new chapel, the one the king has had built in Whitehall Palace."

"Do you think that's wise?" She halted on the pathway, everything she had learned about Papists rushing into her head.

Henry laughed at her expression. "Helena, I am not going to attend Mass, I merely want to see the building." He scuffed his feet on the gravel and she was about to reprimand him for damaging his shoes, but the words died on her lips. He was no longer her little brother. Circumstances had turned him into a man heartbreakingly too soon. He spoke with care these days, and was no longer the enthusiastic boy who would say the first thing which came into his head.

They turned at the garden wall to begin the stroll back toward the kitchens; Helena immersed in her own thought.

"Are you listening to me, Helena?"

"Oh yes, yes, of course I am. Tell me, Henry. How serious is this interest of yours in architecture?"

His eyes shone. "In what other city in the world are there this many new buildings being constructed?" Everywhere you go there are builders, carpenters and stonemasons.

Helena refrained from pointing out that he was one of few who might feel this an advantage, instead saying, "Father always imagined you would go into the army."

"Which army?" He said cynically.

Helena opened her mouth, and then closed it again. He had a point, and Robert complained constantly of the large numbers of soldiers the king kept in barracks, soldiers whom the king should have discharged after the rebellion.

"I am seventeen, Helena," he said firmly. "I have decided I want to be an architect." He halted beneath an arbor, its leafless branches twisted together above them in a high curve. "If you will agree, I shall ask Master Devereux to find a master to instruct me."

"Is this why you came out here?" At his expectant nod, she felt the prick of tears behind her eyes. He was talking about a career, about leaving. She cleared her throat. "If that is what you want, Henry. But we shall have to tame this." She tugged at a thick strand of fair hair, which, being hatless, he had left to hang loose on his shoulders.

He jerked his head away, laughing in mock protest. "It is what I want, Helena, but I must be sure you are happy."

Helena slowed her footsteps. "I love London. Lambtons is a wonderful place and the Devereuxs couldn't be kinder. But as to my future," she gave a bemused shrug, "I shall have to be married to obtain anything in life, as Celia is always reminding me."

"I would feel better about leaving if you were."

She wondered if he meant happy, or married, but decided not to pursue it. "So tell me, how does one go about becoming an architect?"

Henry brightened. "I need a master willing to take me on for a liking."

"Whatever is a liking?" She bit her lip to prevent herself laughing, but Henry saw it and punched her arm playfully.

"This is serious, Helena." Chastened, she composed her face into an expression of studious enquiry as he explained. "I live with him for a month, to see if we get on well together and to determine if I have aptitude for the work. If he is agreeable, I pay him a premium for a seven-year apprenticeship."

Seven years, that is a lifetime. He will grow away from me completely in seven years. Helena forced a laugh into her voice. "Then shall you build cathedrals?"

His chin lifted in mock disdain. "Eventually, I might. But most likely I shall be a journeyman to gain experience."

"What would a premium cost?"

His gaze slid away from hers. "I shall require lessons in mathematics and drawing, so several hundred pounds would be needed."

Helena substituted a small cough for her initial shocked gasp, the look on his face telling her that any reservation on her part would crush his dreams. She took a deep breath. "That doesn't sound insurmountable. We shall speak to Master Devereux this evening." When he flushed she said, "I assume you have already spoken to Samuel?"

"Last night, yes. Don't look at me like that, Helena. I had to, before he left for Devon, and it was my last chance to. . . "

She held up a hand, halting his excuses, but the situation already felt out of her control. "What did he say?"

"That I would make a better architect than a wool man at any rate." He gave a boyish chuckle.

"I can see you have thought of everything." She had not intended her voice to be so sharp, but he seemed not to notice.

"I knew you would be happy for me and not mind my going." He gripped her arm so hard, she called out in protest. "Let's go in, Helena, I cannot feel my feet."

Mind? Of course I mind. Helena allowed him to bundle her through the door into the kitchen with its steamy warmth and enticing smells.

When Lubbock bore down on them with a tray of freshly baked pasties, Henry fell on them ravenously. Helena nibbled at hers, unable to force it past the lump in her throat. Again, changes were occurring. Would nothing stay the same?

CHAPTER EIGHTEEN

It seemed to Helena it was all too soon before she stood outside Lambtons with the Devereuxs, shivering from the chill, but unwilling to cut short her farewells to Henry.

Master Francis Newman, a city architect with several public buildings to his credit, had accepted an invitation to the Lambtons for supper, and an audience with Robert Devereux. A younger man than either of them had anticipated, he had a pleasant manner and piercing light blue eyes. Over a few glasses of wine and an excellent supper, Master Newman agreed to take Henry on as his apprentice. Samuel had agreed to send the premium required on completion of the 'liking' and Henry was to reside at Master Newman's house in Charles Street to learn the profession.

Henry bounced on the soles of his feet as he thanked Robert and Adella for their hospitality; embracing Celia and Phebe with enthusiasm. Having disengaged himself from Adella's suffocating clinch without giving offence, he gathered his sister's hands in his. "I will make Father proud of me, Helena."

Helena's prepared words of love and encouragement caught in her throat. "I know you shall," she croaked, her eyes swimming with salt tears.

The chair stood on the cobbles with its lid up and door open. Henry climbed inside and the chairmen hoisted the poles between muscled arms, setting off at a trot over the cobbles, calling 'make way, make way there', as hawkers and streetwalkers leapt out of their path.

"Charles Street is a mere step away," Phebe snapped in response to Helena's heavy sigh as they traipsed up the stairs. Celia glared at her sister, who flounced off down the hallway, leaving the two girls alone in Helena's room. Celia chattered happily, while Helena stared moodily down at the sodden garden.

Despite Celia's overt sympathy, Helena could not explain to her that she felt adrift in a world where she had no place. That Lambtons was a colorful stage where she played the part of tragic heroine, daughter of the Rebel whose fate was unknown. Celia and Phebe's interaction with their loving parents was heart-warming, but painful to watch and at night, Helena lay sleepless, listening to the watch calling each hour, her loneliness gnawing at her until the London dawn crept across the ceiling.

* * *

Robert met Helena on the stairs the following morning to offer his arm and escort her to the private dining room. She looked heavy-eyed and knowing how Henry's departure hurt her, he was dismayed. The news he had to impart would not help her melancholy.

Adella looked up as they entered the room together. "Have you told her?"

Helena blanched and Robert tried to send silent signals that this was not an appropriate time, but Adella seemed not to notice.

Robert gave a cough. "Er, not yet my dear." He ushered Helena to the table. "We thought you should hear it from us, instead of through gossip in the dining hall."

"Hear what, sir?" Helena seemed disinterested

"That Lord Grey has been given a Royal pardon." Robert took his seat, wincing when his wife gave her throaty laugh.

"Hardly, Rob," Adella snorted. "He paid forty thousand pounds."

Helena closed her eyes briefly and reached for the chocolate pot. "Even if Father came home tomorrow," she said gloomily. "I doubt we could raise such a sum to free him."

Robert decided to tell all and get the tiresome business over with. "Edmund Prideaux and Nathanial Wade have also been freed." He fiddled with his napkin. "Both have had to pay exorbitant fines."

Helena offered a feeble smile. "I cannot blame those two for surviving in any way they can. But I cannot help feeling my father's fate, whatever that may be, can be put at Lord Grey's door. He was one of the chief instigators." She attacked a pastry viciously with her fork.

"And Lord Grey is attending court balls as if nothing had happened." Adella tossed her elaborately curled head, setting the woven ribbons on her headdress quivering.

Helena demolished the pastry but ate little of it, drinking two cups of chocolate in quick succession. "Perhaps." She looked up as if the idea had occurred to her. "I should find a husband with the qualities required to run my father's business?"

Robert was conscious of her studying him, her pigeon wing eyes bore into his, her cup halfway to her lips. He considered his response carefully. "Not an unachievable ambition, my dear. But don't overlook your personal happiness."

Helena frowned. "Security and position are what I need. To expect anything else in the circumstances is somewhat indulgent."

"Oh, as for you being a social pariah, that will pass, my dear." Adella crumbled a pastry onto her plate, but none of it reached her lips. "Monmouth had many detractors during his lifetime, but in death he has acquired the status of a hero. Everyone I speak to regards you as someone worth cultivating." Her attempt to tease a smile from Helena failed miserably.

"I am still the daughter of a fugitive Rebel. I cannot think many eligible young men would regard me as a suitable wife."

Before Robert could contradict her, she rose to her feet, gave a polite curtsey and left the room.

Robert watched her leave, grasping Adella's hand on the table top. "Having been fortunate enough to marry for love," he lifted her hand to his lips. "I cannot help but advocate similar happiness for all my girls."

"Don't fret about her, Rob." Adella gathered her skirts as a prelude to leaving. "I am sure she will see things differently when an attractive young man comes along." She bussed his cheek. "You are such a sentimental creature."

"Perhaps," he murmured. "Still, I am convinced such cold practicality can only bring her more suffering. I hope, in time, she will reconsider."

CHAPTER NINETEEN

In many ways, Helena dreaded the coming of her first festive season without her family, yet she could feel the anticipation charging the days preceding Christmas at Lambtons. Servants darted through the corridors with laden arms, balancing on ladders to adorn the hallways with boughs of fragrant laurel, holly and mistletoe. Serving men, kitchen maids, cooks, servers and pot-men all worked together with the inimitable Carstairs, to ensure the preparations went without a hitch.

"It smells like a forest in here." Phebe stood in the entrance hall and wrinkled her nose.

"I know," Helena sighed dreamily, taking deep breaths.

Adella directed operations with the air of a duchess, gliding regally between the upper rooms and the kitchens, issuing orders and supervising the preparation of the vast amount of food required for the season.

The cooks and the kitchen maids prepared vast Christmas pies made with game, chicken, eggs, sugar, raisins, orange and lemon peel, mixed together with rich spices. The cauldron of plum 'porrage' bubbled away on the fire, with generous portions of raisins steeped in wine and spice, its rich, fruity aroma permeating the air. Sides of beef, venison pork and various screeching poultry arrived in the kitchens, until the cooks protested they had no more room to prepare it all.

A self-important Lubbock appeared at intervals, carrying the news that Lord 'T' had arrived with his party for dinner, or the Earl of 'S' and his lady wished a private supper in an upper room. Harassed kitchen girls scurried between the tables and serving men bore laden trays at a run up the stairs to upper dining rooms.

In a rare moment of confidence, Phebe revealed to Helena her pre-arranged signaling system with the serving men;

alerting her when a person of consequence was served 'a deux' in one of the private chambers. When it came, the three girls hovered on the landing, waiting for the lovers to appear, giggling and trying to guess who the lady, or even the gentleman might be. "If you wait long enough," Phebe declared confidently. "The entire court of St James will pass along this corridor."

Helena woke on Christmas Day, determined to overcome the sadness threatening to overwhelm her on the first Yule away from Loxsbeare. Consoling herself with the knowledge Henry would be arriving later to eat with them, she threw herself into the festivities, distributing the fruits of her frequent shopping expeditions to the New Exchange amongst her new friends.

When she went to her room in the afternoon to fetch a shawl, she found a tearful Chloe crouched by the fire. "What is wrong, Chloe?"

The maid looked up, her face tear streaked. "Master Dev'ro is so kind, Mistress, he gave me this." She sniffed, holding up a gold chain at the end of which twisted a gold cross.

"It's very pretty, Chloe." Helena noted it was a thin, light trinket and not of the best quality.

Chloe's happiness made Helena ashamed at the extravagance of her own gifts, lined up on her bureau, such as the prayer book bound in white kidskin given to her by Master Devereux. For all his flamboyance and emphasis on wealth and position, Robert was a genuine and devout Anglican.

Adella gave her a turquoise silk shawl and a gold pin studded with jewels of green and blue, fashioned like a peacock. Phebe's gift to her was a hand painted fan and several lengths of ribbon, exquisitely made by the Huguenot weavers in Spitalfields. Helena made a special point of displaying her pleasure over this gift, for Phebe was still unpredictable, as capable of delivering a barbed retort, as she was a compliment.

Celia gave Helena a pair of dancing shoes in gold embroidered blue brocade with latchet ties. "For your first real ball in London," she said, as Helena marveled at the paste jewels attached to the daringly high heels.

Henry arrived with his arms full of decorated pasteboard boxes filled with sugared fruit, spiced almonds, writing paper and new quills; while others held combs and hair ornaments, wig brushes and buttons that he distributed with largesse.

He spent the entire day at Lambtons, eating, drinking and talking with the family and inn patrons, even flirting with Phebe, who at one point was convinced the Duke of Buckingham was in the dining hall, annoyed when no one would believe her.

"Oh, ignore her; Phebe is always searching for famous faces among the patrons." Adella leaned forward provocatively to caress Henry's cheek, which in his mildly tipsy state, he tolerated unembarrassed.

With Celia's encouragement, Helena looked forward to Lambtons' traditional Twelfth Night party. "Father invites all patrons on payment of a subscription to cover the cost of their dinner."

"Mummers perform plays in the main hall, and we have musicians and tumblers to entertain us," Phebe was as excited as a child. "The Christmas cake has the bean and pea of course. Do you have such things in Devon, Helena?"

Helena recalled her previous Christmas with a pang. "Indeed we do, and whoever finds them rule as King and Queen of the festivities."

"Celia was Queen last year." Phebe gave Robert a level stare as if he were wholly responsible for the oversight. "So this year, I insist it shall be me."

"You are too old for petulance," her father scolded, but the soft look in his eyes belied his words. "The fates will decide who shall rule Twelfth Night."

* * *

Helena dressed for the party in a plum colored gown that fell to the ground in silken folds, its skirt split and pulled back to reveal an ivory silk underskirt. Loud chattering and laughter drifted up the stairs as she dressed, accompanied by haunting mandolin music.

The gilded oval of silvered glass on her bureau blurred Helena's features, giving her an ethereal look. Eschewing the paint and patches Adella favored, she brushed a sheet of spanish paper gently against each cheek, rubbing it into her lips to deepen their natural color.

Chloe fastened her square, ruby pendant round her throat, then wound wine colored ribbons into her hair, teasing out the little 'favorites' and 'heartbreakers' onto her temple and neck. Watching her in the mirror, Helena noticed the maid's gaze dance frequently to the door.

"Is something wrong, Chloe?" Helena smoothed cream into her hands to whiten them.

"No, Mistress," Chloe began. "It's jus', there is a party in the kitchen today for the servants, and I thought..." Her voice trailed off.

Chloe wore her best skirt and bodice and her hair was not hidden under hr usual white cap, but dressed in curls fastened with ribbon. Helena took pity on her. "You may go, Chloe, but make sure you are back in time to help me disrobe."

Chloe sketched a hasty bob and hurried away with as much grace as her damaged leg allowed. She pressed her skinny frame against the door on her way out as Celia arrived, all plump and pink prettiness in a yellow-gold gown with emeralds at her throat, a Christmas gift from her doting parents.

"Is it time to go down?" Helena patted her hair and smoothed her bodice.

"There is someone you must meet." Celia joined her at the mirror, their gazes locked in their reflections. "He is not a guest, but you don't know him, so I suppose that makes him a guest, in a way."

Helena placed her hands on either side of her waist, cautiously breathing in and out to see how much leeway her corset would allow. "Who is this guest who is not a guest?"

"Come and see." Celia darted to the door and back again, like a puppy asking to go out.

They descended the stairs to the sound of clinking glass and female laughter drifting through from the public rooms. Bemused, but not intrigued, Helena's gaze rested on a tall young man at the bottom of the stairs. Adella was giving him the benefit of her full attention; her slender hand caressing his arm as she gazed adoringly into his face. Phebe hung onto his other hand and Robert stood to one side, smiling at them benevolently.

As if sensing her presence, the newcomer turned and met her gaze. For a moment, he reminded Helena so vividly of the late Duke of Monmouth, she almost gasped, then shrugged the thought away as ridiculous. Dressed in a sapphire blue long coat with deep turned-back cuffs in pale yellow, a full-bottomed black wig, heeled, and buckled black shoes. White lace frothed at his wrists and carefully knotted cambric cravat around his throat.

"What do you think of him?" Celia whispered at her shoulder, not waiting for a response before rushing on. "He's my brother William, come home from his tour. It's a new fashion you know, for young men to see some of the continent before they embark on a career."

Helena smiled as realization dawned. Adella frequently talked about her son in dreamy tones, regretting his absence and bemoaning the fact they did not possess a likeness of him to show Helena. Now here was the real thing, standing in the hallway, and Adella's motherly pride had not embellished her son's looks at all.

Helena took mental stock of how she might appear to him, gratified that her fashionable gown flattered and her hair had been washed that morning. Robert beckoned her forward and although she tried to remain aloof, Helena found herself drawn into deep brown eyes alight with obvious appreciation.

He bowed over her outstretched hand murmuring, "My pleasure, Mistress Woulfe." He lifted his gaze to her face, but retained a firm grip on her hand. Helena felt the entrance hall recede, her fingers resting comfortably in his palm. They stood no more than a foot apart, appraising each other, William's eyes flaming with silent laughter as he answered the challenge in hers.

Phebe slid her arm possessively through his, forcing him to drop Helena's hand. "Isn't Helena lovely, William?" she gushed, pulling him away. "You must tell us about Italy and France, we want to hear all your stories."

Adella stepped briskly to his other side, and with Robert leading the way, they entered the throng of partygoers. At the door, William glanced backward, his gaze fixed on Helena as if an invisible thread ran between them. Helena returned his look, her strong reaction to him quite unsettling. She tried to fathom why she felt light-headed when Celia jerked her forward, almost pulling her over. "Helena, you are blushing," Celia smiled mischievously.

"Not at all; it is exceedingly warm in here." Helena lifted her chin and this time, she was the one dragging Celia along in her wake.

Wherever Helena found herself during the evening, William never seemed far away. Content to encourage his company, Helena introduced him to Henry, who arrived with Master Newman, his pleasant, homely wife and their eldest daughter Mary Ann.

"What a wonderful party," Mary Ann exclaimed in a musical voice, her hands clasped together in delight.

"How are you enjoying your liking, Henry?" William's gaze drifted to Helena as if seeking approval for the prior knowledge he possessed of her brother.

Henry's mild expression altered to one of eagerness. "Master Newman took me to Stationers Hall this last week, to have my indentures stamped, so I am officially an architectural apprentice."

William turned a laugh into a cough and beside him, Helena resisted the urge to ask Henry if this procedure had been as painful as it sounded. Instead, she observed how pretty the Newman's daughter was. Henry blushed, refusing to look at the subject of his embarrassment.

"Well, do acquaint us with her, Henry," Celia urged, appearing in the middle of his embarrassed stammering.

Left with no choice, but to present his patron's daughter to his employer's, Henry acted with grace and dignity, but a good deal of stammering too.

"Who is that serious-looking man over there, Celia?" Helena tilted her fan toward a tall, elderly gentleman who appeared to be giving a lecture to a group of enthralled guests in the middle of the room. Clothed in black, with a long ebony periwig on top of a narrow face, he spoke in a braying voice, a look of tired cynicism on his face.

"That, is Master John Evelyn. He is a Commissioner of the Privy Seal," Celia whispered. "The short, plump person with spaniel eyes sitting beside him is Master Samuel Pepys, see? He is Secretary to the Admiralty." With a sigh she added, "They are both quite old, but have some fascinating stories of their youth at the court of the old king."

"My Uncle Edmund worked for Master Pepys, many years ago." Helena exchanged a look with William.

He gave a slow nod, evidently impressed.

Celia's eyes flew open in surprise. "I had no idea, Helena, how interesting!"

"He looks very proud." Helena spoke in a stage whisper.

"Master Pepys?"

"No, Master Evelyn, and there appears to be a bad smell under his nose."

The party was gathering pace, with new arrivals entering the hall and noisily greeted by those they knew. The men wore high periwigs in a variety of colors, piled high on their heads with rows of thick curls flowing over their shoulders. Some sported tiny black patches on their faces, convincing Helena they were to disguise scars and blemishes on their skin. Others wore as much face paint as the women, making them look like garish dolls, with splashes of red dabbed beneath their eyes.

"He's an important man." Celia took her arm and led the way through the throng. "Godfrey Kneller painted his portrait, which is something of a privilege, as that gentleman only deigns to paint people of consequence."

"A gentleman painter?" Helena smiled, knowing all about Master Kneller, but Celia's way of describing people was so entertaining.

"Simply a gentleman who paints." William smirked at her from her other side. "That particular one will paint himself into a knighthood, if I am not mistaken."

"He would never paint me, William, I am far too lowly." Celia giggled. "Master Evelyn enjoys the confidence of the king, but I believe he is not overly fond of his majesty."

"Why is that?" Helena asked, liking Master Evelyn immediately.

"He was a close friend of King Charles, and was distressed to hear of his deathbed conversion." Celia's voice dropped conspiratorially. "Though to be anti-Papist is hardly news. It applies to almost everyone in this room." She gave a derisive laugh. "As for his attire, he is in mourning for two daughters he lost this year from the smallpox."

"Two daughters? Oh, how sad for him." Helena felt immediate sympathy, his loss reminding her of her own.

Celia sighed. "Mary, the elder, was a lovely creature. She was to have been one of the Queen's ladies."

"How disappointing for her," Helena murmured, watching William hail some friends on the other side of the hall. He leaned forward to ask her indulgence to leave her company and his wig brushed her cheek, sending a shiver down her back. She found her gaze fixed on the tiny creases in front of his ear.

"Evelyn's a nice old soul," he whispered, his breath warm on her face." But a dry stick. I shall offer the compliments of the season when I have consumed a deal more wine."

Distracted by the contact and with her face growing warm, Helena had to ask Celia to repeat what she just said.

"I asked if you would like me to introduce you?"

Helena frowned, trying to recover her composure. "No, I don't think..."

However at that moment, Evelyn glanced in their direction. "Ah. The elder of Master Devereux's delightful daughters, the pride of Lambtons. How are you, my dear?" He made an ostentatious leg.

"I am well, sir. Do allow me to present Helena Woulfe, Master Evelyn."

The elderly courtier bowed over Helena's hand. "My good friend Robert has spoken of you, my dear, but skimped disgracefully on details." His hooded eyes sparkled with amusement.

Helena's surprise must have shown on her face, for he added, "London is a village, Mistress Woulfe, everything is known here." Still moving languorously, he waved a hand in a small circle as if to include her in the conversation. "We were discussing the worsening plight of the Huguenots, since King Louis revoked the Edict of Nantes." He gazed around at the small crowd of enthralled onlookers. "Abhorring the fact that Protestant churches are being demolished all over France, whole families are being imprisoned and libraries burnt."

"I, too have heard of it, sir," Helena said, watching Adella sidle up to Evelyn and flutter her eyelashes.

"The persecution is barbaric, but the 'London Gazette' remains silent on the subject. All intelligence comes to me by my friends or through letters; such a strange situation I find, for what is still a Protestant Country. Should we not all be up in arms on behalf of our French neighbors?" He held his slender hands palm upwards as if inviting her opinion.

Adella spoke instead, her fan flapping. "Now we have a Catholic king and queen, do you anticipate such persecution will cross the Channel, Master Evelyn?"

Celia glared at her mother and two elderly ladies gasped in horror, leaning on their companions for support, while the gentlemen murmured darkly.

"Protestantism in France is not the same as Anglicanism, my dear." Evelyn placed a finger to his cheek as he considered the question. "Huguenots follow the beliefs of John Calvin, who states God has willed the majority of men to eternal damnation."

"Which some of them richly deserve," Robert interjected; nervous laughter went round the small circle.

Helena glanced sideways to see William walk by, an attractive blonde woman on his arm, but his gaze held Helena's. Embarrassed he had caught her looking at him, she turned away quickly.

"Master Calvin thought so too." Evelyn gestured to a passing server to bring him a glass of wine. "However, they do not discover if they have lived righteous enough lives to become God's elect until they die."

"What would be the purpose of living a virtuous life, if it avails us nothing?" Adella asked reasonably. "It is a thankless religion to my mind." She gave a loud sniff.

Emboldened, Helena spoke up. "Catholic doctrine states a priest can grant direct entry to Heaven, and has the ear of

God." Evelyn turned toward her and she tried not to stammer. "It is little wonder the French king has made Calvinism illegal. It strips his church of its power." Her words earned her several admiring stares, although she dared not turn her head to see if William's was one of them.

A group of mummers dressed in jester's costumes broke through the circle, performing somersaults and throwing wooden hoops into the air, scattering the gossiping crowd around Evelyn. One performer held a flaming wand, which he appeared to swallow, making the ladies squeal. When Helena looked around again, she found herself isolated at the side of the room beside the elderly courtier.

He inclined his head, one hand stroking his chin. "I knew Monmouth quite well you know, my dear. I thought him a lovely person, handsome and of an easy nature. He was contaminated by the greed of others in my view, crafty knaves every one of them." With a low bow, he moved off into the crowd.

As she watched his narrow retreating back, she murmured, "I thought him the craftiest knave of them all."

* * *

The main dining hall sparkled with light from a hundred candles when dinner was served. The Devereuxs and their invited guests settled down to listen to William's tales of foreign countries, impressive architecture, bad roads, intractable foreigners and unbearable weather.

Robert cut the Christmas cake with a flourish and when Helena discovered the pea in her slice, her first instinct was to remain silent. Celia spotted it on her plate and declared her Queen of the Revels. This announcement was greeted with roaring applause from everyone who had made her acquaintance, plus a good many that had not. Thus encouraged, Helena shyly took her place on the decorated chair, which was to serve as her throne. William clapped the loudest and Robert mollified a furious Phebe with the promise of a new gown.

When the 'King' proved to be John Evelyn, he pleaded his age and constitution as being inadequate to the position, so William, amid loud catcalls and suggestive laughter, stepped forward and begged to be Helena's champion.

"I have never been Queen of Revels." Helena leaned toward William to whisper, "What do I do?"

"Simply follow my lead, Mistress." William gave her a broad wink, which made her cheeks flame even deeper.

He proceeded to issue orders for the performance of outrageous tasks, instructing four serving men to carry Helena round the room on a makeshift litter. Then Celia had to polish the buckles on Helena's shoes. A giggling young woman, who Phebe insisted was the mistress of someone important at Court, followed William around the room with his gloves on a silver tray.

William dropped to his knees to present Helena with a bouquet of feathers. "Would that Yule fell in June," he declared. "Then these poor things could be roses in bloom instead." Their audience into tumultuous applause as Helena accepted his offering gracefully, while out of the corner of her eye, she saw Phebe roll her eyes and tap an impatient foot.

As dawn light crept in through the front windows of Lambtons, the taproom emptied slowly of revelers. As the last guests lurched and tiptoed out to their waiting carriages and sedans across icy cobbles; calling the compliments of the season drunkenly to each other as a crisp frost clung to the inn windows.

Robert surveyed the array of empty platters and discarded wine glasses on every surface, abandoning the chaos to the servants to clear up in the morning. "It is no more than the mark of a successful Twelfth Night!" he announced happily.

Yawning serving girls extinguished the candles and as Helena and Celia reached the hall on their way to bed, William appeared, tugging her hand and insisting he escort Helena to her room.

"I think the bottom of the stairs would be quite adequate, sir." She stood her ground and held out a hand, inwardly thrilled.

William stumbled down the three steps he had already ascended, making a clumsy half turn to face her, swaying a little. "Ah, of course, far too forward of me." He gave a discreet burp which made Celia giggle, turning Helena's hand over to plant a lingering kiss on her palm.

His lifted his head, unfocused eyes hovering somewhere on her forehead. Helena wondered why she did not simply walk away and leave him there, but she was enjoying the feel of his hand wrapped around hers.

William staggered to one side, almost losing his balance. A passing footman caught him, twirled him around and supported him up the stairs. The pair took two steps up and three down several times before reaching the landing. At the top, he blew Helena a dramatic kiss over his shoulder.

"William is so amusing." Celia laughed.

Helena didn't respond, but her hand tingled all the way up to her room.

CHAPTER TWENTY

Leaden skies gave way to snow, which swirled into doorways and drifted down the wider chimneys, making venturing beyond the firesides an unwelcome ordeal. Samuel was visiting London and Helena awaited his arrival all during one February afternoon. When his carriage rolled onto the icy cobbles outside Lambtons, she ran outside to greet him.

He looked much as ever, tall and imposing in his 'city peruke' with the remains of a frown on his face, as if he had been berating some unfortunate. Helena hugged him. "And whose coachman have you sent away with boxed ears today, Master Ffoyle?" she teased.

They had exchanged no more than an opening remark before a second figure in a wide brimmed hat emerged from the coach and caught Helena's attention.

"Patrick!" Helena gasped. "I had no idea you were coming to London."

Patrick stepped forward to bow over her hand. "It is good to see you, Mistress Woulfe." His voice sounded a little forced, his gaze shifting to his father, who seemed reluctant to look at him. What is going on between these two?

Patrick reached back into the carriage and as Helena blinked snowflakes from her lashes, long, feminine fingers grasped his outstretched hand and a young woman appeared. Her presence provoked very different reactions in the two men. Patrick solicitously helped her navigate the narrow step, while Samuel set his lips in a firm line and turned away.

Enveloped in a voluminous traveling cape, the girl's white cap beneath the turned back hood was askew. Strands of pale hair blew across her face in the cold wind, but she held her chin high and her light eyes glittered with defiance, and perhaps a little fear.

Patrick stammered an introduction. "Th-this is my wife Amy."

The young woman inclined her head in shy acknowledgment, her gaze flickering to her father-in-law, who was still avoiding her eye.

"Your wife?" Helena was open mouthed in shock, but her questions remained unspoken as Robert appeared at the inn door. Samuel stomped towards him without a backward glance. After a brief exchange, in which Helena heard Samuel, asking, "Is he here yet?" they disappeared inside the inn.

"Father is...displeased with us." Patrick coughed, embarrassed. "Our marriage was something of a surprise." He gave a tense half smile towards Amy, who stared at the ground.

"As it is to me, Patrick." Helena took his arm and pulled him toward the welcome yellow glow spilling from the open door. "Let us go in," she urged. "I am freezing out here."

Neither he nor Amy moved.

"Er, we shall not be staying here, Helena." Patrick glanced self-consciously at the footman who held open the carriage door. "Father has insisted we go to the Red Lion in Holborn."

"Oh, I see," Helena mumbled, not at all sure she did. "Then we shall talk here." She clambered into the carriage and settled herself under the fur rug discarded on the seat. Amy climbed in after her and with a last glance back at the inn, Patrick followed, slamming the door on the surprised footman.

"I am so pleased to make your acquaintance, Mistress Woulfe. I have heard so much about you from Patrick and my sisters-in-law."

"I wish I could express the same sentiments, Amy." Helena felt awkward. "But I am delighted to meet you too."

"Father does not approve of our marriage." Patrick sounded resentful. "I am his firstborn, and he imagined he would choose a wife for me who would bring the greatest benefit to himself."

"Patrick! That's unfair, your father-" Helena paused at the sight of his tense face, thrown into relief from the links on the wall opposite. Bitterness clouded his eyes and his jaw clenched. "But you are married, Patrick, so he must have given his consent."

Patrick gave a bark of laughter. "We gave him little choice."

Amy covered his hand with hers. "I was betrothed to someone else and I saw no reason to object, at the time. My parents wished it."

Helena nodded in perfect understanding. Hadn't the same happened to her?

"Then I realized what I felt for Patrick was far more than childhood friendship."

The newlyweds exchanged a look so charged with emotion, Helena felt uncomfortable, as if she was witnessing something too intimate to be shared.

When she looked back at Helena, Amy's eyes were soft. "Patrick felt the same about me, so we approached my parents to have the betrothal dissolved."

"They refused," Patrick growled, his voice choked with anger. "And when we asked Father to intervene, he would not help us. He said a betrothal is as binding as a marriage."

"But you persuaded him?" Helena studied each of their faces, confused.

"Not at first, no." Patrick's voice held derision. "He informed me I was to come to London to manage his new warehouses. That Amy would be married as arranged, while I was far enough away not to make. . .difficulties. So we did what was necessary to ensure we would be together."

Helena was about to ask for an explanation, when Amy performed a gesture universally understood and laid a hand gently on her stomach.

"Patrick," Helena gasped. "Your father must have been outraged when he found out."

His features were partly in shadow, so she could not see his expression, but the sharp snort he gave spoke volumes. "What else could we do?"

"Samuel is a proud man, Patrick." Helena sighed. "It must have hurt him deeply."

"I know that. But I was angry with him for dismissing us."

"How can you say that? Amy was betrothed."

"I didn't think how it would make us look. I could only think of Amy."

"Or you didn't think of her." Helena regretted her sharpness instantly at the look on their faces.

"I should have behaved better." Amy tucked her arm beneath his. "But the damage was done."

Helena concluded they had had this conversation many times. Hasty marriages and babies born without benefit of clergy were an accepted part of rural life, of any life. However, Samuel was the Worshipful Master of Clothmakers and there was bound to be scandal attached to this union.

Patrick tenderly arranged the fur rug over Amy's knees, the gesture making Helena feel unaccountably lonely.

"Thus I am still to be banished from Ideswell," he said. "But Amy is here with me as my wife."

"He won't forgive you easily Patrick, or you Amy."

Amy sighed. "Four days confined in a coach and sharing lodgings, has been more punishment than you can know." She closed her eyes, as if at remembered indignities endured at the hands of her father-in-law. "No matter, it is over now and when Master Ffoyle returns to Ideswell, we will be alone."

"You appear to view your banishment as a wonderful opportunity."

"Which is the best strategy I find." Patrick's boyish enthusiasm flooded back. "I am to be in sole charge of father's wool distribution, its storing and selling in the capital. Yours too, Mistress," he added. "The warehouse is in Freemans Yard, where father has also purchased a house for us." His involuntary grimace betrayed his disappointment.

"Isn't it a nice house?" Helena thought he could be a little more grateful, after all, Samuel could have sent them to live in cramped lodgings near the meat market instead.

"I am sure we shall be able to make it our home." Amy patted his arm, her words, Helena suspected, more for Patrick's benefit.

"It's near Cornhill and the warehouse district." Patrick conceded. "I should imagine it's suitable, but not elegant or fashionable." He shrugged. "The merchants dealing in woolen goods, millinery and hosiery are situated there. Drapers Hall also has a pleasant garden where Amy can take exercise, which is good for her condition." He gave Amy another adoring gaze. "And Freemans Yard is almost wholly Dissenter." Patrick laughed. "So to plague Father, we could always threaten to attend the Presbyterian Church." He sniggered at his own joke while Amy flapped her hand at him in rebuke.

"He will accept us in time." Amy covered his hand with hers.

Helena hoped their optimism was not misplaced.

"Father is not a cruel man." Patrick seemed to read her thoughts. "If I do well here in London, the whole family will benefit, and Mother will be working on him at home."

"Your mother approves?" Helena felt the first spark of hope.

"Oh yes." Amy's face lightened. "Mother Ffoyle has always liked me, but Master Ffoyle was adamant the wedding would not take place and she could not speak up for me."

Helena remembered the loaded looks Samuel and Meghan exchanged during her stay at Ideswell which told of lively disagreements between them about offering shelter to the Woulfes after the rebellion. Helena suspected those heavy glances had been resurrected as they found a way to live with each other, and what Patrick and Amy had done.

"But you are married, and there is to be a child." Helena tried to sound encouraging.

Two enraptured faces greeted her words, but then Amy looked crestfallen again. "I have yet to buy childbirth linens in preparation; there was no time at Exeter. And of course I should have a winding sheet..."

Patrick gripped both her hands in his. "You are young and strong Amy, do not speak of dying, this child will be born healthy and you shall be safe, I am sure of it."

Helena suppressed a shiver. Childbirth was a perilous business for both infant and mother. It was common for even the healthiest women to greet news of a new life with the chance it might end her own.

"I am well prepared," Amy said. "I have some saffron in my baggage."

"Saffron?" Helena frowned, confused.

"An infusion, taken moderately during pregnancy, facilitates birth." Amy smiled. "Mistress Hannah Woolley recommends it in her household manual. Her advice is invaluable."

Helena would have liked to question Amy more on the subject of Mistress Woolley, but suddenly the carriage door flew open. A flurry of icy snowflakes swirled into the cozy interior and glowering at them from under his black wig, was the angry face of Samuel.

"What the devil is going on out here?" he growled, then without waiting for a response, hauled Helena bodily out onto the drive. "You will catch a chill Mistress, from this foul air!"

Without a word to his son or daughter-in-law, he slammed the door shut again, ordering the coachman huddling on the box to drive off. The wheels began cutting lines in the fresh snow and Samuel called tersely after his son, "Be at the warehouse at eight tomorrow."

Helena's last glimpse of Amy was a white face peering out from under the leather flap before the carriage turned the corner.

Chilled to the bone in her woolen day gown, Helena offered no resistance as Samuel ushered her into the inn and propelled her to the Devereux's private salon. A large fire crackled and hissed in the grate. Helena rushed toward it, rubbing her stiff hands together in front of the flames.

Samuel perched on the sofa behind her, the seconds stretching between them in ominous silence. She hoped he wasn't going to try to ally her against Patrick and turned to face him. "Amy is a very intelligent young woman, Master Ffoyle, I am sure they will be very happy together."

Samuel sat with his feet splayed out in front of him, both elbows resting on his knees, his jaw jumping as he ground his teeth. A bad sign for him.

"Huh, I cannot help feeling he has taken this action to repay me for forbidding him from joining Monmouth."

She cleared her throat self-consciously. "You were proved right about the rebellion Samuel, I am sure he realizes that. But to marry in order to spite you. No, I don't believe he would do such a thing, and..."

He held up a hand to forestall her. "Helena, I will not discuss Patrick with you, he is my problem and I will deal with him. No, there is someone else here who wishes to see you." He rose and went to the door and swung it open. A tall figure stood framed there. "He arrived on the post coach this afternoon but agreed to wait until my arrival before speaking with you." Helena's breath caught in her throat, and for a fleeting second she could have sworn he was...

"Good evening, Mistress Helena," he said in a familiar, deep voice as Tobias Lumm stepped into the room.

Helena stared. "Master Lumm, wh-what are you doing here? I mean, in the city..." she floundered.

He looked as he always had, handsome and totally at ease with himself, seeming almost amused by her discomfort, but not cruelly so. Helena looked from him to Samuel and back again as they exchanged an almost intimate look. These two are friends.

Helena was bewildered to see him there. It didn't make sense, if there was news of her family, surely Samuel alone could have brought it?

"This is quite an alehouse." Tobias removed his hat and gazed around appreciatively. "My room is a virtual palace."

"Lambtons is no ordinary alehouse," Helena replied, offering the standard response without thinking. "I am delighted to see you, Tobias, but if you would forgive me." She looked from his smiling face to Samuel's bland one. "I hardly expected you."

Tobias removed his cloak and set his hat down on a side table, tugging off his gloves he flung them into it, each movement masculine and deliberate.

Samuel made to leave. "I will see you later, my dear."

Helena started after him, but Tobias called her back. "He has left us alone for a reason, Mistress."

She halted and turned toward him, frozen by his tone as the door clicked shut. Tobias surveyed the room, selected a sofa and relaxed back on it, an outstretched hand indicating the empty space beside him. "Please, sit, I need to talk to you."

Helena did as he asked, feeling uneasy. He seemed so confident and, yes that was it, in command. Why had he come all this way? Did he know something about her family?

Before she could ask any of the questions which sprang into her head, he brought a creased piece of parchment from the pocket of his long coat and held it out.

Helena made no attempt to take it from him. "It appears to be a letter," she faltered, playing for time as the sight of the familiar handwriting had set her heart racing. She gabbled on, "Which must have lost its way judging by the condition it is in." It cannot be? Can it?

Tobias held her gaze. "It arrived at Christmastide, and with Lord Blanden resident at Loxsbeare," he paused as Helena flinched. "The messenger was directed to me, as former steward. It is addressed to your mother."

Revealing herself to Tobias felt like an alien thing to do, so she fought the impulse to snatch the parchment and devour the contents. More than anything, she wanted to see what was written on the yellowed pages, yet still she could not bring herself to take it.

Eventually he pressed the paper into her hand. She turned it over several times as if she couldn't believe it was real. Slowly, she unfolded the greasy pages, stained from handling and with the seal broken. The writing was Aaron's. "You have read this?" she asked, but not in an accusing way.

Tobias gave a small smile and nodded, lounging back on the sofa as if to give her the illusion of privacy. Helena began to read.

CHAPTER TWENTY ONE

September 3rd 1685
The Hague
Dearest Mother

This is the first occasion I have had both the resources and inclination to write of the events of these last weeks. I am impatient to assure you I am alive and well, and would I had more welcome news, but everyone at home must know the fate of our expedition.

Our hopes were so high that day we left for Taunton, but before I venture into the worst of it, I must tell you there will always be one light, which shines through my darkest memories, and that is Monmouth, who was everything I remembered from my youth, and more. When he was proclaimed King at Taunton's market cross, no one could have been prouder than myself, or surer the course we had chosen was right.

All too soon did it turn to hopelessness and despair, although the early signs were there, when the squires of the West did not come. Those who gathered under our banner were faithful and determined men, though there was barely a real soldier among them.

Even the weather turned against us, for after the drought of early summer, we faced rain every day for a week, with mud to our knees and our clothes forever sodden. With no proper tents, we slept in the open, and as our supplies diminished, we went hungry more often than not.

At first, it was a true adventure, a test of our spirit and resolve. Copies of Kin James' pardon were handed out amongst the men by kin and clergy, after which the desertions began. We cursed those for sloping away in the night, but I hold no bitterness in my heart for their wish of family and hearth. I longed for it every day myself.

The Royal Army closed in, and we were no longer welcome where we had marched in triumph days before. Warned off by the town authorities, we dodged troopers through hedge and village as they hunted us like rabbits.

Monmouth decided to launch a surprise attack on Feversham's men and I was assigned to Lord Grey's Horse under Capt Jones. A man named Godfrey was to guide us across the moor, but still we got lost among the rhine in the dense, clinging mist.

We found the Langmoor, but as the first horses were crossing, a shot warned of our coming, so Captain Jones took us full tilt against Compton's troopers before the king's infantry could arrive. We put their commander out of action straight away. Not bad for a cabinetmaker wouldn't you say?

I could make out lights ahead, thinking they were of the town in the distance, then an officer shouted they were the tapers for the matchlocks of the Dumbarton's Scots Brigade. Our infantry fired on them with musket and cannon. We killed some of them, though I heard later, Churchill made the Rebels pay for that indignity.

A deafening volley of musket fire from Albermarle's militia terrified the horses which proved our undoing, for they scattered and turned about, stampeding backwards into our own upcoming infantry. My own horse reared, then a musket shot caught him in the neck and he went down like a felled tree. Gentle Strider, companion of my boyhood, he was never meant to be a soldier. I fell with him, jarring my shoulder as I hit the ground, rolling into the path of a dragoon who aimed his musket straight at my face.

I froze, certain I would be killed, but another horse crashed into his and he was crushed beneath both flailing mounts. I got to my feet, scrabbling for my sword as our infantry surged toward the Royal troopers, caught in their forward charge. I saw neither my father nor Uncle Ned during that frantic hour when the fighting was at its worst. Then the dawn came and with it a massive charge by Feversham through the mist, cutting through what was left of our men. Musket balls screamed past me in waves, shredding men and horses with terrifying ease

Wade's boys were driven back to the Langmoor Rhine, and the Taunton Blue's fought like demons, though they must have known they stood little chance. Then Ogelthorpe's horse thundered over the moor, howling and hacking at any Rebels left standing, although there was little sport left for them.

The boom of the guns and hundreds of hooves battering the ground filled my head, I could barely gather thought, much less fight. But rage burned in me then at the sight of our boy's easy slaughter, and somehow I stopped cowering and ran at the troopers, swinging my sword through red cloth and flesh as they came at me. I carried blood on my clothes for days afterwards which was not my own.

I did not see the blow that struck from behind and plunged me into a Rhine, where I lay stunned and soaked by muddy water, some poor drowned wretch beside me. When I came to my senses enough to crawl out, my clothes caked with mud and blood, it was into a field fallen eerily silent.

I breathed in the sharp stink of powder carried on the air, and it seemed like every one of Monmouth's boys lay broken on the earth. Unrecognizable heaps of bloody, dirtied clothes, with pallid faces; the ground littered with discarded weapons, bloodied pikes and scythes, boots, coats and hats, all mixed in with corpses, musket balls and mangled horses.

I staggered away from their twisted features and accusing eyes, trying not to see the hands clutching wounds, convinced some of them reached for me. I know not how long I crouched beneath hedges up to my waist in stinking water while king's men searched the cornfields, shooting or hanging men where they found them.

It took me two days to reach Lymington, where a fishing boat master bound for Cherbourg took me aboard. I would like to think the man enough of a good Protestant to help a distressed Rebel, but I fear the villain only sought to relive me of my gold. I let him think he robbed me, but am enough of Edmund Woulfe's nephew to keep some back and well hidden, I have already discovered the life of a fugitive is very costly.

The voyage in heavy seas in such a tiny, stinking vessel convinced me it would surely be my last. I doubt I shall go to sea again without serious misgivings, but daily remind myself I have life at least, when so many do not.

I am in a poor but Christian lodging here in The Hague, with another Rebel outlaw, an intelligent fellow whose name is Daniel Foe. He is a splendid companion but much saddened at having to leave his young wife in London. I suspect he will not stay long.

I have scant news of my officers, although 'the plotter' is here in our company. They say Matthews and Foulkes are still at large, and we heard Lord Grey is preparing to purchase his freedom in exchange for information, but best I don't dwell on that.

I have heard no news of Father or my Uncle, but they are without doubt the bravest and best men I know, so I pray God has preserved them.

When I have been presented to his Majesty of Orange, I shall write again, although how long before I can return home, I cannot tell. Tales of the savagery meted out to those captured has sickened us all. For York to have murdered his own nephew so callously, then to spread rumors that Monmouth offered to convert in exchange for his life, are beneath contempt.

Surely the Prince of Orange would not allow this travesty to go unpunished, with the Protestant Church in more danger than ever before? When I return, I hope to be among those of like minds, who would make the devil of York account for his cruelty.

I pray you are kept safe, Helena and Henry also, and I long for the day we can be together again.

Your respectful and loving son
Aaron Woulfe

Helena was taken back to the courtyard at Loxsbeare, the morning after Sedgemoor. She could still hear Henry's anguished protest when dirty water spilled on his shoes. Her throat burned with remembered pain that all three of them might be dead. "Oh, Tobias," she breathed. "Aaron got away." Her elation was instantly clouded by bitter disappointment. "Although, he doesn't know where Father is." She gave a choked sob. "And I shall have to tell him about Mother, and Uncle Edmund. He expects-"

"He expects nothing." Tobias cut across her. "He will give thanks you and Henry are safe and well."

Helena shook the fragile pages at him. "He wrote this months ago. He will be wondering why no one has responded. I must-" she broke off to stare at him. Something didn't feel right. "Why are you here, Tobias? Samuel could have brought this to me."

He gave a shrug. "I wanted to be the one to deliver the letter."

"Why?" She let the pages fall into her lap. "You owe us nothing. You lost your livelihood when Loxsbeare was seized. Why would you want to do something like this, for Henry and me?"

"On the contrary. I owe the Woulfes a great deal. And with your permission, I am determined to carry it through and go to The Hague."

Every suspicious thought Helena ever had about Tobias rose in her throat and threatened to choke her for its injustice. That he demonstrated such devotion when her actions toward him at Loxsbeare had been nothing less than spoiled petulance. Her shoulders slumped and with a silent nod, she gave way to quiet, heartbreaking sobs.

Tobias gathered her in his arms like a child, the cloth of his coat rubbing her cheek, the smell of damp wool overlaid with leather and warm skin filling her senses. Familiar, masculine smells, which brought with them the painful realization, that no one had held her for a long time.

When her tears subsided, she pulled away, embarrassed at her lack of control in front of a servant, despite that he was no longer in her service.

His face seemed to reflect her sadness. She could not fathom how or why, but her relationship with Tobias had subtly changed. He had never been a subservient man, it was not in his nature, but he had always treated her insolence with humor and tolerance. He handed her a large kerchief. "If you will give your permission, I wish to go to Holland." Her first instinct was to protest that he need not go, but his tine of voice convinced her that even if she withheld her consent, he would go anyway.

Helena indicated the pages in her lap. "This only mentions the street and the town. How will you find him, and is it safe?" Inexplicably, she did not want him to walk into danger.

Tobias appeared to give her question some thought. "Someone will know where he is residing, and I doubt the king still has men on the look out for messages going back and forth to fugitive Rebels." His soothing words were balm to her distress. "With the king's scandalous promotion of Catholics into key positions, he has more than enough to cope with at home, without worrying about Aaron Woulfe."

"Or Sir Jonathan Woulfe?" Helena whispered, wiping her wet cheeks. "I wish we could find out what happened to him."

"One thing at a time, Helena. I believe Samuel has sent a messenger to fetch Henry so he may be told."

"Oh yes, he will be so happy." She noticed he did not say, Master, but hardly cared. "Thank you, Tobias. Now if you'll excuse me." She rose to her feet and went in search of Celia to tell her the good news before Henry arrived full of questions.

As she hurried past the dining hall, William's familiar laugh caught her attention. With a wide smile she retraced her steps intending to go in, knowing he would be as delighted as she to know about Aaron, he always seemed sympathetic to her worries over her father and brother.

He sat at a table with an attractive young woman Helena had never seen before. On closer inspection, she was not that young, but William pressed his lips to her hand, while fixing her with his amorous gaze. From her delighted protestations, Helena could tell she was receiving the same flattery she had imagined he reserved for her alone.

Before he looked up and saw her, Helena stepped back, almost colliding with one of the serving men, who turned a grimace of annoyance into a gracious smile. She fled up the stairs, the blood throbbing in her head. By the time she reached her room, the moment of disappointment had passed and she went to stand by the window to stare down at the street. The settling snow had been churned to black slush by a combination of soot in the air and pedestrian feet.

She was being absurd. Why should William not flirt with any woman he chose? That very afternoon, when he used that same devastating look on her, she suspected boredom alone drove him to lay siege to her. She thought again he was not a man to be taken seriously, so why was she so shaken?

William was handsome and amusing certainly, but he lived on the generosity of his father and had nothing to offer her which could begin to compensate for what she had lost. He reminded her of a cat, stretching and preening under whoever's hands it found itself at the time.

If I cannot attract a wealthy man, then I need a reliable one with ambition and ability. Not a vain, idle fop, with a roving eye. Surprised at herself for allowing him to disturb her so badly, she refused to allow him to spoil her special day. Helena returned downstairs, resolving never again to be susceptible to Williams' easy grace.

* * *

Tobias wrapped his heavy long coat around his shoulders and huddled on the foc'sl deck of The Sirius. Icy salt spray whipped across his face as it assaulted the main deck and he shivered in the bitter cold; although he would rather brave the prevailing wind, than suffer the nauseating yawing of below decks.

The noise of the gale sounded like an animal in pain, adding to the feeling of hovering doom about the journey; though the cheerful sailors declared it meant an early arrival at their destination. The ship had left Brewhouse Quay on the tide the previous day, and through half closed eyes, Tobias saw the coast of Holland, visible as an uneven gray mass on the horizon, obscured by horizontal rain.

The rain abated as they pulled into the busy port, and the ship ceased it's pitching as it bobbed alongside the dock. The vessel was lashed down with ropes and Tobias disembarked, clumping down a rickety wooden gangplank with a mixed crowd of twenty or so other passengers; none of whom had uttered a word to him throughout the overnight voyage.

His leather bag tucked under one arm and one hand holding down his hat, Tobias glanced around the dockside, wondering which way to go. An old man approached him, narrowed eyes staring out of a wrinkled face. Tobias took him for a sailor, but still grasped his bag tighter, returning the man's stare in silence.

"Waar u bent die gaan?" the old man mumbled.

Tobias frowned, shaking his head

The man tried again. "Kan ik u de heer helpen?"

Tobias decided this was a waste of his time and turned to go, when an English voice behind him spoke, "He is asking where you would like to go, and can he be of help?"

A smiling man of about his own age was perched on a cart pulled by a well built, but elderly horse several feet away. "Thank you, sir, I am looking for a street called..." He pulled a sheet of paper from his pocket on which was scrawled Aaron's address. "Grote Markt."

"It is in the market area." The carter pointed with a curt nod. "I go there. I gif you a ride."

Tobias slipped a coin to the old Dutchman, who nodded thanks and shuffled away. Tobias shivered as he climbed onto the cart, his hand still clasped firmly onto his hat.

"De wint' comes straight from the Russian plains." The man grinned. Tobias rolled his eyes, huddling lower in the seat, distracted from his discomfort by the rows of neat, tightly packed brick built houses with ornamental gables. As the cart rattled along, Tobias wondered if he could have travelled by water instead. Everywhere he looked, the canal weaved along his route, jammed with conveyances piled high with goods and people.

The carter set him down by the main market place and Tobias scoured the streets running alongside the square, until he found what he was looking for. The street led into a narrower one, which in turn led to an alley where a house bore the name Aaron had scrawled on the top of his letter to his mother.

A tiny, wizened man opened the painted wooden door, a black cap covering his head down past his ears. Tobias was grateful he spoke a little English and the mention of Aaron's name brought smiles and nods, together with a pointing finger to an upper floor. He took Tobias to a narrow staircase at the back of the hall and pointed again, indicating he should climb to the top.

Aaron's look of total amazement as he flung open the door was everything Tobias had hoped for. In an instant it was replaced by a wide smile and he slapped Tobias on the back, his gaze raking him from head to foot as if reassuring himself he was real.

"I thought you were a creditor," he offered as if in apology. Then he gave a slow, thoughtful nod. "My letter reached mother at Loxsbeare?"

Inexplicably, Tobias found himself unable to speak, but Aaron did not seem bothered by his silence and stepped back from the doorway. "Do come in Tobias, although I warn you, my humble lodgings are not as salubrious as the manor." He gave a depreciative grin as he drew Tobias under a low lintel, hastily removing a pile of linens from a chair to offer his guest a seat.

Aaron's face looked too thin, his eyes wary under a vivid red scar that sliced through his left eyebrow. He wore his hair shorter, held back in a band at the nape of his neck. But the broad, familiar smile and twinkling blue eyes were unmistakably Aaron Woulfe.

"I have brought letters for you, sir." Tobias, faltered on the 'sir', but Aaron appeared not to notice. "And money." He withdrew the bulky packet from his coat.

Aaron gave a harsh laugh, the privations of the last months clear in its tone. "I appreciate them all, Tobias." He slapped his guest hard on the shoulder. "But have to admit, the money is particularly welcome. As you can see," he indicated his worn clothes, "I wear second hand garments these days."

Tobias assessed his surroundings at a glance. The floorboards were bare, the small, square window held no hangings to keep out the cold wind and the furniture was old and worn. The door of the next room stood open and through it, Tobias spied a narrow bed with meager coverings. His gaze came round to settle on Aaron's face again, all his well-rehearsed speeches deserting him.

Aaron dropped the letters on a table, staring at them hungrily for a moment before turning back to Tobias. "How is everyone at home? I have been worried for them all since the rebellion failed." He took a chair by the window, whose grimy glass looked out onto the closely jumbled rooftops of the city, washed of their color under the winter sky. He leaned his forearms on his knees, his chin jutted forward, a stance so familiar it brought a lump to Tobias's throat. Something in his face must have told Aaron all was not well.

"Is it so bad?" he asked in a whisper.

Tobias nodded. Where to begin? "There has been no news at all of Sir Jonathan."

Blowing air between his lips, Aaron stared at the floor. "I feared as much, but I cannot help be grateful he was not caught and sent for trial. Then there would be no hope." He leveled his gaze at Tobias' face, waiting.

Tobias swallowed. "Edmund Woulfe is dead."

Aaron gave a small groan, then rubbed his hands over his face as if washing it. He stared at the floor and rocked back and forth, like Helena. Finally, he gave a resigned nod. "May his soul be at peace," he murmured. "Was he hanged?"

"He was killed at Sedgemoor." As if the manner of his death made a difference. However it seemed to matter to Aaron, who looked relieved, his lips moving in a brief, whispered prayer.

In the heavy silence, which followed, Tobias knew if he did not say the rest of it, he might never be able to. "Your moth- Lady Elizabeth is also dead."

Aaron's eyes widened and his mouth worked. He looked away, then back at Tobias, his expression darkening as if he were about to accuse him of lying. He rose and flung himself across the room, his lips moving, but making no sound. Eventually he found his voice and it was cold. "How did she die?"

Slowly, haltingly, Tobias told him about the day the militia came to Loxsbeare, recounting the scene in the hall with the soldier snatching her necklace, her fall. The picture so vivid in his head, his voice broke as he described it.

Aaron fists clenched as he talked, his knuckles blanched white and bloodless, the veins on his neck bulging as his whole body tensed in suppressed fury.

When Tobias stopped speaking, he expected Aaron to crash his fist into the wall, or hurl the scanty furniture around the room in a rage; even scream accusations at Tobias. A heavy silence stretched between them until Aaron crumpled to his knees on the bare floorboards, dropped his fair head forward and sobbed like a child.

Once again, Tobias found himself in the role of physical comfort to one of the Woulfes. This time the grief was so deep, so heart-wrenching in its intensity, Tobias found his own face wet with tears. He murmured repeatedly as they clung together like lovers, "I am sorry, I am so sorry, forgive me."

They broke apart finally, without embarrassment, yet knowing neither of them would ever speak of the incident again. "There is nothing to forgive," Aaron murmured, pulling himself to his feet. He strode to the corner of the room and splashed water on his face from a ewer on a low table.

When Aaron spoke again, he seemed chillingly calm, his damp hair darkened at the hairline. "There is a small eating house a few doors away. The food is a little strange." He gave a small laugh. "Mostly cold and consisting of cheese and some odd sort of fish. But it is economical and filling. I have funds, thanks to you. Would you dine with me?"

The brittle invitation tore at Tobias' heart. He accepted with a silent nod. Aaron collected a shabby brown coat from a hook behind the door, and the two men clattered down the narrow stairs and out onto the cobbled street.

They pulled their collars up and hats down against the biting wind from the North Sea which was funneled through the narrow street. The inn was no more than adequate, the food as unappetizing as Aaron had described, but their seats in an alcove by the fire gave them privacy. With orange flames reflected in Aaron's eyes, he listened as Tobias talked.

Aaron accepted the loss of Loxsbeare with naked, but silent grief; expressing his relief his brother and sister were safe, grateful his mother and uncle received Christian burials. He expressed incredulity at Helena's foray into Somerset. "She is an unusual girl, my sister." A tear slid down his cheek, which he palmed away.

Tobias told him about Henry becoming an apprentice architect, and Aaron's face suffused with genuine happiness. "You don't say so!"

The door opened and a face appeared round the jamb. A pair of shrewd eyes scoured the room before alighting on Aaron. The man stepped inside and as he approached their table, Tobias studied him. He was tall and lean with stringy brown hair and a large, Roman nose that sat uncomfortably on a thin-jawed face. His eyes were sharp and piercing and he tended to stoop a little.

Aaron glanced up. "Master Ferguson, do join us."

If Tobias hadn't known his nickname was 'The Plotter', he would have been able to tell it from the man's furtive glance.

Aaron moved his stool to make room, but the newcomer declined with a hand gesture. "I came ta gie ye the news." His accent was so thickly Scottish, Tobias had to concentrate to make out his words. "The king has pardoned us, Aaron." He rolled the name over his tongue, already eyeing the door as if eager to be off to spread the news elsewhere.

Aaron leapt to his feet. "All Rebels?"

Master Ferguson nodded. "The messenger arrived on The Sirius this morning. Tha news'll be posted in the market place later today."

Tobias frowned, wondering which of the men he had shared passage with had been the one.

Master Ferguson leaned both hands on the table and stared into his friend's face. "We cae' go home Aaron." He beamed.

Aaron rose to his feet. "We must tell the others." He followed Ferguson, to the door, and then turned back. "Tobias, will you wait here until I have consulted with my friends?"

Tobias looked bewildered, but he nodded. "The next ship for England does not sail for three days." He glanced around the gloomy taproom. "Might I obtain a room here?"

Aaron nodded, and then with a brief wave, both men were gone.

In the time it took for Tobias to negotiate with the Dutch innkeeper to secure a room, change the linen he had worn for the last two days and have a cold but welcome wash, Aaron had returned.

They took their places at the table in the taproom they had vacated an hour before, Tobias noting a transformation in his companion. Aaron no longer exhibited the burdened man, reeling under the recent loss of half his family. His eyes were determined, and with his self-possession restored, he reminded Tobias of the Aaron he knew.

Their recent close bond had disappeared. This Aaron Woulfe was instructing a servant, with every expectation of unquestioning obedience.

"I am staying here, in The Hague."

Tobias was open-mouthed with shock. "But you have no reason to, you can return to England with no fear of-"

Aaron held up a hand. "I have friends here. Friends who saw what I saw at Sedgemoor and barely got away with their lives, as I did. We shall not go back to England to live under the tyranny of the Papist King James."

"What will you do?"

"You have brought the means with you." He tapped the money pouch inside his coat. "The Prince of Orange sympathizes with our situation. I feel sure he will commit troops soon."

"Troops?" Tobias swallowed nervously, scanning the room to see if anyone could overhear them, but they were virtually alone.

Aaron opened his hands in a gesture of resignation. "I can see you don't understand my reasons, Tobias, but the Protestant religion is in greater danger than ever while this king is on the throne. Can you not see?"

No, Tobias couldn't see. News of the Pardon would be all over England. Helena and Henry would be expecting their brother home. How could he return alone? However he could see by Aaron's eager face, there was no persuading him.

"Would you call on a friend of mine in London? A Master Daniel Foe. Take him to Samuel at Lambtons. He will explain my reasons if you feel you cannot."

Tobias rose wearily to his feet, the long journey and his stressful day combined to rob him of all energy. "As you wish, sir," he murmured. He left the table and stumbled to his room, where he slept the clock round.

Three days later, Tobias stood in the stern of the ship taking him back to England, among his fellow passengers several exiles that, unlike Aaron, were eager to return home. The wind had dropped and the sea was calmer, prophesying a longer crossing, but an easier one.

He waved to the lone figure on the dockside as the ship pulled away, his inside pocket heavy with a new bundle of letters for everyone at Lambtons. Aaron was almost out of sight before Tobias remembered; he had lacked both the courage and opportunity to broach the subject of his birth.

CHAPTER TWENTY TWO

Henry had eaten enough breakfast, despite Mistress Newman hovering at his shoulder with a platter of cold meat. He politely declined, repeatedly, but without success. Her attitude towards him was almost motherly and he appreciated her care of him, it went some way to helping him miss his own mother a little less. He also had good reason to be proud of himself, in that Master Newman had lately expressed more than satisfaction with Henry's work.

Master Newman told him he would be spending less time on building sites and in stone warehouses. Instead, he would learn the more aesthetic aspects of being an architect. Henry thanked him, but forbore to explain how much he enjoyed getting plaster dust on his hands. He liked nothing better than to run up ladders, hang precariously over drops and scramble along buttresses to see how the masons were progressing.

On this particular morning, however, Henry's thoughts were not on stonemasons. Instead, he contemplated Mary Ann Newman's green eyes and rich, glossy hair. She was the most exquisite creature he had ever seen, diminutive and fine boned, she made Henry's lack of height seem dominant and manly beside her.

Her eyes had attracted him first. Wide and luminous, with tiny green flecks within; they reminded him of Helena's. He hesitated to mention this for fear of allotting her the status equal to that of a relative, and with a genuine compliment withheld, it rendered him tongue-tied in her company.

From her position further along the table, Mary Ann flicked glances in his direction from under long, sweeping lashes. Henry couldn't stop looking at her and was drawn repeatedly to her delicate features and her perfect, bowed lips, held in a perpetual smile. He thought she mocked him at first, but as he came to know her, realized she was intelligent and quick witted, so that before long, he included her naturally in conversations.

In contrast, the other Newman girls vied for Henry's attention, performing small tasks to gain his notice, until he was giddy with the gratitude he found himself constantly bestowing.

"I used the tiniest stitches on the tear in your coat Henry," Joanna simpered. Her attempt to look doe-eyed and appealing did not sit well on her rather plump frame. "You must have caught it on a carriage door as you climbed down, it was on the hem at the back."

Henry ducked his head in a polite nod. "Thank you for the effort, Mistress, but I was not aware of it until you mentioned it."

"Do you like the feather I picked for you Henry?" Margaret smiled coyly, brandishing her gift. "The color will suit your new hat perfectly."

With a smile on her lips, Mary Ann slipped out of the room. The void she left felt like a chasm opening up, but Henry forced himself not to watch her retreating figure. He sighed inwardly.

Yes, he had definitely had enough breakfast.

He took his leave of the family and collecting his hat, muff and coat, strode down the hall. Mary Ann stepped out of a side room into his path, opened the front door and slammed it with a resounding bang. Pressing a finger to her lips, she drew him into the room behind her and closed the door silently.

Henry smiled. "I have to meet your father-." She cut him off with a deep kiss, pressing him back against the door.

"I know." She released him, smoothing down his coat with her hands. "But I haven't seen you for days."

Henry traced the line of her chin with one hand.

"Could you get away and meet me somewhere?" she wheedled, bringing the tips of his fingers to her mouth, nipping at them with her teeth.

Henry swallowed. "You are bold, Mistress Newman, you know that don't you?" He tried to look serious, but knew his enraptured expression gave him away.

Mary Ann smiled, jutting her chin in challenge. "I know, but only with you."

"Your father is waiting for me at Christ Church in Newgate. It's almost finished and Sir Christopher will be there. I mustn't be late." Henry insisted, but still he did not move from the circle of her arms.

"Later then," she breathed into his neck. "Think of somewhere we can be alone."

"We are alone." Henry teased.

"You know what I mean." She giggled, leaning into him for another urgent kiss. The door behind him creaked in protest and they sprang apart. "Mother might have heard that," Mary Ann whispered. "She will be coming to see what I am doing." His arms still encircled her waist and she caressed his neck with one hand, both reluctant to act on her sensible advice.

"Perhaps, you could be walking round St James Park, sometime around three of the clock?" Henry suggested.

Mary Ann gave the slightest of nods, then slid past him to open the door, checking the passage before signaling him to emerge. The footman standing in the hall saw everything and nothing, his back ramrod straight as he stared at the wall.

Avoiding the man's eye, Henry slipped past, through the front door, turning to blow Mary Ann a kiss as she closed it behind him.

Outside, Henry's gaze alighted on two chairmen slouching against the wall of a building opposite. He beckoned with his chin, in a fair imitation of Robert Devereux. One nudged his companion before hurrying over, the heavy conveyance slung between their broad shoulders.

Henry settled into the comfy interior, wondering how the workmen on the building site were capable of even flexing their fingers in such weather. He shoved his hands inside the fur muff he carried, his hand closing on a small square of parchment. He frowned, bringing it into the light to read. It was from Mary Ann. The words rambling and meaningless to anyone not bound tightly in the throes of first love. He read it twice, then touched it to his lips before tucking it back inside the muff.

He and Mary Ann had skirted around each other for weeks, with shy smiles and awkward exchanges. He still did not know quite when their attraction had intensified into stolen kisses and secret meetings, but he did not regret one moment of it. However they were in a terrible dilemma neither could face discussing. Henry might have private means, but he was also an indentured apprentice to Mary Ann's father, and it would be unacceptable for him to make advances towards his patron's daughter under the man's own roof. Public ones at least.

They had not talked of the future, it was heady enough snatching private moments in the present. It would be another six years before he could contemplate marriage, although the thought of it occupied his thoughts constantly.

Henry knew if he asked Mary Ann to wait, she would agree without hesitation. However she also needed the approval of her parents and his guardian and without them, what would become of Henry's grand schemes then?

Since the wonderful news that his brother was still alive, news which Mary Ann had been as excited about as Henry himself, he had longed to see him and place his future in Aaron's hands. He still could not bring himself to mention it to Helena, she and those Devereux girls teased him enough for blushing in Mary Ann's company. Aaron might clap him on the back and laugh at his gaucheness, but he would know what to do, and Henry longed for his strong presence again.

He stared unseeing at the interior of the sedan as it rocked and bumped along in the heavy traffic. Henry liked sedans, they could ease through spaces a carriage could not, making his frequent journeys through the city more efficient. He kept the leather flap down, allowing the familiar sights of London to pass him by unnoticed, his fingers gently stroking the square of parchment inside the muff.

They turned a sharp corner and the chair jolted, causing the chairmen to shout a protest. Henry put out a hand to steady himself, but was thrown hard against the padded backboard. He righted himself and threw up the flap, craning forward to scan the street.

They had almost collided with a large handcart, which lay on its side, its load spilled onto the cobbles. Henry joined in the abuse and yelled at the hapless carter gathering up his belongings from the filthy road, ordering the way be cleared so he could complete his journey. A busy man, Henry could not tolerate delays.

* * *

Lambtons was busy and to keep out of the way of continuous running feet, Helena found a private corner in the kitchen parlor to sit. The sounds of raised voices, the clashing of pots and the clunk of cleavers on wood filled the background. A cook shouted at a maid for dropping a plate, a serving man relayed a customer's orders, while the door to the dining room swung open with a creak, then flapped back into place with a rhythmic whoosh.

The kitchen parlor was where Mistress Carstairs ruled her domain, a scrubbed wooden table on one side and a pot bellied stove the other. A narrow shelf circled the room above head height, displaying a collection of blue and white china, sent to the housekeeper by her Dutch son-in-law.

Lubbock could often be found there, sipping tea like a gentleman and gossiping with the housekeeper. Helena would join them on cold afternoons, warming her feet at the stove and chatting to Lubbock.

He reminded her of Benoit in some ways, the cook left behind at Loxsbeare, with his fastidious nature and vanity about his appearance. His temper was equally as volatile, although he cursed in English, not French and was an excellent dining room host.

Helena sat at the table writing her journal, a dish of coffee beside her. The doors on both sides of the room stood open, the kitchen side revealing the cooks bullying the serving men, while the other gave onto the clamor of the dining areas. I n a sudden flurry of movement, Lubbock scrambled to his feet, bowing respectfully. "Good afternoon, sir."

Helena turned and found herself staring into William's laughing eyes.

"Mistress Woulfe, I thought I might find you here." He leaned against the doorframe, arms crossed over his chest, his black periwig arranged artistically over one shoulder.

"You have found me, sir." She tucked a hand beneath her chin. "With my favorite gentleman at Lambtons."

William pretended to be offended, pressing hand to his chest. "And I came hot-foot from Wills, leaving my coffee untouched, in my haste to be the first to bring you the news."

"How thoughtful." She pulled her gaze away from his reluctantly. "And what news is this?"

"King James has issued a general pardon to all those who fought in the Western Rebellion."

"Everyone?" Helena sprang to her feet, all traces of the coquette gone. "All pardoned?"

William's eyes told her no. "Those who came over from Holland with him are excluded, as are a few Rebels. Like your father." Helena's face fell. "Aaron Woulfe, however, is a free man."

"Oh, thank you, William, that is good news." Helena felt her cheeks grow warm and told herself it was for Aaron's sake, but the feel of William's eyes roving over her face and slipping down onto her bodice made her quiver.

Lubbock made a mumbled excuse about having duties to perform and slipped away. From the periphery of her vision, Helena saw Mistress Carstairs appear at the door, only to be pushed back the way she came by Lubbock.

Helena suppressed a smile as William flicked up the back of his coat and sat down at the table. "Is this coffee still hot?" he asked a passing serving girl. The waif flushed deep red and nodded, then scurried away.

Helena resumed her seat and poured some for him. Her fingers brushed his as she passed him the cup, a sharp jolt running through her. She looked up, the sudden flare in his eyes showing he had felt it too.

She withdrew her hand with an inward sigh, wondering why he created such mixed feelings in her. When he was kind, and treated her with genuine affection it seemed churlish to resist him so strongly. Then he would make a frivolous joke at someone else's expense, talk disparagingly of an enamored lady in her company, or lose a vast amount of money he had not earned at a gaming table, and her heart would harden against him.

They were still staring into each other's eyes when Celia arrived, Phebe on her heels. "Oh there you are Helena, why are you sitting here in this horrid little room?" Celia gaze flicked around with distaste. "Do come into the salon, there is a lovely fire in there."

Celia pulled Helena to her feet and with her siblings following, wandered out into the hall. "Have you heard about the amnesty?" Celia asked as they reached the salon.

"Yes." William and Helena replied simultaneously.

She clasped her hands together. "Isn't it wonderful? Aaron can come home."

Helena smiled to herself as they took their places on the sofas and chairs around the welcoming blaze, appreciative of Celia's enthusiasm for someone she had not met.

"Do you think he could stay here, at Lambtons?" Phebe asked, positioning herself behind her brother's chair, her long fingers caressing his shoulders.

"I expect he would prefer his own establishment." William said, his gaze still on Helena.

Celia's hand flew to her mouth. "Oh but, suppose he insists you go and live with him?"

Helena began to reassure her, and then stopped short. As head of the family, Aaron could indeed command her as he wished and she would have no choice but to obey. She wondered why this idea held no appeal, then pushed the thought away.

"Will Aaron know about the pardon?" Helena asked.

William laughed. "No doubt all the Rebels in The Hague will have heard it and be crowding every available ship out of the harbor as we speak." He was still looking at her and she reveled in his appraising scrutiny, unable to tell if the thrill she felt was due to her brother's imminent return, or William's smile.

Robert and Adella arrived to join in the general celebration, and while they were speculating with their daughters as to where Aaron might live, Helena listened distractedly, hearing only snippets of their conversation.

William was being his most gracious, his high backed chair positioned so close to hers, their toes almost touched. "I hope you will allow me to escort you to the Pleasure Gardens at Fox Hall when the weather improves, Mistress? They are particularly pleasing in the Spring."

Helena feigned interest in a piece of embroidery she had discarded on a table the previous evening, giving him a nod she hoped was not too eager, nor too dismissive. "That would be most agreeable, Master Devereux." So intent on how she looked to him, she pricked her finger.

William's gaze lingered on her with a half mocking smile. Her cheeks grew warm, her pulse quickening. He had a habit of locking gazes with her as if she were the only person in a room, daring her to be the first to look away. When she could forget the sheer physicality of him, she found him excellent company. He sought her out often; their companionship giving Helena a thrilling sense of her own feminine power as they exchanged teasing banter, dancing together, then away again in flirtatious jousts.

While Robert was busy calling in every favor he possessed to find gainful employment for his son, the object of all this industry had so far expressed nothing but boredom at the prospect of work.

"What about the Navy, William?" Robert looked up from his newssheet. "I can purchase a commission for you with little trouble."

William wrinkled his nose and waved the suggestion away, not bothering to respond.

"But, my dear, the uniform would be so flattering do you not think?" Adella pointed out with mild regret.

His father uttered a deep sigh. Helena suppressed a smile.

"You are not enough of a gentleman, William," Robert jabbed the air with the stem of his pipe, "nor are you rich enough to be able to idle your life away."

Helena looked down at her sewing, recalling how William, for his part, whiled away his days wherever young men went, to bet fortunes on the turn of a card or the progress of a louse up a wall hanging.

Then there were the lengthy drinking sessions with his friends in the public rooms, or the nights he joined a group of affluent young fops in one of the private rooms upstairs; catcalling from the balconies to passers by below, until Robert called a halt to their rowdiness.

Helena glanced up to see William drumming his fingertips on the table. A smile tugging at her lips at his obvious boredom. He got to his feet with a sigh, staring moodily out of the window with his hands held loosely behind his back. After a moment, he appeared to make up his mind and turning on his heel, bowed to the ladies, saying he was off to visit a coffee house.

"Which one, Will?" Phebe asked, following him out. Helena suspected she did so to retain his attention, but they were at the door before he answered, so his reply was inaudible.

When he had gone, Celia sidled up to Helena, perching herself on the edge of a chair. "I cannot understand you, Helena. How can you remain so unmoved, when every female who lays eyes on William, falls instantly in love with him."

Helena smiled. She had seen those ladies he charmed, then immediately forgot, hanging on the fringes of his company at gatherings, hoping to rekindle his interest. If he noticed their existence at all, his glance would skim over their earnest faces with a vacant smile, and they would forgive him, call him a rogue and sigh after him.

"I like him very much." Helena shrugged, pretending to wrestle with an intricate stitch. "But he is only flirting with me, there is no real attachment."

"I was hoping you would marry him." Celia fiddled with Helena's box of sewing threads. She had lowered her voice and glanced at her father, who had his nose buried in the newssheet. Adella sat farther away, reading one of her novelettes, her brow creased in concentration.

Celia prattled on, "You would settle him down, dearest. He spends too much time gaming, and drinking and-."

Helena arched an eyebrow and Celia whispered, "yes, well, probably whoring too." Her light tone indicated this was a minor fault. "But if you were married, he would not need such...entertainment. You would mould him into a stable and respectable husband."

Helena did not reply, one hand hovering in mid air as images of a life being married to William paraded through her head. Then the face of the vapid blonde woman loomed in front of her eyes and she stabbed the linen viciously with her needle.

She decided Celia's clumsy matchmaking was the result of the final settlement of her betrothal to Master Ralf Maurice. The future bridegroom called at Lambtons almost daily, making it clear he could not wait for them to be married.

Helena observed them with amusement, intrigued that a pleasant, but undistinguished and shy man, had overnight become Celia's romantic dream. The bride-to-be tripped around the inn with a beatific smile, bestowing goodwill on everyone. Phebe, exasperated with her sister's cloying sentimentality, flounced out of the room whenever marriage was mentioned.

"William might offer for you, Helena, if you gave him encouragement," Celia suggested.

Helena held up an imperious hand. "I don't want a husband. Well certainly not yet." And not that one.

CHAPTER TWENTY THREE

When Tobias returned to London with a companion, it was disappointingly obvious to Robert that the self-conscious stranger at the table in the dining hall, was not Aaron Woulfe. By the time Helena appeared, Tobias confirmed what they already knew. Aaron was still in The Hague.

"Do sit down, Helena," Robert greeted her, pre-empting the question he saw she was about to ask. "I have invited Master Foe to take a libation and discuss the purpose of his visit in comfort. Henry is on some building site or other, but he can join us later."

Robert asked a serving man to inform Adella and Phebe of their visitor. He knew that if he did not include them, they would insist he repeat whatever Master Foe told them when they finally did arrive.

Helena took an empty seat, which happened to be beside William, adding her gaze to those already putting the stranger under close scrutiny. Master Foe looked pale and insignificant sitting beside the handsome and colorful Tobias. He appeared to be in his middle twenties, with a swarthy complexion on a long face that threatened to turn to fleshiness in later life. His chin and nose were both sharp, and there was a mole beside his full mouth. He wore a good quality wool coat, which Robert surmised was originally made for someone broader. His linen, if frayed, looked laundered, although shadows of old stains remained.

"It was kind of you to attend us here, Master Foe." Robert tried to put the man at ease, but this proved unnecessary when the newcomer returned his look with pride and a little arrogance.

"Er, actually, sir." Foe gave a cough. "I returned to London late last year. I escaped to Holland from Sedgemoor."

His gaze flicked round the room, as if the word itself might rouse troopers from the corners. "Aaron gave me passage money he could barely spare, but I was eager to return to my wife. I also had some pressing family business requiring my attention."

"You were not afraid of the soldiers?" Helena demanded.

Foe's eyes clouded. "I feared being brought to account for my involvement, certainly. In fact, my name is on the Petty Jury List for Cornhill Ward. I am in the process of negotiating with a Master Penne to have it removed for a . . . a consideration." He blushed. "Which ah, Aaron has provided, since his fortunes lately have altered."

"Why has Aaron not come home?" Helena fixed their guest with slate eyes. She appeared calm, but Robert could feel the displeasure coming off her in waves.

Foe turned admiring eyes on her. "I believe, Mistress, from the letter Master Lumm brought me, he feels the loss of his mother and his uncle keenly. He will take time to recover from the dreadful news."

This seemed to annoy Helena even more, while Robert inwardly congratulated the man on his divertive powers.

Foe rested his elbows on the table and steepled his hands. Robert wondered for a moment if he was preparing a prayer for them all. But instead he said, "Aaron feels the time is not yet right to return to England, not when our present monarch still occupies the throne."

Helena gave a groan of dismay. "He is not coming back at all?"

"Has Master Woulfe been presented at the Prince of Orange's Court?" Adella asked, revealing rather more décolleté than their guest seemed comfortable with, as Foe flushed and looked away.

"The-the Prince of Orange keeps a close eye on the situation here," he stammered.

"And how does that concern my brother?" Helena demanded.

Foe's eyes filled with righteous fervor. "As it should concern every Anglican!" He scanned each face in turn. "The king's closeness to French Louis; a standing army in peacetime, his promotion of Papists into high office. All indicate he intends bringing the country back to Rome, and by force if necessary."

"I disagree." Robert grew indignant. "I know no one in London who has found life more difficult as an Anglican since the succession."

"Perhaps, sir." Foe gave a wry grin. "But Catholics seeking office have found it considerably easier of late."

"Actually, Father." William ignored his mother's warning glare. "Evelyn complains of seeing Popish pamphlets on the streets, yet no moves have been made to have them banned, or the publishers imprisoned."

Robert opened his mouth to respond, but William had not finished. "The king is aware his preferment of Catholics is making him unpopular. His failure to have the Test Act repealed proves that. Master Foe may be right, the king may well be arming himself against his subjects."

Robert gave a derisive snort, turning in time to see William give Helena a slow wink that she pretended not to see. He began to wonder if his son's fanning of the political flames had been to impress their beautiful guest, or simply to annoy him.

"If the king is not preparing to bring us all to Rome by force, why then does he keep over thirteen thousand soldiers in barracks?" Foe held up a finger to emphasis his point. "Their regiments should have been disbanded after the rebellion."

Robert gave a signal to a serving man, who detached himself from the wall and scurried off to fetch more wine. He used the interval to consider Foe's words. Aaron Woulfe and this young man had been closeted with their fellow fugitives for far too long, with time lying heavily on their hands. The only use they appeared to have made of it, was to imagine plots and counter plots coming out of Whitehall against the entire Protestant world.

With a wife to distract him, Foe would adjust to normal life again in due course, he imagined. However, the longer Aaron remained in Holland, the more romantic a figure he would become in his own eyes, if not those of Helena and her brother. In Robert's view, Aaron should return to England as soon as possible, to take up the ties of responsibility he still had left.

"And tell us, Master Foe, what does your future hold in London?" Robert asked, determined to divert the conversation away from religion.

"I am a hosiery merchant," Foe replied. "Although, I have had a great deal of time to think these last months."

"I should imagine you have, sir," Robert muttered under his breath, passing his guest another glass.

"Pamphleteering is rewarding, but can be somewhat dangerous." Foe took an appreciative gulp of Robert's best claret. "I also write for the Review, but I have a novel in mind."

Robert raised an eyebrow, political or religious rhetoric perhaps, but a novel?

"And what shall this novel be about?" asked Adella. Robert smiled. His wife spent a great deal of her free time consuming novelettes, the more racy the better.

"I have not yet a story in my head, Mistress Devereux." Foe's face softened at being the focus of Adella's dazzling smile. "However, when I was hiding from troopers after Sedgemoor, I found myself huddled beside a gravestone with a most unusual name inscribed upon it. I have never forgotten it, and since then have had a notion to name my hero after that dead man."

"What was the name?" Tobias asked.

Daniel Foe stared off. "The gravestone bore the inscription, 'Here lies Robinson Crusoe'."

"Strange indeed," mused Robert. "I wonder what manner of story one could write around such a name?"

* * *

Helena woke next morning in a sour mood, having spent most of the night conducting angry exchanges with Aaron in her head, where she confronted him on his virtual abandonment of herself and Henry.

"What does he say, dearest?" Celia had asked, referring to the letter Master Foe had brought her. Helena had been delirious with joy, up to the point she had read it aloud to her friend. "He says Master Foe will explain everything to me and he hopes I am conducting myself respectfully in my guardian's home."

"Oh dear." Celia's voice fell. "Does he have nothing nice to say?"

Helena read on, 'I must thank you for the service you have performed in bringing our dear Uncle Edmund's body back to Devon.' She broke off angrily. "He writes as if I were a stranger! Listen! He says has been received by Prince William and they have discussed the need to, protect the Protestant religion." She parodied the final words.

"It sounds dangerous," Celia murmured.

"It's practically treasonous," Helena cried. "I cannot believe that after all he has been through, all we have been through, he is taking such a risk!"

She tossed and turned in the bed, twisting the sheets round her body until she was hot and irritable. How could Aaron have been so cold? She could hardly believe her handsome, sunny brother had written to her in this way. All those nights she had lain awake after the Rising, sending messages into the heavens for him to stay alive, keep safe and come home to her. He knew her better than this.

And worse, he had heard nothing of father, '...our father appears to have disappeared into the mud and mist of the battlefield.' Shivering at the image he conjured, she told herself he was wrong, their father still lived, somewhere.

The dreams were so vivid, she could still feel the hurt and disappointment when, blind to her tears, Aaron refused her entreaties to come home.

Chloe seemed to sense her need for silence and dressed her without her usual chatter. When Helena wandered downstairs, she found Tobias in the entrance hall, talking to Lubbock. Tall and imposing in an emerald green long coat, strands of his peruke were tied into knots with colored ribbon arranged over one shoulder. He drew several blushing glances from the serving girls who passed him.

His eyes creased at the corners when he saw her. He strode forward to grasp her hands and invited her to break her fast with him. "If you have not yet dined, of course." His expression was guarded, as if he presumed too much.

Helena accepted his proffered arm with genuine pleasure, glad of the opportunity to discuss Aaron with him alone. Lubbock showed them to a table in a corner of the dining hall, the room almost deserted so early in the day. A serving man brought buttered bread and hot chocolate for Helena, while Tobias was served ale, fresh bread, cheese and cold meat.

"What do you think of Lambtons?" Helena asked, noticing he took no more than mild interest in his food. The room was cold, but without being asked, Lubbock set a brazier near their table. The air began to lose its bite, nevertheless, Helena pulled her shawl tighter, wrapping her chilled fingers round her cup of chocolate.

Tobias gazed round the elegant room. "I wonder what my patrons at The Ship would think of this." He grinned. "When Samuel told me where you and your brother were going to live, I never imagined anything so grand." He held both hands palm upwards in an expressive gesture.

Helena looked around her, trying to see what he saw. Lambtons surprised everyone on their first visit, but she was accustomed to its unexpected luxury. "Samuel told me you were back at your father's inn. It must be very different from Loxsbeare," she tried to keep her voice steady, but saying the name brought a lump to her throat.

He glanced at her over his tankard, and then set it down with a nod. "How could it not be? But I shan't talk about it, if it upsets you."

"No, I don't mind," she lied, forcing a smile. "But I would rather hear about Aaron. How is he really?"

Tobias wiped his mouth on a linen cloth and relaxed back in his chair as if giving himself time to consider. "He is changed. Still handsome and charming, but his personality is darker somehow."

Helena did not respond. She had already come to this conclusion herself.

"His hatred of the king colors his judgment, I feel. It reminds me almost of..."

"Of my uncle, Edmund Woulfe?"

His face lit with surprise, and then he gave a slow nod. "Having to tell him about your mother was the worst thing I have ever done." He turned from her to stare morosely into his ale.

"They were very close," Helena murmured, her hands trembling as she reached for the chocolate pot. The container came up light in her grasp and she indicated to a server to bring more. "Is what he is doing dangerous?"

"I cannot say, but Prince William of Orange strikes me as a man who will not act until certain of a favorable outcome." His voice held a cynical note.

"And there is still no news of our Father?"

Prevented from speaking by the arrival of the server, Tobias smiled at her as the man removed the empty plates and replenished the ale and chocolate. With a nod and a smile at them both, the server slid a plate of tiny biscuits onto the table.

"They have been experimenting in the kitchen again." Helena indicated the plate.

Watching idly as he examined a biscuit before biting it, the action struck a chord in her head. His mannerism was familiar. Similar things had occurred to her before, but she had not known what to do with the information. Her curiosity got the better of her and she blurted out, "Why were you and Father so close during your tenure at Loxsbeare?"

He stared at the biscuit, turning it over in his fingers. "What do you mean?"

You know what I mean. "You and he were always together, laughing, talking in a way no servant talks to his master."

"My relationship with Sir Jonathan bothered you?"

Helena nodded. "I was jealous." Having admitted it aloud, all her misgivings spilled from her. "You were always in his company. Out on the estate and in the house. You went with him to Exeter and Plymouth, when he always used to take . . ." she faltered, unwilling to admit the one he often took was herself. Her father's neglect had hurt her. "I distrusted you."

"I know." His gaze held hers with something like compassion. She saw no anger there or denial either. He brushed crumbs from his breeches with the back of his hand. Watching him, Helena's eyes narrowed. He reminds me of someone. But who?

"Why did you want to bring me the letter, then go all the way to Holland to see Aaron?"

His thought processes altered his expression, at which Helena gave a gasp, banging a fist on the table, her voice carrying across the room. "Who are you, Tobias Lumm?"

To Helena's amazement, Tobias smiled, a slow, beautiful smile, bringing tenderness into his face and softness to his eyes. The corners of his mouth crinkled and a dimple appeared. Helena saw it, and everything became clear.

He leaned until their faces were inches apart. "Sir Jonathan met my mother a year before he married Lady Elizabeth."

"Go on," she whispered, her heart hammering in her chest.

"He was young, younger than I am now. He was handsome and wealthy with a whole city paying him homage as Thomas Woulfe's son. There was some rivalry between him and his twin when they were younger, I believe, so. . ." He gave a shrug as if explanations were unnecessary. "My mother was pretty, flirtatious, and flattered when he paid her attention."

"Father told you all this?"

Tobias nodded. "Yes, when I first came to Loxsbeare."

"What happened?"

"When she discovered she carried me?" At Helena's nod, he went on. "What you would expect. Thomas Woulfe visited my grandparents, and between them they convinced Jim Lumm to make an offer for my mother. Your grandfather put money into the Inn and he sought a betrothal for your father."

"To my mother, yes I see. When did you discover you were not his?"

Tobias gave a snort. "Mother burdened me from birth with the knowledge Jim was not my father. She would taunt him with it when he tried to discipline me, so he let me run wild and saved his fathering for my four half brothers." He saw her frown and hurried on, "But he was a good father. I never had to suffer the beatings my brothers did, and it spoiled me." He indicated his embroidered burgundy vest beneath the green wool long coat and breeches. The perfectly tied cravat and lace at his wrists. "She encouraged my vanity as you see." He laughed a full, happy laugh, revealing even, white teeth.

"When you were young, did you know who your father was?"

"No, not until Sir Jonathan offered me the stewardship of Loxsbeare."

Helena's emotions were a mixture of wonder and fascination. Her father had another child, and she had not known. Strangely, she felt no anger, yet at the same time knew she would have if they were still at Loxsbeare. She was such a child then, even though it was mere months ago. Had mother been aware of him?

"Your mother knew."

It was almost as if he had read her thoughts. "She always treated you kindly." Her tone was defensive, forestalling any complaint.

His smile was reassuring. "She was a true lady and always behaved graciously toward me. Although she had every reason not to do so." Helena's throat hurt as he talked, painful memories flooding into her head. "When Samuel Ffoyle suggested Sir Jonathan employ me at Loxsbeare, she agreed willingly."

"Master Ffoyle knows?" Helena gave an incredulous laugh. "Of course he does, Samuel knows everything."

The tables began to fill as the morning diners stepped in from the cold wind. They greeted Lubbock jocularly, calling for mulled wine and hot pies to keep out the cold.

Helena stared at the new arrivals without seeing them, too occupied with her own thoughts. Then something occurred to her. "Have you told Aaron all this?"

"I intended to." Tobias sighed. "When news of the pardon came. I imagined I might bring him home, to you and Henry. But my plans went somewhat awry, when he decided to use his inheritance on intrigue in Holland."

The word 'inheritance' worked on Helena's brain. "Father managed to keep some of his estate back for us. Did you know that?"

Tobias reached across the table to take her hand. Helena surprised herself by letting him, even welcoming his touch. We could be lovers on a secret tryst. The look he gave her was certainly loving, but not lover-like. The more she looked at him, the more of herself she saw in his features.

"He left me the property your grandfather owned near Bedford House." His gaze searched hers as if seeking approval.

"He was your grandfather too, Tobias, and I'm glad he gave it to you. I am glad too that you are my brother."

His devastating smile reappeared. "Thank you, Helena. I thought you would be angry."

"I would have, a year ago. But I have lost too much of my family to be in a position to reject someone who actually wants to be connected to me." Her happy laugh caused several gazes to swivel in their direction.

"I wanted to tell Aaron all this," Tobias relaxed back in his seat, "but seeing his grief for your mother, it did not seem appropriate somehow."

She looked down at his hand, which rested on the table between them and felt a lump in her throat. He had Aaron's hands.

I shall keep your secret, Tobias. Aaron had not wanted his confidence, and Henry was living his own life with the Newmans. She had never admitted to herself before, that despite her having encouraged him, her younger brother's decision to leave was a small betrayal.

They parted outside Lambtons later that morning with new affection and promises to write often. Helena watched him walk towards the Rose Inn, his lone bag slung casually across his shoulder, his hat tipped back on his head.

"I told you he was a strange one," Chloe snorted at her shoulder.

Helena returned Tobias' backward wave. "Stranger than you know," she murmured.

CHAPTER TWENTY FOUR

Celia's wedding to Ralf Maurice was to take place in April. Helena was curious as to what precipitated this sudden culmination of Robert's plans.

"Spices and sugar, I think." Celia sneaked a slice of bread and butter from Helena's breakfast plate.

The two girls sat by the window overlooking the garden in Helena's room, attired déshabille in loose, flowing gowns tied over soft linen petticoats, sipping hot chocolate and nibbling pastries.

"You are making no sense, dearest." Helena wondered if her friend was being innocently spontaneous, or possessed a wit she was unaware of.

Celia rearranged her gown around voluptuous shoulders. "Ralf's great uncle died last spring, which is a tragedy of course," she waved the bread in the air. "Although Ralf hasn't seen him since the age of five or perhaps six, I cannot recall." She stared at the ceiling, a finger at her cheek.

"Celia!" Helena prompted.

"Oh, sorry. His will stated when his ship returned from the West Indies, the proceeds of the cargo were to go to Ralf." Her light eyes sparkled as she told the story. "Everyone imagined it must have been lost to a storm, or pirates or something; but the 'Emerald' came into port last week and at auction, the goods it brought from the islands sold for four thousand pounds." She dragged the words out for effect. "We are to marry immediately. Is that not wonderful news?"

"Did Ralf ask if you were agreeable to marry earlier than planned?"

"Should he have done?" Celia asked, devouring another slice of buttered bread.

Helena sighed and changed the subject. "Which church shall you be married in?"

She grimaced, licking butter from her fingers. "Why, we shall marry here of course, in Lambtons. No one of quality gets married in church." Celia's mouth twisted in distaste. "The ceremony would have to take place during divine service, when everyone who cares to may come and watch. Then there would be a charivari to endure, and Mother would be mortified."

"What is that?" Helena asked.

Celia wrinkled her delicate nose. "A charivari my dear, is where a band of complete strangers gather outside the bride's window with drums, whistles and such and make as much noise as they can until they are paid to leave."

Helena conjured up an image of Adella Devereux discovering such a spectacle outside her Inn, and smiled. She suspected she knew who would suffer the most as the result of such a confrontation.

"Father has to pay the clergyman twenty shillings for us to marry outside canonical hours." Celia rolled her eyes. "There seems to be a fine for everything one wishes to do these days." Barely pausing for draw breath she gabbled on, "Ralf is taking me to see his house tomorrow."

"He has bought a house?" Helena felt a little envious.

Celia frowned. "Well no, the uncle left it to him. An old retainer lived there who, according to the will, could not be dislodged. However, he has died, so the property belongs to Ralf. Is that not convenient?" Celia's eyes shone with excitement.

Helena fell silent, her mind on the demise of the servant, which appeared to have no effect on Celia at all. It came to her that a year ago, she would not have given a thought to a servant. Everything was different after the events of the summer and Helena wondered if this new sympathy was good or not.

She poured herself more chocolate, pondering on how complicated life had become, when there were so many things to feel sad about. She could hardly remember the days when all that concerned her was how her new gown looked, or if her father would take her riding. It had never occurred to her before how easily and swiftly fortunes could be turned.

The fact she was living comfortably with generous people brought home to her there could have been a far worse alternative. In fact, had Master Devereux expected her to work as a serving girl in his inn, she would have been in no position to complain. The thought made her shiver.

* * *

On Celia's wedding day, Helena and Phebe dressed in identically styled gowns. Phebe made the process considerably tiresome by insisting the design did not suit her. However when Chloe weaved sprays of rosemary and bay dipped in scented water into her curls, Phebe caught sight of herself in the long glass, and her features softened. "We look like wood nymphs," she declared, smiling for the first time that day.

Lambtons was hung with ribbons, branches, hothouse blossoms and wildflowers like an enchanted garden. Helena wandered through the halls admiring it all as serving men and girls bustled around like insects amongst the blooms in response to Adella's shrill orders.

Adella appeared for the ceremony late, attired in a fuchsia silk gown, her still youthful face painted and patched like a courtier. Helena could not help admiring her ability to make a grand entrance as she glided past all the guests to take her place beside Robert. The invited guests thronged the main dining hall, while the taproom regulars peered in at the windows to wish the bride happy.

Ralf wore nut-brown velvet, sumptuously embroidered with leaves and spring buds to match the season and complementing the design picked out on Celia's cream bodice. Ralf stood only slightly taller than Celia, looking young and nervous, despite being eight years her senior, with gentle eyes and boyish, clear skin. His ebony wig did not suit his pale coloring; although his clothes were expensive and well made.

After the ceremony, the principal guests surged forward to shake hands with the happy couple to show approval for an alliance well forged, congratulating themselves for the part they played.

Helena enjoyed her role and chattered to each guest dutifully as they devoured the elaborately prepared supper: roasted meats, savory pies and pasties, puddings and sallets, with apple pies and cheeses, nuts and fruit, together with the excellent wines, ales and spirits Robert had been stockpiling for weeks for the occasion.

The light began to fade. The wedding party trooped noisily to the newlywed couple's chamber to prepare for the bedding ceremony. Celia stood shyly in her negligee as a loud knocking came at the door and a male voice called, "Ho Madame, let us in. We have a groom to put to bed!" The door flew open, and a group of young men crowded the room, pulling a blushing Ralf after them.

Celia's garters were of the finest blue silk. "They shall be worn on the bridemen's hats for weeks afterward and I shall not have anyone say my girls wear cheap ribbon." Adella declared. She also made a point of untying them before the men arrived. "We cannot have young men hunting disrespectfully beneath your skirt, Celia."

Helena joined the festive group as the bridemen removed Celia's garters and the riotous process of tying them to the men's hats followed, hampered by the copious amounts of wine everyone had consumed.

There followed loud and suggestive toasting, mostly at the groom's expense, then a blushing Celia and self conscious Ralf clambered onto the canopied bed with as much modesty as they were able, when it stood three feet from the floor. Celia smiled coyly, and Ralf looked proud as Phebe and Helena took up positions at the bottom of the bed, each clutching one of Ralf's stockings.

"Why are we doing this again?" Helena whispered to Phebe.

Phebe rolled her eyes, obviously scornful of the entire process. "Tradition states that if one of the stockings lands on one or both of them, the thrower will be married within the twelvemonth."

Helena gave the superstition no credence, but was happy to join in the general hilarity. On an indiscrete cue from Adella, the stockings flew through the air accompanied by tipsy cheers. Helena's draped itself across Celia's face, but Phebe threw hers short, offering a mock innocent shrug in response to her mother's exasperated scowl.

When the ritual was reversed, the bridemen had to conduct the throwing of the bride's stockings. The procedure was a good deal noisier. Henry toppled over as he threw, drawing rowdy laughter and clapping as the stocking slid to the floor.

William, looking handsome in navy blue silk, led his group of inebriated young men to even more raucous behavior, teasing the bride and making lewd suggestions to the groom. To Helena's admiration, Ralf clapped for silence and, nightshirt notwithstanding, firmly ordered everyone out.

Loud groans of dismay followed, but the mob complied, emerging onto the landing flushed and laughing. Helena stood to one side, pausing to catch her breath as the guests surged past her down the stairs. Easing her shoulders luxuriously, she stretched her neck to release tense muscles, at the same time taking care not to disturb her elaborate coiffure.

She sensed rather than saw a movement on the periphery of her vision, and turned to see a young man step from the shadows to lean nonchalantly against the wall, blatantly observing her. He wore a wine colored suit, with polished gilt buttons and a white silk cravat. Wigless, his brown hair was tied back and an enigmatic smile pulled at his lips, his arms folded over a broad chest.

The first thought that came into her head was he waited for her. Then she dismissed it, certain they had not met before. To the accompaniment of the wedding guests laughing and calling to one another all the way down the stairs, they stood scrutinizing one another.

Her admirer smiled, pushing himself away from the wall to join her at the balustrade. His calm appraisal gave her a surge of confidence, and she returned his scrutiny with a bold stare. She raised a hand to the rail, knowing the pose showed her off to advantage. "I don't believe we have been introduced, sir."

He was taller than she, even in her heeled shoes-an agreeable quality in any man. He was handsome certainly; his face possessing a strong symmetry with penetrating brown eyes beneath well-shaped brows. There was a firm masculinity about him in the set of his shoulders, the way he stood, as if he was not expecting attention, but commanded it.

He responded in a soft, measured voice, "Actually, the bridegroom performed that ritual earlier." His gaze held reproach.

"Sir, I-I am not aware..." she stammered, feigning embarrassment. Even Phebe could not have dissembled so well. Helena found it not at all unpleasant being the object of his attention, and when she realized her gaze traced his lips and had come to a halt on a tiny dimple on his chin, she felt her face grow warm and looked away.

"I have accepted the slight, and shall have to learn to live with it." He gave a mock sigh, the corner of his mouth twitching.

"Forgive me, sir, I have had duties to perform today." She glanced down at her gown for emphasis. "However, as there is no one present to do so for a second time." She glanced round at the deserted landing. "I am-"

"I know who you are. It is I who has been overlooked, remember? Guy Palmer, at your service." He made her a slow and elegant leg, which would have done justice to any courtier. "I am a goldsmith banker, like my friend Ralf; although he has the advantage of a late, great uncle to accelerate his way in the world."

Helena detected a cynical note in his voice; but it disappeared quickly. "I, on the other hand, shall have to work a little harder, in a less salubrious part of Hatton Garden to catch up."

"Do you resent the circumstances which separate you, Master Palmer?" Having become aware of the inequality of the world, Helena was intrigued as to how these differences affected lives.

"Not at all, one could never resent Ralf, he is a dear fellow."

"I am sure you will do admirably," Helena said. "Even without the uncle."

"I intend to." His lips curved but there was no smile in his eyes. "And I do in fact have an uncle, but he is very much alive."

Helena grinned, pretending to study the closed doors of the ground floor salon, from where muffled sounds of noisy revels drifted out.

"Ralf deserves happiness, and by the acquisition of a presentable wife and companion, his life is sure to be enhanced in every way."

Helena bridled. "You know the bride well, sir?"

He looked sheepish. "Truthfully, I have spoken to the lady but once." He held up a hand in mitigation. "However, today I have had the opportunity to observe her physical attributes for myself, and like to count myself among the confirmed admirers of Mistress Maurice."

"You make her sound like a horse instead of an ideal wife." Helena laughed, throwing back her head.

"Both should be assessed carefully and with an eye to the long term," he replied, his gaze never leaving her face.

"Indeed? Like a financial investment?"

"Ah, I see you understand me perfectly." He met Helena's indignant surprise with a broad smile. "Finance is a subject at which I am particularly astute."

Helena accepted his proffered arm, allowing him to escort her back to the party.

"Master Palmer, when you said before you knew who I was-"

"You are Mistress Helena Woulfe, the daughter of Sir Jonathan Woulfe, a fugitive Rebel wanted by the Crown."

Helena came to an abrupt halt on the staircase, turning a nervous gaze on her companion. With some relief she saw his expression was sympathetic. 'He knows who I am, and yet he appears to have sought me out.'

"I know what it is to have embarrassing relatives."

"Embarrassing?"

He winced at her expression. "A bad choice of words, do forgive me. I was trying to reassure you, we are none of us untouched by the precarious times in which we live."

"I appreciate your diplomacy, Master Palmer, if that was your intention. But I will never regard my family as 'an embarrassment'. High principled, courageous, even misguided, but never embarrassing."

"Your loyalty does you credit, Mistress Woulfe. It is an admirable quality to disagree with someone's actions, and yet remain their champion."

"What makes you think I don't agree?" She tapped her fan against her lips.

Helena watched the pupils of his eyes expanding into black circles as he appeared to search for the appropriate response, and failed. The hallway glittered with a bank of candles along the walls and the liveried footmen standing at attention by the doors. She found herself enjoying the effect she was having on him and their reflection in the wall mirrors showed what an attractive couple they made. Helena slowed her steps to drag out the moment, and then frowned as something occurred to her. "Palmer. That name sounds familiar."

Her companion inclined his head. "Barbara Palmer is my aunt."

At Helena's frown he went on, "She is the Countess of Southampton, and Duchess of Cleveland, mistress of the late Charles II and mother of six of his children," he recited. "It may have been less, due to there being considerable doubt about two of them."

"Do you know her well?" Helena asked, intrigued.

Her companion shrugged. "Hardly at all I am afraid, we are related by marriage. Her husband, Roger Palmer is an uncle, but their marriage was brief, and not a success."

"How could it be?" Helena knew she sounded cynical. "With a king for a rival."

He inclined his head in agreement. "Besides, the lady, and I use the term purely in respect of her title, lives in Paris and has done for the last ten years, since the king turned her off."

Helena had a vague recollection of her parents mentioning the Duchess had converted to Catholicism, but the ploy proved ineffective, as King Charles used the Test Act as an excuse to have her removed from court.

"Are you are a Catholic yourself, Master Palmer?" Helena asked, unaccountably relieved when he responded in the negative.

When they paused outside the door to the party, Helena found herself reluctant to cut short their conversation. "She was reputed to be very beautiful."

"At one time, certainly; however, she is no longer young and has always had a vast appetite for money, and er . . . other things."

Helena did not know whether to look shocked or impressed.

"She returned to England when the old king died, I believe. Probably hoping he had remembered her in his will."

Helena threw back her head and laughed. How different he was from the affected, self-seeking — what was the word Phebe used, 'fops?' — who sought her attention on a daily basis. He was also different to William, whose first instinct when he passed a looking glass would be to look at himself. Whereas, when they reached a mirror, Master Palmer had looked at her reflection.

Should her father return to England when the crisis ended, perhaps . . . She checked herself, we have only just this moment met.

A stiff-backed servant opened the door to the dining hall as a wave of high-pitched female laughter assailed them, together with the oppressive heat and fragrance of sixty warm, confined bodies.

Her new acquaintance bowed her into the room, and then both were claimed by opposite factions. A group of young men clamored around Master Palmer, while Phebe dragged Helena in the direction of the supper table. When she scanned the faces around her a little later, Master Palmer was nowhere in sight.

"He is quite attractive isn't he?" Phebe whispered.

Helena started. "What did you say?"

"Master Palmer, I saw you talking to him."

"Do you know him?"

"Ralf has spoken of him. He is another goldsmith." She shrugged, as if dismissing them as a species. "Handsome enough, but rather serious." Then her eyes flashed. "He has a notorious aunt though, try to guess who she is!"

"I couldn't possibly!" Helena pretended to be offended, watching Phebe's face fall.

There was no opportunity to search out Master Palmer during the rest of the evening, but Helena was confident this would not be an isolated encounter.

CHAPTER TWENTY FIVE

Helena greeted Robert in the salon where the family gathered and took a seat near him. He resembled an eastern Pasha in his saffron yellow silk banyan, having replaced his periwig with a cotton cap.

Adella offered wine, but Helena declined in favor of sweet lemonade as she was feeling the heat. Robert, she knew, also found the city in summer unbearable and looked forward to a quiet evening away from the stifling clatter of the public rooms.

Helena was surprised and pleased to see William lounging on a sofa, then turned to greet Guy, whom she was less surprised to see but was almost as delighted.

Robert picked up his copy of the London Gazette. "I see that due to the unseasonable cold and wet at the beginning of June, the king's troops encamped on Hounslow Heath packed up their tents and retired to quarters. Standing army indeed."

He picked up a clay pipe and looked about for a taper, when Helena saw Adella glare at him disapprovingly. Instead, he fingered the bowl without lighting it, holding it in his hand and stroking it as if drawing comfort from its smooth feel.

Despite Adella's hatred of fresh air, the rear door to the garden stood open to encourage a cool breeze into the room, bringing with it a tang of the city. Helena exchanged polite conversation with Guy, and from the corner of her eye she watched Phebe wander over to William, who sat writing at the table by the window, his back turned on the company. He shielded his writing with a well-placed arm as she approached, simultaneously taking a sip from a nearby wine glass.

"I declare, Will, why cannot I see?" Phebe stamped her foot, her voice petulant. "I'll wager you are composing poetry to some lady you saw across the 'Change and liked the look of."

Helena caught his blush of guilty annoyance as he waved Phebe away, his gaze swiveling to Helena, who dropped her gaze and pretended she did not notice.

Beside her, Guy fidgeted in the heat, occasionally running a finger round the inside of his cravat. Helena flicked her fan back and forth, grateful she had put on muslin that morning, her hair wound into curls brushed off her neck. She caught Robert looking at her, and making an excuse to Guy, rose and strode toward him.

"Did you wish to speak to me?" She lowered herself beside him. When he gave a surprised start, she congratulated herself on her ability to judge his moods.

He removed the stem of the unlit pipe from his mouth. "I was simply wondering, my dear. With my elder daughter settled, and my youngest baulking me at every turn if I so much as mention the subject." He gave an expressive shrug. "What are your own feelings on the subject of marriage?"

Helena brought her fan up to her face to hide the blush she felt sure must be there. "I think it is a very agreeable institution." She flicked her gaze first at William, then across to where Guy sat talking to Adella.

"And what, may I ask, are your feelings on taking a husband?"

"Why, I had not thought, sir." She smiled at him over her fan.

"Nonsense." Robert removed his pipe and pointed it Guy's direction. "That young man has been hanging around for weeks."

Helena did not turn her head, keenly aware both young men must know one of them was being discussed.

"My dear," Robert leaned in close to whisper, "despite Guy Palmer's grasp of financial matters, which is admirable, he does not call to see me."

"He does not?" Helena stopped smiling. "I would value your opinion of him, sir."

"He is an excellent young man, from a respectable family and with a good head for business."

"Respectable? Even his aunt by marriage?"

"Oh, especially her."

Their spontaneous laughter drew all eyes toward them. Adella lifted an inquiring eyebrow, but Robert did not react. Helena speculated he would be required to elucidate for her later.

Robert refilled his wine glass from a decanter on a side table, holding it out to Helena, who declined. "He has a thriving business of his own," Robert pointed out. "Which I am well positioned to promote. Although to his credit, he has not even hinted this has occurred to him."

"It is almost as if you had chosen him for me yourself, sir."

At that moment, William looked up and caught her eye; the intense look he gave her apparently not lost on Robert, who swiveled his head slowly toward Helena with a look of enquiry.

Helena feigned innocence. It would not do to let Robert think she toyed with his son's affections while she treated Guy as a serious suitor. Robert gave a small cough and leaned toward her conspiratorially. "Had I taken against Master Palmer, my dear, he would not still be calling. I thought to see how things are with you on the subject, so I may know how to respond when he offers for you."

"When?"

"Assuredly when. Helena you are becoming quite the coquette."

"Master Devereux?" she began. "If. . .when. . .Master Palmer should offer for me, would it be necessary for you to ask my brother's permission?"

He stared at her, confused. "I don't profess to understand your reasons, my dear, but if you would prefer, there is no need for me to write to Aaron. I am your guardian until he returns to England."

"I would prefer it." She kept her voice firm.

"As you wish." For a moment he looked as if he was about to request she explain herself, so with a curt nod, she left him.

Adella poured lemonade for the ladies. "Henry called this morning." She handed Helena a glass. "He is still upset about Compton's suspension."

Helena laughed. "Henry's concern for the Bishop is focused on how long the work will be held up on St Paul's." She sipped the concoction delicately.

Robert waved his pipe to attract their attention. "It appears the man refused to discipline one of his clergy for preaching anti papist sermons. This had so enraged the king, he was suspended."

"Compton will be back in favor again soon." Adella sounded confident. "The king himself wants the cathedral finished."

"King James is a stubborn man." William slid his writing into a drawer of the bureau and locked it before walking toward them, his hands held loosely behind his back. Helena watched his approach with admiration. The heat did not seem to affect him at all. His clothes were unwrinkled and immaculate as ever, whereas poor Guy was almost wilting beside her. "He wants to allow dons and undergraduates at Oxford and Cambridge to be worshiping Catholics."

"Where did you hear that?" Adella's tone held skepticism.

"At The Grecian." William plucked fluff from his sleeve. "He argues that the colleges were founded when England was a Catholic country, and should therefore be available to Catholics."

Robert lifted his copy of the Gazette. "See here. Sir Edward Hales has been acquitted for holding office in the Army, despite him being a Papist."

William turned from his position at the window, a smile on his face. "The king packed the court with judges who hold his own opinions. Lord Chief Justice Herbert decreed the king was an absolute sovereign, and the laws of England were the king's laws. The verdict was a foregone conclusion."

"Have you read this newssheet before me?" Robert waved the pages at him.

William grinned. "Not all my knowledge is gleaned from the same source."

Robert glared at him and carried on reading. "Halifax was dismissed for daring to say it was illegal to employ Catholics in the Army." He clamped his teeth down on his pipe so hard, it broke off in his mouth. He spat the pieces out and hurled them into the hearth. "The king is making Parliament irrelevant."

William smiled. "Halifax is too clever for him. He is determined the king won't repeal the Test Act."

Robert jabbed a finger at the newssheet. "But another four judges who objected to the repeal of the Test have been sacked."

"I think you will find Parliament will hold out against the king on that issue, sir," Guy assured him.

"What? Oh yes, I suppose you are right," Robert mumbled, though Helena thought he seemed unconvinced.

Helena turned her head to study Guy's profile, impressed with his knowledge and confidence. Robert's earlier words played again. He might teach her a great deal, if he was her husband.

Guy Palmer had become such a familiar face at Lambtons, Helena discovered that to avoid him successfully would have meant her virtual exile from her own home. Yet strangely, when he did not call, she missed him.

Respectful and engaging, he had the ability to judge her mood correctly, so when she felt uncommunicative, he happily chatted to others, bestowing gentle smiles on her from a distance. She had to acknowledge Robert was right, he would make an excellent companion.

William had resumed his seat and was twisting one hand back and forth, studying the way the light caught his emerald ring. She consigned him to the back of her mind. So handsome, a pity he is such a fop.

"Have you heard from your brother lately, Helena?" Robert asked.

Helena brought to mind Aaron's most recent letter. "Yes, sir. He still plots with the Prince of Orange, although he appears to be living well in The Hague."

"He does? Do tell us," Phebe slid along the sofa toward her, her face eager.

"It appears he has purchased a house, which he has thrown open to other fugitives, so they may spend their days in scheming and leisure."

"I almost envy him." William laughed.

Guy arched an eyebrow at her, but Helena refused to apologize if that was what he expected. Her resentment at the fact both her brothers had left her to fend for herself in a world where men made all the decisions still roused her to anger.

The fact her future hung on the good nature of whomever she married, was a truth she found difficult to reconcile herself to. She bestowed her most devastating smile on Guy, who blushed self consciously. She was fond of him, and if marriage was the only way she could regain her status in life, then marry she would.

If Robert was right and Guy declared himself, then she would accept him and put herself out of the influence of both Aaron and Henry. Even if her father should return, he could not overrule the wishes of a husband. She knew those around her were convinced Sir Jonathan Woulfe was dead and despite herself, she was beginning to believe it too.

She glanced at William, who had turned back to his letter. Let him write all the silly verses he wants, he will regret it when I am married.

* * *

Henry accepted an invitation to take a glass of claret with Master Newman in his private sanctum in Charles Street; a small room at the front of the house strewn with maps, plans, lists of building materials, pens tools and miscellaneous cartons piled up in one corner. It was totally different from the rest of the immaculate house where his wife and daughters held court, Master Newman cherished his privacy and Henry appreciated being invited to join him there.

"Is this a special occasion, if I may ask?" Henry accepted the full glass happily. He hadn't been asked to sit, so he leaned against the desk to study a plan of a church lying near his hand.

"Ask away, my boy, ask away." Francis Newman grinned as he poured. "Mistress Newman and I are celebrating a forthcoming marriage." Henry took an appreciate gulp of his wine, not anticipating Newman's next words. "My beautiful daughter is to become a bride!"

A knot of dread descended onto Henry's chest, hovered there and slowly expanded. "You er . . . have five beautiful daughters," Henry stammered, the drawing forgotten. "To which of them are you referring?"

Master Newman guffawed. "Well, with two of them well below marriageable age, one still in the schoolroom and the other not prepossessing enough to attract any young man's fancy." He paused at Henry's startled look. "Although, I dislike being unkind to Margaret, I think you can rightly guess which one is to be the fortunate young miss."

Henry set his glass aside shakily, eliciting an enquiring look from his host.

"Not to your taste?" Newman asked, surprised.

"It is excellent, sir, but I have the headache and don't wish to worsen it. Allow me to congratulate you on your news." He knew his hopes were about to be crushed, but a kind of perverseness rooted him to the spot as he waited for the damning words to be spoken.

Newman frowned. "I am sorry, Henry, I had no idea. You must retire and get some sleep. But before you go, I must tell you that Sir Joshua Holt has offered for my Mary Ann. They are to be married in two months. Is that not excellent news?"

The blood in Henry's ears roared and his mouth opened and closed like a fish. Was it possible his employer did not see how this 'news' affected him? Or did he know all along how he felt about Mary Ann, and this was his way of ensuring Henry never declared himself?

Henry recovered the ability to speak. "I-I don't believe I know the gentleman."

"He is extremely wealthy." Newman's eyes glowed in appreciation. "There is an estate in Hertfordshire which runs to three thousand acres, not to mention a fine town house with at least fifty servants. He has a nephew." This was said almost regretfully. "Who will inherit, as the estate is entailed, but the portion he is settling upon Mary Ann is . . . oh well, perhaps I should not dwell upon it." He gave a sheepish grin. "Suffice it to say, he is a fine match for my girl, and it is a great honor he offered for her."

A dense fog wrapped itself around Henry's senses, but Newman ploughed on. "He is somewhat older than she is." He looked abashed, then a smile twitched at the corner of his mouth. "Actually, he is thirty years older, but what does it signify if he gives my girl a place in society?"

Thirty years! Henry fought to keep his face impassive. The man was a little older than Newman himself. How could he give his beautiful Mary Ann to an ageing lecher, no matter how wealthy and respected he might be? He shook the thought away, realizing how ridiculous that was; were not wealth and society were what mattered to everyone?

To discover he was not penniless and alone after the Rebellion had made a world of difference to Henry. To have at least some of his father's wealth at his disposal, was what enabled him to be where he was: in Master Newman's drawing room, dressed in a gentleman's clothes and drinking a gentleman's wine. It was wealth and society, which would allow him to fulfill his dream and become an architect, visit rich men's homes as an equal and enjoy their society.

For Mary Ann, the question was far simpler. She belonged to her father, to be given in marriage by him, to a man who could provide for her and offer her respectability.

"And Mistress M-Mary Ann, is she agreeable to this match, sir?" Henry hardly recognized the sound of his own voice as he stumbled over her name, but Newman appeared oblivious to his discomfort.

"Eh?" he asked distracted. "Oh, I have not yet informed her of her good fortune, but I don't expect anything but submissive gratitude from that quarter."

Newman paused in thought, the wine pitcher still clutched in his hand. "I admit, I have heard disturbing tales from other fathers whose daughters have given them all manner of difficulties over the subject of marriage. Praise be, I have a dutiful child, who would never go against me or her mother."

Newman topped up their glasses. Henry left his on the table, fearing he would choke. His host was right, she was a dutiful daughter, who adored both her parents and would offer no objections. Mary Ann was lost to him.

The thought of her married to another man was physically painful to Henry, who knew he could do nothing but accept the situation. His immediate problem was to get out of the room before his feelings showed on his face. Pleading his worsening headache as an excuse to cut short the conversation, Henry offered his congratulations stoically.

He lit a candle at the bottom of the stairs and dragged himself up to the second floor. It was late, and apart from his host, the rest of the household slept. As he rounded the corner leading to his room, he felt rather than saw her.

"Henry?" He could tell by that one, choked word she had been crying. Mary Ann detached herself from the shadows, the yellow glow of his candle throwing her face into sharp relief. Her eyes were red-rimmed and she gave a sad sniff, yet she was still the loveliest thing he had ever seen.

"Henry," she sobbed. "The most horrible thing has happened."

He sighed. "Your father said you had not yet been told."

"You know?" At Henry's nod, she gave a tiny moan. "Mother told me." She wiped her eyes with a kerchief. "She imagined I would be overjoyed, and swore me to secrecy." She took a step toward him and burst into fresh tears.

The floor creaked under their combined weight and with a furtive glance down the darkened corridor, Henry ushered her into his room, closing the door firmly behind them. Mary Ann leaned against the doorpost, wilting as if her knees were giving way.

"What are we to do?" Her eyes were pleading.

Henry placed the guttering candle on the low windowsill, where it stilled, and glowed brighter. His face reflected in the glass above it looked drawn, his eyes large as he stared at the shadowy rooftops reaching away into the darkness.

Mary Ann came to his side on a rustle of taffeta, grasping his arm with both hands. "I don't want to marry him. I won't marry him, I-"

"Yes, Mary Ann, you will," Henry's voice was almost cold. He didn't move, nor could he look at her. He felt he would break into a thousand pieces if he tried.

She gasped, the kerchief pressed against her mouth. "You want me to?"

"No!" He burst out in a harsh growl as he turned toward her. Her distraught face was like a knife twisting in his stomach. He lifted his arms with a sob. Mary Ann collapsed against him.

"I could refuse." She lifted her face, eyes full of unshed tears.

"And tell your parents you wish to marry me? The consequences would be devastating." She opened her mouth to speak.

He pressed the tips of his fingers against her lips. "Not just for us, but for our families too."

She stared at him, horrified, large tears spilled on her cheeks.

"Your Father would discharge me from my apprenticeship, and no architect would agree to continue my training," the truth of his own words tore at him. "Aaron would cut me off from my allowance and my father's business. I feel Helena may accept us, but she is in no position to offer practical help. We would have nothing."

"But Henry," she wailed.

He held her away from him, his hands gripping her upper arms as he willed her to understand. "Do you have any idea what it would be like, to be penniless and with no friends? She shook her head, the wispy curls at her temple bobbing. "Well, I saw what my future held without those things. Even if I could stand such a life for myself, I could never do that to you. Eventually, you would hate me for it."

"I could never hate you, Henry."

"We would be shunned, Mary Ann, and how could you bear never to see your mother, or any of your sisters again? Apart from you, Helena and Aaron are all I have. I cannot lose them." He bit his lip, this throat almost closed with pain as she collapsed into his arms, defeated. His eyes stung with hot tears as he realized what he said made sense to her.

"How stupid of me to think we could. . . Oh, Henry what are we going to do?"

"There is nothing we can do," he whispered into her hair.

They clung together in the gloom of Henry's attic room, making oaths and promises to help each other through the future they would spend apart. As the night deepened and their loss became real, they separated, painfully, with fresh tears on both sides.

Henry spent the rest of that night in wakeful misery, imagining Mary Ann crying herself to sleep in the room below his. For the first time since his apprenticeship began, he was not looking forward to the morning.

CHAPTER TWENTY SIX

Guy Palmer entered the sumptuous entrance hall of Lambtons. Taking a deep breath, he instructed a footman to inform Master Devereux of his arrival. The man scurried away and while he waited, Guy stepped in front of one of the long mirrors in the entrance to check his appearance.

Someone tapped him on the shoulder and Guy jumped, turning to come face to face with a grinning Phebe.

"You are looking exceedingly fine today, Master Palmer." With her hands clasped behind her back, she rotated on her heels, a mischievous grin on her face.

Guy made a leg, inclining his head. She was the last person he had wanted to see at that moment. "It is kind of you to say so, Mistress." He prayed for rescue before her questioning began.

He had approached the task he had set himself that morning as he did every other in his life, with meticulous planning, and an escape route if the fates interfered to his disadvantage. He glanced toward the door of Robert's private study, willing the man to appear.

"I could take you to Helena if you wish," Phebe offered.

"Err . . ." he faltered, dismayed. Guy had not prepared a response to this suggestion and searched his brain for an acceptable excuse. To his relief, Robert arrived and bore him away.

Orphaned at the age of ten, Guy spent an insular childhood, brought up by his father's younger brother, a confirmed bachelor with a penchant for exotic travel. Left in the care of a parade of semi-neglectful tutors and housekeepers, he had been quite young when realization dawned that if he wanted something, success at acquiring it lay entirely in his own hands.

His life plan included a family, and as soon as he saw Helena Woulfe, he knew she was the kind of wife he required. He went about winning her with persistence and determination. Calling assiduously at Lambtons several times a week, he found himself looking forward to these visits more and more, his step growing lighter as he approached the inn door. Every time Helena walked into the room and smiled her beautiful, slow smile, he felt an overwhelming rush of pleasure.

It came as some surprise to him to discover, that during his careful courtship, he had fallen in love. At first, these unpredictable feelings disconcerted him, but as his obsession invaded every aspect of his life and thoughts, he searched for her face in every company, bereft if she did not appear.

When he emerged from Robert's study, the older man's arm rested round Guy's shoulder. Conscious his face held a nervous grimacGuy disengaged himself from Robert's embrace and went in search of Helena. He discovered her in the kitchen parlour in animated conversation with Lubbock.

Assisted, he felt sure, by Phebe, the Lambtons' grapevine was evidently in good order that morning. Lubbock diplomatically melted away as he offered his compliments, witnessed by a gaggle of serving girls who peered round the kitchen door, wring.

Helena greeted him cordially, making no move from her comfortable chair, leaving Guy little choice but to perch on the wooden bench opposite. It occurred to him that she always received him in the same way, with mild surprise, as if she had no expectation of seeing him.

After a stilted exchange about her health, and that of her two brothers, his discomfort became evident even to her. With a concerned frown, she asked him if he would like a soothing drink.

"Thank you, no. But I have something to ask you, which I am not finding sy. May I ask you to put down that book and give me your attention?"

She lifted her gaze to his face, startled, dropping the offending article with a small thump. He was horrified for a moment that he had miscalculated; that what he was about to say might be unwelcome. He swallowed, and shifted position on the bench. He had come too far to dissemble now.

"Helena." He savored her name on his tongue. "Would you do me the honor of marrying me?"

Her eyes widened but she recovered quickly; disappointing him by not exhibiting the breathless excitement such an offer was supposed to elicit. Nor was there any sign of discomposure or even a feminine blush. In fact when she did speak, her words were so unexpected, he had to ask her to repeat them.

"I asked, Master Palmer, why do you wish to be married to me?"

Guy uttered the first thing that came to mind. "Why would any young man not want you for a wife?"

Strangely, she did not receive his reply quite as he expected.

"A pretty compliment, sir." She inclined her head, her beautiful eyes pulling him into their depths. "But why do you wish it?"

Guy faltered. "Well...Well, I feel we would make a good marriage as we have a great deal in common."

"Such as?"

"I-I have no living parents, yet I am financially sound." He swallowed, knowing instinctively that this was the wrong thing to say, but it was too late to retract.

Helena's eyes glinted. "Are you saying orphans should marry each other so as not to contaminate society?"

"Not at all," he blustered, genuinely distressed she had misunderstood. "I have grown to appreciate your many qualities, made evident in the way you have conducted yourself since-"

"I know what you mean, Master Palmer." She held up a hand to silence his clumsy explanation. "I asked, because I am curious to know if there is any emotional attachment to your offer."

He blinked, opened his mouth, and then closed it again.

"Oh, no matter." This time a blush did appear. "I am not making myself clear." She began fiddling with the fastener on the journal close to her hand.

Guy bridled, insulted. "Do you imagine I would seek a marriage with someone I did not feel affection for?" His voice was sharper than he intended.

Helena lifted her chin. "I don't know you well enough to make such a judgment."

He leaned forward to place his forearms on his splayed knees to look into her face. "Has it occurred to you, Helena, I have no idea what your feelings are either?"

At the faint pink blush appearing on her cheeks, Guy's nerves disappeared and he felt equal to the task he had set himself. "I am no courtier, and you are not a duchess. Perhaps we are expecting too much of each other."

A small frown appeared, creasing her brow. He reached forward to smooth it away with a caressing finger. She did not shy away from his touch, but gave a coy smile.

The brief contact gave him courage. "Helena, I would not have called upon you so diligently these last weeks, had there been no emotion on my part." He tried to interpret her look. Was it relief? He could not tell.

"You have been very attentive, Master Palmer, but you have never . . ." She left the sentence hanging.

"Professed my undying devotion?" He inclined his head, arching one eyebrow. *Is that what she wants of me? I can certainly give her that.*

"You could profess a little," she wheedled.

He found himself warming to Helena the coquette; not a role she played with him, yet he had seen her behave so with William. It made her seem vulnerable somehow, more in need of him. And he wanted her to need him.

He summoned his next words from a dry mouth, his voice soft with emotion. "I love you Mistress Woulfe, and you will never have reason to doubt my devotion."

Impulsively, he reached across the table to take her hand. She allowed her long, slender fingers to rest in his quite naturally. "When I first saw you at Ralf and Celia's wedding I believe I felt then we would marry." He laughed self-consciously as he absently massaged her thumb. "I even toyed with the idea of asking you that night."

"I might have refused you, then," she teased.

"Does that mean you are not refusing me now?"

Her eyes flashed. "I have forgotten the question."

"Are those serving girls still watching from the kitchen?" Guy asked, without turning his head.

Helena shifted in her seat to look past his shoulder. She nodded, a smile tugging at her mouth.

Guy gave a slow, thoughtful nod, then without lowering his voice, he repeated his proposal. "I asked, Mistress Woulfe, for your hand in marriage."

A ripple of sighs and giggles erupted from behind them.

"I accept your offer, Master Palmer." Helena held his gaze. Then a slow smile blossomed on her face, surprising him at how genuinely delighted she looked.

The mischief in her eyes lit a tiny flame of anger, and he could not help the words tumbling out. "Helena, I have been dreading and anticipating this moment since we met." He swallowed. "I sincerely hope that laying bare my feelings and hopes for the future have been more than a source of amusement to you."

She stared at the floor, her deep blush indicating she was embarrassed. The thought reassured him and when she looked up, her voice was soft, almost pleading, "There are very few times in a girl's life, Master Palmer, when she has the advantage of a handsome gentleman. Surely you would not condemn me for making the most of it?"

Guy sighed, lost to her loveliness. She had the most compelling eyes, sometimes of darkest blue, then slate, like a winter sea with yellow lights in them. His heart soared. "You are forgiven for teasing me. May I inform your guardian we are formally engaged?"

She hesitated. "Yes...you may. If that is what is expected."

Her eyes darkened with a look that Guy did not understand. He decided it was unimportant, what mattered with his objective was satisfactorily accomplished, and he could not be happier.

He strode across the hall in search of Robert, when it occurred to him that he had merely pressed Helena's hand warmly before leaving the room. He gave an inward shrug; as a maiden she probably expected nothing more.

* * *

The cooks chivvied the kitchen girls back to their work and Lubbock had not reappeared. Helena found herself alone and mildly deflated; the interview having not gone quite as she planned. She had fully intended to exploit Guy's discomfort, evident the moment he sat down on the hard bench.

However, the balance of power had shifted at some point in their exchange and Guy had taken control. Perhaps that's as it should be, what woman wants a husband she can bully?

Listening to the familiar kitchen noises in the background, Helena wondered what she was supposed to do. She fingered her journal; toying with the idea of recording the fact she was going to become Mistress Palmer. Like Lady Castlemaine. She chuckled to herself, wondering what Aaron would say about that.

A small knot settled beneath her breastbone that her parents would not see her married. He may not be what you would choose, she addressed them in her head. He has no lands, nor does he have a fortune, but with my dowry and his abilities, we shall neither of us want for anything. She fingered the fastener of the journal nervously, praying she could trust her own judgment.

Then there was Aaron, whose letters took the form of political and religious tracts, with appended instructions about how she and Henry were to conduct themselves in his absence. She dismissed him. He would be glad to have me off his hands.

She was disappointed about Henry, who, instead of relying on her to provide a home for him, was forging his own future. She consoled herself he would welcome another fireside to visit, and a table to eat at during his free evenings.

The prospect of having her own household was a heady one, no matter that it would not be grand, like the refurbished Saffron Hill property Ralf had provided for Celia. She glanced round the snug room where she sat, wondering if she too might have Dutch plates arranged in a rack on the wall, like the housekeeper. She snapped the journal shut.

Helena started at the sound of Phebe's voice behind her. "Whatever are you doing sitting here all alone, Helena?" She stood with her hands on her hips. "You must join the family and tell them you are a betrothed woman." Her eyes twinkled with amusement.

"Did Guy tell you?" Helena laughed, rising from her chair. "Or your father?"

Phebe smirked. "It was Lubbock. He has been hovering at doors all morning hoping to be the first to spread the good news."

"Ah! A far more reliable source." Helena brushed down her skirt.

"Are you happy, Helena?" Phebe asked, as they crossed the hallway with their arms linked.

"What a strange question." Helena looked at her askance. "I have received, and accepted a proposal of marriage."

"Not so strange." Phebe's penetrating stare was like Adella's. "It depends on whether it was a rehearsal, or the real thing."

Helena gave a forced laugh and turned away. Phebe's clear-eyed scrutiny made her uncomfortable.

* * *

William ran into Lubbock in the dining hall, almost knocking him over. The servant recovered his balance well. For a heavy man, Lubbock was surprisingly agile.

"Do you happen to know the whereabouts of my Father, Lubbock?" William asked, rearranging his coat.

"Why, yes sir, they are all in the small dining hall, celebrating Mistress Helena's engagement to Master Palmer. Shall I inform them you will be joining them?"

William raised a hand as if to ward the man off. "Er . . . no. Should anyone ask, I shall be at Jonathan's this evening." Without waiting for Lubbock's bow and murmur of acquiescence, he pivoted on his heel and stumbled out into the street.

William had watched with mixed emotions as Helena received her suitor's attentions. His jealousy was a persistent irritation, but with no idea what to do about it, he took to absenting himself from Lambtons with increasing frequency.

His unease was exacerbated by the fact he liked Guy Palmer. Predisposed to find fault with him, he had discovered Guy to be a man with whom he could discuss goldsmithing in a way he felt unable to do with his father, to the extent he was considering the business for himself.

However, despite the man's excellent character and disposition, William knew in his soul, Guy Palmer wasn't right for beautiful, deep thinking, damaged Helena. Her closeted upbringing and the terrible losses she had experienced meant she was too much in need of exclusive and intense love, to enter into a 'suitable' marriage.

As for himself, he had no alternative to offer her. He liked his freethinking, aimless life too much to present himself as a serious suitor. Instead, as Palmer's courtship continued, he treated her with cool civility. He no longer sought her out for their private talks, even blatantly flirted with other women in front of her. And yet he found himself missing her.

He knew what Celia and Phebe thought about his attraction to Helena Woulfe, that he should marry her and make their comfortable little circle complete. Even Phebe was beginning to get over her inherent jealousy of Helena, yet William had no intention of falling into any romantic plans his sisters might make on his behalf. And they had those in abundance.

Distracted, William's aimless pace annoyed his fellow pedestrians and to display their impatience they jostled him, hard. He pushed back at the culprits, ignoring the protests and sour looks which came his way. When he had put some distance between himself and Lambtons, he paused to take a breath. Somehow the Navy didn't seem such a bad alternative after all.

* * *

That evening, Robert informed his patrons there was a celebration in the offing, aware they would throw themselves wholeheartedly into the festivities. With Helena and Guy as the principal guests, he encouraged them to embark on an extended bout of toasting and drinking.

He hardly noticed the time passing and before he knew it, the watch called eleven and the disconcerting figure of the constable checking for license breaching drinkers, appeared in the entrance.

"Now, Master Dev'ro," he intoned, bringing his painted staff of office down hard on the polished floor. "If ye don't want some 'o these fine gen'elmen spending a night in the Poultry Compter, I think ye should lock the doors."

"Master Cassidy," Robert greeted him affably, although he was the last person he wished to see inside Lambtons. "We are celebrating my ward's engagement," he ushered Helena forward to receive congratulations. "These here are all invited guests at a party," he lied, pleased when the constable accepted his proffered glass of wine happily enough.

Master Cassidy threatened to return if he saw the lights burning in half an hour, so Robert began ushering the guests out. The street filled with sounds of departing coaches, cries of good wishes and the slamming of doors as the inn settled down for the night.

A little later, Helena gave an annoyed groan when she saw her last remaining candle was guttering to a snub. She had dismissed a yawning Chloe, but did not wish to finish her toilette to an accompaniment of scratching from the rats in the skirting. She shrugged into a loose mantoe and slipped downstairs to the deserted hall to collect more candles from the box.

She had reached the first landing on her way back upstairs, when she heard footsteps coming down from the flight above. A low male voice murmured something, and a woman giggled in response, their voices growing louder as they drew nearer.

Helena smiled at the realization that someone had been entertaining a lady in one of the upper rooms. Then she gave a low groan, knowing they would walk past her and she wore only her nightclothes, with her hair undressed and flowing down her back. There was no time to cross the landing before they reached her, so she ducked back into an alcove to wait for them to pass.

The man was taller than the woman, and carried a lit candle, which suffused both their faces with a yellow glow. His other arm encircled the lady's waist and as they reached the landing, her head was tilted back as she laughed throatily into her companion's eyes in total infatuation.

As the couple turned the corner to descend the last flight of stairs, the man must have heard something and he looked over to the alcove where Helena stood. Helena froze as her gaze met William's, and held.

Surprise, then embarrassment crossed his features, and then with a curt nod, he turned away. The woman was too intent on her escort to notice Helena's presence, and as William swept her down the steps in front of him, he cast a lingering, almost disappointed look over his shoulder.

She stared him out, nursing a small triumph that he was more uncomfortable than she. When he was out of sight, she fled back to her room. Clicking the door shut as firmly as she could without slamming it, Helena hurled the candles across the room and launched herself onto the bed. He is a shallow, dissolute rake, with no thought for anyone but himself and his own pleasure.

"I was right about him all along," she muttered, punching her pillows into submission. The idea she might have considered William, for even the briefest of moments, as a prospective husband, made her burn with shame.

Helena heard the watch call two of the clock that night, her bed uncomfortably rumpled before she finally fell asleep.

CHAPTER TWENTY SEVEN

One particular sultry day in late July, and with Chloe in attendance, Helena visited the New Exchange. She liked wandering the stalls at her own pace, without having to listen to Phebe's constant prattle or wait for Adella, who would stop and chat to acquaintances every few yards.

With no parents on either side to make the arrangements on their behalf, Robert insisted their winter wedding would be held at Lambtons. Even with such a small celebration, there was still plenty of shopping to do.

Helena located the shoemaker Adella recommended on the upper concourse. The gentleman proprietor became particularly attentive when she mentioned the name of Devereux. He was a very tall, thin man who looked elongated, almost as if he might snap in the middle if pushed.

His peruke was the color of dirty ash and he kept dipping his head whenever he spoke. Helena might have been discouraged had she not spotted several pairs of exquisite heeled shoes with decorated lappets, which she almost bought there and then. She strode to the far side of the shop to examine his work more closely.

"Are they for a special occasion, Mistress?" he asked, bobbing forward.

"My Mistress is to be married," Chloe answered for her, blushing guiltily at Helena's annoyed frown.

"In that case, I insist I make them for you myself." His ferrety eyes sparkled and his face held such eager warmth, Helena felt disinclined to refuse him. He measured her feet with spidery fingers, scratching figures on a yellow piece of parchment. When she had chosen the exact shade she wanted, they spent a pleasant few minutes discussing whether to adorn them with buckles or ribbons, or even mother of pearl lozenges.

When the entire process was complete, he bowed her to the door again with repeated assurances. "I will have them delivered to Lambtons in a little over a sen'night, Mistress Woulfe."

Helena emerged from the shop feeling light hearted and with Chloe following behind balancing her packets of ribbons and trinkets; she stepped onto the balcony outside the shop. A man stood at a stall a little way along the concourse, in a brocade long coat and wearing a curly periwig. His dress was flamboyant, but no more so than any other city gentleman, He held a brown polished cane and leaned over a tray of men's' gloves held out for him by the stallholder.

Something about him struck a sharp memory and Helena paused mid-stride, its unexpectedness causing Chloe to collide with her.

"Oh, Mistress I do beg your pardon," Chloe righted herself. "Mistress, you have gone quite pale, whatever is-?"

Helena lifted a hand to waist level as a signal for silence, her eyes fixed on the man who was still studying the gloves and seemed unaware of her presence. Then something made him look sideways and his round, slightly bulging eyes lifted to her face.

Lord Miles Blanden raised himself slowly to his full height and took a step forward, the cane swinging lightly in one hand. The stallholder attempted to detain him, but he waved him away.

Helena could hear her own breath hauled into her chest, almost as if she had been running. Hatred welled up inside her and she wanted to cry out, run forward and pound the man's chest with her fists. Chloe must have seen him too as she gave a sharp gasp from behind her.

She could feel an ache beginning in her jaw and found she was grinding her teeth, reciting in her head every name she had ever called him in her rage and bitterness.

"Mistress Helena Woulfe," he drawled, offering her an inadequate, almost insulting bow.

"Lord Blanden." Her voice was calmer than she thought possible. Lifting her chin, she returned his arrogant stare. His expression was not soft or ingratiating, as it had been when she was his future daughter-in-law. This Lord Blanden was self-satisfied, leering even and his thin lips formed a sneer as his gaze flicked insolently over her.

The noise and bustle of the 'Change went on around her, but Helena's ears were filled with a soft roaring sound as she stared at the hard face of the man she had hoped never to meet again.

He arched an eyebrow and the sneer turned to a wry smile. "What a coincidence fate has decreed we should meet thus, Mistress. When Helena did not respond he went on. "You appear surprised to see me in the city," He stared around at the bustling 'Change as if wishing to be heard. "I have business at the Court of St James. Did you not hear I have been made one of his majesty's Commissioners?"

"I did not, sir." She inclined her head. Nor did she care.

Her apparent disinterest seemed to anger him and he stepped forward, bringing the cane up in front of her face. Helena refused to flinch and in a voice laden with menace, he snarled, "I know what Ffoyle did for you and that whelp brother of yours."

Helena didn't respond. Determined not to appear intimidated, she held her ground at his nearness, refusing to take a step back. Chloe moved closer as if to insinuate herself between them. Blanden ignored her, his gaze fixed on Helena's face.

A party of well-dressed women brushed past them like ships in full sail, their laughter ringing round the hall. Shoppers stepped aside to allow them to pass, but Lord Blanden and Helena ignored them.

"Those houses in the Magdalen Road should be mine, and the warehouses on the quay." He almost spat the words out as if he had waited a long time for this confrontation. "Don't think I don't know Samuel Ffoyle's flock of sheep trebled last June as well."

Helena swallowed. "Wasn't my Father's Manor and his land enough payment for your treachery, Lord Blanden?" She dragged out his name insolently.

"I'm not answerable to you, Mistress," his low growl brought a few curious stares their way, but no one intervened. "I have nothing to feel guilty for. I did my duty by our sovereign and my reward," he lifted his fleshy chin in defiance, "will be to attend the king's birthday ball this autumn."

His expression was so smug, Helena had to force herself not to strike the look away with her fan. Nevertheless, her grip on the bone spars snapped one of them between her fingers and the sharp edge cut into her skin.

"I hear you are living in Lambtons alehouse." He gave a cruel laugh. "More than a traitor's brat should expect in my view." His rodent eyes slid over her again. "Although I have to admit you look exceedingly prosperous on it." He sounded almost disappointed.

His gaze flicked to the diamond pendant at her throat and his eyes widened. He tapped her neck lightly with the cane.

"Was that your mother's?" he sniggered. "It's part of the estate, I think, as are all her jewels." He lowered his voice to a whisper, which made her skin crawl. "I'll have those too."

His taunt acted on Helena like cold water, her fear dissipated and she was about to boast of Henry's career and her forthcoming marriage, when her instincts told her that caution was called for. Instead, she expelled an impatient breath. "I am sure it will not surprise you if I express no delight at this encounter, Lord Blanden. I bid you good day."

She stepped past him, but he caught her arm in a vice-like grip. Helena tried to look away but her gaze fixed on a tiny bead of spittle on his lower lip. "I will ruin Ffoyle, as I ruined your father, and he will wish it was he whom you sealed in that vault in St Mary Arches instead of your mother."

"Do not imagine there will be no reckoning with the Woulfes, Lord Blanden." Helena felt her cheeks burn and she returned his glare with all the pent up anger of the last months. "My brothers are young yet, but they will make you pay for your cowardice."

She felt his hold on her arm loosen and uncertainty appeared in his flat eyes. Perhaps he did not know about Aaron? He seemed shocked just now. His reaction gave her confidence. "I would be grateful, My Lord, if you would not die too soon and thus deprive them of their revenge."

Tugging her arm away from his grasp, she marched away. Her head held high. The summer sun flooding through the multi-paned window at the end of the concourse drew her forward.

Chloe caught up with her as she gained the walkway outside. "Mistress, oh, Mistress," she gabbled breathlessly. "I never thought you could . . . I mean, the way you-."

Helena steadied herself against the wall with one hand. "Go and tell our driver where I am, Chloe." The maid fell silent and scurried away.

Helena stood alone amongst the pressing crowds entering and leaving the 'Change, some so close she could smell their sweat and the powder on their faces. Her heart hammered and the tell-tale prick of tears tugged at her throat. I will not cry, I will not give him the privilege.

Long minutes passed, during which she expected Lord Blanden to appear and renew his taunts, then the coach drew up beside her and she clambered inside.

"I had no idea he was in London, Mistress," Chloe gabbled.

"Nor I, Chloe." Helena stared unseeing out of the window. How dare he insult her after all he had done? And why would he want to hurt Samuel? He got what he wanted, although by his threats it seemed that still wasn't enough. How he must have hated the Woulfes. But why? He and Father were friends once, before King Charles died.

Her stomach lurched as a thought occurred to her. She had been going to marry his son. She chewed the base of her thumb in agitation, relieved Chloe had stopped talking. Could Lord Blanden do what he threatened and wrest the remainder of the estate from them? If he succeeded, she and Henry would have no income at all. How would Henry continue with his training as an architect, or Aaron remain in The Hague if Samuel was unable to send him money? Would Guy Palmer still want to marry her if she had nothing?

A tiny groan escaped her and inwardly she cursed Miles Blanden. The summer's day was ruined; her pretty parcels and the shoes she had ordered for her wedding, all receded into a world of comfort and tidiness, where evil men had no power to instill such dread.

As soon as the carriage pulled into Lambtons' stable yard, her feet touched the cobbles and she was running through the hallways in search of Robert. She found him in his study, one ankle crossed over the other, a clay pipe in his hand and a light periwig draped over one shoulder.

"Ah, my dear Helena, how-goodness child you look distraught. What has happened, tell me this instant." He rose and approached her with his arms outstretched.

She almost fell into his embrace, sobbing into his shoulder, her hands gripping his coat as she poured out her anguish.

Adella arrived on a cloud of silk-clad fragrance and bustled to her side. "Lubbock told me she was here," she addressed her husband. "And the state she was in. What has happened?" Her intelligent calm acted like balm on Helena's nerves as Robert repeated her story.

"Stupid, evil man," Adella almost snarled. "How dare he behave so after all he has done already?" Her words mirrored Helena's thoughts so closely, she felt almost reassured.

"He threatened to ruin Master Ffoyle," Helena forced the words through her tears, still horrified by the encounter.

"Nonsense, Samuel Ffoyle is an influential man, far more so than Lord Blanden." Adella spat the name out as if it might poison her.

"My dear wife is quite right, Helena." Robert patted her shoulder. "Samuel Ffoyle has faced more powerful men than he, and prevailed. I believe Blanden's threat to be an empty one."

Helena began to doubt their reassurances. "But he has been made one of King James' commissioners. Suppose he appeals to his majesty for the rest of my family's estate?"

Robert looked troubled. "If he has the ear of Jeffreys . . ." He tapped a finger against his cheek. "I shall have to give this problem some thought."

Helena was disappointed; somehow she had expected an instant solution to her dilemma, but if anything, Robert seemed bewildered. She forced herself to calm down so she could think, her initial shock at being confronted so unexpectedly giving way to indignation. If only she could talk to Samuel. He wasn't even aware he had an enemy. One thing she was sure of, Blanden wouldn't hurt her, or her brothers, ever again.

"He would be unwise to try," Adella snorted, indicating she had spoken aloud.

* * *

Helena pleaded the headache and desultorily picked at a tray of food sent to her room. It was not a lie, she had gone over and over Blanden's words so often, they began colliding inside her head, making it throb.

Even if he only possessed a fraction of the ability he boasted, there was still considerable damage he could inflict on them. She and her brothers depended on the warehouses, the properties in Magdalen Road and the income from the wool business, which Samuel sent regularly. If he took that away, and if Samuel . . .

She paced the room restlessly, emotionally battered and furious all at the same time, yet helpless to do anything. Well, maybe not completely helpless. At her bureau, she pulled a sheaf of parchment from the drawer, her hand sliding across the journal, which had been her best friend during the days at Loxsbeare while she waited for news of the rebellion. She weighted it in her hand, running her thumb over the familiar leather cover, her resolve hardening as she carefully set it aside. Dipping a quill into a pot of black ink, she began to write.

CHAPTER TWENTY EIGHT

Helena observed the bustling activity in the street from the upper landing opposite her room. The sky on that September morning was a bright blue, but at street level, a sharp wind buffeted between the buildings. Passers-by barely paused to acknowledge acquaintances, hurrying between carriages and houses, grimly hanging on to flapping cloaks and lifting hats. The food peddlers and hawkers had left early, most likely searching for warmer alleys and more sheltered squares.

As the church bell sounded in the distance, Helena released a nervous breath. It was time. Striding into her room, she scooped up her cloak; informed Chloe she would return before dinner and closed the door on her polite, "Very well, Mistress."

In the hallway, she asked Lubbock to order a hackney, feeling quite daring that she was attempting the journey alone. When it arrived, the carriage doors were cracked and the paintwork scarred, but she paid no attention as she climbed into the musty interior.

When the driver deposited her outside the Palace gate next to the Banqueting Hall, her apprehension turned to quivering nerves. What if he wouldn't see her? Or he dismissed her request, saying there was nothing he could do? Perhaps she was being unreasonable to think a court officer would favor her petition over that of Lord Blanden?

The ornamental entrance, one of several leading into the Palace yard, spanned the road and towered above it. It was an impressive structure, with two rounded towers at either end, a pedestrian arch beneath each, with a larger one in the center to allow carriages to pass through.

She thrust her hand into the pocket of her gown to finger the sheet of parchment, which had arrived by messenger the previous day, ready to produce it for the guard to gain entry. Even with her invitation she was uneasy; this was after all the wondrous Palace of Whitehall and it was here, powerful and royal people lived.

Helena need not have worried. When the guard saw the mark of the Privy Seal, he signaled to a footman, who stepped forward with a polite bow. "Kindly follow me, Mistress." He led her through the curved entrance and beside a high wall rising up on their left. Helena had expected long corridors and rows of offices, even an apartment, not this stroll through an endless courtyard. Her nervousness increased and seeing her curious sideways glance, he smiled. "I beg your pardon, Mistress," he shouted above the wind. "The gentleman asked that I should bring you into the Privy Garden."

Helena accepted this information in silence as they turned sharp right through a doorway in the wall. "He will be with you shortly, Mistress."

The door closed behind her with a dull thump and Helena let her hood fall back as she gazed around her. The Royal Privy Garden was totally unexpected; laid out before her in a series of square lawns with straight pathways between, like a chessboard. The Palace buildings formed two sides and with a row of high hedges on the other. The elegant space was completely enclosed, shutting out the buffeting wind and traffic noise from outside.

The squares of lawn each held a stone statue of a classical figure draped in Roman robes. Helena wandered between them, looking up at the blank, serene faces of these mythical gods and goddesses, imagining their blind eyes gazed into the distance to a place where grapes and olives grew in parching sun.

Fat bees hummed in the flowerbeds and birds flapped across the roof tiles. The air was heavy with the scent of late summer flowers and a tiny thrill of excitement went through her as she imagined the Royal family walking in the rooms behind the windows overlooking the garden.

Her sense of unreality faded when several figures bustled between the buildings, none of whom paid her any attention.

"Good day, Mistress Woulfe," a voice drawled from behind her.

Helena swung round, her face relaxing into a smile. "Master Evelyn." She bobbed a curtsey. "Thank you for agreeing to see me."

Still slender and upright for a man in his sixties, John Evelyn looked immaculate in unrelieved black, one hand gently caressing a japan cane. "Have you never visited the Privy Garden, Mistress?" he asked, taking in her awed features.

Helena shook her head. "No, but it's perfectly lovely."

Evelyn bowed in one graceful, fluid movement, accepting the compliment as if it was his due. "I was intrigued by your note, Mistress." He stepped closer. "I hope you do not mind the location of our meeting." He waved a hand at the garden without looking at it, as if immune to its beauty. "I assumed from the brevity and urgency of your request, you would prefer privacy."

Helena relaxed. "Thank you for your understanding, sir."

"Shall we walk?" He extended an arm and with her hand on his sleeve, he guided her along a gravel pathway. "I confess I am not entirely ignorant of the reason for your visit."

Helena stiffened, but she kept her gaze on the garden. He spoke again, this time his tone serious. "I presume you wish to discuss the petition, which Lord Miles Blanden is rumored to be lodging with his majesty."

Helena did not know whether to feel relief at his perception, or terror that he might possess worse information. "Are. . . are you familiar with my situation, sir?"

"I am, Mistress Woulfe. Sir Christopher Wren is a close friend and has a great fondness for your brother, Henry is it?"

Helena nodded. Why didn't she think of that?

"The gentleman I mentioned earlier, is, I believe, seeking to obtain the remainder of your father's possessions in Exeter. Specifically the property and business interests signed over to Master Ffoyle before the Rebellion." He studied a late flowering rose bush as if fascinated, before murmuring, "Have I summarized the man's expectations correctly?"

"It seems you know everything, sir." She felt suddenly defeated. "Is there any possibility his majesty might refuse his demand?" Helena risked a quick glance at his averted face, expecting ridicule. Why would the king refuse to grant one of his own Royal Commissioners what amounted to a traitor's possessions?

A gust of wind swept through the garden, swirling the leaves into a colorful whirlwind. A window banged shut on an upper floor.

Evelyn looked up at the noise. "Ah, Lord Lauderdale's valet has left the window open again." Then he said something quite unexpected. "Tell me, how is that other brother of yours, Master Aaron Woulfe?"

Her surprise must have shown in her face, for he leaned closer. "I am an influential man, my dear. I have ways of discovering such things."

"It was stupid of me to imagine otherwise." Her instincts advised caution, but she may as well be honest. "He is in

The Hague, sir, with . . . " she trailed off, embarrassed, wishing he would answer her original question about Lord Blanden. However, there seemed no urgency to the interview as Evelyn paused beside a sundial that seemed to command his attention.

"This was King Charles' favorite item in the garden." Evelyn tapped the stone podium with his cane.

"It's very beautiful." She wanted to admire the classic lines of the marble column, but it looked plain and unremarkable to her.

"Lord Rochester knocked it over once," he gave a light laugh. "His majesty was incensed, as I recall." He lowered his voice. "I believe, Mistress, Aaron has been in Holland since the summer of '85 where he escaped from Sedgemoor, did he not?" At her weak smile he gave a contemplative nod. "Forgive me if I intrude, but has he mentioned his future plans in respect of the Prince of Orange?" For long seconds his gaze held hers. "Ah! Don't answer that, I can see by your countenance that he has."

She began to feel nauseous and the question she did not want to ask spilled out. "Is Aaron putting himself in danger, sir?"

"If King James discovers proof of a conspiracy against him, and Aaron Woulfe is caught. Then he could be charged with treason, yes."

Helena pushed herself away from the sundial with a small cry. As if she didn't have enough to worry about. The elegant garden began to spin and Evelyn's outline blurred and swayed.

"You look unwell, Mistress." He started toward her with a concerned frown and took her elbow. "Come and sit down, I cannot have you falling into a faint, I am far too old and frail to catch you." He gave a brittle laugh as he guided her to a bench. Lowering himself beside her, he fixed his gaze on the garden as if allowing her time to recover.

Helena fought dizziness and despair, focusing on a fat bee drifting from one late, limp bloom to another, it's furry body dipping and hovering. How could they be talking of treachery in such a beautiful place?

She felt the quiet strength of the man beside her; a man, who had seen more than she could imagine. During his lifetime, the first King Charles had been beheaded outside the Banqueting Hall not far from where they sat. He had endured the government of Cromwell and the restoration of Charles the second. He had actually been in the city for the terrible plague and had witnessed the great fire.

Old King Charles had been his friend and although Evelyn abhorred the religion of the current king, still he was a loyal servant and played an important part in his government. Helena suppressed a groan, if only her own family could have put aside their prejudices and acted similarly, how different their lives would have been. She could learn so much from this man. Feeling more in control, Helena twisted on the bench so she could see her companion's face. "What should I do to protect my brother?"

Evelyn stroked his chin. "I will admit that my sovereign's recent preferment of Catholics is a cause for concern. But forgive me if I don't elucidate, my position here, and indeed that of many Anglicans is at risk."

"I understand, sir." She folded trembling hands in her lap and stared off, almost angrily. Why did Aaron have to be such a principled fool?

A small procession appeared on the far side of the garden. Moving slowly, they meandered along the pathway opposite to where Helena and Evelyn sat, halting to form a semi-circle around one man.

Master Evelyn's gaze was fixed on the group and as if the sight of them stirred a memory, he said, "I knew Monmouth you know, Mistress Woulfe."

"I know. You told me at the Twelfth Night party at Lambtons." Helena watched the courtiers talk among themselves, an occasional high-pitched laugh floating across the garden.

He turned to her in surprise. "I did?"

"Master Evelyn, who are those people?" She indicated the group, who appeared to be listening intently to a gesticulating man in a pale brown wig and elaborate suit, as if what he said was of paramount importance. Two footmen stood a little way off, while another liveried man held two small dogs on leads.

Evelyn followed her gaze. "Ah, that, my dear, is King James."

The King. So that was the man who had sent his soldiers to the west against her family. They had killed her uncle and who knows what they had done to her father. He was the reason Aaron was still abroad and not here with her.

Helena felt her jaw tighten as she ground her teeth. She flexed the muscles of her face to put a stop to it. As her father had often told her, she didn't want to end up with a wooden set.

Her throat hurt suddenly and she looked away, but her gaze returned in fascination to study the heavy Stuart features. Evelyn whispered, "The lady beside him is Queen Mary Beatrice. Do you think her beautiful?"

Helena appraised the tall, dark woman whose hand rested possessively on her husband's arm. She gave a small shrug. "Those silks, furs and jewels make a significant contribution to that beauty, sir."

Evelyn gave a gentle laugh beside her.

"Who is that man beside his majesty? The handsome one on the left, with the black peruke?"

Evelyn's gaze rested on the man. "The Chief Chancellor, Lord Jeffries."

An involuntary shiver went down Helena's back and gathering her skirts, she rose from the bench. "I feel I must go, sir." Instantly she regretted the impulse. He had still not told her what might happen with Lord Blanden's petition.

Evelyn held up a restraining hand. "Their majesties will not remain long, my dear, and I doubt they have an inkling of who you might be. Even if they did, they would not assume you posed any threat."

The party wandered off through a doorway and Helena sank back down again. The footman with the dogs lingered while the spaniels sniffed around the path, but before long they had vanished too.

"Am I a threat to them, Master Evelyn?" The thought gave her a modicum of satisfaction.

"Your brother might be, although his majesty has far more weighty personages to worry about." Catching her expression, he went on quickly. "I do understand your concern for Aaron, my dear. I feel you should at least write to him and advise caution."

"About taking action against the king?"

"About whom he tells, he is taking action against the king."

Helena almost laughed. What a sensible, intelligent man Master Evelyn was. There was no judgment in his advice. In fact, he appeared almost sympathetic.

"Aaron believes he is protecting the Anglican Church," Helena said. "He does not see that his actions could be interpreted as treason."

"He must harbor a great deal of resentment for the current regime, my dear. After all, they robbed him of a greater part of his family." Helena gave him a brief, telling glare. He met her gaze and looked startled. "Oh, as have you, of course, but he is young and idealistic."

"He is also foolish, impetuous and headstrong. He has not given a thought to how this may affect me, my brother Henry, or..." She held her hands up in a helpless gesture.

Evelyn gave a cough. "Quite, but as to Lord Blanden. Well Helena, my dear." He paused. "I hope you don't mind my using your given name."

She gave a slight shake of her head and he looked pleased. "I think I can reassure you about that gentleman."

"Really?" She expelled a hopeful breath.

"Lord Blanden may well have the king's ear, being a new convert to his religion. However, the man's petition has first to reach me, as holder of the Privy Seal, and if I can see no merit in it, I shall simply not refer it to his majesty."

Helena felt a disbelieving laugh bubble up inside her chest. Could it really be that simple?

Evelyn's face held a mischievous smile. "I have what is known, Mistress Woulfe, as the power of veto."

"And you would use this power, on my behalf?"

He shrugged his narrow shoulders. "Certainly, if I feel the situation calls for it."

Helena's eyes swam with unshed tears and she had to suppress the impulse to throw her arms around him in gratitude.

Evelyn looked puzzled. "Is that not why you came to see me?"

"I know, sir. But I never imagined . . . ."

He gave a snort. "I hardly know whether to feel insulted or not. As far as I am aware, I have never in my life refused the impassioned pleas of a beautiful woman."

Helena was about to apologize, but the look on his face was of amusement. He braced his hands on his thighs and pushed himself to his feet, extending his arm toward her. Helena took it gratefully, allowing him to escort her back through the garden and out onto the street.

It was an unremarkable street, but for the armed guards stationed at the entrance to the King Street Gate at one end and the Palace Gate behind her.

Evelyn handed her into the waiting hackney, bowing over her hand which he held onto through the window. "Lord Blanden is a stubborn man, Helena," he warned. "I shall do all I can to ensure his failure here is complete, but he won't take it lightly. I suggest you be wary of him in the future."

She considered his words. "I understand. Thank you, sir."

He inclined his head in acknowledgment and waved her away with his cane. On the journey back to Lambtons, Helena replayed everything he had said, making a decision to conceal her brother's letters in a less accessible place. She wondered briefly if she ought to destroy them, then rejected the notion. If fate chose to keep them apart for longer, perhaps forever, she needed something tangible to remind her of Aaron.

* * *

Helena grew restless as the days passéd, her every waking thought filled with the sneering face of Lord Blanden. At night, she laid awake, running scenarios through her head as to what might happen to her and her brothers if Master Evelyn had been unable to stop his petition. Suppose he appealed directly to the king? It didn't bear thinking about.

Lubbock knocked discreetly at her door to announce Guy Palmer had arrived. Helena groaned inwardly, wondering how she could possibly act normally in his presence when their very future together could be threatened.

Despite her distraction, the visit proved a successful one, although it was necessary for him to repeat several questions. "I can see you are pre-occupied, Helena." He patted her hand affectionately. "Can I flatter myself it is our forthcoming wedding which distracts you?"

Helena looked up. "What? Oh yes, yes of course. There is so much still to arrange."

"Then I shall not keep you." He stood and took a gracious leave and she escorted him into the entrance.

The door closed on him finally and Helena released a heavy sigh, jumping as Robert spoke from behind her. "You decided not to tell him then, my dear."

There was no accusation in his voice, merely acceptance, for which she was grateful. "I couldn't." She gave an apologetic shrug. "If Lord Blanden's petition is successful, I will tell him then."

"I cannot imagine Guy would abandon you purely for not bringing him a dowry, Helena. I believe that young man truly loves you."

"Perhaps, but will he agree to not only to support me, but my two brothers as well? That wasn't part of our bargain."

"No, but-"

"And you, Master Devereux, do you relish having a penniless, unmarriageable ward on your hands indefinitely? No, don't answer. I don't want to think about the possibility."

A little before dawn on a muggy September morning, Amy Ffoyle elbowed her husband to inform him testily she had barely slept for the dull pulling in her abdomen. Not understanding the importance of her complaint, but instantly alert, Patrick sent a servant to fetch his mother.

Dismissing the potential dangers of the city in summer, Samuel and Meghan Ffoyle arrived from Devon with their youngest daughter, Deborah three weeks before, eagerly anticipating the arrival of their first grandchild.

With Amy's confinement approaching, Patrick felt himself becoming wholly inadequate and the reassuring figure of his mother ordering his servants in his house, did not hold the threat to his authority it might have once have done.

Meghan took immediate charge, installing her daughter-in-law in the confinement chamber prepared at the back of the house. Although distracted and in pain, Amy had the presence of mind to send for her chosen gossips.

The agitated father-to-be watched the women parade past him up to the first floor, ducking their heads beneath a lintel to preserve their headdresses. His mother observed them from the landing, her upright figure emanating disapproval, which he pretended not to notice.

Patrick retreated to the salon, but he could not settle. He ordered wine, although it was still early and he had not even had breakfast. He couldn't eat a thing.

"Has that midwife woman been called for?" Samuel asked from the sofa.

"Yes," Patrick mumbled, unwilling to enter into yet another discussion about the professionalism, of lack thereof, of London's midwives.

"They are properly licensed," Amy had assured her father-in-law when he questioned the need for one.

"These licenses you speak of, are granted by the diocesan Bishop, not a doctor at all. And testimonies are sought," he jabbed a finger at a bemused Patrick, "not from medical practitioners as to the woman's expertise, but from six honest women who can vouch for their character and moral standing."

Amy had looked hurt at his derision, but in private, insisted she have her way. Patrick had his own misgivings, but was unwilling to upset Amy, and for the sake of peace in his house, had kept his counsel.

Summoned by a messenger, Helena entered the confinement room as Meghan was settling Amy into the high bed. She ran forward to take Amy's other arm and help hoist her onto the pile of stacked pillows. "How are you, dearest?" she asked, almost too afraid to touch her. Amy's response was to grip Helena's hand and give a strangled cry, drawing her knees up to her chest.

Meghan whispered over Amy's head, "I have a feeling it won't be very long."

"I thought first babies were long labors?" Helena heard this somewhere.

Meghan shrugged. "In this case, it seems not." She glared at the three ladies arranged on high backed chairs in their voluminous skirts with tightly corseted torsos. They set out their sewing and played cards as they chattered animatedly.

Deborah flounced into the room, greeting Helena with hugs and sighs. Her gown was a little too old for her and showed a budding décolleté. Her hair was piled into curls fastened onto her head. She was so unlike the country child Helena remembered, she stared at her speechless.

"I am not to be allowed to stay the entire time." Deborah preened, as they took chairs at the side of the room.

Amy looked terrified, her eyes bulged each time a pain hit her, each one followed by drawn out groans. Helena began to feel uncomfortable witnessing her pain and instead, looked around at the confinement chamber. It was not a small room, but with eight people, including the maid, it felt claustrophobic. The curtain at the square window was shut tight, although it was bright autumn sunshine outside. Several candles gave off smoky fumes into the already heavy atmosphere. Where, Helena wondered, would the midwife fit into all this when the time came?

"Shouldn't we do something to help?" she asked, cutting off Deborah's flow of girlish remarks, none were related to Amy.

Deborah laughed. "There is nothing we can do which mother has not thought of. Besides, we are not here to help."

At Helena's frown, Deborah rolled her eyes. "We are to be witnesses to the birth. Should the infant die, our testimony shall allay any suspicions as to the cause of death." At Helena's shocked expression, Debs shrugged. "But we shall, of course, pray for a safe delivery."

Amy begged Helena to be one of her 'gossips', it seemed an adventure at the time, but the cold reality was disconcerting.

If only Celia could have been here, but Adella had forbidden it. She was very early on in her own pregnancy; a birthing room considered inappropriate for her. The words, 'in case something should go wrong', hung in the air during the fierce argument between mother and daughter.

With Amy's labor progressing in earnest, there did not appear to be much of the calm social gathering Helena had been led to expect of such an occasion. Her pains were already frequent and harsh, leaving her gasping and writhing on the bed, unable to follow or take an interest in any conversation. She only spoke to ask for something to slake her thirst or another cushion to ease the painful spasms in her back.

The three ladies, introduced to Helena as Mistresses Hardy and Mold, the other name she did not catch, watched impassively. One of them tied what looked like a stocking to Amy's wrist. "A possession of her husband's," she explained, in response to Helena's curious stare. "Amy must wear it, so some of her suffering might be transferred to him."

At the word 'suffering' Amy's eyes widened in fear, and then another pain must have overtaken her for her face contorted and she gave a full-throated yell.

Mistress Mold looked down her elegant nose at Meghan, saying. "I assume the midwife will be here directly."

"The presence of a midwife is an unnecessary expense," Meghan's tone was scathing. Helena saw the ladies exchange knowing glances, indicating they regarded Mistress Ffoyle's homespun attitude outdated and ill-informed.

Helena felt sympathy for Meghan, who was not an ignorant woman by any means, but when she looked to Deborah for support, she could tell by the girl's rapt expression she would not find it there. Deborah gazed at the three ladies with fascination, her conker-colored eyes going from the impossibly tall fontanges on their heads to the paint and patches on their faces.

When she made her appearance, the much talked of midwife came as a pleasant surprise. Meghan's misgivings had almost convinced Helena she was bound to be an old crone who used the by-products of childbirth in black rituals.

Tall and upright, in a plain gown and spotless white cap, the midwife introduced herself as Jemima Rand, and with well practiced authority, sent everyone but Meghan in different directions to fetch hot water, linen, vinegar, goose fat and wine.

Helena caught the woman's eye at one point and couldn't help smiling. The intelligent mischief she saw there confirmed her suspicion. The frantic activity was to keep everyone occupied and less likely to further distress the laboring girl with their stories; of which the Mistresses Hardy and Mold appeared to have an extensive repertoire.

Mistress Rand's calm authority seemed to soothe Amy, whose cries hardly appeared to affect the other women. They stood around the bed and commented, to Helena's disbelief, that in their opinion the labor seemed easy.

The point at which Helena felt compelled to leave the room, was when Mistress Rand liberally smothered her hand and wrist with goose fat and advanced on Amy, announcing she was going to, "'Ease the child's passage'".

"You could fetch a length of thread," Mistress Rand asked Helena as she saw her edging toward the door. "Make sure it is as fine as possible."

"Take Deborah with you." Meghan pushed the reluctant girl toward her. Helena retreated, a sulky Debs trailing behind. Catching a final glimpse of Amy as the door closed, Helena wondered how it was possible to arch a body at such an unnatural angle. Her footsteps on the stairs made the treads creak, bringing Patrick out of the front salon, a look of anguished anticipation on his face. "Any news yet?"

Helena was saved from responding when Samuel stepped out of the room behind him and ushered Patrick back in again. "You cannot rush these things, my boy." She heard him say as the door closed.

Deborah had disappeared, and when Helena returned to the birthing room, the energy seemed to have intensified. No longer ranged untidily round the room, the company was lined up on either side of the bed, offering encouraging noises. Amy's pain seemed to be much worse. She strained forward with a guttural moan, and then flopped back against her pillows, only to sweat and strain again as the agony took hold of her. Then her scream was abruptly cut off and a wrinkled, slime covered bundle slithered onto the bed, accompanied by a rich metallic odor.

At first, the grayish form lay still in the midwife's broad hands, then it gave a high pitched, wet wail and threw tiny clenched fists upwards and outwards, its puckered mouth turning to root for food.

Meghan snatched the thread Helena still clutched in her hand, tying it around the still pulsing cord. Then an unseemly tussle ensued when Meghan attempted to take Mistress Rand's knife to cut the cord.

Jemima Rand refused to relinquish it. "A midwife's knife," the woman insisted. "Is her symbol of office, and I never allow another to use it."

Meghan retreated, chastened.

The baby was wrapped in a fine blanket and placed in the crook of Amy's arm, while Helena's gaze was fixed on the patches of drying blood and white slime on the wrinkled head. Its eyes were mere slits in a crumpled, shapeless face and it moved its head from side to side, while the new mother stroked each limb and counted fingers and toes.

The midwife leaned over, pressing on her abdomen. Helena tried not to look at what she hurriedly removed, her initial impression being it involved an alarming amount of blood. Helena was relieved when Amy's lower body was covered again.

As if guided by instinct, the baby latched onto a swollen white breast and began to suck, emitting small animal sounds. Amy's face transformed from that of a thin child, pain-wracked and frightened, into a serene and beaming young woman.

Her fair hair was darkened with sweat at the hairline, no longer restrained by her cap; long tendrils clung to her temples and neck. Her eyes, so recently filled with sharp agony, were wide and clear as she gazed in rapture at the bundle in her arms; the anguished hours that went before forgotten.

Helena tugged Meghan's sleeve. "Is it always like this?" she asked in an awed whisper.

Meghan sniffed, nodding. "If the child seems as if it will live, as this one does, it is the purest feeling anyone could have."

Helena accepted her words. Hoping the baby would soon grow pretty, for its own sake, as well as its devoted parents.

Deborah slipped back into the room and chose that moment to ask, "What is it?"

"It's a girl." Meghan breathed.

* * *

Helena found herself wandering listlessly around Lambtons one crisp October afternoon, unable to concentrate on anything.

Robert and Adella had gone out in the carriage and Phebe was visiting Celia at Saffron Hill. In many ways this suited her, she was in no mood for Celia's chatter or Phebe's barbed remarks about her forthcoming wedding.

The new shoes had finally arrived that morning with apologies from the shoemaker for their lateness, despite Helena having sent the first pair back because they did not fit well enough. On her way up the stairs to her room, she heard a hard voice growling at Lubbock. Lord Miles Blanden stood below her in the entrance hall. It was too late to retreat, all she could do was stand perfectly still, watching him shrug off Lubbock's offer to take his sword and gloves.

He glanced up at her with a smirk. "Good day to you, Mistress Woulfe," he drawled, instilling more insult into his voice than propriety. His gaze slid away from her to take in his surroundings, raising his bushy eyebrows in surprise, as if he did not expect such opulence. Helena gripped the balustrade, her knees threatened to buckle but she was determined not to stumble.

He extended a hand, but she remained three steps above him, her arms at her sides so he was forced to drop his awkwardly. Nor did she reply to his greeting. She waited, her heart hammering with terror, yet at the same time furious he had dared to come to her home like this, unannounced and uninvited.

Lubbock hovered close by, a look of suspicion mixed with concern on his face. When she gave him the tiniest of nods, he backed away, but she knew he would remain within earshot and felt reassured.

"I was not aware you patronized Lambtons, Lord Blanden," Helena said, forcing the words through clenched teeth. Three serving men traversed the hall bearing laden trays, and a group of patrons who had recently arrived, were clustered at the entrance darting looks at them and muttering.

He gave a short bark of a laugh. "I dine at Pontacks, Mistress Woulfe." This time his glance around the hallway was contemptuous. "But I have gone out of my way to inform you that I registered my petition with his majesty yesterday, for the rest of Sir Jonathan's estate."

With difficulty, Helena remained calm, her voice light with unconcern. "You can lodge as many petitions as you wish, sir, but you can prove nothing."

His reaction to her composure was one of fury. His face reddened and he took a step forward, the ubiquitous cane quivering as if he were about to strike her.

"I have proof." He spat. "Ffoyle paid virtually nothing for those houses and the warehouse. Nor is there any bill of sale for the sheep, or your mother's jewels."

Helena had to stop her hand from climbing to her throat, where Lady Elizabeth's pearl necklace lay. He stood close enough for her to see fine purple blood vessels running beneath his skin.

The main door opened then and Robert walked into the hall. Helena's relief was so great she thought she might collapse. Then her confidence increased further, for in his wake glided Adella on the arm of John Evelyn. The three of them advanced on Lord Blanden like wolves circling their prey.

"I see you wasted no time at all, sir." Robert carefully removed his gloves, his gaze focused on his own hands. Adella approached from his other side, disdain written across her painted features.

"I was merely paying Mistress Woulfe a call." Blanden sounded almost apologetic. His gaze flicked to Evelyn, a man he evidently recognized. His chest visibly deflated and his eyes looked hunted.

"As what, sir?" Robert's laugh was scornful. "A family friend?"

"Did you imagine Helena to be alone and friendless in London, sir?" Adella rapped Blanden's cheek with her fan so hard, it left a red mark, but he seemed too astonished to react.

"I believe you have been busy lodging petitions." Evelyn leaned his spare frame against the newel post at the bottom of the staircase and crossed his arms across his chest.

He tilted his head to give Helena a slow, knowing wink. A ripple of warmth worked its way through her, like brandy on a cold day. His commanding presence acted like balm on Helena's ragged nerves and she breathed normally again.

Looking down on her antagonist from the step, Helena thought he looked comical with his chest puffed out and his feet spread apart. It came to her then, he was not a gentleman at all, simply a greedy malcontent who took pleasure in browbeating women. He could not even be true to his own faith. And she had been afraid of him.

"It's a valid petition." Blanden almost whined. "The property is rightfully mine, and-"

"Stop blustering man." Robert took a step toward him. "You are a liar and a villain and you will get no more of Sir Jonathan's possessions."

Lord Blanden's chin was stuck forward in what he probably imagined was bravado, but Helena thought it made him look like a child about to have his favorite plaything taken from him. And so he is.

"I have perused the document, my Lord." Evelyn's tone made the last two words an insult. "In my position as Privy Seal, I decreed it held no merit, therefore I have refused it."

"But...his majesty," Lord Blanden spluttered.

"Will not even see it, sir." Evelyn's voice was like a whip, slicing through the man's protests. "It is over, my Lord."

Narrowing his eyes, Blanden gave a guttural snarl, the black cane tapping rhythmically into the palm of his hand as he glared at each of them in turn.

Lubbock chose that moment to step forward and open the street door, giving a small bow as an invitation for him to leave. "I shall be lodging the petition again in Exeter," he growled as he swung on his heel, waving the cane at them. "I am an important man; the magistrates there dare not ignore me."

Robert called after him. "You would be advised to look to what you have already acquired by treachery, Lord Blanden, it can be lost just as easily."

The door swung shut with a resounding bang and a smirking Lubbock retreated in the direction of the kitchen.

Helena took a deep breath, feeling almost giddy with relief.

Evelyn straightened up and flicked a thick lock of his peruke over one shoulder, his thin lips curling in a mischievous smile. "I rather enjoyed that, Mistress Woulfe."

"What an atrocious man." Adella removed her gloves and snapped them against her palm. "Although I was a trifle disappointed he did not put up more of a fight."

Helena descended the three steps on still wobbly legs and Robert put a fatherly arm around her. "He is a cowardly bully, no more."

Helena drew comfort from his embrace, but she was still uneasy. Lord Blanden hadn't been all bluster when he informed on her father; nor was he a coward when he demanded Judge Jeffreys hand him Loxsbeare. She shivered, telling herself it was simply a reaction to seeing him again. "But if he takes his petition to Exeter?" She broke off, unable to voice her worst fears.

"Oh, I doubt he will receive a sympathetic hearing," Evelyn said airily, offering Adella his arm. "Not when it has already been rejected here. I shall send word to the city magistrates to inform them of the fact."

"That is settled then." Adella bussed Helena's cheek as they sailed past her on the way to the dining hall. "Do let us all go in to a well earned dinner and forget all about Lord Blanden. I simply do not wish to hear the man's name mentioned again."

"Nor do I," whispered Helena.

CHAPTER TWENTY NINE

Helena was one of Amy's first visitors at her traditional 'upsitting', which coincided with the baby's christening. The nurse removed the childbed linens and pulled back the curtain, allowing natural light into the chamber for the first time.

Helena voiced her view on such practices loudly. "It is distasteful, and I don't intend submitting to lying on soiled linen for two whole weeks in a darkened room when my turn comes, whatever polite society decrees."

"We shall see." Amy gave her one of the knowing looks she seemed to have developed lately.

Helena perched gingerly on the bed. "How are you, Amy?"

"I am perfectly well." Her stiff tone indicating she had repeated this phrase, often. "Not that anyone will listen. I was permitted a hipbath today, and cannot tell you what a luxury it felt after the poultices and herbal washes the dry nurse brings me. That woman behaves like a constable. Why, even Patrick has to beg permission to see me, and he pays her wages!"

"Does Mistress Ffoyle offer no objections?" Helena asked, bemused at her volubility. Amy was usually such a quiet girl.

"Not one. She is occupied with the baby. Her own and mine." Amy sniffed. Then her face softened. "Have you seen my baby today?"

"Yours or Mistress Ffoyle's?"

"Mine." Amy winced as her hand brushed against her breast and she took on a long-suffering look. "Mother and Father Ffoyle have been wonderfully kind, but I am counting the days when they return to Ideswell."

"They are leaving Deborah behind," Helena warned.

Amy nodded, the arrangement evidently suited her. "Have you seen my Georgiana?" she asked again.

"I have, and she is lovely." Helena smiled. Amy rested back on her pillows with a sigh.

The formidable figure of the dry nurse appeared to stand with her hands on her hips at the bottom of the bed. "One visitor is quite sufficient on your first day, Mistress."

Helena crept out feeling like a schoolgirl to return to the party. She crossed the hallway at the same time the front door flung wide to reveal Henry. Doffing his hat, he made a gallant bow, at the same time pausing to tip the link-boy who had stood between the dirty coach wheels and Henry's new suit.

Meghan almost knocked him off balance as she pulled him inside. "Oh my dearest boy," she cried. "I am so happy to see you, you cannot imagine. Samuel. Samuel," she summoned her husband. "Henry is here, see how fine he looks."

"I could not miss the baptism of my first godchild." Henry adjusted his coat with a wide grin.

Meghan tucked her arm through his and subjected him to rapid questioning about the state of his stomach and his architectural learning. Helena followed behind with Samuel, a bemused smile on her face.

"I swear sure you have grown a hand span since I saw you last," Meghan cooed, while Henry endured having his cravat rearranged and a tendril of wayward hair tweaked behind his ear.

Helena mouthed a greeting, debating whether she should tell Henry about Miles Blanden. By the time Meghan released him, she had decided there was no need to burden him.

Guy appeared at that moment. She tucked her arm through his with a rush of affection. She found his company reassuring and looked forward to being married; daydreaming about their home.

"Isn't it wonderful to be in love?" Celia asked from the door where she stood with Ralf. Helena didn't feel equipped to answer her. Was what she felt for Guy love? How did one tell?

They joined the party guests to discover a discussion of the king's recent visit to Somerset in progress.

"I wonder at the purpose of such a gruesome pilgrimage," Samuel murmured at her shoulder, distracting her.

"The king wanted to see Sedgemoor for himself, I hear." This was from Ralf. "The villagers of Westonzoyland laid a plank over the Bussex Rhine, so he could examine the battlefield."

Helena frowned, summoning the faces of Jane and Gil Fellowes and their comfortable house near Weston church, certain they would not have been a part of such a spectacle, at least not willingly.

"His majesty brought Major Wade with him," Meghan ventured.

"He was Father's commanding Officer," Henry murmured to Helena, who nodded.

"He has received a Royal Pardon in exchange for information, although what that could be . . . " Samuel left the sentence unfinished.

Henry gave a derisive snort, draining his wine in one gulp.

"I heard an interesting adjunct to the Rebellion story," Ralf drew all eyes to him. "That man who murdered Heywood Dare. What was his name?"

"Andrew Fletcher," Henry said loudly, his eyes unnaturally bright.

"That's the man." Ralf held up a finger. "When Monmouth sent him back to the Helderenburg for his crime, he forced the pilot to steer for Spain." He paused to take a cold pasty from a passing server, studying it before lifting it to his lips.

"What significance does that have, dearest?" Celia prompted.

"Eh?" Ralf looked up, confronted by a line of faces waiting for him to continue. "I'm sorry, what was I saying? Oh yes, the ship was not supposed to go to Spain at all, you know. Monmouth had an agent on board on his way to Carrickfergus to contact the dissidents in Ireland and urge a second rising."

"So the Irish were never told?" Helena asked, horrified.

"That was three weeks before Sedgemoor." Henry reddened. "If the ship had reached Ireland as planned . . . "

Helena placed a restraining hand on her brother's arm. "There is no point to this Henry."

"There might have been a different outcome, but for Fletcher," Henry snarled.

Helena drew him away from curious stares. Henry was so volatile lately and he seemed to be drinking rather a lot of wine. She lowered her voice in what she hoped was a soothing tone. "And if Argyll hadn't been captured, and if Lord Delamere had acted as he promised, and if Grey's cavalry had been better schooled..." She stroked a strand of hair away from his forehead. "It is over Henry, we have to get on with our lives."

Guy had positioned himself between them and the party guests, which Helena reminded herself to thank him for later.

Henry turned cold eyes on her. "Unless the Prince of Orange invades England, and brings our brother with him."

"Hush, that's Rebel talk!"

He looked embarrassed and offered a murmured apology, but Helena was distracted by the sound of Deborah and turned to join the conversation.

Whatever was bothering Henry, she did not believe it was the fate of Fletcher.

"We have not yet talked of the wedding, Father," Deborah stared adoringly up at Samuel.

Helena thought how well her green silk gown with its yellow 'echelles' complimented Deborah's red-brown hair. Her tightly fastened corset gave her an imperious, upright stance, which exposed her slender neck and shoulders. "It is not until late next month, Debs," Helena said.

Deborah frowned. "Oh no, I did not mean your wedding, Helena." Catching herself she flushed. "Although, I offer my congratulations, of course. No, I was referring to Susannah's wedding. Has father not told you?" Her face took on a look of mock innocence.

"Susannah is to marry?" Helena looked at Meghan, and then back at Samuel, who nodded. "Why did no one tell me? Do I know the fortunate young man?"

"You do, my dear, and he is not such a young man either," Samuel chuckled. "It is Nathan Bayle."

Helena opened her mouth in a silent 'o'. The Ffoyles had been in London nearly a month, yet no one, not even gossipy Debs had mentioned one word about it.

"I think it is a perfect match." Henry interjected a loud hiccough.

Helena turned on him. "You knew?"

Henry shrugged. "As our family's former servant, Bayle wrote to me out of respect."

"Yet you saw no reason to mention it to me?" Her voice trembled a little.

Henry frowned, as if confused. "It was not my news to give, but as Samuel has made it public, or rather Debs has, I can freely offer my congratulations."

Suppressing a sharp remark, Helena turned to Meghan. "I am delighted for Susannah."

Meghan's gentle smile told Helena she was not fooled by her feigned poise. "I knew her heart had been inclined that way for some time, did not you?"

Helena was about to reply in the negative, when an image swam into her head of Nathan and Samuel poring over ledgers.

Meghan was still speaking, "It amazed me Susannah was able to convince the gentleman that marriage might be a favorable condition."

"He is somewhat older than her." Samuel twirled a glass by its stem. "This gave me cause for concern at the outset."

He glanced pointedly at his son, who looked away. "However, Nathan Bayle is a fine man and an excellent agent, so the situation suits everyone."

"And they shall live at the Manor, so I shall not lose my girl," Meghan added. As if to compensate for her husband's insensitivity, she patted Patrick's arm.

Helena spent the rest of the party brooding; unwilling to admit the emotion she felt was closer to guilt; that after his devotion to her all her life and those days in Weston in particular, she had consigned Nathan Bayle to a time and place she tried not to visit too often.

She was hurt too that Henry had kept secrets from her. But then, had she not kept hers from him also? Unable to help herself, Helena subjected Guy to her bad temper all the way back to Lambtons in the carriage, which he bore with stoicism.

CHAPTER THIRTY

Helena studied the exotically attired gentleman beside Guy at the entrance to Lambtons' dining hall with open curiosity. He was of about sixty years, which he carried well; upright and spare with wind-tanned skin, a long face and kind brown eyes, which crinkled at the corners as if he laughed a lot. His clothes were colorful but not of the latest style, his peruke adorned at the back with tiny plaits fastened with multi-colored ribbons. She was fascinated to see he wore jeweled rings on several fingers; even his gold- topped cane sported a ruby.

If she had not known who he was, Helena could have guessed by the way he surveyed the room as if commanding attention, that he must be Guy's uncle, Arthur Palmer.

When he saw her approach, Guy stepped forward to make introductions. "Uncle has this morning returned from Africa, Helena." He bestowed a glance full of admiring affection on his relative. "I did not imagine he would be here before our wedding, but as you can see . . ."

Helena sketched a curtsey. "I am delighted you shall be present, Master Palmer." When she raised her head, she found she was under scrutiny by piercing brown eyes, identical to Guy's.

Arthur Palmer made a leg. "And this is the young woman my nephew has selected for a wife?" His voice reverberated across the dining room as if he stood on a ship announcing land was in sight.

Lubbock appeared from nowhere to seat them at a table in an alcove. Openly curious, he bowed out of the room, returning with a selection of cold savories and meats, which he set before them. He hovered so long; Helena glared at him to make him leave.

"Traveling the world must be very rewarding, sir," Helena ventured, not quite knowing what to say to this man, who must have seen things she could never imagine.

"I have a great fondness for Africa, it is true." Arthur Palmer folded his hands on the table, the candlelight making his jeweled rings sparkle. "The Gambia in particular, which is fortunate as the London side of the business holds no interest for me." He leaned toward her with a kind smile. "I leave such matters to Guy."

"Uncle has his Africa Holdings to oversee," Guy spoke between mouthfuls of smoked ham. "The goldmines there are very productive."

"Something I once had in common with certain members of the house of Stuart." Arthur Palmer's rumbling laugh brought several querying stares their way.

"The king has goldmines in Africa?" Helena's interest was piqued.

He swung his head toward her to give a nod. The side flap of his peruke shifted, revealing a large diamond earring. Helena was fascinated, and kept darting looks at him in the hopes of seeing it again, speculating whether or not he wore one in the other ear as well.

"Not any more, my dear," he drawled. "Prince Rupert introduced the Duke of York to overseas trade; before he ascended the throne of course. He and his sisters, Henrietta of Orleans and Mary of Orange were early backers. They formed a company to mine Gambian gold under the Royal African Company." The brown hand, which patted hers, resembled a leather glove. "His majesty gave it up in favor of the more lucrative black gold trade some time ago. Gold mining needs a personal touch, and I love the Gambia, so it suits me." He beamed.

"Black gold?" Helena turned enquiringly to Guy.

"Slaves," Guy murmured. "For the plantations in Barbados."

Helena dropped her gaze to her plate, uncomfortable with the concept. Many families had young slaves in their London houses, working as pages and footmen. When they grew to adulthood, they were sent back to the islands as laborers. Lady Harbourne brought her Blackamoor when she dined at Lambtons, a tiny boy with blue-black skin. He sat on a stool at her knee when she ate.

Guy leaned toward her, his eyes alight. "Uncle has given us his house in King Street."

Helena sat up straighter, experiencing a thrill of anticipation. Guy insisted his Lincolns Inn lodgings were inadequate for a married man, and she knew he was scouring the neighborhood for a suitable place for them. But he never mentioned a house.

"To whom else would I give my possessions?" Master Palmer laughed, expertly opening an oyster with a curved knife and tossing the delicacy down his throat in one movement.

Guy's face took on an ingratiating quality. "Do you not like the idea, Helena? It is a very comfortable house. Not large, but well appointed."

"Of course I am. It simply-"

Uncle Arthur cut across her. "It used to belong to my cousin Barbara, you know."

Helena's hand hovered in mid air; the slice of beef she had lifted to her lips fell back onto the plate with a slap.

"Oh!" Helena swallowed. "Lady Castlemaine's house?"

Arthur Palmer nodded, the ribbons hanging from his peruke flapped like multi colored butterflies. "The very same, my dear."

Helena was unsure whether she should feel thrilled or disappointed. She decided not to appear either.

"She has not lived there for over twenty five years, but it still retains a certain reputation." He laughed throatily. "And perhaps some of its former energy, also."

Helena considered this comment when Guy spoke again. "It is close to the Palace of Whitehall. We shall be in illustrious company."

Helena doubted all the occupants of that particular establishment could be called illustrious, but remained silent. "When will I be able to see this house?"

"This very afternoon if you wish." Arthur Palmer's hopeful smile showed how important it was for her to like it. She smiled back, finding herself pleased she would be having this vibrant man in her life, even if only rarely.

"Shall I ask Master Devereux if we might use his carriage?" Helena asked, knowing Robert wouldn't mind.

"Not necessary, my dear." Arthur Palmer answered in his clipped tone which Helena was learning was an idiosyncrasy of his. "It is but a short ride, and a hackney is very convenient, if not quite so comfortable." He turned concerned brown eyes on Helena. "Would you mind it?"

Helena assured him a hackney would be perfect and left Lambtons on the arm of her new relation with curious stares following her.

When they arrived in King Street, entertained all the way by stories of Uncle Arthur's latest sea voyage, Helena found herself charmed by both the gentleman, and her first view of the house.

The road was very narrow, with room enough for the carriage and a small mule to pass by on the other side. Helena noticed this fact only briefly, for her gaze was fixed on the large stone gate with two round turrets, spanning the end of the road; reminding her of her interview with John Evelyn in the Privy Garden.

"The Kings Gate," Arthur Palmer murmured when he saw her staring at it.

"Oliver Cromwell owned a house here. I know not which one." He stared around, a hand to his mouth. "And Judge Jeffreys, although he occupies a property in nearby De La Hay Street, which the king is having altered for him."

"Altered? In what way, Uncle." Guy did not seem to notice that Helena gave a shudder beside him.

"He is having steps built so the Chancellor can access St James Park more easily. You will recognize it if you go and look, it is the only one so modified."

Helena had no intention of doing any such thing, instead she studied the property they had come to see. Built of brick with timber gables, it was four storeys tall with a wide, single frontage and sat between two others of different heights and sizes. Tall windows on the ground and first floor opened with Dutch style sashes and the upper floor overhung the street level by at least four feet.

There appeared to be a coffee house five or so doors away with a large leaded bow window on the first floor, and at one end was an inn with a hanging sign with what looked like a large grayish pig painted on it.

"The Blue Boar Inn," Guy informed her. "The Kings Head is at the other end of the street, so we are well served with hostelries."

Helena was unsure as to whether this was an advantage or not, but at least she would be able or order an 'ordinary dinner' to be delivered at short notice if her housewifely skills were not up to standard.

"It stands on a slight incline, as you can see." Arthur Palmer waved his cane at the street as they went through the front door. "The kennel running down the center carries the worst of the filth away from the house, so you are spared the nastiest smells."

In the ground floor rooms, Arthur Palmer flicked a red kerchief uselessly at the shelves. "It has been empty for some time, however, it will be cleaned and polished in preparation for your wedding."

Helena wondered how all this could be achieved in two weeks, but Guy looked pleased, so she remained silent as they peered into the musty front parlor, which held a charming fireplace covered in cobwebs.

Arthur Palmer beckoned them through the low kitchen door into the rear yard, picking his way over a row of strategically placed flagstones. The square yard was surrounded by a high brick wall with a wooden door in the center, which their guide told her opened onto an alley leading to the stables and coach house.

Inside the neglected coachhouse, Helena surveying the empty stalls, her foot nudging a clump of old hay. She wondered what had become of Verity, her mother's mare; blinking back tears as an image loomed of her riding the little horse in the park on fine days. She pulled herself up short, hiding her distress. The mare would have hated the confinement of the city.

After first ensuring they were out of Uncle Arthur's earshot, Helena tugged at Guy's arm. "Is your uncle aware of my family . . . circumstances?"

"My dearest Helena, Uncle Arthur is as anti-papist as anyone. Besides, he would never hold a man's politics against his daughter." The implication he might do so if she had been his son went unspoken.

She bridled slightly, irritated by his flippancy. "We do not know my father's fate. Should he return to England, I shall welcome him into my, forgive me, into our home, unreservedly. Would you and your uncle accept that?"

"Well y-yes, of course, my dear," he stammered, apparently taken aback at her vehemence.

As the coach rumbled back to Lambtons, Helena could not help wondering if his ready agreement was because Guy did not expect Sir Jonathan Woulfe to ever appear at his door. But then, did she even have any hope of it herself any more?

* * *

Helena leaned her hands on the wooden sill, breathing the sharp night air through the open window, listening to the bustle and clattering of the cooks and serving men downstairs, preparing her wedding dinner. In her linen shift and underskirt, she waited for Chloe to arrive and help her dress. The winter wind lifted her unbound hair, tugging it away from her face.

Since morning, daylight had strained through a layer of yellowish cloud drifting northward from the industrial city fires south of the river. With coming dusk, the inn lamps were lit, throwing a welcoming glow onto the street. The cobbles were slick with ice which clung treacherously, thawing during the day to freeze again as the temperature dropped near dusk.

She watched with excitement as torches were lit in the side street in preparation for the arrival of the guests, who would have to pick their way through a layer of grimy water between their carriages and the main door. The larger dining hall was shut off from the curious public for the nuptials, and by evening, the intense cold had dampened down the worst smells of the city.

Helena's gaze drifted to a small canvas propped up on her bureau, depicting a scene of Exeter's North Gate with the road leading up to the Weare Cliffs; a view Helena knew intimately. She had shed a quiet tear when she saw it; the letter that accompanied it had warmed her heart.

The entire city is talking about Blanden's ghost, Tobias wrote. He tells a strange tale of Lady Blanden having seen a shadowy figure hovering on the landing. Having complained for months about disturbances in the house at night,Blanden was jumpy with nerves, so when her scream brought him out of his bedchamber with a loaded musket, he fired.

His listeners speculate it must have been an intruder, but Blanden insists that when the house was roused and the candles lit, there was nothing there, not even bloodstains. Adamant he had aimed true, he claimed it was a demon; one that couldn't die and would be returning to kill them all.

Rumor has it he has lost his mind, which is no more than he deserves for the way he treated the Woulfes. His Catholicism is a particular cause for censure, as is the sad looking old priest living at Loxsbeare.

Go into your marriage with an easy mind, dear sister, and be happy.
Your loving brother
Tobias.

Be happy. She had barely considered her personal happiness. It had been enough to be offered a secure home with a man who gave every indication he cared for her and would be kind. Did being happy, mean simply not being miserable? Or was there more? She shivered, wrapping her arms around her upper body, but it was not the night air that turned her blood cold. "I wish Mother was here," she whispered.

A sigh of disapproval and the distinctive scent of bruised roses reached her, announcing the arrival of Adella. She sailed across the room to slam the catch shut, muttering to herself about unhealthy practices.

A smile tugged at Helena's mouth; she had never been able to explain to a city dweller like Adella that sometimes, she longed for the clean air of Devon and would dream about filling her lungs with the scent of cut grass and damp leaves.

Adella's navy blue silk mantoe was crossed over her bodice at the waist, revealing a cream silk underskirt. Her wired fontange tilted forward from her crown with ribbon bows and lace. Such a high headdress would have looked ridiculous on some women, but she carried the new fashion off beautifully.

"There is something I need to discuss with you, Helena," Adella said, arranging herself on the sofa at the end of the bed. "I regard you as my own daughter, and as such feel I owe you a certain courtesy."

Helena stared. Adella had never sought her out in such an intimate way before and she found it strange. Her gaze drifted to a brown, leather-covered book in Adella's hands. Oh no, not Mistress Hannah Woolley?

Seeing her expression, the lady threw back her head and laughed. The infectious sound restored the charming, flirtatious woman she admired.

"I know what you are thinking." Adella smirked. "And no, this is not the scribbling of that jumped up lady's maid with literary ambitions. My dear, this is a far more interesting work. It is called 'Aristotle's Masterpiece'."

"I don't think I am familiar with it." Helena frowned.

Adella's eyebrows rose. "I would be most surprised if you were. This book contains everything a girl should know when they become wives. Or mistresses," she added mischievously.

Helena's cheeks flamed. "I-I appreciate your sentiments, Mistress Devereux, but-."

Adella cut across her. "I don't deal in sentiments, as well you know. This book," she slapped the leather cover, "is the font of knowledge for an inexperienced woman." She paused to fix Helena with a hard stare. "I presume you have no knowledge of men?"

Helena gasped, horrified. "Never!"

"Not even with that young man, Blanden, was it?"

"We were no more than children."

"That is no safeguard in my experience." Adella sniffed, flipping the pages. "I wanted to show you this part especially, which is may be of particular interest to you, as a maiden."

Helena caught a glimpse of something she never imagined to see on a printed page, and certainly not on her wedding day.

"There are...drawings." Helena sucked in a shocked breath.

Adella gave a long-suffering sigh. "My dear, later this evening you will be expected to know at least something of what is laid out here. You should at least be forewarned."

Helena opened her mouth to protest, but Adella held up a hand. "There is nothing more disconcerting to a red blooded man than a partner who is horrified with the whole procedure. It takes away his pleasure when he has to make explanations and calm ragged feelings."

Helena bridled. "I feel sure Guy will make my duties in that direction clear when we-."

"Huh! Then you will be more fortunate than many women. Oh don't glare at me with such an injured expression, Helena. It will not harm you one whit to read what Aristotle has to say."

Helena's curiosity battled with her indignation, but before she could decide how to react, Adella slammed the volume shut with one hand and swept it into her arms and rose to her feet.

"Well, no one can say I did not try, but if you choose to walk into marriage with the ignorance of a lamb, I refuse to take the blame for any anguish it may cause you."

To her utter astonishment, Helena found herself pleading with the lady not to go. "Perhaps you are right. May I at least see?" What was it she was asking to see?

Adella inclined her head in a gesture of condescension and resumed her seat, patting the space beside her. Helena sat.

"I can spot Guy's ilk at a glance," Adella paused to give her musical laugh, "he needs encouragement from you, for he will be reticent to make the first move."

"From me?" Helena asked nervously. "What sort of encouragement?"

"He needs to know you aren't averse to the physical side of your duties."

"I-I have made it clear I shall be his true companion," Helena stammered, hurt.

Adella regarded her with sympathy. "He doesn't want a companion, my dear, he wants a lover."

"But I am to be his wife, not some tavern girl!"

"Ah, that is where so many young women misjudge the nature of marriage. You should be civil and respectful towards him in the public eye and a saucy, forward wench in the bedchamber."

Helena's eyes widened in disbelief, wondering how she should refute it, but Adella waved her protests away. "I know what I know, and you, my dear, shall do well to put away your injured pride and pay attention."

Helena felt her cheeks burn and Adella softened her tone. "Helena, I understand you wish everything to be perfect, but I imagine you have no real idea of what true intimacy is."

Unable to contradict this reasoning, Helena listened in silence. "Some men are quite direct in what they expect from a wife, so if Guy has not broached the subject-"

"He has not," Helena assured her.

"And as a gentleman, he would not expect you to have the proclivities of a courtesan."

"Would I knew what those were, I might anticipate married life with a little less apprehension." Helena surprised herself at her sharpness. She had never admitted, even privately, that the prospect of married life sometimes filled her with stomach wrenching dread.

"Then, my dear, I and my friend Aristotle will show you."

Together, they leafed through the pages: Adella enthusiastically, Helena with shaking fingers. "It says here," Helena ran a finger along a line of text. "A wife must never be sorrowful or despairing when she lays with her husband as should she conceive, the child would have a malevolent temper." She frowned. "Could that be true?"

"It would certainly explain the disagreeable character of some of my acquaintances." Adella's laugh sounded again. "The knowledge that their parents conceived them in sorrow, makes me less inclined to dislike them so much." Her exuberant mood was so infectious, Helena found herself laughing with her.

"And what of this, Mistress Devereux?" Helena asked, that, 'A man derives much more satisfaction in the embraces of a loving wife, than in the wanton dalliances of a deceitful harlot."

Adella gave an expressive sniff. "I would not place all my faith in Aristotle's wisdom."

"Oh! But it appears to me," Helena ventured with more confidence. "The majority of this advice is aimed at those seeking to start and retain a pregnancy, as if that were the only purpose of marriage."

"It is the reason for life after all, apart from one's duty to God, of course."

Helena was about to agree with considered seriousness, when she saw Adella's lips twitch mischievously, sending them both into a bout of almost hysterical laughter.

All traces of Helena's embarrassment were forgotten at the heady excitement of being part of the world of married women and their secrets. Without Adella's revelations, the life she had imagined leading with Guy was mere play-acting. Keeping his house and preparing his meals, was stuff of girlish fantasies compared with what Adella was telling her.

"And this is all quite necessary?" Helena asked, their reading finished.

"Not all. But it will contribute much to his pleasure, and to yours."

"Mine?" Helena lifted her eyebrows in surprise.

"Of course. Do you suppose physical pleasure is solely a man's domain?"

Helena knew she must have looked doubtful, at which Adella gave a bark of laughter. "It most certainly is not, I can assure you of that."

The door opened again and Chloe sidled into the room, her pale eyes fixed nervously on the chatelaine of Lambtons.

Adella's smile was almost a criticism. "Ah, here is your maid, come to dress you for the ceremony." Rising to her feet, Adella hefted the volume into her arms, her eyes dancing with mischief as she delivered her parting shot. "I shall see you later, my dear, but remember, Aristotle and I will be waiting should you ever need us again."

* * *

Attired in black and cerulean blue, with a white silk shirt and perfectly unwrinkled hose, Guy could not help his pride and happiness showing on his face as Helena walked toward him dressed in a gown of peacock blue silk, its underskirt embroidered with birds and flowers in shades of white, silver and ivory.

From the corner of his eye, he saw the ladies present dabbing at their cheeks and blinking hard at their own memories, he assumed, or maybe their respective disappointments.

At Guy's insistence, and Henry's chagrin, Helena and Guy were spared the undignified 'bedding' ceremony, but all too soon the celebrations were over and they left to embark on the short journey to King Street.

The night was pitch black by the time the Devereux coach pulled outside the house. The front door opened to reveal a fairly young, serious looking manservant. Yellow light from a double candle he held spilling onto their faces. "Good evening, sir." The man stepped deferentially aside. "And to you . . . Mistress."

"Thank you, Glover," Guy responded with more confidence than he felt and ushered Helena inside.

Helena sent Chloe off to her new quarters and Glover asked, "May I serve you a nightcap, sir?"

"A splendid idea, Glover. We shall take it in the parlor." Grateful for the manservant's foresight, he escorted Helena inside; impressed at how Glover had marshaled the cleaning crew he had engaged to transform the house into a welcoming home.

They sat together eating tiny cakes and sipping wine, their conversation flowing as if they were still in the salon at Lambtons. Helena seemed to be more tactile than usual, with extravagant smiles and her hand on his arm whenever he moved within reach. However, as the candles burned down, Guy became more self-conscious, aware this was the first time they had been alone in each other's company.

Guy's experience with women was the usual kind for a young professional man in the city, mainly confined to tavern girls or working ladies who expected little from him by way of manners, or even much consideration.

He believed his abilities were more than adequate, but when he looked into the startling eyes of the woman who was now his wife, he found himself wondering if the fulsome praise might not have been part of the bargain. As the fire burned down and the candles guttered, Guy's nervousness increased.

Helena shivered. "It is growing cold. Guy. Shall we retire?"

Her eyes were unnaturally bright and she seemed unsteady on her feet as he followed her out of the room. When they reached the chilly hallway, they both ran lightly up the stairs, like children on a mission of mischief.

Guy looked back from the landing and in the light from a wall mounted candle, he caught Chloe smirking at him from the lower floor and glared at her until she scurried away.

Helena's surprised pleasure was obvious when she stepped into their chamber for the first time. The bed hangings were red velvet brocade, a thick rug cushioned their footsteps and a glowing fire threw a glowing orange circle of warmth onto the carpet.

She leaned against the door until the catch clicked home, arching her head back invitingly to reveal a white and slender throat. "I think I have drunk a little more wine than is my usual custom."

"Master Devereux is an excellent host, Helena. Did you not notice he provided first pressed wine for the wedding?" He inwardly cursed himself at how pompous that must have sounded.

Helena did not appear to notice, pulling him toward her with one hand, the fingers of the other tugging at the ribbon ties on his shirt.

The movement was so swift and unexpected, Guy found himself grinning with delighted surprise. He had never stood so close to her before, discovering the fragrance of her hair and the feel of her skin a heady combination. He traced the line of her jaw with his fingers, his breath quickening as she gave him her beautiful, slow smile.

Then she stumbled, almost falling against him; whispering in a slurred voice that she would appreciate his guidance. Her slender arms entwined about his neck and the fragrance of wine was on her breath, her breathing shallow as if, she too, were nervous.

An overwhelming protectiveness flooded through him at her vulnerability, combined with his growing physical arousal. It surprised him at how natural it felt to hold her, and with her shoulders tucked comfortably beneath his encircling arms, he dropped his head to meet her upturned mouth.

Her soft lips were almost demanding as she strained against him, her tongue sliding along the inside of his upper lip so lightly, he shivered, releasing an involuntary groan.

He lifted her away then stared into her eyes. If he did not say the words he practiced, the opportunity would be lost in the physicality of what was about to envelop him. "Helena," he said, breathless. "I intend to devote my life to making you happy."

"Of course you do, dearest." She gave a tiny belch, covering her mouth with her fingers, giggling. "But I have dismissed Chloe and I cannot remove this corset without help."

Bemused, he unlaced her, wondering why he had never realized what an enjoyable task releasing a woman into his hands could be. His fingers were shaking so much; he almost tore the delicate lace trimming.

Helena stepped away as the garment fell to the floor, reaching for her nightgown. She slipped the filmy length of muslin over her head, making no attempt to fasten it. His gaze slid over her slender outline, watching as the almost transparent material clung to her girlish curves.

She flushed a little when she saw him looking at her, ducked her head and turned away. Holding her arms out to steady herself, she lifted a foot to climb the double step onto the bed, but overbalanced, sending the wooden contraption skittering across the floor. Laughing, she scrambled onto the coverlet, tossing her long hair over an exposed shoulder.

The sight of that nightgown slipping ever lower sent a thrill of anticipation into Guy's groin; he found he did not need the step to assist him up onto the mattress at all.

* * *

Helena woke the next morning in her husband's arms, lying within the warm darkness of the closed bed hangings, not daring to move in case she woke him. Through a chink in the fabric, she saw it was not quite light outside. She teased the hanging closed again with a bare foot to shut out the frigid cold.

Feeling the roughness of Guy's chin on her forehead made her smile, remembering the power that had been hers when he took such delight in her. Using phrases she had never repeated aloud, she had submitted to him with uninhibited grace and curiosity. She had observed his responses in an almost detached way, marveling as his eyes grew smoky and his breathing quickened into an urgent moan as her fingers run across his bare skin.

Disjointed images replayed in her head of pale skin glowing red from the firelight, their combined taut, urgent hands pulling at each other. His broad, naked shoulders and the swish of sheets combined with the low creak of the bed frame beneath her.

She gazed at the prone figure beside her, his arm heavy across her hip and tried to identify what is was she felt for this man, who was to be her companion for the rest of her, or his life.

No desperate longing tugged at her heart, nor did the prospect of his absence fill her with dread, but there was safety and warmth in his presence. She reveled in their new intimacy, which gave her license to run her hand across his naked shoulders, stroking the soft hair at the nape of his neck.

Recollections of their first night together sent ripples of warmth into parts of her body she had barely been aware of before. She hoped it would all be repeated, often. She stretched luxuriously under the coverlet, whispering to herself, "I am his wife at least."

"Is something amiss?" Guy groaned sleepily into her shoulder.

Helena smiled. "Nothing at all husband. Everything is as it should be."

The End

Duking Days Revolution

The sequel to Duking Days Rebellion

Helena Woulfe Palmer has managed to put behind her the horrors of the Monmouth Rebellion and look forward to the future as the wife of Guy Palmer, a London Goldsmith Banker. Her husband grows more prosperous and their marriage is happy, until Helena's discovery of her husband's weakness drives her into an unwise liaison and she learns there is a price to pay for recklessness and keeping secrets.

As the country reels between Catholic and Anglican sovereignty, will the three Woulfe siblings ever learn the fate of their missing Father or reclaim their family estates?

Above all, will Helena be able to keep what is important to her?

Release Date: Fall 2007

Read More/Talk to Author

www.enspirenpress.com